WITHDRAWN

UNWARRANTED

CRAVE *the* NIGHT

Lara Adrian

Delacorte Press | New York

CRAVE *the* NIGHT

Midnight Breed Series
Book Twelve

Crave the Night is a work of fiction. Names, characters, places, and incidents are the products of the author's imagination or are used fictitiously. Any resemblance to actual events, locales, or persons, living or dead, is entirely coincidental.

Copyright © 2014 by Lara Adrian, LLC

All rights reserved.

Published in the United States by Delacorte Press, an imprint of Random House, a division of Random House LLC, a Penguin Random House Company, New York.

DELACORTE PRESS and the HOUSE colophon are registered trademarks of Random House LLC.

LIBRARY OF CONGRESS CATALOGING-IN-PUBLICATION DATA
Adrian, Lara.
Crave the night / Lara Adrian.
pages cm — (Midnight Breed series ; book twelve)
ISBN 978-0-345-53263-3
eBook ISBN 978-0-345-53264-0
1. Man-woman relationships—Fiction. 2. Vampires—Fiction. I. Title.
PS3601.D74C83 2014
813'.6—dc23
2014012935

Printed in the United States of America on acid-free paper

www.bantamdell.com

2 4 6 8 9 7 5 3 1

First Edition

Book design by Virginia Norey

To my readers,

with eternal gratitude for your devotion to the Midnight Breed series and for your willingness to accompany me on new adventures as well.

This book, like the ones before it and all the rest still to come, is for you.

Acknowledgments

Thank you to my publishing teams in the United States and around the world, to the booksellers, online retailers, and reader communities who have so generously embraced my work and helped to spread the word about my books. I appreciate all of your effort and support!

Thanks also to my home team: Paula, Heather, and the rest of the folks who not only keep me on track but keep me sane. I couldn't do it without you!

And to John, for holding my hand in every joy and crisis, and for holding my heart in every moment in between. I love you!

CRAVE *the* NIGHT

1

THE UNDULATING CROWD PACKED ONTO THE DANCE FLOOR IN-
side the throbbing Boston nightclub seemed to collectively sense that
death had entered the building.

Nathan took only the barest notice of the sudden change in atmo-
sphere. As one of the Breed, he'd long grown used to the reaction he had
on humans.

As a warrior member of the Order and a first-generation Breed
male—the most powerful of his kind—Nathan's presence often put
even other vampires on alert.

But it was the other part of his nature, the fact that he was born and
raised a Hunter, one of a dark legion bred for killing and stripped of all
emotion or attachment, which broadcast an unspoken, visceral terror
into the room. He saw it in every pair of eyes that furtively glanced his
way now through the swirling dance lights in the darkened club.

"They don't look happy to see us," quipped Rafe, one of three other
Breed warriors who reported to Nathan as their squad captain.

"I doubt Cassian Gray will welcome the Order with open arms either." This from Nathan's lieutenant, Elijah, in the slow, laid-back Texas
drawl that belied the vampire's quick skill with any one of the blades or
firearms bristling from his weapons belt.

From the other side of Eli, Jax, the third member of tonight's patrol,
quirked a slender black eyebrow over his almond-shaped eyes. "It's not
like we left on the best of terms last time."

No, they hadn't. The last time Nathan and his crew had stepped in-

side the former church that was now one of the city's most popular—
and least reputable—hot spots, it ended with the club's proprietor,
Cassian Gray, calling in an armed unit of the Joint Urban Security Taskforce Initiative Squad. The Order didn't have time to deal with any
public or political fallout from JUSTIS tonight.

And if Cass thought he could hide behind the palms he'd greased so
well within that combined Breed and human police organization, he
was wrong. Dead wrong, if that's the way he wanted to play it.

The Order had recently come across intel indicating Cass might have
other, unknown allies in his pocket. Allies who would make his law
enforcement and criminal underworld connections seem like worthless
puppets.

Tonight, Nathan and his squad had been tasked with bringing the
mysterious club owner in to the Order's Boston command center for
questioning.

"Come on. Let's go find the bastard." Ignoring the sharp spike of
adrenaline and anxious perspiration injected into the general mélange of
stale liquor, smoke, and perfume that hung like a fog in the club, Nathan
gestured for his team to follow him deeper inside. "Eli, you and Jax
search the public rooms. Rafe and I will take the offices in back."

With the two warriors heading off on his instructions, Rafe fell in
alongside Nathan to cut a path through the crowds on their way to La
Notte's owner's quarters. There was no security to stop them once they
reached Cass's office, suggesting the man was either working the floor of
his club as he so enjoyed or not in the building at all.

Nathan hoped it was the former. If not, this unannounced visit was
sure to get back to Cass one way or another, and the Order didn't want
to give the son of a bitch any cause for alarm. They wanted nothing to
send him to ground before they could interrogate him about who—or,
rather, *what*—he truly was.

Nathan stalked up to the black-painted steel door with the word
PRIVATE scratched into it from the tip of a serrated blade. The dead
bolt and secondary lock were no trouble at all for the power of his Breed
mind. Nathan freed the bolt and the other tumbled open with little
more than a second's concentration.

He pushed the door wide and Rafe followed him into the darkened
office. Neither of them needed artificial light; Breed eyesight was flawless, all the more so in the dark.

Nathan made a quick visual scan of the empty room and cursed. "He's already gone."

No sign of Cassian Gray at all. The desk was cleared of all papers and personal effects. No computer tablet lying conveniently in the open for them to confiscate. Nothing but a carefully vacated office.

If Nathan had to guess, he figured Cass had been gone for several hours at least. Maybe a full day or more.

"Dammit," he gritted through clenched teeth.

Rafe meanwhile had broken into a cabinet of paper files and ledgers on the other side of the room. "Just a bunch of accounting records and supply receipts in here. Bar equipment, liquor invoices, band contracts for the club." The blond vampire shot Nathan a wry look. "Where do you suppose Cass keeps the books for the real moneymaking parts of this operation? Nothing in here at all that mentions the fight arena downstairs or the gambling, pimping, and blood trading. Nothing in here about the other pursuits La Notte caters to either."

Nathan grunted. Cass's illegal and other unconventional activities provided in the restricted-access lower level of his club were no secret, but criminal or not, he was careful to protect the interests of himself and his clientele. The records for those parts of his business were surely kept somewhere far more secure than his office at the club.

No, Cassian Gray was a man who knew when and how to keep his secrets.

Rafe had now abandoned the file cabinets to move farther into the gloomy office space. "Hey, check it out," he called over his shoulder to Nathan. "There's another door over here."

The warrior opened it and blew out a whistle. "You gotta see this, man."

Nathan walked over to find a bedroom on the other side of the door. A king-size four-poster bed draped in black satin sheets dominated the room. The rails between the posters dripped with leather straps and an assortment of manacles and buckled restraints, a few bearing sharp metal spikes.

Rafe barked out a laugh. "Whoever Cassian Gray is, he's one twisted fuck."

Nathan stared at the accoutrements of sexual deviance and torture while his friend and comrade stepped inside to jingle one of the studded harnesses. "Leave it alone, Rafe. We're wasting time. Cass isn't here, obviously. Let's go find the others and get out of here."

As Rafe dropped the leather strap and they prepared to leave, Jax rushed in to meet them. His face was drawn and grave. "We've got a problem."

"You find Cass?" Nathan asked.

Jax shook his head. "Apparently, we just missed him, if you can believe any of the club staff. The problem is Aric Chase. He's downstairs at the cages. With Rune."

"Jesus Christ," Rafe hissed, coming up beside Nathan.

"Eli's trying to break it up," Jax said. "But Aric won't stand down. Shit's about to get ugly."

Nathan growled a curse. "Is Carys here too?"

"Not tonight," Rafe said. "She's at the art museum with Jordana Gates. The two of them are hosting a patrons' reception. They've been planning it for months."

Nathan gave a tight nod, grateful for that small mercy. The last thing Carys Chase needed was to see her twin brother take a beating from the cage-fighting killer who'd recently begun sharing her bed.

If the Breed fighter and the daywalking female had shared anything else—namely a blood bond—Aric wouldn't be the only member of the Chase family determined to kick Rune's swarthy ass. Hell, Nathan would likely be willing to join that fight himself too.

He took off at a dead run, heading with Rafe and Jax for the cage arena in the lower level of La Notte. Shouts and roars and bloodthirsty applause thundered from the bowels of the former church.

And no sooner had he descended into the illegal sporting den than Nathan spotted Aric and Rune. They stood in front of the cages, Eli positioned in between them, mostly holding Aric back. Both Breed males were flashing fangs, eyes glowing bright amber in the dim light of the arena.

Nathan scowled at Jax. "What the fuck's going on?"

"I'm not sure. It was already getting heated when Eli and I got down here."

Another of La Notte's fighters, a blond, long-haired Breed male named Syn, met Nathan's hot glare from nearby as the din ratcheted up even higher among the spectators gathered in the arena. "Better rein in your baby warrior before Rune leaves him in bloodied shreds."

"What's Rune's problem with Aric tonight?"

Syn smirked. "Rune's problem?" He shook his head. "Rune was mind-ing his own business, just taking a breather and enjoying some *refreshment* before tonight's first match."

The way Syn leaned on the word *refreshment* told Nathan that when Aric found him, Rune was likely feeding from one of the paid human blood Hosts employed by Cass to serve his fighters and VIP clientele.

"Your boy started talking shit," Syn went on. "Started telling Rune the Order had its eye on him. That he'd better watch his step or he was gonna get ashed."

Holy hell. Nathan acknowledged that this confrontation probably shouldn't surprise him, but Aric's personal dislike of the brutal cage fighter had nothing to do with Order business.

Not yet, anyway. If Aric and Carys's father, Sterling Chase, ever found out his daughter had taken up with an unapologetic underworld player like Rune, Nathan had no doubt the Order as a whole would definitely have something to say about it.

Nathan, Rafe, and Jax pushed through the jeering crowd just in time to see Aric lunge past Elijah to grab hold of Rune. Aric body-slammed the big fighter into the nearby cage, fangs bared and eyes aglow with fury. He threw a couple of wild punches, each deftly avoided by Rune. Aric's anger opened him wide for a punishing blow.

Rune didn't hit back. He was glaring lethally, his savage face twisted in rage. But under his shaggy mane of dark brown hair, the undefeated fighter with more kills to his name than any other before him stayed his hand.

Nathan shoved past the onlookers so he and Rafe could peel Aric off Rune. No easy feat, that. Although just twenty years old, Aric was Gen One like Nathan. He was strong as hell and deadly powerful, especially now, when his whole body was electric with animosity toward his sister's unsavory lover.

"What the fuck, man?" Rafe shouted at his friend. "You lost your mind, Aric? What are you doing down here?"

Aric continued to glower at Rune. He jabbed his finger at the deceptively cool fighter. "You keep to your own. Stay away from her. She's better than this, better than you."

Now Rune's lips twisted slowly, into an ironic smile. "I tell her that all the time. She seems to think otherwise."

As Rune spoke, one of La Notte's blood Hosts sauntered over to drape her nearly naked body around him. She took Rune's earlobe between her teeth, whispering something against his dark, stubble-shadowed cheek. Rune gave her thong-strung behind a meaningful swat and told her to wait for him in one of the nearby booths.

Aric went apeshit. Snarling and seething, he struggled to break loose of his comrade's hold.

Nathan shot a hard look at Rafe. "Let's get him out of here."

"A wise move," Syn agreed, as Nathan and his crew wrestled Aric away from the cages and out of Rune's reach.

They hustled the furious vampire out of the club and back onto the street outside. He tried to lunge for the door, but Nathan and Rafe blocked him. He shook them off and rocked back on his bootheels.

"She has to know this can't go on. Carys has to understand that asshole is beneath her. I can't stand by and let her get hurt by gutter filth like Rune." Aric cursed, low and savage. "Goddamn it, I won't stand by."

Then he bolted. Not for the club again, but out into the street.

"Shit," Rafe muttered, raking a hand over his head. He glanced over at Nathan. "You know where he's going."

The museum reception. Nathan didn't have to guess. But he hated like hell to acknowledge it. No more than he hated to acknowledge that he and his patrol squad were going to have to abandon tonight's search for Cassian Gray and instead go after one of their own.

One of their own who was about to earn the wrath of his beloved sister, if Aric followed through on his threat to see Carys and Rune separated.

And going after Aric meant coming face-to-face with something else Nathan would rather avoid, especially under these circumstances.

Jordana Gates.

The beautiful, Darkhaven-raised female he'd been trying to bar from his thoughts for the past week—ever since she'd pressed her mouth against his in an entirely unexpected, totally unforgettable kiss. A kiss that had unsettled him and, yes, enraged him.

Disturbed him on a level he was still struggling to comprehend.

"The art museum's on Huntington Avenue," Rafe said beside him.

Nathan's reply was short, almost a growl. "I know where it is."

He knew more than he had a right to about lovely Jordana Gates and the places she frequented. Primarily so he could take steps to avoid them.

But there could be no avoiding her now. Not with Aric charging off to defend his sister's virtue.

Nathan rubbed his palm across his clenched jaw. "Fuck it. Let's go."

As reluctant as he was to follow the path where this night was heading, Nathan was the first to step off the curb and race for their destination.

2

ON FOOT, GIFTED WITH THE PRETERNATURAL SPEED OF THEIR Breed genetics, it took all of three minutes for Nathan and his team to arrive in front of the museum across the city.

Aric was ahead of them, already shoving his way past the sputtering human doorman to barge inside. Nathan, Rafe, Jax, and Eli followed quickly behind him, but not fast enough to stop Aric from completely disrupting the invitation-only social event.

Storming through the knots of men garbed in tuxedoes and women swathed in elegant gowns and glittering jewels, Aric roared his sister's name. "Carys!"

Conversations halted abruptly. Heads turned from all directions, Breed and human alike. Only the string quintet in the gallery overhead seemed capable of ignoring Aric's intrusion on the private gathering. They played on, Mozart's spirited *Serenade Number 13*, an odd accompaniment to the current of alarm now spilling across the main floor of the museum.

With Nathan and his squad of warriors trailing close behind him, Aric stalked past the sculpture and art displays arranged specifically for the wealthy patrons assembled there tonight. "Carys Chase!" he bellowed. "Dammit, where are you?"

Nathan was right at Aric's heels. Nathan reached for him, his hand coming down hard on Aric's shoulder to halt him in his tracks. "This is not the time or the place," he warned his comrade, low under his breath, prepared to yank the young Breed warrior out of there bodily before things got any worse.

He would have. But at that same moment, Nathan's senses came to a full stop as *she* emerged from within the shelter of a nearby throng.

Not Aric's sister, Carys.

Jordana Gates.

Tall, slender, wrapped in a gown of sheer, pale blue fabric that floated around her body like a silken cloud, she stepped away from the throng of society's most privileged elite and met Nathan's eyes across the several yards that separated them. Her oceanic blue gaze locked on him in what he guessed to be surprise at first—then confusion—beneath the complicated twists and delicate spirals of her upswept white-blond hair.

The gauzy dress she wore hugged the swell of her breasts and her tiny waist, skimming the gentle flare of her hips. She was stunning, like a vision from an enchanted other world. And she was nervous, not because of Aric's furious disruption of her swanky society party but because of Nathan.

Because he was standing there in front of her now.

Even at this distance, he could see the way her pulse kicked harder in the hollow at the base of her creamy throat as she looked at him. He could practically feel the acceleration of her heartbeat as he held her in an unapologetic stare, drinking her in from head to toe.

He could almost taste her mouth on his again, soft lips crushed against his in a startling kiss he never would have allowed. A sweet, reckless kiss that never should have happened.

Not with someone like him.

No, Jordana's anxiety wasn't misplaced at all.

She'd had no idea what she'd done, kissing him like that. The way his thoughts had been turning in the days since then, she damned well should be nervous around him.

"Carys!" Aric called once more into the crowded reception.

His deep, booming voice made Jordana jump, one delicate hand coming up to her throat in alarm. In the gallery above, the music faded, then halted altogether. The museum patrons began to murmur and shuffle about to gape at Aric's spectacle, though none of the tuxedoed men seemed eager to play hero and take on the threat of a seething warrior from the Order by themselves.

Aric shouted for his sister again and tried to shake loose of Nathan's hold.

"Not happening," Nathan said, digging his grip deeper into the meat of Aric's shoulder. Rafe, Eli, and Jax were right behind him, waiting for his orders. "Come on," he said to Aric. "You need to cool down. Let's take this outside. All you're going to do is piss her off—"

"Aric?" Carys Chase rushed through the unmoving crowds, panic in her normally calm voice. Dressed as elegantly as Jordana and the other women, she gaped at her brother as she charged forward to meet him on strappy sandals that echoed the geometric cut of her curve-hugging copper silk gown. "What are you doing here? What's wrong?"

While Jordana's beauty was diamond bright and icy fair, Carys Chase was earth and fire combined. Her eyes simmered with a fierce intelligence, and her caramel blond mane of hair swung around her face and shoulders like liquid bronze.

Of course, the differences between the two females went beyond the physical.

Where Jordana Gates was a Breedmate, half human in addition to the other, more elusive genetics that made her different from her mundane *Homo sapiens* cousins, Carys Chase was something rarer still. She was Breed, and a daywalker at that.

The same as her twin brother.

"Aric, are you okay?" she asked him, reaching up to touch his rigid jaw. She glanced at him then, studying him in a quick instant. Her shrewd eyes narrowed. "Where have you been tonight? Why is your shirt torn?"

"We need to talk," Aric snapped at her.

Carys blinked. "Now? Can't you see I'm in the middle of some—"

"Now," he snarled, finally breaking out of Nathan's grasp to grab hold of his sister's arm. "This is fucking serious, Car. I'm not gonna let it wait."

He tried to maneuver her away from the onlookers, but Carys dug in her five-inch heels and stood her ground in front of him. "Have you lost your mind? Let go of my arm." She wrenched loose, outrage sparking in her eyes. When she spoke, Nathan glimpsed the tips of her emerging fangs. "For God's sake, Aric. You're embarrassing me."

Across the room, Jordana started to move away from the others, toward her distressed friend. She was prevented from getting any closer by a man who stepped up behind her now. He was Breed, tall and attractive, with clear blue eyes and golden hair.

One of the shiny people who belonged in this place.

The male's hand came to rest protectively—possessively—at Jordana's waist as he gathered her to him, subtly holding her in place. As if she belonged with the man.

Nathan observed this with cool logic and understanding, even if his blood spiked with an unwelcome jolt of disdain for the male who touched Jordana like he owned her.

He stared at her, watched her cheeks flame a little redder under his scrutiny before she abruptly glanced down and refused to look at him again.

Was this the source of her nervousness in front of Nathan tonight?

Not merely Nathan's presence tonight, but his presence when she was in the company of someone else.

This man, whose hand had drifted from her small waist down to the tempting swell of her hip, fingers idly caressing her even as he retrieved a comm device from his tuxedo jacket pocket and held it at the ready to make a call.

Jordana's gaze never lifted, not even as the conflict rose to troubling heights between Aric Chase and his sister.

"He's using you, Carys. Can't you see that? Trash like that will only hurt you in the end."

She scoffed, exhaled a curse under her breath. "What are you talking about?"

"Rune." Aric practically spat the name at her. "You need to end it now. Before it goes any further with him. Before I have to kill the bastard for thinking he can touch you."

"You don't know anything about Rune and me." She glared, fury igniting in her pretty face. "And you have no right to interfere—"

Aric cut her off with a harsh snarl. "I'm your brother—your twin, Carys. And I love you. That gives me every right."

She slowly shook her head, glancing around at the silent spectators who made no effort to hide their rapt interest in the night's other, unplanned exhibit. When Carys looked back at Aric, her pupils had transformed from dilated circles to thinning, vertical slits. Although she projected total outward calm, Nathan and every other vampire in the place could plainly see the Breed female was furious.

Carys's voice was quiet, but as she spoke, her long fangs glinted razorsharp and lethal in the low lights of the museum reception. "Go home, Aric. For now, I'll forgive you because you claim you're doing this out of love for me. But this conversation is over."

The man at Jordana's side cleared his throat, an awkward interruption, and late as well. "Shall I call JUSTIS for assistance here, Carys?"

"No. That won't be necessary, Elliott," she replied coolly. "My brother and his friends are leaving now."

Rafe stepped up beside Aric to take his other shoulder in a firm grasp. The two warriors were as tight as brothers, just like their fathers before them, Dante Malebranche and Sterling Chase, both long-standing members of the Order. When Aric didn't budge, Rafe cuffed him none too gently on the biceps. "Come on, man. This is messed up and you know it. Let's get out of here."

Aric relaxed but kept his hard glare trained on his sister. "End it, Carys. Don't make me do it for you."

She stared at him, wounded but unbowed. "If you so much as try, then I'll no longer have a brother."

The siblings faced off in tense silence, neither of them willing to bend to the other. Having watched the twins grow up within the extended family of the Order, Nathan had seen them lock horns on many occasions, but never like this. Their bond as brother and sister had always been iron strong and unbreakable, no matter how powerfully they clashed.

Tonight, Aric had stepped far over a line he had never crossed with his sister before. Not that he seemed willing to retreat.

Finally, Carys was first to let go of her fury. Head held high, she slowly pivoted away from Aric and strode back toward her friend Jordana and the rest of the stunned gathering as if the confrontation had never happened.

Aric stared after her for a moment, then wheeled around and stalked out of the museum. Rafe, Eli, and Jax fell in behind him, leaving Nathan alone to face the one other person still rooted to the floor and unmoving across the room.

At last, Jordana lifted her gaze to meet his once more.

Some savage, undisciplined part of him imagined how she would feel against him if he closed the distance now and hauled her into another uninvited kiss—his, this time. On his terms.

At his mercy.

A dangerous temptation.

But that didn't make it any less intriguing.

Jordana held his stare for longer than he would have guessed she could. Longer than any woman would have dared, if she sensed the dark direction of his thoughts.

Her full lips parted on an indrawn breath as she looked at him, but she said nothing. She gave him nothing, standing there unmoving, her eyes locked on his as the music from the gallery began again and the reception resumed around her. Conversations buzzed once more, the crowds of museum patrons already putting the night's interruption behind them.

And still those ocean-blue eyes refused to let Nathan go.

It wasn't until the Breed male at Jordana's side cupped her bare nape in his palm that she finally glanced away. She smiled pleasantly at her companion, gave him a small nod. Then he took her hand and gently coaxed her back into the fold where she belonged, with the rest of the gilded elite.

3

ALTHOUGH SHE KNEW IT WASN'T WISE, JORDANA COULDN'T KEEP from glancing over her shoulder as she was led away from the scene of the night's disruption.

Nathan was still there.

Still watching her, his eyes simmering beneath the harsh black slashes of his brows, intimate and penetrating amid the very public throng of museum patrons. The massive Breed warrior was a study in darkness and intensity, from the severe cut of his military-style ebony hair, to the impossibly broad shoulders that topped a body honed of pure muscle and powerful, deadly menace.

Even his face was severe, if devastating, in its rugged male beauty. Fathomless dark eyes stared out of a face carved with a blade's precision. High cheekbones, proud brow, a squared, rigid jaw. His mouth was his softest feature by far, sculpted and lush, generous lips that called to mind all sorts of wicked ideas, even for a woman of Jordana's limited experience.

Nathan exuded a confidence few men seemed to possess. Perhaps that was why not even one male in the room made any move to confront him now. The women, however, practically vibrated with interest.

Not that Nathan seemed to notice any of the attention he drew.

He stared solely at Jordana. There was no mistaking the heat in his dark gaze; he looked ready to devour her. As if the thought of the crowd around them was of no consequence to him whatsoever.

Jordana struggled to find her breath under the weight of that piercing gaze. Her senses were keenly, instantly aware that if this powerful Breed male—this warrior she'd so foolishly kissed the other night—were to decide he wanted something from her right now, not even the hundred men in the museum tonight would be able to keep him from her.

Even more alarming was her heart's reaction to that idea.

Save me, her pulse seemed to drum in her veins.

Take me.

The thoughts caught her unaware. Startled her, they were so unbidden and ridiculous.

Save her from what?

Take her where . . . or *how?*

Her body answered that question with a warm throb deep in her core. The memory of their brief kiss replayed in her mind, only her imagination embellished the details now, turning an impulsive meeting of their lips into a passionate tangle of mouths and limbs and sweat-sheened, naked bodies.

God.

What was wrong with her that her mind would wander onto such a disturbing path?

And yet a swift, intense craving bloomed inside her as the mental picture filled her senses with an aching, terrible desire.

"I don't like the way he's looking at you."

The baritone voice, muttered from close beside her, snapped Jordana out of her unwelcome musings like a splash of cold water to the face. She glanced away from dark, unsettling Nathan to blond, familiar Elliott Bentley-Squire, her self-appointed protector and date tonight. His handsome features were pinched into a disapproving frown. "What do you know of that warrior, Jordana?"

"Nothing," she blurted, flustered by Elliott's notice and the still-burning sense of Nathan's eyes on her. Although her answer wasn't quite a lie, it left a bitter taste on her tongue. She shook her head and gave Elliott a vague shrug. "I don't know him at all."

"Good. Trust me when I say you wouldn't want to know that one. It's no secret that he's a killer, Jordana. One of those laboratory-raised monsters the Order seems so willing to recruit into their ranks."

As Elliott steered her farther toward the museum guests, Jordana chanced another look back to where Nathan stood.

He was gone.

Why that should disappoint her, she didn't even want to guess.

As for Elliott's warning, she knew he wasn't exaggerating. Nathan had been born and raised under awful conditions. She'd heard a little about his background from Carys over the past few days, information she'd attempted to mine as casually as possible, afraid to let on even to Carys that her curiosity about Nathan was anything more than passing.

And it was only a passing curiosity, she insisted to herself now, despite the pang of sympathy she felt for the coolly remote warrior in light of his horrific upbringing.

Born to a Breedmate who'd been abducted as a young woman and forced to breed, like many other captives who'd been imprisoned in the lab of a madman named Dragos, Nathan had been created for one purpose: killing. As a baby, he and the other boys born into the program were taken away from their mothers and raised to be soldiers in Dragos's private army.

Worse than that—they were born and raised to be emotionless machines. Assassins to be deployed on Dragos's whim to murder his enemies without mercy or remorse.

Nathan had eventually been rescued by his mother and the Order, and he now led a squad of warriors for the Order's command center in Boston.

"A Hunter," Jordana murmured belatedly.

Elliott frowned at her again. "A what?"

"Hunters. That's what they were called."

He scoffed. "*Hunter* is too polite a term for what he is."

"What he *was*," Jordana corrected him quietly, but Elliott wasn't listening, no longer interested in Nathan now that he was gone.

"I'm sorry they ruined your reception," he said. "You worked so hard to make it perfect."

She dismissed the concern with a smile she didn't really feel. "It's not ruined." She gestured to the room full of well-heeled patrons at the private, invitation-only showing. The drone of conversation, even light laughter here and there, vibrated around them in the museum's main level. "See? Everyone's already moved on to enjoy the rest of the evening. You should too, Elliott. You worry too much about me sometimes."

"Because I care," he said, reaching out to stroke the side of her face. "And you should worry more than you do, particularly about the company you keep. What happened tonight will likely be gossiped about for weeks, if not longer."

Jordana drew away from his touch and his censure. "If tongues wag over this, it'll be free publicity for the exhibit. Museum contributions will probably double."

Elliott's look was skeptical, but he offered her a smile. "I still think it was a mistake having Carys Chase host this event with you. The exhibit is your baby, Jordana. You've been working on it for more than six months—too long to let anything, or anyone, jeopardize its success. After all, how many times did you cancel or stand me up because your work kept you late at the museum?"

Too many times to count, and Jordana inwardly winced at the reminder. Although Elliott was keeping his tone light, she knew it had wounded him that she'd become so preoccupied and distant in recent months. She didn't want to hurt him or disappoint him.

Although they'd never been intimate in the year they'd been dating, Jordana did care deeply for him. She loved him. Of course, everyone loved Elliott Bentley-Squire. He was kind and attractive, wealthy and charitable. Everything that any woman could possibly want in a mate.

He was also a longtime family friend, having been her father, Martin's, attorney and business associate for several decades.

Jordana's father, a male who had adopted her as an infant yet had never been inclined to take a Breedmate for himself in all his century of living, had hardly concealed the fact that he hoped Jordana might develop a fondness for Elliott. Despite that he was easily three times her age, being Breed like her father, Elliott Bentley-Squire was physically as fit and youthful as a thirty-year-old.

As for Jordana, her twenty-fifth birthday loomed less than a couple weeks away—a date her father had emphasized since she was a child, reminding her constantly of the sizable trust she would be granted on that date, but only if she were mated and settled by then.

Not that she cared at all about the money. Neither did Elliott, who had already accumulated his own considerable riches.

No, their relationship had not been based on commerce or social standing. It had been the most natural thing in the world to assume that she and Elliott might one day seal their long-term friendship with a blood bond and take each other as their mate.

Except . . .

Except the closer their relationship came to that eventuality, the more absorbed Jordana became in her work. It wasn't unusual for her to be at the museum seven days a week, including most nights. In her spare time, she served on a handful of charity boards and had picked up a couple of seats on city improvement boards.

She'd developed a keen, consuming interest in a variety of things that had kept her too busy for any kind of social life. The upcoming art museum debut was only the most demanding of her long list of obligations.

"I'm sorry I've been so tied up with the exhibit, Elliott. But you should know that Carys has worked on this as hard as I have. She deserved to host with me tonight. Besides, she's my best friend."

Jordana scanned the reception for Carys and found her near the rear of the exhibit, smiling and chatting with a deep-pocketed doctor and his wife. Although she was the picture of poise and professionalism now, Aric's awkward confrontation had to have upset her.

"I should go make sure she's okay," Jordana said.

Elliott halted her with a small shake of his head before she even started to move. "You should attend your guests, Jordana," he advised gently. "They're here for you. Look around, they're all waiting for you. Carys will be fine until everyone is gone and the party is over."

He was right, and although she bristled a little at his hand now positioned at her elbow to guide her, Jordana nodded and fell in beside him as he led her toward a number of patrons she had yet to speak with that evening.

"Carys Chase is not like you, Jordana," Elliott said quietly as they crossed the room. "You must see that, don't you, darling? She's too wild. Reckless. Whether that's due to her unusual Breed genetic makeup or an overly indulgent upbringing, I can only guess."

"Indulgent?" Jordana nearly choked on a laugh. "Have you met her father, Sterling Chase? Or her mother, Tavia, who's also Breed? Carys has always been held to exacting standards by her parents." That was one of the things that had made Jordana and her friend so close. Although they seemed very different on the surface, Carys being a bit too adventurous and Jordana suffering from chronic overcautiousness, the two young women had much in common. "Carys and I may be different in some ways, but that's what I happen to enjoy so much about her. Is being a little wild and reckless such a bad thing?"

She'd said it playfully, a small volley of flirtation in Elliott's direction, just to test the waters. His mouth flattened and his blue eyes leveled on her from his sidelong look. "Wild and reckless usually gets someone hurt. You're smarter than that, Jordana." He reached over and gave her nose a light tap of his fingertip. "And that's what I happen to enjoy so much about *you*."

"Counselor," called a jovial, elderly man who chaired one of Boston's biggest banks. In addition to being one of Elliott's human clients, he was also one of the museum's most generous donors. His contributions to Jordana's exhibit had helped her add ten more pieces to the sculpture collection.

"Counselor, good to see you!" the old man exclaimed, from beside his group of equally prominent colleagues representing the elite of both Breed and human society. "Come here and give us an excuse to talk to your lovely fiancée about Italian sculptors."

"It would be my pleasure, Mr. Bonneville." Elliott chuckled and steered Jordana toward the men. She forced a pleasant smile, allowing Elliott to take her hand in his warm, firm grasp as he practically pulled her along beside him. Dutifully, she shook hands with the banker and his colleagues, and with the other patrons who soon came to join their little circle.

Jordana smiled and laughed at all the appropriate times, hoping no one could tell that her heart was now battering around in her breast like a caged bird that would find a way out or die trying.

At the urging of Elliott and her growing audience, she regaled them with a discussion of her favorite works in the exhibit by Italian masters Bernini, Canova, Cornacchini, and other lesser-known artists.

God knew she needed the distraction.

Because if she didn't have something keeping her feet rooted to the floor, Jordana was afraid she might be tempted to do something really wild and reckless.

She might walk out of the place—out of her perfect life—and never look back.

4

THAT NEXT MORNING, NATHAN AND HIS TEAM SAT AROUND THE
large table in the conference room of the Order's command center in
Boston, reviewing their failure to locate Cassian Gray and putting together a new plan for their patrol set to begin again at sundown. Boston's district chief, Sterling Chase, had every right to hand Nathan and
his men their asses for returning to base empty-handed last night, but
he seemed distracted today, his head not quite in the game.

Unusual for the experienced warrior who had twenty years with the
Order and another few decades of Breed law enforcement under his belt
before that.

Tavia Chase, Sterling's mate and a member of the Order in her own
right, was also present in the morning's mission review and also less
than fully engaged. She was seated with her spine rigid against the back
of her chair. Her arms lay crossed in front of her, but the fingers of one
hand drummed ceaselessly on her toned biceps. Her green gaze was
distant, shadowed with a troubled preoccupation.

Had Aric and Carys brought last night's anger home with them? Nathan was by no means an expert on reading emotion or weighing famil-
ial strife, but he had to wonder if that was the problem here today for
Chase and Tavia.

Aric hadn't betrayed his sister to their parents; that much Nathan
did know.

The younger warrior had gone straight to the weapons room of the
command center to work off steam after Nathan and the others brought
him back to Headquarters. No doubt, he would be at it for a while, not

only for the way he'd been frothing but also because Aric wasn't part of the team's morning conference.

Fresh out of training and not yet a full-fledged member of the Order, in a few weeks he would find his own squad of warriors in Seattle, when he was scheduled to report to Dante Malebranche, Rafe's father, the head of that West Coast command center.

When the heavy mood in the room lengthened, Chase finally cleared his throat and brought the meeting back on task. "When we wrap up here, I have to call Lucan Thorne in D.C. and tell him we came up empty on Cassian Gray last night." Chase's shrewd blue eyes swept each warrior at the table, pausing the longest on Nathan. "I know I don't need to tell any of you that the Order's founder does not like failure. I don't fucking like failure much either. But I hate excuses even more. So I'm not going to ask how the best team I ever trained—my most effective squad leader—pulled a patrol before either seeing it through to completion or running full-stop into daybreak."

Neither Nathan nor his comrades spoke. Even if Chase had demanded to know what had caused the mission to search for Cass to be aborted, none of them would have thrown Aric under that bus.

Besides, Nathan agreed with his commander: Blame solved nothing. And the truth was, Nathan felt equally culpable. He'd gone easily enough to the museum reception after Aric.

And while he was admitting damning truths and personal derelictions of duty, Nathan had to count among his the fact that his curiosity about Jordana Gates hadn't ended when he returned to Headquarters with his team.

While Aric had vented his fury in the weapons room, Nathan had spent several hours online and in the Breed nation's International Identification Database, researching Jordana's apparent date at the event.

Or, rather, her imminent mate, Elliott Bentley-Squire.

Nathan had delved into every documented fact and figure he could find—all told, hours of digging. But he'd found no reason to dislike the wealthy, socially acceptable male.

Nor did he care to acknowledge that he'd been looking for cause to despise the trusted friend of Jordana's father, simply for the way she had let Bentley-Squire touch her, even though her eyes hadn't seemed able to break Nathan's gaze from the moment they first saw each other at the party.

The look in Jordana's eyes haunted him, even now. As if she'd been silently pleading for him to rescue her . . . to claim her.

Until her would-be mate noticed her distraction and Jordana had denied even knowing who Nathan was.

If he needed a reason to convince himself that beautiful, tempting Jordana Gates was a bad idea, certainly this was it. Nathan preferred his sexual dalliances to be uncomplicated, impersonal. A biological satisfaction of something his body needed in order to perform at its peak.

The way he viewed it, fucking was no different than feeding.

And he preferred to do neither close to the place he called home.

"We did learn something about Cassian Gray last night," Nathan said, bringing his thoughts back in line where they belonged. "Cass's office at La Notte was orderly, too much so. Anything of value to someone looking into him or his interests had been removed."

To the left of Nathan at the table, Rafe smirked. "His private apartment had been vacated too, except for an interesting collection of restraints and spiked collars in the bedroom."

Elijah and Jax chuckled along with Rafe, but Nathan remained serious, glad to put his mind back on the trail of their quarry. "Cass already knows he's being pursued. His employees at the club said we'd just missed him, but it's probable they were lying to us. My guess is he cleared out of there days ago."

"I wonder if Cass realized he'd been outed the moment Kellan touched him." This from Tavia, her first comment of the entire morning. "He might be fully aware that the Order suspects he's not human and would come after him soon enough."

Nathan nodded with the rest of the warriors around the table. Kellan Archer was recently reunited with the Order and since mated to Mira, one of the few female squad captains. The couple had been at La Notte on a mission of their own no more than a week ago, when Kellan and Cassian Gray became embroiled in a brief altercation. Kellan pushed the club owner, tactile contact that had roused the Breed male's unique psychic gift to read human intention with a touch.

Cassian Gray had been a blank slate.

Cass wasn't Breed; there was no mistaking that fact. But Kellan had realized at once the man wasn't human either.

He hadn't been sure what else Cass could be—no one had been— until a few nights ago in Washington, D.C., at a global peace summit event that had ended in an act of terror meant to sabotage the gathering and blow hundreds of Breed lives away in the process.

Lucan Thorne and most of the Order's elder members included.

The individual who'd tried to carry out the plot under the banner of a shadowy organization called Opus Nostrum hadn't been human or Breed.

No, Reginald Crowe had been something else entirely: Atlantean.

Known publicly around the world as a billionaire business magnate with holdings all over the globe, Crowe was, in actuality, one of a powerful race of immortals that had existed on Earth unknown for millennia. They had been as much a secret to the human population as the Breed.

And now the Order understood the Atlanteans to be an even greater threat than any enemy they'd ever faced before.

"It's been three days since Crowe's death and it's still trending on all the news outlets around the world," Jax said, spinning one of his hirashuriken stars on the conference table. "If Cass is Atlantean, the killing of one of his own by the Order would be enough to send him to ground."

Eli exhaled a drawled curse. "Unfortunately, Crowe's death—and all the shit that went down before that—was a little too public to be contained."

The ultraviolet bomb at the summit had been only one of Crowe's crimes in his role as Opus Nostrum's leader. Before plotting to derail the gathering and ash every Breed dignitary in the building, Crowe's cabal had arranged for the murder of a brilliant human scientist and that man's uncle, a senior member of the Global Nations Council, the governing arm responsible for ensuring peaceful relations between the vampire and human populations of the world.

"It's true, we're at a disadvantage right now," Chase interjected. "The only good to come of the exposure of Crowe's actions and his death is the fact that now the public, Breed and man, is united in their fear of Opus Nostrum. Only the Order is aware of the Atlanteans and the bigger threat Crowe divulged before he died."

The threat of a brewing global war being plotted at the hands of the Atlanteans and their exiled queen.

"The Order has already waged a battle—and won—against a sinister member of our own race," Tavia murmured quietly. "To think that another, more insidious enemy has been lurking in the shadows all this time . . ." She slowly shook her head, unwilling or unable to finish the grave direction of her thoughts.

"And we'll win again, love." Chase reached over to stroke his mate's cheek, then he turned his steely, determined gaze on Nathan and the others. "Lucan is making a very public show of working with human and Breed law enforcement to root out Opus Nostrum. However, the Order's primary mission is something far more crucial, more covert. If what Crowe said is true, then everything we've been through to this point in time—including our hard-won battle with Dragos—was merely preparation for the war still to come."

"If Cassian Gray knows anything about Crowe's threat," Tavia added, "worse, if he's part of it, he has to be contained. We can't let him get away."

"He won't," Chase assured her. "Lucan has arranged for each of Crowe's former wives—his widow and the five exes who came before her—to be quietly interviewed at the D.C. headquarters."

Rafe grunted, his mouth spreading into a wide grin. "Invitations to tea, followed by a friendly game of twenty questions and a mind-scrub?"

Chase slid him a wry look. "Something like that, yeah. If any of the women who knew Crowe best have any knowledge about his true nature or his dealings as part of Opus Nostrum, we'll find out soon enough."

"As for Cass," Nathan said, "we'll find him too. We'll bring him in. His employees, his known allies and associates—we'll leave no lead unturned. Tell Lucan, neither Cass nor his secrets will elude us for long."

Chase gave him a tight nod. "Excellent," he said, and dropped his open palms to the table in finality. He rose from his seat, and the rest of the group stood up with him. "If there's nothing else, Tavia and I have some personal business of our own to contend with this morning."

"It's Carys," Tavia volunteered to Nathan and the other warriors. "She's moving out. Today."

"Moving out," Nathan murmured guardedly, surprised by the news, though surely not as surprised as the young woman's parents must be. "That seems like a sudden decision."

As he spoke, he caught the uncomfortable looks exchanged between his teammates as all three made a hasty exit from the conference room.

The bastards.

He'd punish them later for abandoning him to this unwanted drama.

"Carys says she's been considering this for a while now," Chase replied. "But I know my daughter, and she's holding something back. I've already asked Aric if he knew of any reason she might be upset about something—or upset with us—but he's been no more forthcoming than her."

Nathan grunted. "Do you know where she's going?"

Tavia answered him. "She's moving in with Jordana at her apartment across town. Nathan, do you know anything about this?"

He gave a slight shake of his head. "It's the first I'm hearing of it." The answer was as close to the truth as he could slice it without betraying the sibling conflict of the night before.

"I realize Carys is an adult, and she's free to live her own life," Tavia reasoned aloud. "She's always been impulsive, but this just doesn't seem like her. More than that, I don't know if I'm ready to let go of her," she added, turning a baleful look on Chase. "I know, I'd never truly be ready for this day to come, but especially not now, knowing dangerous people like Cassian Gray are skulking around, unaccounted for. Who knows what he or his cage-fighting thugs might do if they realized one of the Order's children—a female, no less—was living somewhere in the city away from our protection?"

A growl vibrated in Chase's chest now. "I'll forbid her to leave."

Tavia sighed. "You can't and you know it. Trying to force her will only make her dig her heels in harder. Carys is a headstrong young woman—not that either of her parents should be surprised by that."

"No," Chase replied, his eyes gentle on his mate, even if his tone remained firm. "But if she's leaving because she's got a head full of steam over something, or if she's in some kind of trouble—"

Tavia shook her head. "If she's upset or in any trouble, you know she'll only try to shield us from worrying about her. Nathan, what do you think? Are we being too protective if we try to make her stay?"

Fuck. How he'd found himself in the role of family mediator, Nathan had no bloody idea.

But it was difficult not to be moved by Chase and Tavia's obvious love and concern for their child, even if Carys was a full-grown woman, twenty years old. She was stronger than most later-generation Breed males, and more than capable of taking care of herself.

"You raised her to be independent—Aric too. If Carys feels she's ready to live on her own, she's going to do it. No matter what anyone says or thinks. But if you'll sleep better knowing my team and I will keep a close eye on her, consider it done."

"Thank you, Nathan," Tavia said, exhaling her relief while Chase gathered his mate close and gave Nathan a brief nod of appreciation for his offer. The three of them exited the conference room to the corridor outside. They paused there, and Tavia lifted her head from where it rested against Chase's shoulder. "I still think it can't hurt to talk to her one more time, see if I can persuade her to change her mind."

Chase grinned. "Your powers of persuasion may work flawlessly on me, love, but good luck dealing with your daughter. And you'd better work fast. She's upstairs now, packing up her things with Jordana."

Nathan stood there as the couple excused themselves and strolled away hand in hand.

Jordana Gates was there right now, upstairs in the estate. Helping Carys collect her belongings, a task that would likely keep Jordana under the same roof as Nathan for the next couple of hours at least.

Christ.

He pivoted abruptly and stalked down the corridor in the opposite direction of Chase and Tavia, toward the passage that would lead him to the weapons room.

It was about as far away from the living quarters of the mansion as he could get. A few hours of physical training was just what he needed. Hell, the way his blood was churning through his veins now, he might not come up for air until the night's patrol was ready to head out.

With any luck, by the time he surfaced, Carys and her new roommate would be long gone.

5

JORDANA BLEW OUT A SIGH AS SHE CAME TO A STOP IN A LONG, empty corridor—one of many confusing arteries in the Chases' sprawling estate.

Had Carys said to turn *left-left-right-left* once she was in the Order's command center wing of the mansion, or *left-right-left-left?*

Shit.

A simple quest to fetch more packing tape for her friend had now delivered Jordana deep into the warriors' domain. It wasn't like she'd wanted to be there. Not when the odds of encountering Nathan in that part of the mansion seemed a bit too likely for her peace of mind.

But Carys had been insistent. She'd made it seem like no big thing at all: "Just run down to the central supply room and grab another roll of tape for me, will you? Take you not even ten minutes round trip, and I'll have this box of shoes ready to go by the time you get back."

Fifteen minutes later, Jordana was still wandering the corridors, becoming more turned around with each step she took.

She was sure she'd followed Carys's directions correctly . . .

Whether she did or not, she was definitely in the wrong place now. Ahead of her at the far end of the passageway was a set of steel double doors with a security access panel mounted to the right of them on the wall. Above the doors, the dark, unblinking eye of a surveillance camera stared down at her.

"Dammit, Carys," she whispered. "Next time you have a fool's errand to run, you're doing it yourself."

Jordana edged backward a few steps, hoping she didn't look as uncomfortable or idiotic as she felt to whoever might be monitoring the corridor. Then again, it was probably too late to worry about that. She just needed to get out of there, before she wandered any farther afield.

Spinning on her heel, she hurried back the way she came. She was jogging at a good clip by the time she reached the end of the hallway and rounded the corner—

Only to run full tilt into a wall of unmovable, warm flesh and bone. Nathan.

Oh, God.

He caught her by her upper arms, muttering a curse that didn't sound happy to see her either. "I might've guessed," he growled, more to himself than her. "Never did have much faith in luck."

Jordana struggled to find her voice for a second. "Excuse me?"

Caught in his grasp with only inches between them, she stood there immobile, her hands splayed on his broad chest. Though he was wearing a T-shirt, her palms burned with the heat rolling off the firm planes and bulges of his body beneath the soft black cotton that covered him.

His eyes bored into her, and she realized she never knew what color they were until now. Deep, greenish blue, they looked like the sky just before the arrival of a brutal storm.

That same dark, arresting stare had held her across the room of the museum last night.

Demanding.

Possessive.

Even now, she found it hard to tear herself away from Nathan's unnerving gaze. "I, um . . . I was looking for packing tape for Carys," she blurted. "She gave me directions for the supply room, but I must be lost."

He grunted, one black brow lifting almost imperceptibly.

Jordana rushed on, hating how he unsettled her. "Usually when I'm here at the mansion, I keep to the residential areas."

"As you should," he said. "You don't belong down here."

The words were rough gravel, a deep rumble that vibrated through her spread fingers, which were still pressed against his chest.

The low thunder of his voice traveled into her limbs. Into the suddenly quivering center of her body.

Jordana yanked her hands away from him, cradling her crossed fists to her breast. "I'm just . . . I'm going to go now, then."

God help her, but he kept on staring at her, watching her dangle on the strings of her own unease around him. His harsh, handsome face was so unreadable, she wondered if he was actually looking at her or through her.

The way he studied her, Jordana felt . . . exposed. She felt stripped and vulnerable under his penetrating eyes. Completely at his mercy.

His dark eyes drifted to her mouth and she was instantly reminded of the kiss they shared. Well, not shared exactly, considering she was the one who'd done all the kissing.

Nathan had stood there much the way he was now, rock solid, unshakable.

Maddeningly cool and in control.

Jordana wondered how he did it—how he could seem so unaffected yet hold her in a gaze that made her instincts come alive with an anticipation bordering on the profane. Ever fiber in her body was tuned to him, even though her head was telling her to run away. Telling her to avoid this dangerous man and the dark temptations that lurked in his stormy eyes.

What did her senses know about Nathan that her mind had not yet grasped?

Maybe if she kissed him again, she could figure out what it was about this Breed male that had her so flustered and confused.

A low snarl gathered at the back of his throat now. "Come with me."

It wasn't a request. It was a command, and even though she wanted desperately to refuse, her feet were already moving beneath her, following his gruff order.

Jordana assumed he was bringing her back to the residential wing of the estate. Instead, she soon found herself trailing him down another snaking corridor, heading for a closed door near the end of the passageway.

Nathan opened the door, then turned to her. "Inside."

She glanced past him to the unlit room on the other side of the threshold.

And apparently her body still trusted him more than her head, because she walked into the inky gloom without so much as a word of doubt.

He followed her in, so close she could feel his body heat searing the length of her back.

It was impossible not to acknowledge the danger of walking into a dark room in a long, empty corridor with the most lethal man she would probably ever know.

And yet her pulse was kicking in her veins. Her skin felt tight, too warm. Not with fear, even though it should be.

Expectation was a taut coil, twisting in her stomach . . . and lower still.

When would he touch her?

It wasn't a question of *if;* she knew that in the same way she knew that when he did finally put his hands on her, she would let him.

Jordana waited to feel his fingers against her skin, his breath in her hair. She craved it, wanting it so badly in that moment, she could hardly breathe.

Nathan shifted behind her. He moved even closer now, and Jordana closed her eyes, lungs frozen.

A light flicked on overhead.

After the engulfing darkness of a moment ago, it blared jarringly bright, illuminating the small, enclosed surroundings.

"The supply room," Jordana whispered, trying to convince herself she was relieved.

Nathan stepped past her and prowled over to a tower of sturdy metal shelves. He grabbed a thick roll of clear tape from among a variety of stacked office products and tech equipment.

He returned, tape in hand, but drew it back when Jordana reached to take it from him.

"Carys is moving out today." When Jordana nodded, he narrowed his eyes on her. "Because of what happened last night between her and Aric?"

Jordana shook her head. "No. Because it's time. She wants to live her life."

Nathan made a dubious noise in the back of his throat. "What kind of a life do you expect she'll have with a male like Rune?"

"It's not my place to judge," Jordana replied. "Besides, she's moving in with me, not him. What happens between Carys and Rune is their business."

"Until he hurts her. Or worse," Nathan warned.

"Rune would never hurt Carys. He loves her—"

Nathan scoffed. "That what he's telling her?"

Jordana frowned. "He's told her as much, yes. But I see it when they're together too. Carys and Rune are deeply in love."

"And you're some kind of expert in that emotion, I suppose." Something dark glimmered in his unwavering gaze. "You can tell what's in a man's heart just by looking at him?"

Jordana had to work to keep from squirming in his presence. He wasn't talking about Rune and Carys now. She knew that, but imagining he might be talking about himself was a path she didn't dare tread.

Not here.

Not when she had nowhere to escape, even if she wanted to.

"Carys is a grown woman," Jordana said, hoping to put the focus back where it belonged. "If she decides to be with Rune—even if she takes him as her blood-bonded mate someday—that's entirely up to her. No matter what you or her family thinks would be best for her."

"If you really believed that, I doubt you'd be with someone like Elliott Bentley-Squire."

Jordana couldn't even try to hide the fact that she was totally taken aback. "You know Elliott?"

He lifted his shoulder in a negligent shrug. "I know everything I need to know about him. I don't find him all that interesting. Which makes me wonder why you do." It was an impolite question, but Nathan didn't seem to care. "You and Elliott Bentley-Squire have been a foregone conclusion for the past year, give or take."

"Yes," she answered.

"Long time," Nathan said. "And yet no blood bond."

Jordana frowned, feeling a need to defend herself. Elliott too. "He and I have known each other forever. Elliott has been a family friend since I was a child." When Nathan's face remained impassive, she said, "We'll make things official when we're ready. We're in no hurry."

"Apparently," he agreed, but his tone was anything but light. "From what I've seen of the man's professional résumé, it doesn't indicate an inability to close a deal. So I'm guessing the problem must lie with you."

"There is no problem," she insisted, surprised at how desperately she wanted to convince him of that. Right now, standing just a foot away from Nathan in the seclusion of the supply room, she needed to convince herself that she belonged to Elliott Bentley-Squire. Jordana lifted her chin. "You seem to think you know a lot about Elliott and me. Do you make a practice of invading civilians' privacy?"

"No. Only women who make it a practice of kissing me, then insisting to their presumptive mates that they have no idea who I am."

Oh, God. Before he left the museum, Nathan must have heard her deny knowing him to Elliott. Jordana winced, remorseful now. She gave a mild shake of her head. "I'm sorry."

He shrugged. "If you have to lie to Bentley-Squire to keep him happy, it's none of my concern."

"No," she said, ignoring the jab. "I mean, I'm sorry about that night in my apartment . . . when I kissed you."

"Are you?" He didn't believe her. His tone was cool and level, but it contained a dangerous edge.

"Of course I'm sorry. I don't know what came over me. I've never done anything like that before."

"Then why did you?"

She glanced down, searching for an answer that would make sense to herself as well as to him. "I did it because I was afraid."

"You didn't seem afraid, Jordana."

"I was afraid of what you might do if you found out Carys was there with Rune that night. I only wanted to stop you from finding out. I just wanted to distract you."

His face darkened in challenge. "There were a dozen different ways you could've done that, none of which would've involved putting your mouth on mine."

She groaned, feeling her cheeks go warm and red. "I know. I've already apologized. It was a mistake, and I'm sorry, Nathan."

The way he looked at her brought every nuance of their kiss back to life in her senses—the cushion of his mouth beneath hers, the softness of his lips combined with the rough abrasion of his dark-shadowed jaw. The powerful stillness of his body as she threw herself against him.

Punishing muscle and lethal strength caged inside a rigid, total control.

Some brazen part of her she barely recognized throbbed with the want to know that kiss again—to have a taste of what it would be like to press against this deadly male and see if he ever let his iron discipline slip, even a little.

More uncomfortable heat flooded her face at the uninvited direction of her thoughts.

And deep inside her, another unsettling heat bloomed . . .

Nathan's gaze lingered on her, those eyes seeing everything about her. Knowing everything. Ruthless in their study of her.

Jordana grew anxious suddenly, afraid that Nathan might touch her.

Afraid he might kiss her.

Afraid he wouldn't.

"I'll take that tape now," she said, her voice thick and raspy.

He didn't give it to her, didn't move. "Tell me what you see in Elliott Bentley-Squire."

Jordana stared up into Nathan's dark eyes. She shook her head.

"Tell me," he insisted.

Although talking about Elliott was the last thing she wanted to do in that moment, Jordana drew a breath and tried to conjure words. "He's kind and affectionate," she murmured lamely. "He's loyal and steady and attentive . . ."

Nathan's lips twisted with dark amusement. "That's how I'd expect you to describe a pet, not the man who's fucking you."

The frankness shocked her, embarrassed her. But she was also unwillingly aroused by Nathan's lack of delicacy. There was a rawness about him that was unlike anything she was accustomed to.

She was playing with fire where this dangerous male was concerned, and it only made her want to dance closer to the flame.

"Elliott and I are not lovers," she said, pushing the words out of her mouth before she was too afraid to bite them back. "I've never been with him in that way."

Something flickered in the depths of his dark eyes. "And you don't want him like that either."

Jordana frowned, hating that Nathan could know that about her so easily. "I've never wanted anyone like that. There's been . . . no one."

"No one?" Nathan seemed to go even more still where he stood. The only movement she could detect in him was the ticking of a tendon along the line of his jaw. "He wants you, this Elliott Bentley-Squire. He's waited a year to bond you to him by blood. How long do you think you can keep him from claiming you, Jordana?"

"Elliott is a patient man. He'll wait until I decide it's time."

Nathan gave a harsh grunt. "Then he's not the kind of mate you need. Not the kind of male a woman like you deserves."

She collected her courage enough to meet his challenge with one of her own. "What could you possibly know about what I need or deserve?"

He stepped in tighter to her, crowding her backward with the massive breadth of his body. "Have you ever kissed Elliott Bentley-Squire the way you kissed me?"

She didn't answer, couldn't form words with him this close to her.

"Has he ever made your cheeks flame just by looking at you, or made your pulse beat like a hammer in your veins because of the things you wish he'd do to you?"

Jordana swallowed. She exhaled a shaky breath edged with a humiliating whimper. Somehow she managed to find her voice amid the tumult of confusion and dark, unwanted desire that was swirling like a tempest inside her. "I suppose you're arrogant enough to believe that I should want someone like you instead?"

He chuckled then, low and humorless. "No, Jordana. I'm the last kind of man you should want in your life . . . or in your bed."

And yet he didn't move away from her. He just kept her caged with his body for a seemingly endless moment of time.

His irises crackled with tiny sparks of amber as he stared at her. Only the barest tips of his fangs were noticeable behind the lush line of his upper lip.

Jordana felt him reach between the scant distance of their bodies to take her hand. His fingers were warm and strong, so large and commanding as he held her in his firm, guiding grasp.

He uncurled her loose fist, only to place something hard and round, cold and sleek, in her palm. Of course. The roll of packing tape.

"Go back to where you belong now, Jordana." He drew away from her at last, leaving her standing in a chilled, confused state of arousal and rejection. "Get out," he said, a warning in the curt command.

Jordana held the tape to her chest and could hardly scramble for the door fast enough.

As she started to rush for the corridor, he added, "That kiss was a mistake, Jordana—for both of us. But don't expect me to believe you're any more sorry than I am that it happened."

6

IF HIS MORNING HAD STARTED OFF IN A BAD WAY, BY AFTERNOON it hadn't improved a bit. After his encounter with Jordana, as much as Nathan craved an outlet for his tightly leashed aggression, he didn't want to risk killing any of his teammates if he joined them in the day's combat exercises in the weapons room.

Instead, he'd spent the bulk of the day in the command center's technology lab, digging into public records—and some not so public—in his search for intel on Cassian Gray.

All he'd discovered was that the man was proving to be as elusive on paper as he was in person. For all the lack of information, it was as if Cass had been taking careful steps to cover his tracks from the moment he first surfaced in Boston twenty-some years ago.

As if he'd been planning all along for the day he'd need to vanish.

Nathan downloaded what little he had on Cass to a mission intel file, then shut down the computer and left the lab. With sundown just a few hours away, he had time to get in some solo training and prep his weapons for the night's patrol with his team.

His body was still tense, aggression still riding him, and he knew damn well it had less to do with frustration over a stymied mission than it did a certain platinum-haired, Darkhaven beauty he had no right to desire.

An unschooled virgin besides.

Fuck.

Never mind the fact that she was Carys Chase's best friend—as of today, her roommate besides—and the darling of Boston's high society, Breed and human alike. Never mind that she had all but promised herself to another male, out of obligation or naivete, it didn't matter.

No, Jordana Gates was off limits for many reasons, but most of all this: Because she was pure. She was innocent.

He wouldn't be the one to take that from her.

He couldn't take that from anyone, not the way his hungers ran.

He hadn't been merely trying to scare Jordana when he told her that he was the last man she'd want in her bed. It had been a warning. One he hoped to hell she took to heart, because God help her if she trusted him to be the hero.

On a curse, Nathan stalked into the vacant armory of the Order's weapons room. He stripped off his black T-shirt and powered himself through a punishing hour of solo exercise with a pair of long daggers. The exertion woke up his muscles and bones, reminded his body of what it was trained to do.

More important, it woke up his Hunter's mind, put his thoughts in ruthless focus on executing the patrol ahead of him in the city tonight.

Elsewhere, in the main arena of the weapons facility, he could hear Rafe, Eli, and Jax still running one another through the paces of mock combat. A fourth voice—Aric must have joined them at some point— whooped as blades clanked and sawed together, steel meeting steel.

Nathan finished his solo maneuvers and hit the shower. He hoped to be in and gone before the other warriors wrapped up their work in the adjacent room, but no sooner had he stepped under the hot spray than footsteps falling heavy on tile and lighthearted insults sounded in the locker area outside.

Elijah's low drawl echoed over the rest of the men. "Damn, someone tell me why I thought that fifth round of hand-to-hand and blade work was a good idea." A moment later, the brown-haired vampire swaggered naked into the showers, slanting Nathan a casual nod of greeting.

Eli took his place across from Nathan and turned on the spray, groaning as the hot water coursed over him. Blood ran in thin, diluted rivulets down Eli's *dermaglyph*-covered arms and legs from wounds he'd sustained in the practice, but already the lacerations were beginning to heal.

Minor injuries were of no consequence to their kind. Cuts and contusions vanished in minutes, sometimes less time than that.

"Don't be such a sore loser," Aric Chase taunted. Grinning, he strode in and took a spot two down from Elijah. Rafe and Jax followed him inside, briefly acknowledging Nathan before going to separate corners of the showers. "What's the matter, Eli," Aric pressed, "don't want to admit you got trounced by a trainee?"

"Trainee," he said, smirking as he glanced at the younger warrior and sluiced water off his face. "Daywalking, smartass punk, more like it. You're good with a weapon, I'll give you that. But don't think I didn't notice you waited to take me on until after I'd already gone four rounds with two warriors who actually know how to fight."

Aric chuckled as he soaped up and shot a look at Rafe across the room. "You know, for a Texan, he's sure got a fragile ego. Must be that weaker, late-generation Breed blood in him."

"The hell you say." Eli snorted, his drawl thicker now. "Ain't nothin' fragile about me. Next time you ask me to spar, I'm gonna drop you on your daywalker ass before I kick it from here to the Alamo."

Aric laughed and rinsed off the suds. "Tell you what. If it'll make you feel better, I'll give you a handicap next time."

"I'll give you a handicap right now, sunshine." Elijah flashed his fangs at the other vampire and made a fast swat at Aric, cuffing his flaccid dick. It was a jest and a challenge—one Aric tried to return, but wasn't quick enough.

Both laughing now, Eli grabbed him in a headlock under the water and let him sputter for a few seconds before letting him go. Before long, Jax and Rafe joined in the skirmish, the four big males wrestling around like a close-knit wolf pack.

Like the tight band of brothers they were.

Nathan watched for a moment, detached from the camaraderie. For all his expertise in stealth and combat, game play was a concept that eluded him. It went against his nature. Against the rigid discipline that had made him a consummate killer by the time he was seven years old.

He chased.

He conquered.

He destroyed.

His training as a boy in the Hunters' cells permitted nothing less. And although his rescue at age thirteen had saved Nathan, a part of him had never come out of Dragos's lab and likely never would.

He was the fighting dog, rescued from the squalor and violence of the betting pits and brought into a kind, loving home to live a better life.

He had been spared, given a new chance. He had parents and friends he cared for. He had fellow warriors who would die for him, as he would for them.

Yet, like the dog removed from the ring, when a hand reached out to him—in play or in comfort—it was all he could do to keep from biting it.

The distance between who he was now and what he'd been raised to be was a thin razor's edge that he toed with meticulous discipline each and every day. No one knew the effort it took for him to seem normal. To appear that he fit in with decent people, that he belonged.

They saw what he wanted them to see, and nothing more.

No one knew him beyond what he'd allowed them to perceive.

No one took anything from him that he wasn't prepared to give up.

No one ever had, until Jordana Gates.

His blood ran hot at the thought of her, their conversation—and the all-too-tempting memory of her body in such close proximity to his—making his veins light up with hunger.

If he'd thought the beautiful Breedmate an unwanted distraction be-fore, crossing paths with her this morning had only confirmed what he'd been striving so hard to deny.

Jordana Gates was going to be a problem for him.

She already was. After one brief kiss and a couple of chance encounters—all told, only a few minutes' time in her presence—she had aroused a fierce desire in him. She was impacting his focus, diminishing his concentration.

Making him burn with the need to seek her out and take what he craved.

Nathan cursed under his breath and cut off the water.

With his squad and Aric trading insults and banter along with their punches and body checks on the other side of the showers, Nathan stalked out to dry off and dress in the other room alone.

Rafe came out as Nathan was pulling on a fresh black T-shirt. The blond vampire grabbed a white towel from a folded stack and wrapped it around his lean hips. "Something going on with you that I should know about?"

"No." Without looking over at his comrade, Nathan rubbed his towel over the damp black spikes of his hair.

"You sure about that?" Rafe walked over to the lockers next to Na-than and leaned one beefy shoulder against the metal. "Something's bugging you. I noticed it in the meeting this morning. Your head is somewhere else."

Christ. Nathan wasn't accustomed to being read by someone, let alone getting called on it. He bristled at the weakness in himself but shot his cold glare at Rafe as he slammed his locker shut. "You got issues with my leadership, take it up with Commander Chase."

Rafe blew out a curse and scowled, studying him closer. "This isn't about the team, you asshole. I'm asking as your friend. You've been wound tighter than usual all day. Actually, ever since that night we went looking for Carys and ended up at Jordana Gates's place."

Nathan froze, a muscle ticking in his jaw as he faced Rafe's steady, knowing blue gaze.

"You do know she's to be mated soon, don't you?" Rafe pressed. "Some good ol' boy Darkhaven lawyer who's been sniffing around her skirts practically since she came of age, according to Carys."

Nathan growled at the reminder. "Like I said, there's nothing going on that you need to know about. Nothing I can't handle. And as *your* friend, I'm asking you to trust me on that."

It took a long moment before Rafe finally nodded his agreement. He turned away and started getting dressed. "Any further word from D.C. today?"

"Nothing yet," Nathan replied, glad for the change in subjects. "They're still arranging the meetings with Crowe's widow and exes. When I spoke with Gideon at Headquarters today, he said they expect to have the interrogations completed within a couple of days. Which is better than I can say about our mission to bring in Cassian Gray. I've been digging into the bastard's records all day and coming up empty. No personal records, no past, no kin. The man's a fucking ghost."

Rafe grunted. "He's got property. La Notte."

Nathan gave a dubious shrug. "Maybe, maybe not. I hit a wall trying to chase down the title holder of the club. Records are private, sealed. Far as I could tell, there's about half a dozen layers of lawyers and holding companies in the way."

"That's a lot of anonymity and subterfuge for a nightclub," Rafe remarked. "Cage fighting is illegal, but it sure as hell doesn't warrant that kind of paranoia."

Nathan nodded. "That's what Gideon said when I told him what I'd found. He's running some hacks now, said he'll report back as soon as he turns up any leads."

As the Order's longtime chief intelligence officer and resident genius, Gideon in D.C. hadn't run field missions in many years, but the vampire was an absolute killer behind the keyboard.

"Gonna take a hell of a lot more than lawyers and corporate shields to keep Gideon from exposing Cass and whoever he's hiding behind," Rafe said. "There's never been a database in existence that he couldn't crack."

Nathan agreed, but time spent waiting was time wasted. While Headquarters was hacking into Cass's life from D.C., Nathan and his team needed to keep up the pressure locally.

"Tell Eli and Jax we'll meet in fifteen for a review of tonight's patrol. We may not know everything about Cassian Gray yet, but there's one obvious constant in his life and that's La Notte." Nathan headed for the exit. "We need to start disrupting his business, rattle the hive, and see what it stirs up. And we start tonight."

Jordana walked the exhibit floor at the museum, taking a slow measure of the entire collection and jotting notes on her tablet. Last night's patron preview had been a means of thanking the various donors and community supporters, but it had also been a dry run for the exhibit in preparation for its public opening in just a few nights.

She perused the pieces and their placement, making minute adjustments to temperature and humidity settings, double-checking text cards and lighting levels for each of the displays.

Anything to keep her mind from straying to her unsettling encounter with Nathan earlier that morning.

He'd been crude and confrontational. Impolite and far too bold. He was terrifying, not because of his profession or his past but because of the way he seemed to see straight into her soul and lay her bare.

He was dangerous for so many reasons.

And yet she couldn't stop thinking about the things he said to her. She couldn't stop thinking about the way he made her feel. Her pulse quickened at the memory of being alone with Nathan in close quarters.

He hadn't even touched her, yet her body had thrummed with the need to feel his hands on her.

Have you ever kissed Elliott Bentley-Squire the way you kissed me?

Nathan's words came back to her in a heated rush, making the ache return again now. She tried to will it away, but it was already taking root deep inside her. In truth, it had never fully ebbed in all the hours since she'd seen Nathan at the mansion.

Has he ever made your cheeks flame just by looking at you, or made your pulse beat like a hammer in your veins because of the things you wish he'd do to you?

Jordana idly brought her free hand up to her lips, finding it all too easy to imagine it was Nathan's mouth brushing against hers, not the tips of her suddenly trembling fingers. He had been right about that too—she didn't regret kissing him. Not even after the things he said to her today.

Not even after the mortifying things she'd admitted to him about her relationship with Elliott and her lack of experience in general.

God, why had she told him that? What had possessed her to admit so much to him with so little provocation? Nathan knew more about her now than anyone besides her best friend. What more might she be willing to tell him—or willing to do—if she ever saw him again?

I'm the last kind of man you should want in your life . . . or in your bed.

She didn't doubt that for a minute, yet her blood still throbbed in her veins, kindling the knot of heat that pulsed in her core. Her nape tingled beneath the loose chignon of her upswept hair, the pulse points in her neck echoing in her ears with each heavy beat of her heart. Warmth spread down her throat and across the tops of her breasts, making her light silk blouse feel as hot and confining as a winter sweater.

"Hello? Earth to Jordana." Carys's voice broke into Jordana's thoughts like a splash of cold water. "Did you hear a word I said?"

"Sorry," Jordana blurted. "I was just finishing a note on this display."

Carys cocked her head and narrowed her eyes slightly, as if she didn't quite buy the excuse. "I've got the temps and humidity readings you asked for on the French tapestry displays." She tapped her tablet screen and sent the data to Jordana's device.

Jordana scanned the report and nodded her approval. "This looks good, Carys, thank you. I would like to see the lighting muted a bit on the Beauvais pastoral piece. I noticed last night that we were losing some of the more subtle colors of the weaving."

"Okay," Carys replied. "Are you still rethinking the placement of the Roman mosaics?"

Jordana glanced over to the display of ancient tiles encased in a multi-tiered tower of Plexiglas in the center of the exhibit. She considered for a moment, then gave a nod. "Yes, let's have that switched with something else. *Sleeping Endymion* would be a better focal point for that section of the exhibit, don't you think?"

Carys smiled. "Your favorite piece. Sure, I think it's a great idea."

They walked over to the clear case that housed the Italian sculpture that was more than three hundred years old. The terra cotta depiction of the mortal shepherd Endymion reposed in eternal slumber where he waited for his lover, the lunar goddess Selene, had enchanted Jordana from the moment she first saw it. Donated anonymously, the sculpture had been part of the museum's permanent collection for at least two decades.

It wasn't the most valuable, or even among the most historically important pieces Jordana had known. But the simple beauty of the work, and the myth it represented, never failed to move something deep inside her.

Jordana stared into the display at the handsome mortal who slept forever under the delicate sliver of a crescent moon. Just looking at the piece made a sadness swell in her chest. She glanced down at the inside of her left wrist, where she bore a small scarlet birthmark in the shape of a crescent moon with a teardrop falling into its cradle.

Her Breedmate mark.

Unlike Endymion, she wasn't fully mortal. She, like the other half-human females born with the teardrop-and-crescent-moon symbol somewhere on their bodies, could live agelessly once blood-bonded with one of the Breed.

Such an incredible gift, to entwine two lives forever. And yet it could also be an inescapable shackle.

"Can you imagine sleeping through your entire existence?" Jordana murmured as Carys came to stand beside her, looking at Cornacchini's sculpture. "Have you ever felt as though your life were taking place around you, outside of you? That everything was moving faster than you could catch it—as if you were asleep and anchored to the ground like Endymion?"

"No," Carys replied, zero hesitation. "If I want something, I reach for it. I don't let anything stop me."

Her careful tone drew Jordana's gaze to her. "Never?"

"Never."

Jordana gave a mild nod. "It's different for you, Carys. You're Breed. You didn't grow up in the Darkhavens, or with a father who's been drumming into your head since you were a child that he expected you to be blood-bonded to a suitable mate by the time you were twenty-five."

"True," Carys said around a laugh. "If my father had his way, he'd have chained me to the mansion banister until I was twice that age. Life is meant to be lived, Jordana. And we only get one shot at it, whether we're Breedmate, Breed, or basic *Homo sapiens*."

Jordana smiled at her friend, loving how sure Carys always seemed about what she wanted and where she was heading. "I wish I had your bravery. You've never been afraid to leap, no matter how deep or dark the crevasse beneath you."

Carys shrugged, grinning. "It's only deep and dark if you pause first to look down. Besides, you've got your own kind of bravery, Jordana. I mean, look what you're doing here with the exhibit."

Jordana took in the collection she was so proud of, all the pieces she had lovingly, painstakingly, curated one by one. It was her joy, and she threw herself into her work wholeheartedly.

While she'd made a rewarding, promising career for herself, sometimes she wondered if her father and Elliott would both be happier if she'd spent her time in philanthropic or social pursuits like most of the other young Breedmates of the area Darkhavens.

But she'd been a disappointment to them there too. She wasn't like most other Breedmates, no matter how much she or anyone else wished she were. Hell, she wasn't even sure what her unique ESP ability might be, a gift most women like her came into by puberty or earlier.

Jordana pulled her thoughts back to the exhibit and Carys's bolstering praise.

"This is all your vision, your work," her friend pointed out. "No one handed this project to you—you wanted it, so you went after it and you made it happen."

"That's different," Jordana demurred. Her gaze drifted back to the sculpture under the glass. "What if you don't know what you want? What if you wake up one day and realize that you never had a clue what you wanted? That someone had always been telling you what you needed or what was expected, and now all you want to do is close your eyes again and pretend you're still sleeping?"

Carys's bright blue gaze softened. "You want me to tell you what I think, honestly?"

"Yes." Jordana nodded. "Tell me, please."

"I think you know what you *don't* want. And I think that's what you're afraid to admit to anyone, even to yourself."

Jordana blew out a slow sigh as she glanced away. "That's what Nathan said to me too. Well, not in so many words. He was far less polite about it."

"Nathan," Carys said. "So you did see him at the mansion this morning."

Hearing the obvious lack of surprise in her friend's voice, Jordana shot a frown at her. "You knew?"

Carys smiled, devilish. "I thought you might have. You came back with the packing tape looking kind of flushed and out of breath. I didn't think it was because you'd been running around in circles down in the command center. Even though my directions to the supply room might've gotten you a bit turned around . . ."

Jordana's eyes widened. "You *did* give me bad instructions! I knew it. I ended up so lost, I might never have found my way back."

Carys grinned. "Civilians don't go unnoticed on the warriors' turf for long. I knew someone would help you find your way."

"I can't believe you deliberately sent me down there like that," Jordana said, appalled but not angry. "You couldn't possibly have been hoping I'd run into him?"

"I saw the way you looked at Nathan last night at the patrons' reception. And I saw the way he looked at you. I found it . . . interesting. So I decided to take a little chance." She arched a brow at Jordana. "I took a leap, thinking maybe you might need help taking one too."

"With him?" Jordana scoffed. "Please. He's the rudest man I've ever met. He has no social skills whatsoever. He's coarse and cold and menacing."

"And yet you kissed him a few nights ago."

She hardly needed the reminder. Jordana felt her forehead crease harder with her deepening scowl. She'd never been particularly comfortable in her own skin, had felt practically all her life that she was different somehow. That she was merely pretending so hard to be normal—to be the good daughter, the exemplary woman, the pleasant Breedmate—goals that seemed always just out of her reach.

No matter how hard she strived to be what everyone around her expected, inside she felt she was only going through the motions. Acting, not living.

Pretending to be something she wasn't and maybe never could be.

She'd never felt that lack so markedly as she did in Nathan's company. He had the uncanny ability to strip her bare, to pare her down to her bones with just a glance. He had the unnerving power to unravel the tentative constructs of her life with just one uninvited touch.

"He scares me, Carys. When Nathan looks at me, I feel as if he's seeing all my flaws, every crack in who I am. When I'm near him, it's as though I'm standing naked in the middle of a raging storm. He makes me feel as if I'm on the steepest cliff, about to lose my footing. That if I step too close to him, I might never get back on solid ground."

Carys stared at her. "And this is a bad thing, the way you see it?"

"Yes, it's bad. It's the worst thing," Jordana said, uncertain who she needed to convince more: her friend or herself. "I'll be better off—safer—if I stay far away from Nathan."

"Maybe you're right," Carys replied after a long moment. "It would be safer for you if you steer clear of him."

"Yes," Jordana said, pushing out the breath she'd been holding. Having her best friend's agreement was just the confirmation she needed. "I'm glad you understand."

"Oh, believe me, I do," Carys said. Her lips curved into a wry smile. "Because what you just described? That's how Rune made me feel from the moment we first met. I stepped off that cliff with him, and so far, I haven't missed solid ground beneath me for so much as a second."

7

CASSIAN GRAY STEPPED OUT OF A TAXI AND INTO THE LATE-afternoon sunlight on Commonwealth Avenue in Boston's Back Bay. He ambled up the street at a casual pace, even though daytime was ending in less than two hours and he had every reason to hustle his ass to where he was going.

This close to dusk, it was a risk for him to be out and about. Although he hadn't been in touch with anyone at La Notte in a couple of days, he had no doubt the Order was on his trail. He'd suspected his cover had been blown from the instant one of their warriors—an errant comrade-turned-rebel-leader named Kellan Archer—had body-blocked him during a minor confrontation in the club.

Cassian didn't know what the Breed male's unique psychic talent might be, but something told him the warrior's touch had outed Cass as being other than human.

That bit of shitty luck had nearly been enough to make Cass cut and run from the life he'd made for himself in Boston, but it was the more recent bout of bad news—the death of Reginald Crowe—that had Cass skulking around the city and constantly looking over his shoulder like the fugitive he truly was.

Crowe's attempt to disrupt the Global Nations Council summit several nights ago had made headlines all over the world. So had his slaying at the hands of the Order. As much as Cass dreaded the possibility of being captured for interrogation by Lucan and his warriors, there was another, equally lethal army of soldiers that he hoped to elude.

His Atlantean kinsmen.

Cass had been on the run from them for far longer than he had from the Order. Hiding in plain sight had worked well enough all these years, and it was that same method of concealment he employed now, as he made his way to an important appointment in the city.

As he strolled nonchalantly by a coffee shop window on the avenue, he caught his reflection and smiled to himself at how different he looked. His short crown of hair was dyed a nondescript brown and combed into an obedient side part. Dark sunglasses masked his eyes.

He'd traded his usual public camouflage of leather and metal for thrift store denim and a faded Red Sox logo T-shirt that had probably started showing its wear a decade ago. Scuffed loafers covered his feet, their soles so thin he could feel every pit and bump in the concrete of the sidewalk as he made his way toward the designated meeting spot.

He looked more than passably pedestrian, hardly distinguishable from any other civilian man in his thirties. To anyone seeing him on the street today, Cass was unremarkable, forgettable. Just as he'd intended.

No one would think that he and the platinum-haired, black-leather-clad Goth nightmare proprietor of La Notte were one and the same.

Nor would any of the humans around him on this stretch of crowded pavement ever guess that he was an immortal on the north side of a thousand years old.

Only his fellow Atlanteans might sense he was one of them, and he'd been careful to keep his head down in the time since he'd left their realm and come to Boston. He'd constructed an all-new identity, a facade he'd carefully maintained for twenty-some years, from his unsavory occupation and all the underworld connections that went along with it, to his offputting appearance and the presumed kink of his carnal proclivities.

Cassian Gray, proprietor of La Notte, was a mask he'd perfected over a long period of time. Keeping his ear to the ground, his fingers busy greasing palms and pulling various strings in the shadowy underbelly of the city were cautious necessities of his new life.

He'd had to be cautious, because he was a wanted man. A hated man. A defector.

A traitor to his queen.

He'd taken something of great value to her when he fled, and her wrath knew no limits. She'd called for his death. Then again, he'd given her little choice. His death was the only hope she had of ever getting her hands on the precious treasure he stole away from her.

If Cassian had anything to say about it, not even his death would assure the queen of that goal.

He figured it was only a matter of time before someone caught up to him—his immortal comrades or the Order's warriors. There was nowhere completely safe for him now, and so long as he stayed in Boston, his presence alone posed an added risk to the very thing he'd worked so hard to shield and protect.

Which was the reason for his clandestine appointment today. He needed further assurances that his interests would continue to be looked after, even if he was gone from the picture altogether.

Cassian rounded a corner at the end of the block and made his way onto Newbury Street. He headed into a swanky sim lounge, bypassing the hostess before she could tell him what the current offerings were in each of the club's experience rooms. Cass wasn't there to spend time or money playing in the virtual reality realm with tourists looking to become spaceship captains or fairy-tale creatures at the rate of a couple hundred an hour.

He walked to the back of the club as had been arranged earlier that day. The individual he'd come to meet was already waiting in one of the private VIP rooms.

Garbed from head to toe in dark, UV-protective clothing, the Breed male waited with his driver, a human—hired help, by the anxious look of him. No doubt the driver's tip would come in the currency of a mind scrub once the meeting was concluded and his fare was delivered safely back to his home elsewhere in the city.

Cassian strolled in and faced the vampire's obscured form. "My old friend," he said, extending his hand to the vampire who knew all his secrets and had kept them faithfully. "Thank you for agreeing to meet me on such short notice."

"What do you think?" Carys spread her arms wide and gestured around her to the display of French tapestries when Jordana sought her out a few hours later, as the museum was closing for the day. "I had the guys mix the halogens with a few low-watt LEDs. If you think it's too dark now—"

"No." Jordana shook her head. "No, it's perfect like this. Good work."

Carys beamed. "Thanks. I also picked up the interior signage from the printer. It's in your office. They said they'll deliver the digital placards and exterior banners in the morning."

"Excellent. I have a placement mock-up almost finished for all of the banners and digital signs. I know it's getting late, but it shouldn't take me too long to wrap up. You want to wait for me? We can grab some carryout from the Thai place on the way home and a bottle of wine. Seems like we should do something to celebrate your moving in today, right?"

"Oh," Carys said slowly, her expression wilting in apology. "Jordana, I'm sorry. I made plans with Rune earlier this week that I'd be at the club. He's got a big match tonight and I want to see him before he goes into the cages. I hate watching him fight, but I can't bear to not be there, you know?"

Jordana gave a mild shrug. "Sure, I understand. You should be there."

"Come with me instead. We can celebrate and have dinner there."

"No. That's okay." Jordana was disappointed, but she knew how Carys worried herself sick when Rune was in the cages, despite the fact that the brutal Breed fighter had never lost a match.

Jordana could hardly stomach the fights either. And she hated to support an establishment whose proprietor made his living off the spilled blood and broken bones of others. Besides, it wasn't as if she didn't have plenty of work to keep her busy anyway.

"You go on and be with Rune tonight," she said. "We can celebrate another time."

Carys frowned. "Are you sure?"

"Positive. I want to tie up a few loose ends before I head out anyway. I'll order takeout instead and bring home the leftovers for you in case you're hungry when you get in."

"Thank you." Carys pulled her into a quick, warm hug. "I'll see you later, then. And when we do go out to celebrate, it's my treat. Deal?"

Jordana nodded. "Okay. It's a deal."

She went back to work as Carys gathered her things and left the museum. Two hours later, Jordana had finished the signage map for the exhibit and eaten half a container of veggie pad Thai, stowing the rest in the department refrigerator down the hall. The museum was quiet, everyone but her and the twenty-four-hour security guard on post in the lobby having long since left the building.

Jordana saved the signage map on her computer and sent a copy to

Carys's tablet for the morning. She got up to stretch her legs and walk to the restroom before she would have to make the drive home across town. When she returned to her desk, she had a voicemail from Elliott.

He didn't sound happy that she was working late again. "Apparently, I've missed you most of the day, darling. Did you get the message I left on your mobile a few hours ago?"

Shit. She'd been so busy, she hadn't bothered to check the damn thing.

"I want you to call me as soon as you get home tonight, Jordana. I want to know that you're safe." He cleared his throat, and she thought she heard irritation in his tone. "When I didn't hear from you today, I called your building and spoke with Seamus. Maybe you can tell me how it is that I had to find out from your doorman that Carys Chase has moved into your apart—"

Jordana disconnected from the message on a furious curse. What the hell was Elliott doing checking up on her behind her back?

She was half tempted to return his call right now and ask him that herself. But she knew if she did, she might also say something she could never take back.

Angry now, she deleted the voicemail and closed up her office for the night.

She took the elevator down to the lobby, said good-bye to Lou behind the reception desk, and walked out to the parking lot.

Hers was the only vehicle there, the pale silver compact car gleaming under the overhead lamps at the far end of the pavement. Jordana got halfway across the lot before she remembered the Thai food in the refrigerator upstairs.

"Dammit."

She turned to go back and froze. A pair of eyes was trained on her in the dark; she could feel it.

There—a shadow near the building.

It skulked away quickly when she peered in its direction, though not soon enough to escape her notice. Someone was there, watching her. Waiting for her?

The hairs on her nape rose in a wave. Fear shot down her spine like a cold electrical current. Her heart raced, palms going damp.

Someone was there.

Hiding, but not gone.

Watching her, even now.

Who was it?

What did they want?

She wasn't about to go back to the building and find out. Carys's leftovers weren't going anywhere tonight.

As for Jordana, the idea of going home alone to an empty apartment while her pulse was still jackhammering in fear didn't sound very appealing. Of course, she could always call Elliott. He'd come over in a moment's notice if she asked it of him. But she didn't want Elliott.

The sad fact was, she never had wanted him.

And he deserved to know that.

But that was a problem she'd have to deal with soon enough.

Right now, Jordana just wanted to make it to her vehicle in one piece. She needed to go somewhere public, somewhere she knew she'd be safe among friends.

She hurried across the dark pavement and hopped in her car, then peeled out of the parking lot.

Her penthouse was just a few blocks away from the museum, but Jordana passed her building and kept on going, heading deeper into the city, to La Notte.

8

NATHAN LED HIS TEAM INTO CASSIAN GRAY'S CLUB AT THE height of the evening's most lucrative hour. The dance floor and bar on street level were jammed with people who'd shelled out the steep cover charge just to get in, but the real commerce—Cass's bread and butter—was taking place in the cages below.

With fearful glances and anxious murmurs rising in their wake, the heavily armed patrol squad cut a path through the crowd upstairs and headed down to La Notte's arena.

The fights, and the sizable bets that accompanied them, were already well under way. Rune always drew the largest numbers, and tonight appeared to be no exception. The immense, dark-haired Breed male was matched against an opponent almost his equal in size and menace.

At six and a half feet tall and 300-plus pounds apiece, the two vampires dressed in little more than leather breeches and locked in brutal hand-to-hand combat inside the cage was a sight few humans would ever see in their lifetimes.

So much the better that the Breed-on-Breed blood sport could be enjoyed from the perceived safety of the club surrounding the steel-reinforced arena.

The crowd gasped as Rune drove a hard right hook into his opponent's jaw. Bone cracked and blood spewed from the vampire's slack mouth.

The blow was punishing, catastrophic, given that each fighter wore titanium-spiked, fingerless leather gloves in the ring. The metal was meant to increase the savagery of the contest, but it also served to discourage the fighters from doping their performance with excessive feeding before a match.

If a Breed pushed himself into Bloodlust—the addiction only a rare few had ever beaten—the titanium of his opponent's knuckle spikes would enter his diseased bloodstream and kill the vampire faster than any pounding he might suffer in the cages.

With the spectators cheering wildly, Rune's opponent sank down onto his knees on a low howl of anguish. Nathan assessed the damage with a shrewd assassin's eye. Another strike like the last one and Rune's kill count would increase along with the stakes on him at the cashier.

Rune didn't seem interested in beefing up his record or his worth. The big male stood back, allowing the other vampire the choice to either hit the mercy button on the cage and deliver Rune a jolt of electricity to the U-shaped steel collar each fighter wore around his neck or continue the match without the benefit of the handicap. Shouts of disapproval traveled the crowd near the cages as their champion refused to end the bout with an easy, but unnecessary, kill.

As the fight resumed, Nathan gestured to his squad to begin clearing the place out. It took only moments—and the flash of fangs from a group of combat-ready Order members—to send the bulk of the club's clientele in the direction of the nearest exits.

But the intrusion also got the swift attention of La Notte's security staff. Nathan and his men played rough with them tonight, no need to pretend they weren't there to stir things up and make their presence known.

Elijah, Jax, and Rafe bounced a few Breed guards into the brick walls of the place, while Nathan soon found himself going hand to hand with a couple of the other fighters employed by Cassian Gray.

He disabled both in seconds, stopping just short of killing them. He wheeled around to face yet another of Cass's fighters, but Syn made no move to take him on. Just shy of Nathan or Rune's size, and handsome to the point of being pretty, the blond Breed male held his own impressive record in the cages. But he seemed to know better than to invite further problems with Nathan. All around them, the club was emptying out.

"Tell your boss we're gonna come back every night and toss this place until we hear from him," Nathan warned. "The longer he takes, harder the Order's gonna push."

Syn merely stared, unfazed, watching the arena empty further. Only the drunks and diehard fight fans remained now, a clot of about forty people still riveted to the match winding down in the cage.

Nathan stared into that crowd and felt his veins go tight as his gaze locked on to a pair of young women in the front row of the straggling spectators.

Holy hell.

Carys was easy enough to spot. Her loose caramel waves bounced around the shoulders of her form-fitted black sweater as she cheered on her man, dark denim hugging her backside. She jumped up and down on high-heeled black boots, clapping her hands and whistling as the clock ran out and Rune's victory was assured.

The other female was a surprise Nathan neither wanted nor needed tonight.

With her back to him, Jordana Gates stood beside Carys, dressed by contrast in a soft gray pencil skirt and pale pink silk blouse. Her long white-blond hair was gathered into some kind of knotted updo at her nape.

Jesus, she looked like she belonged in a boardroom meeting uptown, not a blood match down in the cages of Boston's least reputable club.

Except Jordana seemed as rapt as Carys with the match taking place tonight. Neither woman paid any attention as Nathan left Syn standing behind him and made his way toward the pair. He smelled liquor on them even before he was halfway across the room. And now he noticed that the women were less than steady on their feet, even Jordana in her conservative pumps.

When the bell on the match rang out, Carys and Jordana cheered Rune's name along with the handful of spectators around them. Nathan stalked forward, idly aware that Rune had peeled off his gloves and collar in order to catch Carys as she threw open the cage door and flew into his arms.

He felt Rune's dark gaze light on him in disapproval for the Order's interruption of the night's commerce, but Nathan's focus was trained elsewhere now.

Jordana went still suddenly, then slowly turned around. Her gaze collided with Nathan's glower, a connection he felt like a lightning strike that sent heat straight to his groin.

If he'd thought Jordana looked suited for a board meeting from behind, facing her now threw that lame comparison out the window. Her blouse was carelessly untucked in front, the first three buttons unfastened, creating a tempting plunge of bare flesh that ended just between the perfect swell of her breasts.

Her skin there was flushed, a pretty rose hue that traveled up her throat and into her cheeks now as well. He couldn't help imagining her blood rushing through those delicate capillaries. Hell, he could almost taste it. His mouth watered at the thought, making his fangs punch out of his gums.

Desire ignited in a flash, hot and consuming. His cock answered the surge of need coursing through him, suddenly straining behind his black combat fatigues.

Nathan knew his pupils were winnowing down to narrow slits as he drank in the sight of Jordana's disheveled beauty. The amber light of his transforming irises bathed her face in a dim glow.

His body's swift reaction shocked him. And he was more than a little disturbed that he couldn't seem to master his urges when it came to this particular woman.

Never one to back down, however, Nathan advanced on her. He called a command to his teammates to sweep out the back rooms and VIP lounge, ordering them to send every last person out of the place.

"The party's over," he snarled, his eyes still rooted on Jordana.

She scowled up at him, planting her hands on the tempting curves of her hips. "What right did you have to do that?" she demanded, her words sounding thicker than normal, no doubt thanks to the alcohol she'd consumed.

Nathan held her annoyed stare. "Don't tell me you didn't notice this place makes its profits off illegal blood sport and gambling. Not to mention other deviant amusements you'd rather not know about," he added. "It's about time someone shuts this hellhole down."

"No," she said, tossing her head back and forth. The motion collapsed her loosely gathered mane and sent the platinum waves tumbling around her shoulders and down her back. "No, I'm talking about you, Nathan. What right did you have to storm into my life and mess everything up?"

He frowned, taken aback, not only by the question but by the sound of his name on her lips. "I stormed into your life?"

"Yes, you did." She moved closer to him, until there was hardly an arm's length between them. Then closer still. "You're a dark, dangerous storm, Nathan." She tilted her head back, her glacial blue eyes arresting, even in the darkness of the club. "If I'm not careful, I'm going to leap off a cliff with you."

He blew out a curse, peering harder at her. Christ, just how much had she had to drink tonight? She might be speaking nonsense due to one too many cocktails, but her steady, searching gaze and parted lips were communicating to his senses clearly enough.

"You're the worst thing that could ever happen to me, Nathan."

"At least we agree on something." She listed toward him and he growled, whether with need or irony, he wasn't sure. "Collect your things, Jordana. I'm going to have one of my men take you home."

"No," she murmured, shaking her head. "No, I don't want to go home to my apartment alone. I want to wait for Carys."

He glanced over, recognizing that Carys was in no better shape herself. Plus, she was wrapped around Rune in one of the booths outside the cages. It didn't appear she would be leaving for a while, and Nathan had no intention of allowing Jordana to hang around the club in the condition she was in now.

And despite Carys's obvious trust and affection for Rune, there was no way in hell Nathan would leave Jordana's well-being in that male's hands.

Fuck.

Her apartment wasn't far. He could drop her off safely and be back on task with his patrol team in no time.

"Come on," he said. "Let's go."

Nathan clamped his hand around her wrist and took her with him outside.

9

FIVE MINUTES LATER, JORDANA WAS SEATED ON THE PASSENGER side of her car, watching Nathan navigate the Back Bay's maze of one-way streets en route to her apartment. "It really wasn't necessary for you to take me home. I could've managed on my own."

"Out of the question," he said, his stern profile bathed in the milky glow of the dashboard.

His deep voice brooked no argument, and she was instantly reminded that Nathan was no Darkhaven gentleman. He was an Order squad captain. A Gen One Breed male and former assassin.

A man adept at killing in God only knew how many ways. And yet here he was, playing designated driver to her after she'd foolishly over-imbibed.

Already she was sobering up, the mild alcohol buzz replaced by the twitchy flutter of her pulse as she sat beside Nathan in the dimly lit vehicle.

"Anyway, thank you," she murmured belatedly, unable to tear her eyes from him.

He was handsome in a harsh way, his cheekbones too sharp, his jaw too square and unyielding. His eyes were stormier than ever as he sped her home, a blue-green thundercloud under the severe slashes of his black brows.

His mouth was easily the softest of his features, his lips far too full and lush for the cool, almost constant grimness of his expression. Jordana knew all too well how warm those broad, sculpted lips could be.

As she looked at him beside her in the vehicle, she was wildly tempted to taste them again.

He glanced her way, no doubt feeling her eyes on him. "I wouldn't have guessed La Notte was your kind of place, considering what goes on there."

Jordana shrugged. "I don't spend much time at the club normally. The only reason I went tonight was because I knew Carys was there with Rune."

"Looked to me like you were having a pretty good time up there in the front row outside the fighting cages."

She frowned, hating that she'd let herself get caught up in the seedy entertainments of the club. Elliott would be upset if he found out, but her father would likely go apoplectic if he found out she knew the place even existed, let alone that she'd been inside.

"Of course, I don't condone the violence of the matches," she murmured, "nor the fact that profits are being made off spilled blood. It's an appalling business."

He grunted. "The fights aren't the only way La Notte's owner fills his purse."

Jordana knew he wasn't talking about the bar and dancing at street level, nor the sim lounge where people could slip into their choice of several virtual reality landscapes at a hefty hourly rate. "You mean the BDSM dens downstairs."

Nathan swung a dark look on her. "You know about the sex rooms?"

"I haven't actually seen them," she hedged. "Carys told me about them."

He cursed, low under his breath. "Don't tell me Rune has taken her in there. For fuck's sake, tell me he doesn't do that with her—"

"No." Jordana gave a dismissive shake of her head. "No, of course not. He might make his living in the cages, but Rune's nothing but gentle with Carys. He's protective of her, always. He wouldn't even want her near that part of the club."

Another grunt from Nathan, this time with a mix of relief and something else that Jordana couldn't discern. He seemed to grow more tense now, staring back at the road ahead, a muscle ticking hard in his jaw. "If Rune truly cared about Carys, he'd make sure she never stepped foot in La Notte at all. It's no place for you either."

Jordana arched a brow. "Now you're starting to sound like Elliott. He's all but forbidden me from the place."

Nathan gave her a sidelong look. "And yet you went there tonight."

"Elliott Bentley-Squire doesn't own me. I'm perfectly capable of handling myself." She scoffed lightly, realizing how perfectly incapable she must appear to Nathan right now. "Well, I can usually handle myself. Tonight was an exception. I'm embarrassed that you feel you have to see me home."

"It's nothing," he replied.

But it was something to Jordana. It was a chivalrous gesture from a man who hadn't exactly struck her as the noble type. She would not have imagined he'd had it in him, considering he was more accustomed to combat and brutality and death.

There was probably a lot she had to learn about Nathan, and as she studied his grave profile, she found herself hoping she might have the chance to understand everything about the remote, unreadable man.

"Before we left the club," Nathan said, "you told me you didn't want to go home alone. What was that about?"

Jordana tried to wave off the question. "It was silly. Something happened at work tonight as I was leaving, and I got spooked. I'm sure it was nothing."

"What happened?" Nathan was all warrior now, no longer posing a light inquiry but demanding an answer.

"I thought I saw someone outside the museum tonight, as I was heading for my car. I thought he was watching me." It sounded foolish to her now, even though at the time she'd been more than a little rattled.

"He," Nathan said, his deep voice edged with suspicion and a protectiveness that surprised her, warmed her. "Did you see this man? Did he threaten you in any way?"

"No," she replied. "No, nothing like that. I saw someone standing outside the museum as I was leaving, that's all. As I said, I'm sure it wasn't anything but my imagination running away with me."

Nathan made a noise in the back of his throat that sounded less than convinced, but he didn't press any further. "We're here," he announced, slowing down as they approached her building. He drove around to the underground parking, then found Jordana's assigned space without her telling him where it was.

She stared at him from the other side of the vehicle as he killed the engine and handed her the remote starter. "I can't decide if I'm impressed or unnerved that the Order not only knows where I live but where I park my car."

"Not the Order," he said, slanting her a look that made her nerve endings tingle in response. "Just me."

Nathan didn't give her much chance to process that information. Before she could stammer a reply, he was already out of the car and coming around to the passenger side. He opened the door and took her wrist to help her to her feet. His strong fingers clamped around her in a grasp that was equal parts command and comfort.

Heat sizzled through their connection, and Jordana struggled to appear unaffected as she came to stand in front of him with hardly two inches of space between their bodies. "Well," she said, forcing a lamely polite smile. "Thanks again for seeing me home, Nathan."

"You're not there yet."

When she would have demurred, he released his grasp on her and gestured toward the elevator leading to the lobby of her building. He strode alongside her to the waiting lift and rode up with her.

Seamus was on duty, as usual. The doorman rose from behind his wide reception desk and gave her a welcoming nod as she stepped into the quiet lobby. "Evening, Miss Gates."

"Hello, Seamus," she greeted, trying to walk nonchalantly across the polished marble floor.

"Mr. Bentley-Squire's looking for you, Miss Gates," Seamus informed her. "He called several times tonight to ask if I'd seen you, even stopped by a short while ago—"

The doorman abruptly clammed up the instant he noticed Jordana wasn't alone.

"Thank you, Seamus," Jordana said, keenly aware of Nathan's presence as he followed her out of the elevator and across the lobby, neither waiting for permission nor asking for it.

She saw the middle-age human guard warily eye the dark and dangerous-looking Breed warrior at her heels. It wasn't every night that Jordana traipsed through her building in the company of a man, let alone one dressed in patrol gear and bristling with deadly weapons.

And it didn't help that she likely carried the unsavory fragrances of the club on her as she sailed past Seamus's desk.

The doorman cleared his throat. "Everything okay tonight, Miss Gates?"

"Yes, of course. Everything is fine. Good night, Seamus."

She gave him a practiced smile, one that invited no further comment, as Nathan proceeded to trail her to the penthouse elevator in broody silence.

As soon as the polished steel doors closed behind them, Jordana closed her eyes and blew out a sigh. "The whole building's going to know about this tomorrow. Seamus is sweet and well meaning, but discretion isn't one of his strong suits." She slowly shook her head, then pressed the button for the penthouse floor. "I can only imagine what he must be thinking about me right now—"

"Why do you care what that human rent-a-cop thinks?" Nathan's low voice was little more than a growl as he moved so he was facing her inside the lift. "Why do you care what anyone might think of you?"

"Because I'm a Gates." An automatic answer, a standard she held herself to from the time she was a child. "Certain things are expected of my family. And of me. I have to care what people think."

"Bullshit."

Startled, she looked up into Nathan's stormy gaze, realizing only now just how close he stood to her. Heat radiated from the large, muscular bulk of his body, sending a flush to her cheeks and down between her breasts. Then lower still.

Nathan didn't need to say anything—he didn't need to do anything—and yet his presence was so dominating, it seemed to suck all the air out of the small space.

Although some insane compulsion drew her toward all of that heat and power, Jordana inched backward, not stopping until her spine bumped against the rear of the ascending car.

He was right there too, crowding her physically, forcing her to hold his probing stare. "That's bullshit, and you know it. You hide behind the crutch of your family's name and whatever obligation you feel toward it, but that's not what I'm asking you. I want to know why you hide."

He moved closer, leaving her no room to escape. No room to avoid his piercing eyes or the chaos of her own senses as every nerve ending inside her came alive with awareness of this man and her dangerous craving for him.

"I want to know why you feel the need to clamp a hard lid down on who you truly are, Jordana. The woman who kissed me in this very building last week. The woman who looked at me at the museum party last night like she was drowning under the weight of everything that was expected of her." Nathan came closer still, until his chest brushed hers, his body searing the length of her. "I want to know why you try so hard to deny the woman you truly are, Jordana."

"I don't know what you mean." Her voice sounded very small, unconvincing, even to her own ears. "I'm not hiding behind anything. And you don't know the first thing about me."

"Don't I?" His dark eyes flashed with amber. When he spoke again, she spied the razor-sharp tips of his fangs behind his sensual upper lip. "You wanted me to take you out of that party last night. You would've fought me and denied it, but in the end, we both know you would've gone with me."

Oh, God. He was right.

Even so, she gave a sharp toss of her head. "No. I would have done no such thing—"

"Yes, Jordana, you would have." He smiled now, a confident, knowing smile that gave her no mercy at all. "And today in the supply room of the command center, you wanted me to touch you, to kiss you. To do whatever wicked things I wanted to you."

She swallowed hard, her mouth going dry under the scorching heat of his gaze.

"You waited for it," he said. "You crave it now, as much as I do."

A sound curled up from her throat, but if she'd hoped to be able to deny what he was saying, the soft moan that slipped past her lips was a pitiful effort. "Don't say such things. You have no right—"

"Why not, Jordana?" he pressed. "Why not say it if it's the truth? Why should either of us pretend we can stop what's going on between us?"

"Because—" She sucked in a breath, searching for the strength to refuse him.

"Because, why?" he asked, more gently now, yet no less commanding. "Tell me why you'd rather scurry back behind your family name and the obligations you've constructed into your own prison?"

Jordana brought her fingers up to her lips, trying to bite back the words that would betray her. They spilled out anyway, a whispered rush. "Because I'm afraid."

Something flickered over Nathan's stern features—shock or understanding, sympathy or pity; she couldn't be sure.

He reached behind him and hit the stop button on the elevator. With a soft rock, the car came to a cushioned halt inside the shaft.

Jordana's eyes went wide. "What are you doing?"

Nathan didn't answer. "Tell me what you're afraid of."

Anxiety shot through her. "Seamus will notice that we've stopped. He'll wonder what's going on in here."

"I don't give a fuck," Nathan growled. "Neither should you."

"He can see us," Jordana pointed out, glancing past Nathan, toward the small security camera lens staring down at them from the ceiling of the lift.

Although he didn't so much as flinch, the tiny red light on the monitoring device blinked out, snuffed by the power of Nathan's Gen One Breed mind. "Now it's just you and me, Jordana. I'm the only one who can see you. I'm the only one who will hear you. Are you afraid now?"

When she looked down in silence, Nathan's warm, strong fingers came to rest beneath her chin. He lifted her face, refusing to let her hide even her gaze from him. "Are you afraid of me, Jordana?"

She gave a weak shake of her head, astonished that it wasn't fear she felt with this man right now. It was something far more powerful than that. More powerful than the desire he stirred in her as well. She trusted him.

Nathan didn't have to demand she bare her soul to him; his turbulent blue-green eyes and unexpectedly gentle touch compelled her with equal measure. "My father's had a very strict path laid out for me to follow from the time I was a child. He wants things for me. Expects me to act a certain way, to achieve certain goals he's set for me. He does it out of love, I know that. He only wants what's best for me."

"I'm sure he does." Nathan closed the scant distance between them, a towering wall of muscle and dark, simmering intent. "What do *you* want?"

"I don't know," she admitted quietly. "But sometimes I'm afraid I'll never be the daughter he wants me to be. I'm terrified I'm going to wake up one day and realize I no longer want the things he thinks are best for me." She let out a soft sigh, still holding Nathan's stormy gaze. "I'm afraid I already have."

He growled a curse, something low and dark, under his breath. His features sharpened, making his face more fierce, as profane as it was handsome. Jordana lifted her hand, wanting to brave a touch of his angled cheekbone and rigid jaw.

Nathan caught her in midmotion, wrapping his fingers around her wrist before she could make contact. His grip was warm but firm. Wordlessly, he raised her hand up and away from him, pinning it over her head against the back wall of the elevator car.

Jordana didn't know what to say—she didn't know what to think—as he then brought her other hand up as well and held it there. She tested his hold and found it unyielding. As unbreakable as iron.

Staring up at him, she swallowed, all too aware of how her current position left her totally at Nathan's mercy. With her hands held above her head, her spine pressed against the solid wall of the elevator car, the only place she could possibly move was toward the crowding heat of his body. Her breasts strained against the buttons of her conservative silk blouse. Her legs were spread slightly to keep her balance, and cool air tickled up the bare lengths of her calves and thighs, making her even more aware of the moist heat pulsing at her core.

Every feminine particle of her being thrummed in response to Nathan's presence, anticipation pounding in her blood.

He switched his grasp so that one hand shackled her wrists, leaving his other free to roam. He stroked the backs of his knuckles along the slope of her cheek, then down along the swells of her breasts, hardly touching her yet making her burn with sensation. "Are you afraid of me now, Jordana?"

"No." Her reply was little more than a gasp, breathless not from worry but from the startling sense of her own vulnerability.

Nathan held her completely under his control. She couldn't have broken loose of his hold if her life depended on it. Nor did she want to.

He owned her in that moment, and damn him if he didn't know it too.

He reveled in it; she could see the dark pleasure in his eyes as he drank her in from head to foot in the tight confines of the lift. Amber sparks pierced the thundercloud color of his irises. His broad mouth was grim yet sensual, barely concealing the growing length of his fangs.

He bent toward her and took her mouth in a scorching, commanding kiss.

Jordana had no experience with such hard passion, such hungered demand. She could only surrender to it, moaning as his lips covered hers, claimed her. His tongue pushed at the seam of her mouth, and she opened to him, submitting to this further claiming with a shudder of raw pleasure that rippled through her, then pooled molten hot between her thighs.

She'd never been kissed like this. She was lost to it, her limbs languid and boneless, her veins lit up and electric.

Where Elliott's kisses were earnest, even passionately inflamed at times, Nathan's mouth was wild and untamed on hers. Possessive and fevered. His kiss branded her in a way that left all other comparisons in ashes.

When he abruptly broke contact and reared back from her, Jordana couldn't contain her cry of dismay. Nathan stared at her, his dark eyes glittering with bright amber light that swamped the thin vertical slits of his transformed pupils.

She wanted more. Jordana tried to reach for him, only to remember that he still held her hands in the manacle of his iron grasp. She frowned, struggling a bit more determinedly against his hold.

The corner of his mouth quirked with dark amusement, but his eyes were serious, unflinching, as he gave her an admonishing shake of his head. "Tonight we play on my terms."

Jordana stood there, panting and confused. So alive with desire, she thought she might explode if he didn't give her more.

"Everything all right, Miss Gates?" Seamus's voice came over the emergency speaker inside the elevator car, the intrusion unwelcome but no surprise. "Looks like the lift's not moving for some reason . . ."

She knew she should answer him. If she had any hope of saving her dignity—of lessening the man's suspicions of what might be going on inside the elevator—she needed to assure Seamus that they had halted the lift by accident.

But to do so meant she'd have to push the intercom button on the panel on the other side of the car. And that meant she'd have to insist that Nathan let her go.

He stared at her in waiting silence, seeming to understand her inner struggle, even if his smoldering gaze said he had no intention of offering her any mercy.

"Miss Gates?"

Jordana couldn't speak. She couldn't break the hot connection of Nathan's eyes as he leaned into her in a full-body press that ignited her every nerve ending and made her acutely aware of just how masculine and powerful this Breed warrior truly was.

He cupped her nape with his free hand, stroking the pulse point of her carotid with the pad of his thumb. So tender, even as he restrained her, even as he tempted her to shred her reputation and her virtue in the same reckless moment.

And yet Jordana swayed into his touch, as helpless to resist him as a sapling bending for the wind.

He splayed his fingers into her unbound hair, then gathered the mass of platinum waves into his hand, winding her tresses into a coil around his fist. He slowly pulled her head back, baring her throat to his hot gaze. Jordana gasped, shivering with a heady combination of fear and arousal.

Danger gleamed in Nathan's otherworldly amber eyes. His fangs were enormous, as sharp as daggers. He bent forward in aching deliberation, then kissed a searing trail from the underside of her chin to the sensitive hollow at the base of her throat.

"Miss Gates, can you hear me?"

"Oh, God," she whispered, letting the doorman's concerned voice fade into oblivion as Nathan delved deeper and began to lick and nip his way down toward her breasts.

10

NATHAN HAD LONG CONSIDERED DISCIPLINE TO BE HIS GREATEST strength—even more so than any of his Breed-born abilities or his myriad lethal skills that made him one of the most dangerous of his entire race.

But as he dragged his mouth along the silky arch of Jordana's throat, then down, toward the delectable valley between her pert breasts, he clung to his self-control by a thin tether.

She was sweet against his tongue. Responsive to his every touch. Open and compliant, her trust a gift he hadn't expected and was certain he didn't deserve.

She was so damned hot and sexy, it took all he had not to rip away her boardroom blouse and sensible skirt and bury himself to the hilt inside her beautiful body.

Nathan released the thick rope of her hair only because his palm itched to feel the pebbled buds of her nipples. His other hand stayed locked around her wrists where he still held them pinned above her head. She moaned as he fondled her breasts over the fabric of her blouse.

She gasped a moment later, when he put his hand inside and cupped one rounded, perfect globe.

"Nathan, please," she whispered, testing his grip on her hands. "I want to touch you too."

He gave her a dark look and a sober shake of his head. "My terms tonight, remember?"

Her ice-blue eyes went a bit wider, but she didn't deny him. Her tension leaked away, and Nathan went back to the business of her breasts, hissing with the pleasure of her warm heat filling his palm.

He squeezed and caressed, then pinched the little knotted peak between his fingers. It wasn't a gentle tweak—he wasn't capable of softness under the best circumstances, and right now he was on the verge of a need that could easily consume him if he allowed it.

Despite what he told her, all it would have taken from Jordana was a flinch and he would have released her. One shudder of fear or uncertainty and he would have known enough to stop.

He would have accepted that this thing that burned between them could go no further than this moment.

But she didn't fight him.

No, she submitted to him now. Sweetly. Trustingly.

Dipping her chin, she watched him roll and tug her tender nipple in his fingers, her eyes heavy-lidded, their color gone from cool blue to the shadowed hue of dusk. She cried out, breathless and panting, her gaze rooted to his as he lowered his head and suckled the abused bud between his teeth and fangs.

"Miss Gates, do you need help?" The doorman's voice had taken on a more anxious tone now. No doubt the aging human worried that his building's most attractive, high-society tenant was being devoured by the blood-drinking monster she'd brought in with her tonight.

Nathan smirked as he drew Jordana's breast more deeply into his mouth. Devouring her definitely had its appeal.

"Miss Gates, please," the rent-a-cop urged. "I need to know if you're all right in there."

"Are you, Jordana?" Nathan's voice was a rough snarl in his throat, sounding more savage than normal for the way his veins were throbbing, his fangs filling his mouth. He glanced up at her in sensual challenge, the amber light of his irises washing her pale skin in a burnished glow. His cock ached, growing harder, more demanding, with each hammered beat of his pulse. "Are you all right in here, or do you need Seamus to save you from me?"

She whimpered, squirming against him as he slowly rose before her and caged her with his body. When she spoke, the words tumbled out in a breathless gust. "Oh, God . . . I shouldn't be doing this. I shouldn't want this . . . shouldn't want you."

"Then tell me to stop." He pressed himself against her, fusing them from chest to thigh as he licked the fluttering artery on the side of her neck, then took her earlobe between his teeth. "Tell me to let you go, Jordana."

He stroked his free hand down the front of her body, then around her backside, squeezing one firm cheek over the fine wool weave of her skirt. When she parted her lips on an indrawn breath, he took her mouth in a deep, heated kiss, at the same time delving his fingers into the cleft of her ass.

She gasped against his mouth, tensing for a moment, before she accepted his wicked caress. He slid deeper along that crevice, reveling in the way she quivered under his hand. He didn't cease until his fingertips were nestled in the juncture of her thighs. Her sex was a furnace against his palm, tantalizingly soft.

He wanted her bared to his touch, couldn't stand the impediment of her clothing. But some shred of reason warned him that to see her naked, here and now, in his current state of need, was a temptation not even his iron will could withstand.

Instead, Nathan satisfied his craving by gathering up the hem of her pencil skirt and slipping his hand beneath it. The hand that held Jordana's wrists began to tremble as he used his other to sweep aside her delicate panties, uncovering the moist haven between her legs.

"Oh," she sighed, exhaling a thready cry as he stroked her mound and the slick seam of her core. "Oh, my God . . . Nathan . . ."

"Tell me I go too far, Jordana." He dragged in a slow breath, inhaling the sweetness of her arousal. "Ah, Christ. Say the words and this will stop right here and now. Say you don't want it, and this is the last you'll ever see of me."

Was the mercy he offered now—rare though it was—intended more for her or for himself?

He didn't know. He hadn't intended for the night to end up like this. This thing with Jordana had never been fully in his control, and seducing her like this wasn't going to make it better for either one of them.

That realization alone should have been jarring enough to cool his need. But it was impossible to deny himself the satisfaction of pleasuring Jordana. She shuddered under his touch. Her flesh was wet and lush, her petals open to him, welcoming all he had to give her.

He wondered how far he could push her. How much of his dark urges could she take?

When would she break—if not in denial, then in climax?

Her cream coated his fingertips as he started to slide one finger inside her. He met with a slight resistance, reminded at once that Jordana was not the kind of experienced partner he had always preferred.

"Fuck, Jordana," he groaned. "You are so tight. You're so wet." Her virginity made him want to protect her and claim her at the same time. He inched his finger in only a fraction, exercising caution despite the fact that everything male in him was rampant with the urge to possess, to plunder.

But not here. Not like this.

For now, he spared her untried body, stroking her tender flesh as he smoothed the pad of his thumb over the swollen pearl of her clit. She arched into him, whimpering as he began a slow but building rhythm. She trembled and bucked, her soft moans growing more intense as he steered her toward the orgasm he felt rising in her with each fevered pound of her veins.

"Miss Gates, please respond," the guard in the lobby insisted now.

"Oh, God," she moaned. "Oh, God . . . I've never, not like this . . . Nathan, I can't hold on any longer . . ."

Her body quaked with release as Nathan stroked her deeper, harder. She uttered something raw and wordless in the instant she shattered, her pale blond hair tossing around her shoulders as she was caught up in a powerful climax.

Nathan watched her splinter in wave after wave of pleasure, unable to curb the satisfied curve of his lips for knowing that she came for him. Her first time, by her own breathless admission. He had the sudden, fierce urge to show her many other firsts, each one more wicked than the next.

"Miss Gates, since I can't be assured of your well-being, I'm going to override the system and bring the elevator back down to the lobby—"

"Shit," she gasped, panic instantly replacing pleasure on her pretty face. "Let me go, Nathan." When he didn't immediately release her, Jordana's voice rose. "Dammit, let go!"

As soon as he had, she flew to the other side of the elevator car and hit the intercom switch on the emergency panel. "It's okay, Seamus. There's nothing wrong. I'm perfectly fine."

"Are you sure, miss?"

"Yes, of course." Her voice sounded more than a little out of breath to Nathan, but the guard downstairs didn't seem to notice enough to remark on it. Jordana canceled the stop button and the lift resumed its ascent. "We're moving again, Seamus. I don't know what the problem was, but everything's back to normal now."

Back to normal.

Nathan studied the woman who'd been writhing and moaning under the illicit touch of his hand just a minute ago. Now Jordana smoothed her skirt back in place with crisp efficiency. She reached up to finger-comb her loose platinum waves, then adjusted her disheveled blouse. Crossing her arms over herself like a shield, she blew out a long sigh.

She was trying to become Jordana Gates again, retreating back into her carefully constructed, perfectly proper cocoon. She glanced at him now, no longer watching him through passion-drowsed eyes but eyeing him with a look that was equal parts bewilderment and shame.

Nathan said nothing to ease her discomfort. His body was still raging with hunger for her, and there was a darker side of him that wanted to see how quickly he could have Jordana surrendering to him again, panting and crying out in pleasure, once he had her alone in her penthouse.

He moved up close behind her, giving her a good long feel of his stiff erection against her backside. He ground into her with his pelvis, wanting his intentions to be clear. With his head lowered, he placed his mouth near the delicate pink shell of her ear.

"Until I say otherwise, we're still on my terms, Miss Gates," he warned her, his voice rough and thick with promise. "Don't think I'm finished with you yet."

She shivered as he spoke his erotic threat, and he could sense her slow, spreading smile as the car came to a stop on her floor.

The doors slid open, revealing the black wrought iron grate that secured the white marble vestibule of Jordana's lavish apartment.

The grate was ajar. Someone waited inside.

A Breed male, seated on a delicate, velvet-upholstered antique chair, his head down, forearms braced on his knees. A dark wool coat was folded over his lap as if he'd been sitting there for some time.

"Elliott." Jordana practically squeaked the vampire's name.

He lifted his head at once, worry etched deeply into his face as he stood up to greet her. "Jordana, thank God. I—" His eyes narrowed the instant he spotted Nathan behind her. Disapproval and suspicion ate away his look of concern.

Jordana stepped off the elevator and walked into the vestibule. "Elliott, what are you doing here?"

He didn't look at her at first, instead stared coldly at Nathan, lurking behind her.

Nathan didn't so much as blink under the outraged scrutiny of Jordana's would-be mate. Part of him flared hot with the urge to haul Jordana against him and kiss her like he had in the elevator—show Elliott Bentley-Squire that she would never belong to him.

But a possessive display like that was unnecessary.

The other Breed male could smell freshly spent desire on Jordana as easily as any of their kind, and Nathan's still-rampant erection—to say nothing of his amber-swamped eyes and elongated fangs—was equally hard to overlook.

Nathan would have ripped apart any male who had the bad judgment to lust after a woman he cared for, let alone touch her. Yet the Darkhaven lawyer seemed to let the affront slide with little more than a bitter scowl.

Nathan had a mind to throttle the undeserving man simply for his lack of reaction.

Bentley-Squire swung his frown on Jordana. "I tried reaching you tonight, several times. When you didn't return any of my calls, naturally, I became worried something might have happened to you. Did you get my voice messages?"

"I worked late," she murmured. "Did Seamus let you in?"

He scoffed. "I don't need a human to give me permission to make sure you're all right, Jordana. Where have you been?"

Panic spiked in her, a feeling so intense and visceral, Nathan could practically hear the sudden race of her heartbeat from where he stood near her. She swiveled her head in his direction, and there was misery in her wintry blue eyes.

"I was out, with Carys. We were at La Notte." Her voice quieted then, an apology swimming in her gaze. "I had one too many drinks, so Nathan kindly offered to drive me home."

Bentley-Squire grunted, his lips pressed flat in disapproval. "I didn't realize the Order was running a chauffeur service." Sneering, he glanced once more at Nathan. "How much do I owe you for taking care of my lady tonight?"

Vibrating with menace, Nathan had already calculated ten different ways he could kill the male. He said nothing, half hoping Bentley-Squire would be fool enough to try him.

Jordana must have realized the dangerous direction of his thoughts. She pivoted back around to face him.

Please, she mouthed silently, giving him a nearly imperceptible shake of her head.

If she hadn't looked so desperate, so terrified of what he might do in that moment, Nathan might have acted on the anger simmering just below his deceptively cool surface.

"Thank you for seeing me home safely," she told him, her politeness grating after what had happened between them just a few minutes ago.

"Jordana," Bentley-Squire said from his position behind her in the gleaming finery of the vestibule. "I'm sure this warrior has more pressing business to attend to tonight. You've delayed him from his work long enough, don't you think, darling?"

Nathan ignored the other vampire, his blazing eyes locked on Jordana. If she gave him any inkling that she didn't want to be there—if she looked at him even remotely like she had last night at the museum reception, when her gaze seemed to all but beg him to take her somewhere, *anywhere*, else—Nathan would have dragged her back into the elevator in that same instant.

"I have to go," she murmured softly. "Please try to understand."

She stepped away from him, back to the Breed male who was part of this other world she inhabited. The world that drew her back into its orbit, even while Nathan could still her hear climax in his ears, could still smell her sweet juices on his fingertips.

He didn't like the anger that seethed in him as he watched her fade out of his reach.

He wasn't accustomed to letting emotion rule him.

He'd survived his childhood by learning to master his feelings—by learning to master every facet of his life with ruthless control and punishing discipline.

He wasn't about to let that hard-won control slip out of his grasp now.

Without a word, without acknowledging Jordana or the sting of her retreat, Nathan stalked into the elevator and hit the down button.

Elliott Bentley-Squire had been right, after all. Nathan did have more pressing business to attend to tonight, back in his own world.

About damned time he got back to it.

Forcing her feet to remain rooted to the floor, Jordana watched the elevator doors close behind Nathan.

Instantly, she regretted that she hadn't had the nerve to walk right in with him. Not to follow him like some passion-blinded fool but to taste some of the freedom he seemed to enjoy as someone who walked his own path, controlled his own destiny.

And yes, she had to admit, there was a wild, reckless part of her that did want to taste some of Nathan's freedom firsthand, as the woman at his side. As the lover in his bed, abandoning herself to his every power-ful, wicked whim.

But he hadn't promised her anything tonight. Even if he had, she couldn't throw her life away on an impetuous impulse.

Why not? some dangerous voice whispered in the back of her mind.

How long could she act as if she wasn't slowly suffocating under the burden of what everyone in her life expected of her?

Nathan's words came back to her in a rush—all the intimate truths he seemed to know about her, when a few days ago they'd been all but strangers to each other.

His words had made her angry. Even in his absence now, she felt cor-nered and exposed, stripped bare in a way no one had ever done to her before.

His touch had made her burn. Tonight Nathan had made her feel as if she'd been living and breathing for the very first time in all her nearly twenty-five years.

And she'd simply let him walk away.

Not that it had taken much for him to go.

Jordana hadn't missed his seething reaction to her attempt to pre-tend nothing had happened between them—that he hadn't just given her the most explosive experience of her life.

She'd done it out of fear, and out of a feeble respect for Elliott. She didn't love him, but that didn't mean she wanted to wound or humiliate him. Even so, Elliott was an intelligent man, and Jordana knew only an imbecile would mistake the intense, erotic energy that sizzled between Nathan and her for anything other than what it was.

"Jordana," Elliott said now, his tone soothing as it broke into her pri-vate torment. "Darling, you can't intend to stand out here all evening. Come inside with me."

She glanced at him over her shoulder, a frown etching into her brow. "Aren't you upset with me about what happened tonight?"

He blinked at her slowly, then gave a mild shake of his head. "You're home safe, and that's all that matters to me."

Was he serious? A bubble of hysteria climbed into the back of her throat. "It doesn't matter to you that I was with another man?" At Elliott's prolonged silence in response, she exhaled a sharp laugh. "My God, it doesn't bother you at all. You don't love me."

There was no venom in her words, only a sense of disbelief that she'd never realized this truth until now. The discovery didn't upset her. It liberated her.

"You never really wanted me at all, did you?"

He sighed heavily, his expression patient, kindly indulgent. "Are you trying to provoke me, Jordana? Of course I care about you. I always have—"

"Yes," she said, seeing it now. "You care for me, the same way my father does. The same way a dear uncle would. Like a child, a ward in need of guidance and protection. Not the way you would if I really meant something to you."

He cursed now, but there was no passion there either. "Come inside, Jordana. I forgive whatever went on between you and that miscreant from the Order. Let's put this night behind us where it belongs."

"No. I can't do that." She crossed her arms over her chest, her feet refusing to move, even when Elliott came over and tried to guide her away from the elevator. He put his arm around her shoulders, and she ducked out of his embrace. "I can't do any of this anymore."

"Any of what, darling?"

"This. Us. All of it." God, she hadn't imagined she'd be standing there, ending the farce of her relationship with him like this, but it felt good to let it go. It felt right, for both of them. "I'd like you to leave now, Elliott."

"Leave?" He studied her cautiously for a moment, then shook his head in denial. "No, I don't think I will, Jordana. I understand. It's late, and you're upset. I don't think you realize what you're saying or doing right now."

She barked out a sharp laugh. "Stop telling me how I feel, Elliott. Dammit, I wish everyone would stop telling me what they think I should do and think and feel!"

He stared at her like he might look at a furious, hissing snake suddenly dropped in his lap. "This kind of outburst isn't like you, Jordana. You're only proving my point that you need someone to look after you right now. I really think it best that I stay awhile—"

"Fine," she replied. "Then I'll go."

She punched the elevator call button, half hoping it would come back up with Nathan still inside. But when the doors whisked open a moment later, the car was empty.

"Jordana, you're being ridiculous," Elliott said as she stepped into the lift. "This kind of behavior isn't like you at all."

"No, it isn't," she agreed. "But maybe it should be."

"Jordana—"

"Good-bye, Elliott." She pushed the down button, feeling a sudden surge of exhilaration—her first taste of newfound freedom—as the doors slid closed in front of Elliott's incredulous expression.

11

NATHAN MADE THE TREK BACK TO LA NOTTE ON FOOT. NOT EVEN the brisk run through the cool night streets managed to curb the rawness of his need for a woman he should never have pursued in the first place.

He was a man used to being in control of every situation, especially when it came to sex. He fucked who he wanted, when he wanted. He called the shots. He controlled the rules, the pace, the boundaries. He decided how things started and ended—all of it, every time.

And then *she* came along.

Jordana, and that impulsive kiss that had ignited a flame in him that he couldn't seem to put out.

Taking things as far as he had tonight had only made that heat flare hotter. If he'd expected to have a taste of her only so he could finally get her out of his head—get the need for her out of his blood—then he'd just proven himself a goddamned fool.

He could still see her face as she pleaded with him to keep his silence, to play along with her where Elliott Bentley-Squire was concerned. It shouldn't have mattered to him, but it did. What she had with the other Breed male was a fucking farce that burned Nathan almost as much as the fact that he still craved her with a fierceness he could hardly reconcile.

She had made it pretty clear that she intended to keep to her own, even if she had to do it unhappily. So now Jordana was back at her place with a male who didn't deserve her, and Nathan was hoofing it into Cassian Gray's seedy club with a raging hard-on and a deadly bad attitude.

He found Rafe down in the empty arena of the old neo-Gothic church, questioning a trio of humans employed as blood Hosts to serve the club's vampire clientele. As Nathan strode in, the blond warrior lifted his chin in acknowledgment and dismissed the group with a low command.

"Got the place swept out, except for the fighters and some of the staff," Rafe informed him. "Nobody's giving up anything on Cass, though. We've questioned everyone. They're all telling the same story—no one's seen hide or hair of the son of a bitch for the past several days."

Nathan grunted, his voice gravel in his throat for the way his blood was still pounding in his veins. "Maybe the disruption of tonight's revenue stream will get his attention."

Rafe arched a tawny brow. "Right now, that's all we've got. Where the hell did you go? I looked for you an hour ago, but you were gone. When I saw Carys with Rune a few minutes ago, she said she thought you left with Jordana Gates."

Nathan bit back the ripe curse on his tongue. Barely. "She was in no shape for driving, so I brought her home. Took longer than planned."

His friend and teammate studied him, then blew out the curse that Nathan strived to contain. "You and Jordana. Jesus, Nathan. Do you really think that's a good idea?"

"No, I don't," he replied, not interested in explaining himself, nor in reliving what had gone on between Jordana and him tonight. "I think it's one bad fucking idea. And after tonight, it's not happening, so feel free to drop the subject and tell me what you and the rest of the squad have been doing while I was gone."

As Rafe gave him a quick rundown, one of the club's other service workers came out of the back corridor that led to the BDSM dens. Dressed in a few straps of black leather held together by silver metal rings, the brunette female sashayed into the arena in a pair of tall, glossy boots with sky-high heels.

She'd taken care of him once or twice at the club, one of the many nameless partners who had long been his preference. The sex worker spotted him now and her hips took on a more languid, inviting sway as she headed to the bar a few feet away from him.

"We cleared the sim lounge and dance club upstairs," Rafe said. "Eli and Jax are giving Cass's office and private apartment another once-over. I came down here to see if I could squeeze anything useful out of the service staff, since Syn and Rune and the other fighters are less than cooperative."

Although he was listening to the report, Nathan couldn't help but notice how the woman leaned over the bar to reach for a bottle of liquor, giving him a good long look at her ass and the leather thong wedged between her cheeks. His body was still fevered from want of Jordana, and it responded to the obvious invitation from this other woman the same way his fingers would reach to scratch an itch.

And she worked hard to get his attention. Grabbing a bottle of whiskey from the bar, she poured herself a shot and checked to make sure he was watching. As she tilted her head back and downed the amber liquor in one long, open-throated gulp, Nathan saw another delicate neck in his mind.

In a hard, heated instant, he relived the sight of Jordana's pale, pretty throat, bared to him as he'd tugged her head back, the silky platinum rope of her hair wound around his fist.

Hunger drew his fangs out, and he wondered how long it had been since he fed. About as long as it had been since he satisfied the other craving that was gnawing at him, both made worse after the way his encounter with Jordana had left him feeling.

The sharp, nagging edge of his twin needs aggravated him, but even more disturbing was the fact that everything male and primal in him demanded he head right back to her place and slake the need she stirred in him—even if he had to tear through Elliott Bentley-Squire to have her.

Dangerous thoughts.

And a craving he could not permit himself to act on, no matter how tempting.

The leather-clad female plopped her shot glass back on the bar and sauntered past him, an inviting look in her eyes as she slinked back to the corridor leading to the BDSM dens.

Rafe stared after her too and let out a low, approving whistle. "Maybe I should do a more in-depth interrogation of some of the backroom staff. Wouldn't want to leave any stone unturned."

Nathan slanted him a dark look. "There's nothing more for us to do here tonight. Go tell Jax and Eli to wrap things up. I'll be right behind you."

Rafe shrugged, then took off to carry out his captain's order.

Once he was gone back up to the club at street level, Nathan crossed the arena floor on a direct course for the VIP rooms in back.

The brunette was waiting for him, already arranged for his pleasure on a red leather settee with her legs spread wide and her hair gathered off to the side to give him open access to her carotid. "How can I serve you tonight, sir?"

Nathan stepped inside the room. A pair of buckled restraints hung from a hook on the wall near the door. He took them down, then kicked the door closed behind him with the heel of his combat boot.

"What do you mean, you walked out on Elliott?" Carys's voice sounded incredulous on the other end of the line. "What happened? Does this have something to do with you and Nathan? I saw you leave the club with him. Did something happen between you? Is Nathan with you right now?"

"No. He's gone." After the way she'd acted, probably gone for good.

Jordana hated the way things had ended tonight. She'd been a coward and a fool, and she owed him an apology at the very least. She hoped he would accept it, if she ever saw him again.

If she was being honest with herself, she hoped for far more than that.

While she hadn't broken it off with Elliott because she expected anything from Nathan, she'd be a liar if she tried to deny her attraction to him.

Attraction? Good lord, the way her heart raced at the thought of him—the way her body still hummed with electricity from the wicked things he did to her, things he warned that he intended to continue before they'd come face-to-face with Elliott at her apartment—Jordana had to admit that what she felt toward Nathan was a pull as fierce as the tide to the moon.

He was darkness, as cool and untouchable as night itself, and she craved to know him, to be close to him, like nothing she had known before.

Tonight he'd taken her to the edge of that cliff she feared, but she'd been too terrified to step off.

Jordana blew a sigh past the receiver of her phone. "It's a long story, Car. One I don't particularly feel like reliving at the moment."

"Are you okay?" Jordana heard her friend whisper the gist of the situation to Rune. "So, if you left Elliott at the apartment, where are you?"

"On Commonwealth, just outside my building," Jordana said, her low heels clicking on the sidewalk. "And I'm fine. I just needed to get out of there."

Part of the problem with making a dramatic exit, she had realized pretty quickly, was the need to have someplace else to go.

The thought of going home to her father's Darkhaven didn't hold much appeal. It was late, and although she would have been welcomed with open arms, Jordana didn't want to show up on her father's doorstep to disappoint him with the news that she'd failed at the relationship he wanted so badly to work for her.

Ordinarily, she might have gone to the museum to escape. It had been her secret refuge on numerous occasions in the past, but she hadn't quite been able to shake her sense of unease about being watched as she'd gone to her car in the parking lot earlier that night. And although her cocktail buzz was long past, Jordana wasn't about to climb behind the wheel and drive aimlessly through the city so late at night.

"Come back to the club," Carys told her. "From the sounds of it, the Order has the place pretty well shut down, but I'm still here with Rune. We can both crash in his quarters overnight and sort everything out tomorrow."

"Oh, Carys. I don't know—"

"You're not far from the train. It'll get you here in less than ten minutes. I'll be waiting for you. Come around back and I'll let you in through the staff entrance."

"Carys—"

"Let me take care of you for once, okay? Be here in ten, or I'm sending Rune out to drag you here."

Which is how Jordana found herself getting off the train in the old North End some seven minutes later and walking the short block to La Notte's rear door.

Carys was there before she even had a chance to knock, opening the door and pulling Jordana into a warm embrace. "You're shivering," Carys pointed out. "Come in, and tell me what's going on."

Jordana walked with her friend into the back corridor, feeling relieved to have come, now that she was there.

But the feeling was short-lived.

No sooner had she stepped inside when a door opened farther ahead of them in the gloomy passageway. A man walked out and strode in the opposite direction of Jordana and Carys.

No, not just a man—a Breed warrior. Six and a half feet of sinew and dark, stormy menace. Jordana knew that massive build and prowling swagger anywhere.

She could still feel his hands on her. She could still hear the sinful rumble of his deep voice against her ear.

Nathan.

God help her, she almost called his name out loud.

But then, in that next awful instant, a woman came out of the room behind him.

More naked than not, she strutted out on spiked boots, her breasts strapped into a complicated web of black leather and metal rings, another skimpy, punishing-looking set of straps emphasizing the round globes of her bare behind.

There could be no mistaking the brunette's line of work. Nor the fact that she and Nathan had been in the room together behind the closed door.

The woman glanced over her shoulder and spotted Jordana and Carys gaping at her in the corridor. In the sex worker's hand was a wad of cash, which she ceremoniously slipped beneath one of the tight black strips of leather on her bosom before sauntering off.

Jordana felt sick. If she'd been afraid of how she'd left things with Nathan tonight, apparently she shouldn't have worried. He certainly hadn't wasted any time finding a replacement for her.

Disappointment and hurt roared up on her. She was pissed too—at him, but even more so at herself, for caring enough to be upset.

"Get me out of here," she whispered to Carys.

Her friend looked equally miserable. "Oh, God, honey. I had no idea. I never would've told you to come—"

"He can't know I was here," Jordana hissed urgently. "Don't let him see me, please. He can't know that I saw him here tonight."

"Of course not." Carys took her hand. "Come on. Rune's quarters are this way."

Jordana followed her friend down another length of dark hallway, feeling as if that cliff she'd been so afraid of had suddenly broken away under her feet and left her falling.

12

"YOU TRYING TO CLEAN THAT FIREARM OR RUB OFF THE SERIAL number?"

Jolted, Nathan swung his head around from the table and chair where he was seated and found Sterling Chase leaning against the jamb of the open weapons room door.

Jesus Christ. He'd been so engrossed in his work, his head full of steam and troubling realizations, he hadn't even heard the commander arrive.

It was early morning at the Order's Boston headquarters. Most everyone in the compound and the connected estate would be in bed. Nathan, however, had been awake and twitchy ever since he and his team returned to base last night. A couple hours ago, he'd finally given up the idea of sleep and decided to make some productive use of his restlessness.

He met Chase's stare. Years of old training schooled his expression to a bland, unreadable mask before he went back to cleaning and lubricating the field-stripped black Beretta 9 mm. "Didn't expect to see you down here at this hour. How long you been standing there?"

"Couple of minutes," Chase said. "Long enough. You wanna talk about it?"

With nimble fingers, Nathan reassembled the pistol and set it aside. "Nope."

Chase strode into the room now and took up a position next to Nathan's worktable, his thick arms crossed over his chest. He wore a white short-sleeve T-shirt and loose gray sweats, his trim golden hair rumpled.

At the moment, Sterling Chase looked less like the impeccable, tight-ship captain he was and more like a man with troubles of his own. Troubles that dragged him from the comfort of the warm bed he shared with his mate at an unholy, early hour.

"Looks like you've been up for a while yourself." Nathan glanced at him sidelong. "Maybe you wanna talk about it?"

"Not really." Chase smirked and blew out a short sigh. "I guess I'm still trying to get used to the fact that Carys moved out. Tavia doesn't like it either, but she says we have to give her time. Give her space." A growl rumbled in the vampire's chest. "If anything happens to her . . . if anyone hurts her now that she's living outside my direct protection—"

"She's doing all right," Nathan said. "She has people looking out for her."

Chase scoffed. "Jordana Gates may be well connected in the Dark-havens, but no one she knows is going to keep my little girl safe the way her mother and I can."

"Your little girl is a full-grown woman," Nathan pointed out. "She's making her own choices. You have to trust her. Hold her too close and you'll only make her pull away harder."

"Philosophy at this hour—and from you, besides?" Chase chuckled, then gave a nod. "It's good advice, Nathan. Gonna be damned hard to follow it, though. And if Carys ends up getting harmed by anyone in any way—"

"Then she'll have you and all the rest of the Order making sure someone pays," Nathan said.

"Damn straight she will," Chase agreed, his blue eyes glittering with menace. He went quiet for a moment, then cleared his throat. "My daughter's actually not the only reason I'm pacing the halls this morning."

Nathan glanced up. "What's going on?"

"Gideon called a few minutes ago from D.C. One of Crowe's exes surrendered some interesting news under tranced interrogation today. Seems Reginald Crowe had a mistress."

That was the most promising intel they'd uncovered so far. "Who? Where can we find her?"

"Ireland. Dublin, according to the former Mrs. Crowe," Chase said. "As for the who of it, we're still trying to figure that out. We don't even have a name yet. All we know is that Crowe's ex claims he saw this woman frequently during their marriage and that it had been going on for quite some time."

Nathan's veins lit up with the instinctive, predatory spark of his assassin past. "We've got to find her. We've got to find her now. I can be ready to roll out anytime, if you need me to go in solo and see this done."

"You're best utilized right here in Boston, going after Cassian Gray. Besides, we have boots on the ground over there already. Mathias Rowan's team in London will be mobilizing at sundown tonight. Lucan's put this in their court for now." Chase narrowed a look on him. "You've never walked away from a mission. You're not looking to do that now, are you?"

"Absolutely not," Nathan replied, a brisk denial, even though his conscience pricked him.

Had he been hoping for a reassignment? One that would put a whole continent between him and Jordana Gates?

Fuck, he didn't know what to think about that.

Chase studied him now. "You seem . . . unfocused, my man. Like you're walking a dangerous edge. What's going on with you? When's the last time you fed?"

"I was with a blood Host last night," he replied, the unwanted reminder of the brunette from La Notte's BDSM club making his voice darken to a growl.

Chase seemed to consider for a long moment, his shrewd gaze lingering for longer than Nathan liked. But his commander didn't challenge the lie, even if he suspected it.

"I'll leave you to your work," he said, and headed for the door. "Good job last night. If nothing bubbles up to the surface on Cassian Gray today, let's hit him even harder again tonight."

Nathan gave him a vague nod. Only after Chase was gone back up the corridor did Nathan release the curse that had been burning like acid on his tongue.

Although Chase seemed satisfied with his answer, Nathan knew the elder vampire had seen through him. Self-directed anger heated Nathan's blood at the dishonor he'd shown the other Breed male just now. He had never been compelled to lie to his comrades, least of all his commander. His training as a Hunter would have deemed a breach like that suicidal.

And while Nathan was many years away from the brutality and punishments of his handlers, their lessons had never left him.

He didn't expect they ever would.

No one knew what he had endured as part of his shaping into the killer he became for Dragos. Not even his mother, Corinne, who rescued him from that life, or her mate, Hunter, a Breed male brought up in the same program as Nathan decades earlier.

Not even Nathan's closest friends and teammates in the Order knew what he went through—no, especially none of them. They would never see him the same way again if they knew how he'd been degraded, shamed.

He'd kept that corrupted, dirty part of him a secret all his life. Stuffed it down deep, the only way he was able to move on, move past it.

And he intended to keep it there forever.

As for Jordana, he would turn his deadly skills on himself before he would ever let her know his truth. Ironic that he'd pressed her so hard to open herself to him when he had no intention of truly letting her in.

It was a small mercy that he hadn't been able to seduce her completely last night. He might have done things he could never take back.

Far better that he slake his carnal appetites elsewhere. That had been his thinking when he went with the female at La Notte. But his effort to purge his hunger for Jordana with another woman had only made him want her more.

He hadn't taken the sex worker's vein, as he'd implied to Chase. He hadn't taken anything from the woman, in fact, but he'd paid her just the same.

And after he and his team left the club soon afterward to search the city for leads on Cass, Nathan had made sure his path took him past Jordana's building. Just to assure himself she was safe, he'd told himself, but it had taken all of his increasingly questionable restraint to keep his feet from carrying him inside and back up the elevator to her penthouse.

But the apartment had been dark from the street.

He'd moved on but spent the rest of the night's patrol trying—and failing—to keep her out of his thoughts. Recalling her orgasm with him was only slightly less tormenting than picturing her home in her dark apartment with Elliott Bentley-Squire.

Nathan didn't like the violence that perked to life inside him at the thought of another male being with Jordana. Especially one with less obsession for her than him.

Not that Nathan was worthy of her. His background made him unfit for anyone, but particularly a woman as pure and clean as Jordana.

He had already brought her too close to his world. And he knew he would have taken things much further last night if not for running into her undeserving, would-be mate.

He had to be done with Jordana Gates.

Already she was starting to mean more to him than he cared to admit, and that, if nothing else, was cause enough for him to keep his distance.

Even if that meant watching her bind herself in blood and vow to a male she would never love.

By five o'clock that afternoon, Jordana had already put in an eleven-hour day at the museum.

She'd gone in alone, hours before anyone else had shown up for work. After everything that had happened the night before, the solitude of her workplace had been welcome, even more needed than sleep.

Jordana had eventually left La Notte around two in the morning, accompanied back to her apartment by Carys and Rune. Elliott had been long gone by then. He'd politely turned off the lights and locked up for her, apparently departing her life as ambivalently as he'd entered it.

Jordana wasn't sure how she would break the news of their split to her father. Then again, dutiful Elliott probably had taken care of that for her too.

Instead, she had chosen to put all of the drama and emotional stress on hold for a while, letting her work at the museum absorb her. It was the one thing she had that had always been hers all on her own, historic art being her passion.

Her personal sanctuary and escape.

Fortunately, her work was giving her plenty of things to think about, aside from the sudden mess of her private life. The exhibit's grand opening was little more than twenty-four hours away and was nearly sold out. She and Carys had reviewed the final list of preparations top to bottom twice today, ensuring that everything was in place for a successful event.

Still, that didn't keep Jordana from obsessing over the details yet again. She was in her office on the phone with the local florist when she felt a queer prickling of the fine hairs at her nape.

Was someone in the closed exhibit room outside?

It couldn't be Carys. She'd left just a few minutes ago to pick up a last-minute printing order across town. As for the rest of the museum staff, most would be packing up and preparing to close for the night.

But there was definitely someone in the exhibit. Jordana felt the presence like a cool hand settling against the back of her neck. She felt observed somehow, much as she had been in the parking lot the other night. Anxiety spiked through her as she ended her phone conversation and walked out of her office.

A man stood inside the closed exhibit.

Dressed in a rumpled, rain-dappled gray overcoat, he pivoted to face her as she approached. He was tall and fit beneath the drooping coat, worn jeans, and faded T-shirt. His short, bland brown hair was combed neatly to the side.

Everything about him was average and nondescript, except for his eyes. An arresting shade of peridot, they held her in an unrushed, considering stare.

Although nothing about him broadcasted a threat, Jordana's senses remained alert, expectant in some odd way. "I'm sorry, but the exhibit hasn't opened to the public yet. You can't be in here."

"I won't stay long," he said. "I only wanted to come in and have a quick look."

She frowned. "I'm afraid I have to ask you to leave. We have tickets for sale at the museum website, or you can come back tomorrow evening at the grand opening and purchase a ticket at the door."

He didn't acknowledge the offer or her request for him to go. Slowly, fluidly, he strolled from one art display to another.

"A Canova," he said, walking over to the clear case containing a marble bust of Beatrice from the famous, epic poetry of Dante Alighieri. "An impressive piece."

Jordana followed the man to the sculpture, taking in his modest attire more closely now. None of his clothes looked newer than a decade old, and they fit him like they'd been broken in on someone else and cast off years later. His brown leather loafers were scuffed and scarred, faded and timeworn like the rest of what he wore.

"Canova is considered one of the greatest neoclassical sculptors," Jordana said, unable to resist sharing her knowledge of the collection. "He was probably the most famous artist of his day, but I don't find many people who know his work on sight. Particularly the lesser-known pieces like this one."

"More's the pity." Her uninvited visitor's mouth curved in a faint smile. "Canova's work is exquisite, no question. There is a calmness to his sculpture, from the smoothness of his subject's skin, to the fluid form of each curve and the flawless stroke of every line."

Listening to him speak so eloquently and so well informed, Jordana suddenly felt awkward for insisting he'd have to pay to view the art that belonged by rights to the world. In spite of her earlier misgivings about him, she found herself intrigued.

He went on, still studying the sculpture. "The perfection of Canova's work—the pure idealism of it—invites the eye to linger, to study and admire." The man glanced to Jordana. "Wouldn't you agree?"

Jordana shrugged. "Honestly, I find it too perfect. His art is too . . . I don't know. Too controlled, I suppose." She gestured to a neighboring marble piece, one of the collection's most important acquisitions. "Take this Bernini bust, on the other hand. Look at the energy of his work. It's unsettling, unrefined. Aggressive."

The sculpture they looked at was *Anima Dannata*, depicting a condemned soul staring into the abyss of hell. Jordana drew closer to the display. "Bernini shows you every crag in his subject's face, every livid vein and hair standing on end. You can actually see the torment in the man's face—you can feel it. You can almost hear the scream of horror from the man's open mouth. Bernini shows you everything. He dares you to experience it."

The stranger nodded. "You take your art very seriously."

"I love it," Jordana admitted. "It means everything to me."

Something flickered in his unusual green eyes. "We share that in common, then. I am a lover of art myself. And today, a newfound appreciation for Bernini. Your favorite piece, I take it?"

"Oh," Jordana said, shaking her head. "No, there's another sculpture that I like even more. But it's not as important as either of these."

"Will you show me?"

For a moment, Jordana forgot all about the fact that the exhibit was currently off-limits to anyone but museum staff. She led him to another of the pieces housed inside a Plexiglas display.

"Cornacchini's *Sleeping Endymion*," he said, a smile on his lips.

Jordana noticed he hadn't needed to read the placard. "You know this one too?"

"It's been in the museum's collection for many years, I believe."

"Yes, it has." He must be a longtime patron of the museum, to be so familiar not only with art in general but with this particular piece as well. "*Endymion* came to us by anonymous donation a couple decades ago. It was in another exhibit most of that time, but when I began planning this collection, I had to have it." She gazed at the reclining human shepherd, sleeping under Selene's crescent moon. "There's not another piece in the entire museum that I love more than this one."

A cryptic smile played at the corners of the stranger's mouth. "I can't imagine it being in better hands."

Jordana considered the odd compliment, her curiosity about the man deepening the longer she spoke with him. He couldn't be more than thirty years old, she guessed, but he had a wisdom about him—an indefinable aura that made him seem far older than his age.

He wasn't Breed; he had no *dermaglyphs* that she could see, nor would he be walking around during daylight hours without being wrapped in yards of UV-protective gear, if he was one of Nathan's kind.

And yet her senses seemed to resist the notion to call him human.

Flummoxed, she extended her hand to him. "I'm Jordana Gates, by the way. The exhibit curator."

He hesitated momentarily before taking her hand in a warm, firm grasp. "Yes, I know who you are." At her uneasy look, he indicated the ID badge hanging from the lanyard looped around her neck.

"Oh." Jordana laughed nervously. "I'm sorry, but . . . who are you?"

At first, she didn't think he would answer. Then, carefully, he said, "Cassian." No more, no less.

Did she know that name from somewhere?

She couldn't be sure, but Jordana knew she'd never seen this man before.

Jordana withdrew her hand from his. "Well, Mr. Cassian, I really have enjoyed talking with you. But it's getting late and no one is supposed to be in the exhibit before it officially opens tomorrow, so . . ."

"Of course," he replied politely, even dipping his head slightly in an almost courtly bow. "And I assure you, Jordana, the pleasure has been all mine."

She took in his shoddy attire again and felt a pang of regret for the way she'd discounted him on sight. And she couldn't just push him out the door, especially not knowing how much he enjoyed the exhibit. "Wait here a moment. I'll be right back."

She didn't pause for his answer. Impulsively, she pivoted away and hurried back into her office. Riffling through her desk, she grabbed a pair of complimentary tickets to tomorrow's grand opening event and full-day admission to the museum.

"I just remembered I had a couple of leftover passes in my office," she said as she returned to the exhibit room. "I'd love for you to have—"

He was gone.

"Mr. Cassian?" Jordana scanned the area, then made a quick search of the nearby exhibits.

He wasn't there.

She hurried to the gallery overlooking the museum's main entrance lobby.

Nothing.

He had left.

No, he'd vanished.

Mysterious Mr. Cassian was gone, as swiftly and cleanly as a ghost.

13

HE HAD RISKED FAR TOO MUCH.

Cass made a hasty dash through the city streets, oblivious of the rain that soaked his thrift store clothes and cheap, soggy shoes.

He was across the city from the museum now, unsure where he was headed except that it had to be away. Far away. As far as he could get, and he had to go at once.

He hadn't expected to linger as long as he had. In his mind, he'd imagined entering the museum for a few short minutes—just long enough to visit the treasure that had branded him a wanted man, traitor to his queen and his kind.

A treasure that he was giving up today . . . forever.

Of course, the anonymous donor of the *Sleeping Endymion* sculpture twenty-five years ago was no mystery to him. He couldn't deny his satisfaction—his relief—at knowing that particular treasure was in a safe place, and had been all this time.

But the terra cotta figure wasn't the only secret he'd been keeping since he'd fled the Atlantean queen's court.

Either one of his secrets could have gotten him killed.

The risk of discovery was too great now. He was jeopardizing all he cherished by remaining in Boston.

He'd almost chanced this visit to the museum a couple of nights ago, but he'd lost his nerve and instead skulked outside the building like a wraith. He'd barely gotten away without creating undue notice.

But he had to look upon his greatest, most precious secret one last time—an indulgence he had been careful to avoid at all costs for nearly a quarter century.

Now he was content. He had to be, because today he was leaving for good. He could only hope that his secrets—and the treasure he cherished most of all—would be safer for his absence.

Cass had placed his trust in an ally who had proven his loyalty through years of silence and sacrifice. That trust had been reaffirmed at their meeting a couple of days ago.

Another ally—this one across the globe—one who risked as much as Cass in aiding him, had agreed to look out for Cass's interests once he'd fled for his permanent exile.

An exile that would begin now.

Resolved, Cass pulled up his collar to shield himself from the slanting rain as he ducked down a side alley.

That's when he noticed them—the trio of dark figures that had fallen in behind him.

He glanced over his shoulder and his stomach went cold.

Atlantean soldiers.

The three immortals were disguised in pedestrian street clothes, much as he was. But their purposeful stride and menacing presence were unmistakable.

And beneath the long hem of one of their sodden trench coats, Cassian spied the glint of an Atlantean blade.

There was a time he might have turned around and faced this threat. A time when he would have fought it, even unarmed as he was now.

But today, he knew true fear.

Not for himself, but for the secrets he would die to protect.

Cass took off running, leading the legion guards as far away from the museum as he could, calling upon every ounce of his preternatural agility and speed.

The queen's men were close behind him—too close. They zigged and zagged as he did, never losing sight of him for a second.

In minutes, Cass and his pursuers were in the city's old North End. He hadn't intended it, but his feet had carried him to the only home he'd truly known since coming to Boston.

La Notte was just ahead. Through the rain, Cass saw the back entrance of the club a few hundred yards in front of him.

The Atlantean guards had split up at some point.

Cassian lost track of one of them.

He didn't see the assassin until it was too late.

The soldier from Selene's royal court appeared out of nowhere, standing in front of him, long blade gleaming.

I'm dead, Cassian realized. *It was over now.*

He knew it, even before he felt the ice-cold kiss of Atlantean steel biting into the side of his neck.

"A toast," Carys said, raising a glass of red wine across the table from Jordana at one of their favorite Italian restaurants in the city's old North End. "To the exhibit grand opening. I know it's going to be a huge success."

"I hope so." Jordana sighed and clinked her glass against her friend's. "Did you check to make sure the placard on the French tapestry was corrected? And now I'm wondering if I shouldn't have moved that display of Roman pottery from where we had it for the patrons' reception. Do you think it should go back to its original place?"

Carys grinned and rolled her eyes. "It's perfect, Jordana, all of it. You thought of everything. The exhibit couldn't possibly be in better hands."

"Thanks." Jordana smiled at the compliment, but she couldn't help being reminded of her odd visitor, Mr. Cassian, and the fact that he'd said something very similar to her.

Carys gave her a quizzical look. "Did I say something funny?"

"No, it's just . . ." Jordana shook her head. "A man came in to view the exhibit this afternoon."

Carys frowned. "Someone you know?"

"No, I'd never seen him before. He apparently just wandered in from the street."

"But the exhibit doesn't open to the public until tomorrow night," Carys pointed out.

"That's what I told him." Jordana took a sip of her wine. "He didn't seem bothered that we weren't officially open yet."

"Weird," Carys said, twisting some pasta onto her fork. "What did he want?"

Jordana shrugged. "I suppose he wanted to look at the art. That's what he said, anyway. We talked for a while about Italian sculptors and compared some of the pieces in the collection, then he left."

Carys eyed her over the rim of her wineglass. "Like I said, weird."

"He was . . . nice," Jordana said, taking a bite of her scampi as she thought about the man and the short time she spent with him in the exhibit.

He was a stranger, a peculiar one at that, and yet she'd felt almost instantly at ease around him. Despite his oddness and his uninvited presence in the museum, she had felt comfortable with him; safe, in some indefinable way. And she would have enjoyed talking with him a bit longer, had he not left the museum without explanation as soon as she turned her back.

Vanished, more like it.

Maybe Carys was right, there *was* something weird about the man.

Jordana's musing was interrupted when her friend's comm unit pulsed on the edge of the table with an incoming call.

"It's Aric." There was a note of bitterness in Carys's voice as she spoke her brother's name. Her fingers hovered over the device for less than a second before she drew her hand back onto her lap with a shallow sigh. The comm unit buzzed again, but Carys remained still, her mouth pressed into a flat line.

Jordana studied her across the small table. "You can't shut him out forever, Car." The Chase siblings hadn't spoken since their heated confrontation over Rune the other night, and Jordana knew it was killing Carys to have a wall standing between her and her twin.

The device vibrated again, and with reluctance written all over her face, Carys finally picked it up. Before she even had the chance to utter a word of greeting, Aric's deep voice came over the receiver. "Carys, where the hell are you right now?"

"Hello to you too, brother dear."

His response was clipped and dark. "Are you at La Notte?"

"Since when do I have to answer to you, Aric?" Amber light sparked in the Breed female's blue eyes. "Where I am is no business of yours. I thought I made that clear to you."

"Dammit, Carys! I'm not playing a fucking game here," he snarled, and suddenly it was obvious that Aric's demanding tone wasn't about anger but something more visceral. Something more urgent than that. He was calling out of fear and worry for his sibling. "Carys, tell me you're nowhere near that goddamn place right now."

Carys's voice dropped to a near whisper. "What's going on?"

Jordana could no longer hear Aric on the other end, but judging from his sister's stricken expression, the news wasn't good. Carys inhaled a sharp breath, her fingers coming up to her mouth for an instant before relief flooded back into her features. She listened for a moment, her face grim, then she quietly ended the call.

She glanced across the table at Jordana. "There's been a killing at La Notte."

"Oh, no," Jordana murmured. "But it wasn't—"

"No." Carys shook her head. "Not Rune, thank God. Aric said it wasn't any of the fighters, but he didn't have any more information than that. Some of the warriors are heading there now to investigate. Aric told me to stay away from the club tonight."

And yet Carys was already pulling out cash enough for the bill and a generous tip from her pocketbook. "I have to see Rune," she explained as she got up. "I just need to see for myself that he's okay."

The depth of Carys's love for the fighter was evident in her eyes. So was her fear. The strong Breed female trembled where she stood, visibly shaken by the news of a death at the place where her lover risked his life every night in the cages.

And while Jordana had no wish to be anywhere near the Order if it meant she might run into Nathan, she wasn't about to let her friend go there alone.

"Come on," Jordana said. "I'll drive."

Carys managed a faint nod and followed Jordana out to her car.

They made the short trek across town, arriving at La Notte's block in mere minutes. The club was closed, the arched wooden doors of the old church building barred.

A pair of immense bouncers was parked at the top of the steps leading up to the place, standing shoulder to shoulder in the dark beneath the thin lamplight at the front entrance. As the club's usual stream of patrons arrived to party upstairs or do other, less savory things in the lower level, the two bouncers turned them away on arrival.

"Drive past and turn down the side alley," Carys instructed Jordana as she slowed outside the club.

They rounded the corner and found the alleyway access blocked by one of the Order's huge, unmarked black patrol vehicles. Carys hopped out of the car the instant Jordana brought it to a full stop. Jordana followed her, only to be halted along with Carys by one of Nathan's team.

"Out of my way, Jax," Carys said as the pantherlike Asian vampire moved out of the shadows to intercept the women.

"Captain said no civilians, Carys. We've got a crime scene back there."

"I know. Aric called me. I just want to see Rune."

Jax gave a shake of his dark head. "He's around back with some of the other club staff, but you ladies are gonna have to stay out here for now. Trust me, you don't wanna see—"

"I'm going back there." Carys shoved past the warrior, breaking into a bolt before he was able to react.

Jordana followed her, jogging to keep up as her friend rushed around to the rear of the building. Rune may not have been injured here tonight, but it was obvious there was no one, not Carys's brother or any of the Order itself, who could keep the female away from the fighter she loved.

"Rune!" Carys called to the dark-haired Breed male as she and Jordana rounded the back of the club. Standing among a few of the other fighters and La Notte staff gathered in the gloom behind the old brick church building, Rune glanced up at Carys's shout.

His hard face was grave, his eyes shadowed and grim as he broke away from his colleagues to meet her as she and Jordana approached. Carys launched herself into his arms.

"Rune, I was so worried! Aric called and told me someone died at the club. Even though he said it wasn't you, I had to see for myself. I had to be sure—"

"Shh," the brutal fighter soothed, stroking his broad palm over the back of Carys's head as she clung to him. "It's okay, baby. I'm right here."

While the couple embraced, sharing private words of comfort and affection, Jordana drifted away from them. Although she'd never been to a crime scene before, and didn't want to be at one now, she found herself drawn toward the dark stretch of pavement where the apparent victim lay, surrounded by the team of warriors from the Order.

Her heels ticked hollowly on the asphalt, an odd sense of dread snaking around her with every careful step. Death hung in the air, cold and cloying. It lifted goose bumps on her arms, put a chill knot behind her sternum.

Although she didn't want to look—didn't want to know what kind of violent end someone had met with a short while ago—Jordana couldn't keep her gaze from peering between the warriors at the slain individual on the ground.

She caught a glimpse of baggy, worn denim on the skewed legs of the victim. The brown loafers on the man's feet were scuffed and aged . . . familiar.

Oh, no. It couldn't be . . .

She was holding her breath. She knew that even before the ache in her starving lungs forced her to suck in air.

Even before she saw all the blood on the asphalt, and the object lying next to the body. An object that looked unmistakably like the dead man's—

Before her horrified mind could confirm what her eyes were seeing, a deep voice was at her ear. "Holy hell." A pair of strong arms swept her away from the scene, a firm hand holding her head against a rock-solid chest covered in black combat fatigues. "Jesus Christ, Jordana. What the fuck are you doing here?"

Nathan's words were rough and dark, but his hands were warm and gentle on her as he held her close, keeping her face averted from the carnage. She didn't want to acknowledge how welcome his touch was in that moment. She meant nothing to him, so feeling his comfort now only added a deeper sting to the shock she was feeling.

She pulled out of his hold on a ragged cry. "It's him," she murmured. "I know him."

Nathan's black brows crashed together over his stormy eyes. "Who?"

Jordana gestured in the general direction of the victim, too stricken to look again. "That man. I was just talking to him a couple of hours ago."

Nathan's scowl deepened. "You talked to him?" His dark voice went from concerned to demanding, almost bordering on suspicious. "You saw him today? Where, Jordana? When?"

"Jordana," Carys said, walking over now with Rune. "What's the matter, honey? Are you all right?"

"It's him. The man I met in the exhibit this afternoon. He was alive earlier today and now he's—" Jordana's stomach lurched, choking off her words. Her chest ached with a sense of loss she could hardly reconcile for a stranger she'd known only a few minutes. "I don't understand how this could happen. Why would anyone want to kill Mr. Cassian?"

A swift, uncertain look passed between Carys and the two Breed males. Even in her distress, Jordana noticed the change in the air.

"Mr. Cassian?" Carys asked gently. "Jordana, that man over there is Cassian Gray."

When Jordana didn't react, Nathan added, "La Notte's owner. Until tonight, no one would admit to having seen the bastard or to knowing where he might be." He slanted a dark look at Rune. "I guess the Order wasn't alone in trying to track Cass down."

The fighter held the warrior's stare. "Like everyone told you, Cass dropped off-grid for a few days without warning. It wasn't that unusual for him."

Nathan grunted and turned his attention to Jordana. "Why was Cass at the museum today—did he tell you that? What exactly did he say to you? What did he want?"

Jordana shook her head, confused. She hadn't known the club's proprietor by name, had only glimpsed him once or twice from a distance on those rare occasions when she'd gone with Carys to watch Rune fight.

What she vaguely recalled was a man with a shock of stiff, white-blond hair and black leather clothing bristling with metal studs and buckles. Not the drab-dressed everyman she'd met today.

"There has to be some mistake. I don't know the man who runs this club. He's not who I saw in the exhibit. He doesn't even look like him—"

"It's Cass," Nathan insisted. "He'd altered his appearance and stayed out of the public eye, no doubt because he knew the Order was after him. Maybe he did it because someone else was after him too. The one who chased him down and took his head tonight."

Jordana winced at the reminder. "The man at the museum today wouldn't have those kind of enemies. He talked to me about sculptors he admired, about art and some of the pieces we have in the collection. He seemed like a decent, nice man—"

"He was a criminal," Nathan cut in. "More than likely, far worse than a criminal. If I'd seen him anywhere near you, it would have been my blade biting into his neck."

She stared up into his sternly handsome face, into stormy blue-green eyes that kindled with the faintest embers of amber light. She didn't know what skewed reality she had to be living in that would make the kind of possessive, violent remark he'd just made seem like a pledge of affection. Certainly not in her reality—the one she'd chosen to retreat back into after she'd let Nathan nearly seduce her in her building's elevator.

He cared for her about as much as he might care for any of his bed partners here at La Notte's sex dens. Possibly less.

Jordana forced herself to break his arresting eye contact. "If I'm sup-posed to be flattered that you would use me as an excuse to murder an innocent civilian, you're sadly mistaken."

His thundercloud eyes narrowed on her. "He was no innocent, Jor-dana. Trust me on that."

"Trust you?" She scoffed. "I don't even know you."

She turned and started walking away, needing space to breathe, to process everything that had happened today. She felt sickened by the death of the man she'd genuinely enjoyed meeting—whoever he truly was. And she couldn't deny that seeing Nathan again, even under these awful circumstances, had affected her more deeply than she cared to admit.

In spite of how it hurt her to see him at La Notte with another woman so soon after he'd left her, Jordana couldn't keep her pulse from beating a little harder around him. She couldn't keep her foolish heart from wishing things had gone differently last night, that they could start over again, beginning with that reckless first kiss.

She hurried her pace, hoping she could round the corner and make it to her vehicle before the weight of everything she was feeling over-whelmed her.

While Carys and Rune stayed back, she heard Nathan's long strides coming up fast on her heels. "What the hell is that supposed to mean—you don't even know me?" His already deep voice dropped to a lower, arrestingly intimate tone. "Seems to me we got pretty familiar last night."

She stopped abruptly and wheeled around on him, struggling to keep her voice controlled enough so that only he would hear. "Please, don't remind me about last night."

He halted where he stood, his square-cut jaw rising a notch. "You're upset with me. Because of what happened between us in the elevator, or the fact that Bentley-Squire interrupted us and we didn't get the chance to finish what we started?"

Jordana exhaled a sharp, outraged laugh. "I wish last night had never happened."

"That makes two of us," he said quietly, his face hard and unapolo-getic.

So he regretted it too? God help her, but she didn't want to feel wounded by that admission. She wanted to feel only anger that he could bring her to the crest of something so incredible—something she'd shared with no other man before him—then turn around and slake his need on one of the trained professionals at the club.

Jordana spotted the leather-clad brunette sex worker near the back door of the building, one of several La Notte employees who'd since come out to gawk at the crime scene. She couldn't help picturing Nathan's hands on the female.

Equally painful to imagine was the thought of what the brunette might have done for him to earn the fistful of money Jordana had seen the woman tuck away after Nathan left one of the club's private BDSM dens.

"I never should've kissed you," Jordana murmured. How much simpler would her life be if she'd just stayed on the safe, secure little path that had been laid out for her?

How much happier would she be if she'd never let herself reach for something reckless, something as dangerously seductive as the Breed male standing before her now?

"I never should've let you touch me, Nathan. I wish I could take it all back."

A low growl escaped his throat as he reached for her. She pulled back, avoiding the contact. "No, don't. Stay away from me."

He studied her for a moment, his eyes locked on her. "Tell me you really mean that, and I will."

"I mean it." She forced herself to hold steady, in spite of the widening ache in her breast. She had to do this. For her own sanity, she had to put him out of her mind and out of her life. "I don't want to see you again, Nathan. I wish I'd never met you."

He said nothing. Just stood before her in agonizing silence, his inscrutable gaze seeming to cut straight through her, as cold and unfeeling as a blade. His face was unmoving, impossible to decipher if he was relieved or insulted by her rejection.

The walls she'd so naively thought she might pull down were in full force as she looked at him now, perhaps rising even taller than they had been before. Nathan wasn't someone who let others in easily; she'd sensed that about him early on.

Now that she was pushing him away, he would shut her out completely. And she knew once he did, there would be no getting back inside.

One of his teammates—Aric Chase's best friend, Rafe—called to Nathan from back at the crime scene. "Captain, heads up. Squad from Joint Urban Security is en route from downtown. This place'll be crawling with JUSTIS officers in less than ten minutes."

Nathan acknowledged the report with a vague lift of his hand. In flat, maddening silence, he stared at Jordana for what seemed an eternity.

Then he simply turned away from her, walking back to his waiting crew of warriors and the grisly reality of his dark world.

14

NATHAN LEANED BACK AGAINST THE ORDER'S PATROL VEHICLE next to Rafe, trying to pretend he wasn't brooding from his confrontation with Jordana as he idly watched a team of six officers from the Joint Urban Security Taskforce Initiative Squad process the crime scene outside La Notte.

Shit, he was worse than brooding. He was pissed off and bewildered.

She wished she'd never met *him*? She had no idea. The best thing she could do for him was take her haughty indignation and all-too-tempting body and stay far the hell out of his way.

Out of his head.

Out of his life.

And the fact that he was stewing over the female an hour after she'd gone only jacked his frustration higher. He wasn't used to letting anything, or anyone, get under his skin. His Hunter training had conditioned him to ignore distractions, to dismiss anything that might sway him from his course. Any obstacle in his path was either shoved aside or trampled beneath him, left behind and instantly forgotten.

It was how he survived. It was how he came through the fire of his childhood, his mind and body equally honed, his heart as ruthless as a blade.

He was a master of control, and yet Jordana Gates had somehow begun to chip away at that impenetrable foundation. Like a small trickle of water through a mountain of stone, she'd managed to find a breach and slip inside.

Try as he might to put her out of his thoughts, to close himself off to the desire he felt for her—to deny his maddening need to possess her, now that he'd had the first taste—he couldn't get her out of his head.

The best thing she could have done for him was storm off in justifiable fury, determined that she never see him again.

And yet he brooded.

He stewed.

Told himself to let her run back to her safe life with Elliott Bentley-Squire and consider it a bullet dodged.

He tried to pretend that every muscle in his body wasn't twitchy with the hunger to go after Jordana right now and take her down beneath him, show her pleasure like no other man ever would.

With more effort than he cared to admit, Nathan wrestled his focus back to the situation at hand. While most of the combined human/Breed JUSTIS unit stood around trying to look important as they made phone calls and manned crime scene blockades set up around the club, they'd tasked one of their junior members with the unpleasant job of photographing the evidence. The twenty-something human, an obvious rookie, had already vomited twice since his team arrived an hour ago.

Rafe chuckled beside Nathan as the young officer butterfingered his camera and nearly dropped it into the blood pool surrounding Cass's headless body. "Twenty bucks says the new guy doesn't make it back to his squad car before he passes out."

As Rafe spoke, Elijah strode over with Jax to join them. "Now, that's just mean, picking on the human." Eli grinned. "I got forty on the Breed detective over by the club door. He's been trying to hold his shit together, taking statements from the staff and fighters, but that vampire's gonna need an assist before the kid does. I give him about two minutes before he goes all fangy standing around this much spilled hemoglobin."

Jax grunted. "Hell, we don't get out of here soon, I'm about to sprout fangs myself."

Although the blood was dead and no longer viable to any of their kind as sustenance, there was hardly a Breed in existence who could ignore the prolonged sensory torment of the lake of blood surrounding Cassian Gray's remains. Even Nathan felt the throb of his lengthening canines and the sharpening of his pupils as he stared at the headless body across the dark, wet pavement.

Then again, blood thirst was only part of his problem tonight.

The bigger instigator to his dangerous mood was more than likely tucked away safe and sound in another male's arms right about now.

Nathan growled at the thought.

The unbridled sound of aggression drew his team's gazes, Rafe's more questioning than that of the others. "You okay, Captain?"

"No," Nathan muttered. Refusing to acknowledge the reason for his lingering discontent, he jerked his chin in the direction of the crime scene. "Instead of putting Cassian Gray's ass in an interrogation cell back at Headquarters, I'm watching JUSTIS mop up our best potential source of intel on Reginald Crowe. Hell, Cass might have been our best source of intel on the Atlanteans themselves as well."

Rafe's nod was grim. "True, but this slaying did answer one question. How many deaths by decapitation do we see on average?"

Eli arched a brow. "Not counting Crowe's little helicopter blade mishap on that rooftop in D.C. last week? Exactly none."

"Someone was making a statement here," Jax suggested.

Nathan had to agree. "As we suspected, Cass wasn't human. Whoever killed him obviously knew that too."

Rafe met his gaze in the dark. "But who would want Cass dead— Opus Nostrum? Or someone Cass might've crossed in his business dealings at La Notte? No doubt the man took a lot of secrets with him tonight."

"Could be whoever wanted him dead had a secret of their own to protect," Eli added.

Nathan stared at the carnage across the way, considering all of the disturbing possibilities where Cassian Gray's murder was concerned. "Someone knew what he was and how to kill him. This was an execution. But even so, that doesn't tell us why."

And there was another question still gnawing at Nathan.

What the hell was Cassian Gray doing at the art museum today?

That the bastard had gone there within hours of his being killed was suspicious enough. But to have gone there and merely chatted with Jordana about art, when he was so concerned with being found out he'd changed his appearance and been MIA from his club and staff for nearly a week?

What business did he have at the museum? It didn't make sense that he would spend precious time—not to mention risk coming out of hiding—to go there today.

Nor did it sit well that Jordana was evidently the last person to see Cass alive.

What did he want with her? Because Nathan was damned certain it wasn't coincidence that put the elusive club owner at Jordana's exhibit. He'd had a reason to go there. She may not realize it, but Cassian Gray left something with her today. He did something, said something—something Nathan was determined to find out.

And if he was looking for that answer, what was to say Cass's killer wasn't doing the same thing?

For all he knew, Jordana could be in the crosshairs already.

Holy fuck. If Cass had put Jordana in harm's way, intentionally or otherwise—

A murderous flare of rage shot through Nathan at the thought, a deep protective instinct that he had no right to feel where the Darkhaven female was concerned. Still, the ferocity of his emotion stunned him.

But his fury was self-directed too.

He'd let Jordana walk away from him tonight. Hell, he'd all but shoved her away.

Bad enough he'd let jealousy and stung pride rule his warrior's logic in neglecting to debrief a possible intel source. But in allowing Jordana to leave the crime scene, he'd left her completely unprotected, should Cass's killer trace the Atlantean's steps back to his visit to the museum.

That logical part of him that had been missing earlier tonight tried now to remind him that Jordana likely wasn't without a Breed male to keep her safe from imminent harm. She had her de facto mate to protect her—a choice she'd willingly made last night.

As if Elliott Bentley-Squire were capable of looking after a woman like Jordana.

She needed a better male, a stronger male. The kind of male who would throw down his life for her in an instant.

The kind of male who would have leapt on Nathan last night and pounded him into a bloody pulp for the liberties he'd taken with her in that elevator.

Nathan snarled low under his breath. Told himself the current of urgency coursing through him was more about protecting a potential Order asset than assigning himself as a personal bodyguard to the woman he craved so fiercely, so unwelcomely.

The woman who just a short while ago had insisted she wanted nothing more to do with him, and rightly so.

As the JUSTIS officers cleared the crime scene and packed up the body, Nathan ordered his team to report back to base. Then he pivoted away and began to stalk across the dark pavement.

Rafe jogged after him. "What's going on?"

"Jordana," Nathan stated simply. "She was the last person to see Cass alive."

"Jesus," Rafe muttered. "Are you sure? How do you know that?"

"She told me. Cass showed up at the museum this afternoon. She spoke with the bastard."

Rafe frowned. "About what? Why the hell would he go there?"

Nathan kept walking. "That's what I intend to find out."

"You mean *we*," Rafe said. "As in the Order. As in we call this in to Headquarters and let them decide how best to proceed with the female." When Nathan didn't respond, Rafe grabbed his shoulder. "Jordana Gates is a civilian and a potential intelligence lead now, Nathan. You know the protocol on something like this."

Yeah, he did.

He knew Order procedure and protocol inside and out. Hell, he'd lived and breathed it for most of his life. But that didn't keep his feet from moving in the opposite direction of what he knew was the right and proper thing for a warrior to do.

"Holy shit," Rafe murmured. "You really care about her."

Nathan didn't have the patience to try to deny it. Not that his friend would believe him, even if he wanted to pretend it was true.

All that mattered in that moment was getting to Jordana, making sure she was safe.

"Dammit, Nathan. You know I have a duty to report this."

Nathan picked up his pace. He heard Rafe's curse behind him, low and incredulous, in the instant before Nathan vanished into the darkness.

The teakettle started to howl in the kitchen as Jordana sat on her sofa, sweeping fresh tears from her cheeks. The sweet ending of the romantic comedy she was watching shouldn't have inspired more than a smile or a satisfied sigh, yet as the credits rolled, she was about two seconds away from breaking down into a full sob.

Not that the movie was what had her so emotionally on edge. She'd been shaken up since she arrived home tonight. The long bath she'd taken when she first got there had helped calm her nerves, but she didn't think she would ever be able to purge the memory of what she'd encountered outside La Notte.

She had cried inexplicably for Mr. Cassian—for Cassian Gray, or whatever his true name was. She'd never been so close to death before, and she hated that the kind man she'd spoken with had met such a seemingly senseless, violent end.

No matter what he'd apparently done for a living, the odd stranger Jordana had found inside the exhibit had appeared to be a decent, interesting person. What he could have possibly done to earn the death he'd been dealt tonight, she couldn't imagine.

Sniffling as she got up from the sofa, Jordana padded barefoot to the kitchen to rescue the whining kettle. She had donned lavender silk pajamas after her long soak in the tub. Beneath a loosely tied matching robe, the light tank and shorts felt cool against her bare skin as she trekked through the empty apartment.

Carys and Rune had checked in on her a short while ago, practically insisting that she come out with them and not sit around the penthouse by herself. But alone time had been just what Jordana had wanted. Except now she felt a sudden, keen ache for the comfort of family. She longed for the reassurance of her father's protecting arms.

Martin Gates would welcome her back to his Darkhaven anytime; she knew that. She also knew that going home would only make her father try to persuade her to move back in permanently. And that was a conversation she didn't want to have with him again. Especially not tonight, when learning where she'd been and what had happened would send him into a fit of worry.

Although the wealthy Breed male had brought her up selflessly as his daughter from the time she was an infant, providing her with anything she could possibly ever need in life, Martin Gates could not seem to fully adjust to the idea that Jordana had become an adult woman. She was nearly twenty-five years old, yet he still wanted to direct her life as if she were a child.

God, her birthday. Jordana poured a cup of tea and groaned, thinking about the trust that would become hers in less than a couple of weeks. A payoff her father held out to her as incentive to settle down and take a mate—so long as that mate was the Breed male of his choosing.

As much as she loved seeing her father, if she went home tonight, she would never hear the end of how disappointed he was that she'd rejected a fine male like Elliott. At times, his desperation seemed so great, Jordana half expected she might be physically forced into the bond with Elliott. But her father loved her too much to do something so unforgivable, no matter how deep and misguided his belief was that she needed to settle down.

Jordana had to start taking steps on her own path. Walking away from a relationship she didn't want and couldn't honor with her whole heart had been a good start to that goal.

Halting her dangerous attraction to Nathan had also been a step in the right direction.

A good, sensible step.

Except telling Nathan tonight that she didn't want to see him ever again hadn't done anything to curb how she felt about him.

She couldn't begin to deny that she was attracted to him. After the pleasure he gave her in the elevator, her traitorous body only wanted more.

But worse than her physical need for him was her interest in him emotionally. He intrigued her. He frustrated and infuriated her.

He confused her, enflamed her, made her crave things she hardly dared think, let alone act on with anyone but him.

And he'd hurt her more than anyone ever had too. A pain that shouldn't have surprised her so much. Shouldn't have wounded her so deeply.

She'd felt more for Nathan in a period of a few days than she had for Elliott in all the years she'd known him.

Everything about Nathan was intense, from the rugged perfection of his face and bleak, thundercloud eyes, to the seductive power that clung to him as menacingly as the darkness of his Hunter past.

And she must be a fool of the highest order to imagine she might have gotten close to him without getting burned.

Thankfully she'd come to her senses before she'd done something really stupid, like letting him into her bed.

Or worse, letting him into her heart.

Too late for that.

"No, it isn't," she muttered to herself, scolding the all-too-eager, all-too-knowing voice of her conscience.

And dammit, that merciless little voice was right. It was too late to pretend there was nothing between Nathan and her.

Too bad she was the only one feeling it.

Jordana took a sip of her tea, grimacing at the bitterness. Stirring in a large spoonful of sugar, she scowled into the swirling tendril of steam rising up from the cup. "Anyway, he's gone now, so what does it matter?"

Her cup of tea clutched in both hands as she sipped the sweet brew, Jordana stepped out of the kitchen, back into her living room.

And felt her grip go slack as she nearly collided with six and a half feet of black leather and dark, simmering male.

Nathan caught the cup as it slid from her grasp, not so much as flinching when the hot tea sloshed over his strong fingers. Stormy eyes held her startled gaze beneath the slash of his raven's-wing brows.

Seeing him sent a surge of emotions flooding through Jordana, but the first one to leap to her tongue was outrage. "What do you think you're doing here?"

Damn him, he didn't even blink. "Proving a point," he replied, his deep growl doing all kinds of bad things to her heart rate. "This is how quickly you can go from thinking you're safe and secure, to pushing out your last breath."

Jordana hiked up her chin. "I thought I told you I didn't want to see you again."

"You did."

He might as well have shrugged one of those bulky shoulders for the lack of apology or excuse in his tone. How dare he think he could just ignore her wishes?

"Breaking into my apartment hardly qualifies as staying away from me."

No acknowledgment, but as he set her steaming teacup down on the sofa table next to them, his dark gaze flicked past her briefly, toward the kitchen. "Is someone here with you? Maybe I'm here at an inopportune time . . . again."

"What?" She frowned, unsure what to make of that comment. Did he think Elliott was with her? "No one's here with me. Why?"

"You were talking to someone as I came in."

Oh, God. Talking to herself. Trying to assure herself that if she never saw Nathan again, it would be too soon. And now here he was, standing in front of her in the middle of her apartment, questioning her like a jealous lover and making her blood race like wildfire through her veins.

"I'm here by myself. As if it's any concern of yours," she added, grasping feebly for anger when his dark gaze—his very presence—had her breath coming shallow and fast, her heart pounding frantically in her breast. She crossed her arms as if to contain her body's eager reaction to him. "What do you want, Nathan?"

The corner of his mouth quirked slightly, more scowl than smile. "I doubt you really want to know the answer to that question, Miss Gates."

Was he toying with her, getting some kind of twisted enjoyment out of her discomfiture the way he got other thrills from the women who serviced him at La Notte?

Jordana swallowed hard, half tempted to make him tell her so. But she couldn't let herself fall back into that trap. She was nothing to him; he'd demonstrated that clearly enough last night.

"You need to leave now, Nathan. I'm not interested in playing your games, and I certainly don't appreciate you breaking into my apartment."

"I don't play games," he said, crisp and cool. "Nor did I break in. I leapt up to the balcony from the street. The slider was unlocked, which only helps to prove my point. You're not safe. I might just as easily have been whoever killed Cassian Gray tonight."

Shit. She wasn't actually in any kind of danger, was she? Dread knotted in her belly as she glanced to the slider across the room. The large glass door was locked now, the latch securely in place.

She looked back at Nathan, hating that she now had to add gratitude to the list of unwanted emotions his unannounced visit was stirring inside her.

"Haven't you tormented me enough already?" She paced away from him, suddenly needing some distance in order to keep from leaning into his warmth. "You didn't have to come here like this and scare me nearly to death."

"It wasn't my intent to scare you, Jordana." A pause behind her, then his voice, soft but demanding. "What do you mean, I've tormented you enough?"

Forget it. No way was she about to explain that reckless slip of her tongue. If he didn't know how he'd affected her since the moment their paths first crossed, then she would gladly take that knowledge to her grave.

"I want you to go," she said, not looking back at him as she marched barefoot across the living room toward the vestibule where the penthouse's private elevator was located.

The elevator where less than twenty-four hours ago, Nathan had given her the most intense climax of her life.

God, she should not be thinking about that right now.

"I told you tonight that you had to stay away from me, Nathan."

"Yes, you did."

He was right behind her now, so close she could feel his big body throwing off heat and coiled male power. The thin silk of her robe and pajamas was no barrier at all. From head to toe, her skin felt too exposed, seared, every nerve ending tingling and alive with awareness.

Everything female within her was tuned on him implicitly.

"I know what you told me, Jordana. I know it's a bad idea for me to be here." He swore under his breath. Firm hands came to rest on her shoulders and he slowly turned her around to face him. "Unfortunately for both of us, when Cassian Gray decided to spend some of the last hours of his life with you, he put you in the middle of my investigation for the Order."

Jordana stiffened in his grasp but couldn't quite find the will to pull herself away from the contact. "So you're just here in an official capacity, is that it?"

"I think we both know better than that," he answered, deliberate and calm. So maddeningly arrogant. But he drew nearer then, and the heat of him, the leather and dark spice scent of him, nearly made her moan with pleasure.

His eyes smoldered, locked on hers as he closed the distance, leaving scant inches between their bodies. Amber light sparked in the murky blue-green depths of his gaze. His normally hard-to-read face was harsh with grim purpose, his angular cheekbones seeming more pronounced under the subtle blaze of his mesmerizing irises.

As she looked up at him, his pupils began to narrow, the tips of his fangs just visible behind the fullness of his lips. Along his neck, the intricate pattern of *dermaglyphs* that tracked over his smooth skin and into the ebony hairline at his nape began to churn and surge with rising hues of indigo and gold.

Nathan may have been born and raised a Hunter, but he was Breed as well, and not even his cold origins or discipline seemed enough to mask the desire Jordana saw in his transformation.

His hands still holding her, he moved in closer, crowding her with the delicious heat and scent of him. "Nothing about my being here right now is official in nature. But that doesn't change the fact that you're currently my best potential source of intel on Cass's final hours. Why was he at the museum? What did he do there, how long did he stay? What did he say to you? These are all things the Order will need to know. I'm going to need you to tell me everything, Jordana."

"You already interrogated me once tonight," she reminded him. "I don't have anything more to tell you, so you might as well leave."

His nostrils flared. Eyes flashed with brighter flames. "I didn't come here to interrogate you."

"Then why are you here?"

"I came to make sure you were okay." His expression tightened as his gaze swept over her, fierce yet gentle. He blew out a low curse. "I needed to know that you were safe, and I trust no one else to make sure of that but me. Fuck, Jordana . . . I don't want to see you get hurt."

He didn't want to see her get hurt?

As tender as his words were—as deeply as she wanted to believe the concern in his voice—Jordana stared up at him, unable to bite back her quiet scoff. "I'm not your responsibility, Nathan. It's not your job to look after me."

"No, it isn't. But by Christ, I'm going to protect you, no matter whose job you think it is to keep you safe. Whether you like it or not."

She didn't like it. At least that's what she tried to tell herself as he held her in his strong hands, in his possessive amber-flecked gaze.

She didn't want to like that flare of raw hunger she saw in his expression. Didn't want to ache with want to feel his mouth crush down on hers while he kept her captive in his grasp.

Her shallow breaths mingled with the hot gusts that rolled out of him, her heartbeat pounding furiously, frantically, while his thrummed as hard and steady as a drum.

He was saying all the right things, acting as though she mattered to him. Drinking her in just now as though she belonged to him.

But she didn't belong to him.

She couldn't belong to him, not if she wanted to keep her heart intact. Their worlds were too different. She saw that last night.

And no matter how much she wanted to believe him now, to trust what he was telling her with his words and hands and eyes, Jordana clung to the tiny shred of sanity that warned her she was looking at the very thing that could hurt her more than any other potential threat of danger.

She dropped her head and let a sigh slip out of her, chagrined to hear it manifest as a pained moan. "You don't have the right to do this to me, Nathan. You can't come into my home uninvited and say things to me like that. You don't have the right to appoint yourself my protector. You're not my anything."

"That's true," he answered, but instead of drawing back from her, he leaned closer.

To her combined agony and delight, he removed one hand from its loose grasp on her shoulder only to bring the backs of his fingers toward her face in a caress so light it robbed her of both breath and good sense.

His touch drifted lower, along the side of her neck, then down the length of her silk-covered arm. "It's all true, Jordana. I don't have any right when it comes to you."

And yet her veins were throbbing as she stared at him, warmth rising up her throat and into her cheeks, igniting in her core. The heavy beat in her veins was nothing compared to the deep pulse centered between her thighs. Her sex ached with a longing that spread through her limbs, making her legs feel unsteady and boneless.

He leaned closer, his mouth very near to her ear. "Tell me how I tormented you."

She shook her head, all the response she could muster as his free hand moved around to the silk sash that loosely tied the front of her robe.

"Tell me, Jordana." A command, not a request, even though his deep voice was pure velvet. "I tormented you. That's what you said. Now tell me what you meant."

"No." The refusal rushed out of her, airless and desperate.

She didn't want to explain how he'd hurt her last night after giving her so much pleasure. It was too humiliating to admit how easily she'd been wounded. Or that she was too inexperienced to participate in the kind of wicked pursuits he seemed to enjoy.

She didn't want to be that sheltered, untried girl. Not with him.

And she supposed that made her an even bigger fool.

With one deft hand, he worked the knot of her robe's sash loose, then coiled the twin lengths of silk around his fist, forcing her to step toward him now, until there was no space left between them at all. Her breasts pressed against the hard muscles of his chest, and lower still, his thick thigh parted her legs to nestle firmly against the molten core of her body.

"How have I tormented you, beautiful Jordana?" When she tried to glance away, he caught her chin in his other hand and guided her gaze back up to him. "You won't say it?"

When she gave him a wordless, weak shake of her head, his gaze flashed with amber fire and a dangerous smile curved his grim mouth. "Then I'll have to guess. Was it torment when I kissed you like this?"

He bent toward her and took her mouth, swallowing her breathless gasp in a kiss so deep and fevered, she nearly collapsed in a quivery puddle on the floor. His tongue invaded, pushing past her teeth in a profane rhythm that made her hips respond in time with his movements, answering some primal call she had no will to resist.

It wasn't torment. Not until he drew back, denying her any more than a heart-stopping taste of what she craved.

"Was it torment when I touched you?" he asked, pulling her to his body by the hand wrapped tight in her sash, while his other hand slipped inside her robe and beneath the loose pajama tank to cup her bare breast in the heat of his palm.

He caressed her breast, tweaking the hard nipple with his thumb, pinching it with a pleasure-pain that made her sink her teeth into her lower lip as her body shuddered with excitement.

God, she could hardly take it, the dark need he stoked in her. She was already half mad with desire and mounting pleasure when he abandoned her breast to begin a descending trail along her ribs and abdomen.

He met with little resistance from the drawstring waistband of her silk shorts. His fingers delved between her thighs, into the slick juices of her sex.

"Was the feel of my hands on you last night—inside you—a torment, sweet, wet Jordana?" He stroked the swollen pearl of her clitoris, making her moan in pure abandon. "Tell me you didn't enjoy what we shared last night. Tell me it was torment. Torment enough to send you running into the arms of another male, is that right?"

"No," she gasped, too lost in sensation to deny him now. "No, that's not right. You were the one . . . you ran to someone else. Not me."

He reared back as abruptly as if she'd slapped him. His sharp amber-drenched eyes narrowed on her, suspicious and questioning. "I ran?"

"Back to La Notte," she replied, still panting, her body still throbbing with need.

She didn't want the pleasure to end, but it was too late to call it back. Nathan was staring at her in a dark, dangerous silence, his jaw clenched.

He released her, let the silk ties of her robe fall away from his grasp. In the sudden quiet, Jordana felt a coldness sweep over her, replacing the heat she'd been enjoying so thoroughly a moment ago.

"I know you go to the BDSM dens at the club," she said lamely. "I know what you do there."

He didn't try to deny it, which was a relief in some small way. "Rune told you?"

Jordana shook her head. "It wasn't him. It doesn't matter how I know. I only wish I'd understood how interchangeable I was to you before I let you touch me last night." She blew out a jagged laugh. "Then again, I knew that today and I didn't stop you just now."

"What are you talking about?" Nathan demanded, his deep voice taking on a thunderous edge. "What the hell makes you say I think you're interchangeable with anyone?"

"I know you were with one of the club's sex workers after you left me with Elliott last night. I saw you, Nathan. That's what I meant by torment."

She tried to pivot from him, but he caught her, didn't give her the chance to get away. "Are you saying you were there? When? Just what do you think you saw, Jordana?"

"I saw you with her—the brunette," she blurted, glad she didn't know the woman's name for fear that she would sound even more jealous and injured. "You were in one of the private rooms with her. You paid her a lot of cash and the two of you walked out together."

He listened, more calmly than she might have expected. He didn't say anything, but as she spoke, the hardness began to ebb from his ruthless gaze. His square jaw was still rigid but no longer seemed on the verge of shattering. "You're right, Jordana. I did take one of La Notte's sex workers into the dens with me last night. As you saw, I compensated her for her service."

Jordana stared up at him. Had she really felt relief that he hadn't tried to spare her feelings by lying about what he'd done? Hearing him admit it all so casually seemed to chip off tiny pieces of her heart with each detail he confirmed.

"I think it's best if you go now, Nathan. I hope you'll respect my wishes and not come back again."

He gave the slightest shake of his dark head. "I don't think so."

Jordana frowned. "I want you out of my house."

"No, you don't."

His hand was still wrapped around her wrist. With one flex of his powerful arm, he drew her toward him. Their bodies contacted, his hard and unyielding, hers boneless and melting at the feel of so much hot male power pressed against her.

"You don't want any such thing. You want me to tell you I didn't do things with the human female at the club that you want me to do to you. You want to hear that I didn't fuck her. That I wouldn't have used you last night the same way I've used the workers at La Notte. As a meaningless, interchangeable tool for my release."

"Let go of me, Nathan."

"I'd like to." He exhaled a sharp, humorless laugh. His eyes glittered, sparking with fresh embers. "Believe me, I'd like nothing more than to be able to let you go. I'd like to tell you that I'm every bit the asshole you think I am. I'm no prize, make no mistake there. I did leave here to finish what we started with someone else at the club. Touching you, feeling your tight, wet heat with my fingers made my cock so hard, all I could think about was burying it inside you. God help you, it's all I'm thinking about right now too."

His erection crushed into her abdomen, thick and alive with heat. It pulsed through the thin barrier of her clothing, each heavy throb making her own heartbeat pound deeper in response. Awareness made her stomach clench, turned the ache in her core into a molten yearning.

"I'm a Hunter, Jordana. I don't wait for invitations. I don't ask for permission. I pursue, I conquer. Then I move on and I don't look back. That's how it's always been for me. That's how I live." Cold truth, made all the more cruel when he was stroking her cheek and neck, his thumb moving in maddening little swirls over her throbbing carotid. "I'm not a gentle man. Neither are my needs. You wouldn't like my methods for slaking them. So when I left here last night, it was because I wanted to fuck my need for you out of my head, out of my system. I *had* to, do you understand?"

"Stop," she whispered brokenly.

Despite the harshness in him, despite the fear she knew she should be feeling because of all that he said and all that he was, it was this last admission that was the hardest to accept.

It was all too easy to picture him doing just what he described. His mouth on another woman. His hands giving pleasure to someone else.

Someone else whose heart probably wasn't as foolish as hers.

"I don't want to hear any more, Nathan. I can't do this with you anymore. I'm not like those other females you prefer. Those other females you . . . fuck."

The word felt foreign on her tongue, not something she'd ever uttered in front of a man before. Certainly not to a man who'd had his tongue down her throat and his fingers between her legs more than once in the past twenty-four hours.

A man she wanted inside her with a yearning that bordered on sheer, reckless lunacy.

Nathan growled then, low and deep and lethal.

"No, you're not like them, Jordana." When she tried to look away, to hide her need from him, he brought her face back up, forcing her to meet his gaze. "I wanted to prove that to myself last night. I wanted to convince myself that you meant nothing to me and that my craving for you could be satisfied by someone else. Anyone else. I wanted to . . . but I didn't."

Jordana gaped at him, afraid to believe. Afraid to hope. "But I saw you with that woman. You said yourself you paid her for servicing you."

"Yes," he admitted evenly. "She offered me her vein and her body, for a price. But once I took the woman into the dens, I realized she didn't have anything I wanted. I paid her because the problem wasn't with her, it was with me."

Was he serious? The human female hadn't been with him at all—not even to serve as his blood Host?

Jordana could hardly contain the surge of relief that flooded through her.

His seductive mouth curved in satisfaction and challenge. "Now tell me you want me to leave." He put his face beside hers, the rough scrape of his cheek and jaw a delicious abrasion that sent a shiver up and down her spine. "Last night, you had the excuse of Elliott Bentley-Squire to keep you from taking what you really wanted. He may have saved you from me then, but I don't see him here right now."

With his free hand, Nathan palmed her breast, then splayed his fingers up toward the base of her throat and coaxed her head back onto her shoulders so he could place a hot, deliriously erotic kiss to the pulse point that kicked into a frantic rhythm under his warm, wet tongue.

He growled against her skin, and for the briefest instant, Jordana felt the sharp tips of his fangs dragging over her vein. "Christ," he hissed. "Even if the son of a bitch walked in the door right now, I wouldn't take my hands off you, Jordana. I want him to know he'll never have you."

"No, he won't," she panted. "And he won't be coming here anytime soon because I ended things with him."

Nathan stilled. Then his head lifted, his stormy eyes ablaze with crackling heat. "You ended it."

She gave him a small nod. "Last night. Just before I went after you and found you at La Notte."

For a long moment, he didn't move. Didn't speak a single word.

When his lips parted, his fangs gleamed, the tips as sharp as daggers.

He muttered something dark and hungered.

Then, without warning or excuse, he scooped her up into his arms and headed toward the bedroom.

15

JORDANA WAS LIGHT IN HIS ARMS AS NATHAN BROUGHT HER TO the bedroom at the end of the hallway.

A delicate crystal chandelier hung from the center of the vaulted ceiling, casting soft light in the room. Beneath the elegant fixture sat Jordana's sumptuous king-size bed, which was heaped with fluffy pillows, frothy white coverlets, and fine, crisp sheets. The walls were painted in an equally snowy hue, the plush area rug just inside the door crushing easily under his black combat boot as he entered the room.

Everything about Jordana's private sanctuary was soft like her, pure like her.

And he, the invading darkness soon to defile both.

Crossing the threshold into her bedroom, Nathan recognized the moment now was do or die. Jordana could leap out of his arms and barricade herself inside. Or he could set her down on her feet and make his escape.

Run? Hell, yes. That was exactly what he was contemplating—admittedly, not for the first time where this woman was concerned.

The thought perished swiftly, scorched into oblivion, when instead of fighting to get loose from his arms, Jordana turned her head and buried her face into the crook of his neck and shoulder.

Christ, the feel of her so close to him was arresting. It shot through him like a jagged flash of lightning, impossible to ignore.

And bewildering too. He didn't know what to do with the humid rush of her breath against his throat. The touch was too intimate. Too tender.

Too honest and trusting.

It wasn't too late to stop this. His intellect was quick to warn him of that, but his body had other ideas. With blood pounding furiously through his veins and to points lower, his cock grew even more demanding behind the confines of his patrol fatigues. His lust was vying for control of the situation now, and it had no intention of backing down.

Jordana nuzzled closer, innocently unaware of the depth of her impact on him. The scent of her swamped his nose, drugging him with the combined fragrance of the vanilla soap that she must have used in her bath and the more intoxicating perfume that was simply Jordana. She smelled warm and soft and innocent, yet heady with the scent of arousal.

How would her body taste against his tongue? And if he pierced the tender vein that fluttered so temptingly in the side of her neck, would her Breedmate's blood flow down his throat like sweet nectar or boldly exotic spice?

Saliva surged at the mere idea. His fangs were already filling his mouth, but now they ripped farther out of his gums, the long canines pulsing with an even darker need than the one that practically owned him tonight.

Nathan set Jordana down on her feet beside the bed, his entire being vibrating with a barely restrained hunger.

If she were any other woman, he'd already have her naked and spread open wide to receive him—facedown or tied down, his long-standing requirement of anyone he fucked.

No kissing him.

No touching him.

No watching him as he exorcised the weakness of his flesh-and-bone body.

He fed and fucked because he had to, but he did it on his terms. Always under his strict control, in order to retain the edge of the honed, unfeeling weapon he'd been born and raised, mercilessly trained to be.

Jordana Gates had broken all of his rules.

If she were anyone else, he wouldn't be standing there with a raging hard-on, a need that bordered on savage, and no damned clue how to begin what he'd started here tonight, let alone how to finish it.

She must have finally sensed the threat in him as he stood before her near the bed. She retreated a couple of steps, only until the backs of her thighs hit the mattress and she dropped down onto its edge. She swallowed hard as she looked up at him, her alabaster face and wide blue eyes gilded in the amber glow of his transformed irises.

"You're afraid," Nathan said, the statement rolling out of him like a growl.

She gave a small shake of her head, her long, loose platinum hair tumbling around her like a bridal veil. "Not afraid," she murmured, her voice somehow more steady than his. "You don't frighten me, Nathan."

He grunted, incapable of speech as heat spiked into his bloodstream. Jordana's lavender robe had fallen open, revealing the flimsy excuse for clothing underneath. Her spaghetti-strap tank did nothing to conceal the buoyant shape of her breasts, nor could it hide her nipples, which stood erect and far too tempting under the pale silk. Her loose-fitting shorts were nothing but a whisper of fabric that covered her hips and the tops of her thighs.

Jordana's legs were naked and seemed to go on forever. Nathan followed the line of them with his gaze, drinking in every flawless inch.

He could hear her breath racing now. He watched the rapid rise and fall of her chest and the frantic ticking of her heartbeat at the pulse point in the hollow above her sternum.

His own lungs were soughing hard, air rasping past his teeth and elongated fangs. "I only know one way to do this, and that's me in control," he said, feeble apology or warning, he wasn't sure. "Do you trust me, Jordana?"

"Yes." No hesitation. No waver in her voice or her beautiful, brave eyes.

Nathan swore, low under his breath. He moved closer to the bed, trying to resist the urge to pounce on her. He took off his weapons belt and let the blades and other lethal tools of his profession fall to the floor beside him.

It was all he dared remove for now.

Jordana might truly trust him, but that was more than he was willing to say for himself. He needed to keep a steady hand on the reins; he owed that to her for her trust in him. His focus would be entirely on her.

Nathan moved between her legs, urging them to part wider, and wider still. He drew forward, until the heavy bulge of his erection was brushing against the damp center of her sex.

She gazed up at him, as fearless as a goddess, as pure as an angel. By contrast, standing in front of her now, he felt dirty and unfit. As profane as a demon come to pray in the center of a cathedral.

For the first time in his life, Nathan realized he felt afraid—afraid that he would hurt her, disappoint her. That she would suddenly realize how unsuited he was for the gift of her body, of her passion.

Most especially, for the gift of her trust.

He reached out to move a thick wave of blond hair from where it had fallen into her face. It sifted through his fingers, sleek and shiny as pale, liquid gold.

"Everything about you is so soft," he murmured, winding the thick, gleaming lock around his hand. "Soft but strong."

He released the errant tendril and hooked it behind her ear, exercising a care he never imagined he possessed. "Tonight, I need to see that you're okay at all times. I don't want you to hide your reactions from me, no matter how small. I need to know if I'm pushing you too far. Do you understand?"

She nodded.

"No," Nathan said. "I need you to say it out loud. I need you to be clear, Jordana. I don't want to guess at anything. Not this time."

She nodded again, then surprised him with a smile. "I understand, Nathan."

"Good," he murmured, then he reached down to touch her breasts, rubbing his thumb over one lovely nipple, then the other. "I shouldn't be your first. Then again, I don't think I've got honor enough to stand aside and let you give yourself to anyone else. Not now."

"I want this," she whispered resolutely. "I want you."

She reached for him as she said it, her hands nearly taking hold of his face before he had the chance to elude them.

A cold panic seized him and he reared back, catching her in a firm grasp.

Her wrist tendons tightened. She gave a small flex of her hands, testing his hold.

He didn't relent, not so much as a fraction. Uncertainty flashed in her eyes.

"Last night, in the elevator," he said, trying to keep the hard edge from his voice. "I told you that when we did this, it would be on my terms."

He could see the question in her eyes now. Apprehension washed over her face, flattening her lips and making her already racing heartbeat drum even harder as he held her, unyielding.

"My terms, Jordana."

"Yes."

She relaxed at once. Her hands lay in his grasp easily, her fine muscles loosening, surrendering to him.

He sucked in air, let it out on an approving growl.

Guiding her down onto the bed on her back, he pushed her arms up alongside her head. "Don't move. I want to look at you."

He drew back slowly, and simply gazed upon her.

And Jordana didn't move. She lay there, spread out before him like an offering. Her bare inner thighs were open, warm against the outsides of his legs. Her heat was intense, permeating his combat fatigues and scorching the taut muscles of his thighs.

Need coiled even hotter in him, dangerously close to breaking.

God help him, he wasn't used to taking things slowly. He wasn't sure he could now either. She was so beautiful, so arousing.

Everything male in him was hammering hard with the need to take.

To possess.

To vanquish.

He bent over her and drew her robe off her shoulders, letting his palm rasp over the top of her little silk tank. The pebbled points of her nipples teased the underside of his hand as he caressed her breasts. He almost hated to leave them as he skated his touch lower, over the flat plane of her abdomen.

He could feel her strength in every flex and contraction of her stomach as she breathed, sighed, gasped under his fingers. He lifted the hem of her pajama top so he could touch her without the barrier of clothing and feed his craving for her nakedness.

He knew her skin would be as flawless as the rest of her, and it was—as fair and smooth as cream. Her breasts, which felt so incredible under the silk, were perfection unclothed. Round and firm, tipped with rosy little areolas the same shade as her kiss-bruised lips.

Nathan's gums throbbed in time with his cock, all of his senses fevered with the need to feast on her. He lowered his face to her belly and licked a slow trail along her skin, up the center of her rib cage, before venturing off to the side to capture one of her nipples in his mouth.

He suckled, groaning with the sweetness of her, the purity of her—something he'd never known.

Greedily, he moved on to her other breast, his hand following the path his lips had just blazed. Jordana trembled under his touch, against his tongue. Her fluttering pulse rang in his ears and sent hot need surging into his already granite-hard cock.

As he played the tight bud of her nipple between his teeth, her breath caught. Her hips lifted off the mattress in wordless plea for contact.

Nathan let his hand drift down her body then and beneath the loose waistband of her silk shorts. She moaned as he cupped her sex. She was wet and scorching against his fingers, her juices like liquid velvet. Her petals bloomed even more as he stroked her. Her folds swelled, slickened with each stroke of his fingertips.

The feel of her softness was driving him quickly to the brink. His skin felt tight and overheated, his erection straining so heavy and hard within his clothing, he could barely think straight.

But as demanding as his desire for her was, some distant shred of sanity punched at him with the reminder that she was untried.

As tempting as he found her, she was not at all prepared for the depth of his hungers.

She writhed and moaned with need, but she wouldn't be truly ready to receive him until she was on the other side of that raw ache.

With a restraint nothing short of Herculean, Nathan drew back from her luscious body, slowly peeling off her pajama shorts as he went. Next, he removed her robe and tank, baring her completely for his fevered gaze.

A curse leaked out of him, as coarse and dry as gravel. "Ah, Christ . . . you're so lovely, Jordana."

Lame praise, hardly worthy of her. But it was sincere. One look at him—at his blazing irises, sharp fangs, and very obvious approval of his cock—would be enough to tell her how the sight of her affected him.

He drank her in from head to toe, a long, unhurried appraisal. Her face was flushed and dewy, her eyelids drooping over the dusky, darkened blue of her eyes.

He could practically see the blood coursing through her veins. He could hear it, every heavy throb of her pulse, the rush of red cells flowing like a thousand rivers under the milky white perfection of her skin.

His vision sharpened even more, and he knew that by now his pupils must be all but nonexistent, winnowed down to the thinnest, catlike slits in the ember-bright furnaces of his irises. His *glyphs* pulsed across his body, churning and alive with the intensity of everything he was feeling and seeing. All the carnal things he wanted to do with this woman.

His woman, an eager voice promised him from the lowest depths of his consciousness.

He dragged his searing gaze down to the pale blond curls on her mound and the long legs he couldn't wait to feel wrapped around him as he rode her, buried to the hilt in her wet heat.

The scent of her arousal wreathed him as he moved in closer, unable to resist the temptation of her any longer.

He put his palms on the tender insides of her thighs, exposing her further to him. "Your sex is so pretty, Jordana. So juicy and red and inviting."

He stroked her, groaning in approval at the way she flushed a deeper shade for him, her wetness coating his fingers like honey. She squirmed as he caressed her, a soft cry curling up from her throat.

"I've never seen anything so beautiful," he told her, his voice deepening, sounding too thick for the presence of his fangs and far less human than he cared to admit. "Your petals are so swollen and ripe. And your clit . . . I've never craved anything more, Jordana. It's as dark and glossy as a cherry, just begging to be eaten."

He moved down and sank onto his knees between her legs. The instant his mouth touched her, she sucked in a sharp gasp, arching high off the bed. "Oh, God," she sighed. "Nathan . . ."

He breathed her in as he suckled her, murmuring against her flesh how delicious she was. He slid his tongue through her cleft, growling as her intoxicating nectar hit the back of his parched throat.

One taste wasn't nearly enough. He delved deeper, lapping at her tight opening before licking upward, toward the pert, cherry-dark knot nestled between her folds.

Jordana bucked now, squirming under his mouth. He stoked her even higher, lavishing her with his whole mouth as he teased her with his fingers.

Suckling her clitoris with ruthless demand, he eased one finger inside her. "Holy hell," he muttered roughly, lost to the silken grip of her channel as he worked his digit in and out of her in a tempo he couldn't wait to find with his cock.

Jordana panted and gasped. Her sex clenched at him greedily as he drew her clit deeper into his mouth, sweeping his tongue over her in the same urgent rhythm of his fingers.

She moaned, pushing her hips against him as a tremor wracked her in a head-to-toe shudder. A pleasured scream started to boil out of her, but she stifled it, her head thrashing back and forth on the bed.

She tried to rise up, tried to reach for him again.

Nathan growled and put his hand on her belly to press her back down.

"Let it go," he ordered her. And he kept his mouth fixed on her trembling flesh, merciless in his command of her body. "Let me hear you, Jordana. Don't hide anything from me. That was our agreement."

She whimpered and writhed as he coaxed her toward a higher peak now.

And when she came, it was on a powerful roar, unbridled and raw. The sexiest sound he'd ever heard. She climaxed immediately again, grinding against his face in unabashed pleasure, his name tearing out of her throat like a curse and a prayer.

16

HER EVERY NERVE ENDING WAS CHARGED AND THRUMMING WITH a current unlike anything she'd ever experienced. Her skin felt seared, her limbs trembling, boneless.

Deep inside, the very core of her being had gone molten, all of her thought and logic—every last inhibition and fear—obliterated by the shattering intensity of her release.

And Nathan's scorching gaze promised even more.

Breath racing short and shallow, Jordana lay back on the bed and watched, mesmerized, as he began to strip out of his combat boots and clothing in an economy of movement. Just the sight of his muscles bunching and flexing as he tore off his black patrol shirt and bared his arms and chest to her made more wet heat surge between her legs.

Dermaglyphs tracked all over his light olive-hued chest and shoulders, then lower, along the ridged planes of his abdomen and down below the waistband of his black fatigues. There could be no mistaking he was Gen One Breed. Jordana had seen precious few *glyphs* on other males, but nothing compared to the complicated pattern of interlocking swirls and elegant flourishes of Nathan's otherworldly skin markings.

Nothing so erotic as the way his *glyphs* followed the contours of his body as she yearned to do with her fingers . . . and her tongue.

Her mouth went dry on the thought and she swallowed the urge, her full attention now caught on his hands as he unfastened his dark fatigues. The black fabric slumped loosely on his tight hips. And not so loosely on the massive bulge straining at the front.

She licked her parched lips, her lungs gone still as he let his pants drop and stepped out of them.

The *glyphs* that had her so fascinated with his chest and arms now dragged her gaze farther south, where their pattern continued into the dark thatch at his groin and onto the thick, jutting length of his penis. His muscular thighs were wrapped in *glyphs* too, and all of the swirling, arcing patterns that covered him were alive with deep shades of indigo, wine, and gold—the Breed colors of fierce desire.

Jordana stared at him, at the sculpture of his body and the master-work of his *dermaglyphs*, helpless to keep her hungered little moan from escaping her throat.

In his warrior's garb and weapons, Nathan was forbidding and lethal. Awe-inspiring by the darkest of definitions.

Naked and fully aroused, he was all those things and more.

Immense.

Terrifying.

Heart-stoppingly, dangerously beautiful.

And he was looking at her as if nothing else existed but the two of them in this moment. As if the sight of her nakedness affected him every bit as intensely.

He stepped closer to the bed now, skimming his warm palms along the insides of her thighs as he took up residence between them. She exhaled a tremulous sigh at his touch, at the heated, hard presence of his body positioned so intimately against hers.

"Please," she whispered, the word shaky, more breath than sound.

Nathan grunted, low and contemplative, his smoldering eyes locked on her face. "Please, what, Jordana? Tell me." Demand in his deep, coaxing voice, nothing close to request.

As he spoke, his hands caressed her, moving upward until he reached her damp curls and hypersensitive flesh. He teased her with long strokes and deft fingers, stoking her so easily back to a state of writhing need.

Jordana closed her eyes as pleasure swamped her, pulling her under on another dizzying tide. She let it take her, gave herself up to the bliss of his hands on her, his fingers inside her.

And when she didn't think she could hold on for another second, Nathan's touch slid away, leaving her gasping his name, her body vibrating and fevered with an ache she could hardly bear.

"Oh, God," she murmured, lifting heavy lids to find Nathan poised above her on the bed now, braced on his fists with elbows locked straight on either side of her.

His erection pulsed from its upright position against her cleft, the feel of him like warm steel sheathed in velvet. As if he knew how badly her body craved him, he flexed his hips, sliding his hard length through her wetness, cleaving her folds with his heavy shaft.

Jordana moaned at the torment, growing mad with want. Desire kindled and burned, stronger than ever, and with it seemed to form another awakening within her, this one more elusive but no less powerful.

Something more than physical need, deeper than simple craving.

Something queer and unfamiliar to her, an unfolding awareness, reaching out from the furthest corners of her consciousness for what seemed the first time.

And all of that heat, all of that power, all of that strange, rousing energy arced toward Nathan as surely as a divining rod trained on a font of clear, quenching water.

She felt it in her blood and bones, in her senses . . . in her very soul.

"Nathan, please . . ." She lifted her shoulders up off the bed, her palms hot and itching to feel him. To touch his skin and trace the tantalizing lines of his extraordinary *glyphs*.

But not until after she felt him inside her, filling her with more than just his wicked fingers.

"Make this ache stop," she demanded, her voice husky and rough with desire. She reached for him, prepared to take hold and drag him down atop her if he didn't ease her yearning soon.

But Nathan moved faster than she could even dream to. For the second time tonight, he dodged her touch and captured her hands in his strong grasp.

This time, however, he didn't seem content to merely hold her away from him.

Straddling her now, he rose up onto his knees above her, his fingers wrapped around her wrists like iron clamps. His eyes flared with amber sparks, something hotter than desire or even anger. Something darker, menacing in its intensity.

His face was so serious, his pupils nearly swallowed up by the light radiating from his Breed irises. His sensual mouth was unsmiling, merciless, his fangs gleaming and deadly sharp behind his parted lips.

And yet despite his ferocity and unforgiving hold, he carefully brought her hands toward him, pressing a tender kiss into the center of one tingling, hot palm, then the other.

His thumb stroked the underside of her left wrist where her Breedmate mark resided, a growl curling up from the back of his throat.

Jordana didn't notice he held the tie from her robe until he began to loop the lavender silk sash around both of her wrists, binding her hands together.

He said nothing.

No excuse or explanation.

No request for permission.

She'd come to accept his dominating nature in most everything he did, but now it took on new meaning. Nathan wanted total control when it came to sex.

He needed it, assumed it.

Demanded it.

Jordana could have broken out of her bonds if she tried. But she didn't wish to try. There was something wildly erotic about the satiny abrasion of the tie against her skin.

Even more arousing than that was the idea of surrendering herself so completely to Nathan.

A shiver raced through her, part in trepidation, part in breathless anticipation. She was a strong woman with a strong head. She'd always chafed against even the lightest reins someone attempted to place on her. But with Nathan it was different. *She* was different. After tonight, she knew she would never be the same again.

If she was being honest with herself, she hadn't been the same since the moment she took that first impulsive kiss from him. Nor did she want to go back to the life she had before.

And for now, she was right where she wanted to be—safe with the most dangerous man she would ever know.

Jordana let him ease her back down onto the mattress. Allowed him to push her arms up, so that her bound hands rested above her head as he moved off her.

She submitted to him willingly, unabashedly, when he parted her trembling thighs and gazed upon her, naked, open to him, for the longest moment of her life.

His eyes roamed unhurried over every bare inch of her, a slow lick of flame that left her quivering and overheated, restless for him to quench the burn. He tangled his hand in her loose hair, lifting the pale strands, watching it sift through his fingers and settle back down around her shoulders and naked breasts.

Eyes blazing, fangs glinting as sharp and white as diamonds, he lowered his face to the front of her throat, sending her pulse into a wild hammer.

His breath skated over her tender skin, then his lips closed over the vein that throbbed like a drumbeat pounding in her temples and in her ears.

His tongue soothed, but she could feel the hunger radiating off his immense body. His kiss was gentle, sensual, seducing her body into a boneless state of passion, of fearless, wanton trust.

"Yes," she gasped, giving him the submission his skilled mouth and hands demanded.

At her carotid now, a faint graze of his fangs—whether in his own temptation or to demonstrate to her how totally she was at his mercy right now, Jordana couldn't be sure.

Nor did she care.

He could have sunk his sharp canines into her in that moment, and she would have been helpless to stop him.

God save her, but there was a reckless part of her that would have welcomed Nathan's bite . . . and the eternal blood bond that would come with it.

Jordana moaned his name, caught between pleasure and frustration over the fact that he'd denied her the ability to touch him and kiss him too. She wanted to run her hands over him as he moved, feel the power of his muscles as his strong body covered her. She wanted to feel his hard shaft filling her, claiming her.

She wanted Nathan to do whatever he pleased with her, a wish that should have terrified her but only made her need wrench tighter.

And that peculiar, unfurling coil of energy deep within her seemed to agree.

It rushed up from the center of her like a live current, jagged and white and consuming.

"Now," she said, astonished to hear the growled command push past her lips. "Nathan . . . oh, God . . . I can't bear this. Please, I beg you . . . do it *now*."

His head came up sharply from her throat, his face hard and impassive. Maddeningly, unbreakably in control.

But his eyes . . . they gave him away.

She wasn't alone in the violence of her desire, not even close.

Nathan snarled a curse, amber light flaring hotly in his transformed irises. He moved between her legs, his erection standing thick and upright, terrifyingly large.

Doubt flickered through her mind, a sudden fear making her brace for certain pain. Her breath stopped, heart rate speeding now, as he shifted his hips and the blunt head of his cock slid through her wet cleft, coming to rest at the virgin opening of her body.

Nathan stilled above her. "Open your eyes, Jordana. Let me see you."

She obeyed at once, not even aware she had closed them. Nathan stared at her, eyes locked on hers as another subtle pivot of his hips seated him more fully at her entrance.

"You're so slick and hot," he murmured. He pushed slightly, testing her. Studying her. Patiently allowing her to prepare for his invasion. "Your body is ready for me. I need to know you are too."

"Yes," she replied, her stifled breath gusting out of her on a tremulous sigh as he moved against her, teasing her with the promise of what was still to come.

She bit her lip but kept her gaze trained on his as he'd demanded. Another nudge of his hips coaxed her untried channel to accept more of him. A flood of liquid heat pooled in her core, all her fears drowning quickly in that rising tide.

Nathan's mouth curved in a knowing, wicked smile. His hips drew back slightly, then pushed forward in one sure thrust.

Jordana's body bowed as he entered her, filled her. There was pain, but it was as fleeting as it was sharp. There and gone in a few instants, obliterated by the incredible feel of their bodies pressed tight together, naked and joined as one.

"Ah, fuck." Nathan's voice was rough, guttural. And the raw sound of it only made Jordana's arousal spike higher. He moved inside her, his pelvis rocking smoothly, gently, even as his big body shook with hard tremors. He rasped a low curse beside her ear. "I didn't want you to feel this good. Dammit, you shouldn't feel so right."

He thrust deeper as he said it, impaling her as if in punishment, yet Jordana could only revel in the fullness and the tempo that sent pleasure into all of her senses.

It felt more than good. It felt more than right, Nathan deep inside her, their bodies answering each other's rhythms as if they were meant to be together.

As if they had always belonged like this.

Jordana spiraled toward orgasm, climbing higher and higher as Nathan drove into her welcoming sheath. She cried out as the first wave crashed over her. Gripped by the force of her oncoming release, she arced into each rock of his hips, tugging against the silken bonds that still held her hands above her head.

Nathan showed her no mercy, increasing his speed and depth until she was lost and adrift, every particle of her being turned electric with pure, powerful sensation. She screamed as an explosive climax overtook her, splintering her from the inside.

And then Nathan followed her, pushing deep, grinding his hips against hers at an urgent, violent pace. Lips peeled back off his enormous canines, he bucked into her, riding her hard.

Jordana loved the wildness of his passion. Nathan, the cold, cool warrior—the ruthlessly in-control Gen One male—scorching her with desire-drunk eyes and an expression caught somewhere between fury and rapture. That she had done this to him, turned him so savage with lust, was astonishing. Empowering.

The headiest aphrodisiac she could imagine.

She was already coming again when a fierce shudder gripped him. Nathan roared her name, his voice unearthly, untamed. One hand clamped on her hip, he buried himself to the hilt and yet another coarse shout ripped from between his teeth and fangs as a jet of fluid heat shot inside her.

Jordana lay there, floating on a strange new plane, her senses both satiated and hyperaware. She heard every breath, felt every heartbeat—her own and Nathan's both.

Her body felt loose and relaxed, newborn in many ways, as it recovered from the dull pain of her lost virginity and the even greater pleasure of what she and Nathan had just shared.

He was still inside her, still firm, stretching the walls of her sheath as his erection pulsed with renewed life. The feel of him growing bigger, hard all over again, made her own body react like tinder near an open flame.

She exhaled a deep sigh, moving beneath him in effort to create more delicious friction.

Nathan's muscles twitched, and inside her, he thickened in swift response. Eyes narrowed on her, he lifted his head and uttered a low groan.

"Too soon for you," he cautioned. "Your body needs time to mend, Jordana."

No, it didn't. What it needed was more of him.

But Nathan withdrew and rolled off to the side of her. He reached up and freed her hands from the soft tether above her head. He paused for a moment, the length of silk crushed in his tightly clenched fist.

When his gaze met hers again, she saw regret there. An apology he didn't speak but communicated with his light caress on the bare undersides of her arms, then in the tender stroke of his fingers along her flushed cheek and parted lips.

The torment in his expression pulled at her. He struggled with very private demons; she might have guessed that, in light of his background. Now she saw his internal struggle playing across his handsome, tortured face. A struggle he seemed accustomed to battling alone.

Her heart clenched at that thought. There was so much about this solitary, remote man that she didn't know. Things she wanted to understand.

She didn't know if he would share any more of himself than what he gave her tonight. And despite the real fear of his rejection, Jordana couldn't let her questions go unasked.

"Nathan," she said softly. "Will you tell me . . . why?"

Black brows furrowed—an instantaneous reaction, and one that he swiftly schooled into the cool aloofness she'd come to know and expect in him.

How adept he was at erasing all traces of emotion from his face, even from his eyes. What had he endured that he could mask his feelings with such little effort?

He held her inquisitive stare, almost as if he challenged her to see through him. "I told you what to expect before we began any of this." Mouth flat, grim, he poured the crushed length of silk out of his fist and onto her nude torso. "This is the way it is with me. You can't say I didn't warn you."

Cold words. No doubt meant to freeze her into silence as he pivoted away from her on the bed. His defensive walls had gone up, blocking her out. That is, if he'd ever been inclined to let her inside in the first place.

His bare feet hit the floor and when he went to stand up, Jordana tossed the sash aside and drew up onto her knees behind him. "That's not what I meant. The bondage . . . it doesn't matter to me. Your need to be the one in control doesn't matter."

She took a fortifying breath and crept closer to him, very much aware that of the two of them, only he seemed frozen and silent now. Jordana edged up behind his broad back, with its masterpiece of *dermaglyphs* adorning the flawless canvas of his skin.

She lifted her hand, but drew it back, unwilling to dare that much.

Not when she could feel the caged power radiating off him. A menace so dark it nearly stole her voice.

"Nathan," she whispered carefully. "Why is it that you can't bear to be touched?"

The answering silence seemed to stretch on forever. He sat on the edge of the bed, unmoving. Jordana wasn't even sure he was breathing.

She'd overstepped. She realized that now. They had shared something incredible tonight—something intimate and real to her, at least—and now she'd ruined it by pushing him to open up a part of himself that wasn't hers to examine.

"I'm sorry," she blurted. "I shouldn't pry—"

"Would you want to touch the bloodied edge of a blade?" He spoke without turning to face her, his deep voice even, utterly devoid of emotion. "Or willingly put your hand in the jaws of a fighting dog?"

He slowly pivoted then, his stormcloud gaze flat and unblinking. "I'm not the kind of man you should want to get close to. I don't function the way you expect me to. A weapon doesn't require touch or comfort. And if you reach out to a creature bred and trained to kill, it's liable to be your last mistake."

Jordana swallowed, a keen ache opening up in the center of her chest for what Nathan must have endured as a young man—as a mere child—while he was part of the Hunter program.

She'd heard little more than rumors about the secret breeding labs that had been disrupted by the Order some twenty years ago. There were whispers of neglect and brutality, of terrible abuses suffered on the Gen One boys who'd been created to serve as the private army of one diabolical Breed madman.

Boys like Nathan who, according to Carys, had been removed from his mother as an infant and spent the first thirteen years of his life under those unthinkable conditions.

Jordana's heart broke for that infant, for that tragic little boy.

And for the detached, battle-hardened man who sat before her now. The beautiful, deadly Breed male who had shown her such unexpected tenderness tonight and who had awakened her to a passion that still stirred, potent and alive, within her.

"You're not a blade or an animal, Nathan. Whatever awful things you were forced to do in your past don't define who you are today." She inched closer, braved the smallest caress of his stern jaw. "Nathan, you are not what they tried to make you."

This time, he didn't remove her hand from where it rested lightly against him. But he stared at her with a calmness that chilled. "Yes, Jordana, I am. Don't try to imagine I can ever be like the other men you know."

"I don't." She gave a small shake of her head. "I wouldn't want that."

She'd proven that to herself in recent days, if not to Nathan. All her life, she'd known the warmth of a loving home and the safe embrace of family and friends. She'd had no shortage of admirers, no lack of even the smallest thing she'd ever wanted or required.

And yet she would give all of that up right now, trade her past with his, if it would remove the hauntedness from Nathan's stormy eyes.

Oh, she was in trouble here.

She was falling fast, one foot over the edge of that steep, storm-swept cliff she felt teetering beneath her whenever Nathan was near.

Tonight, she'd given him her virginity. If she wasn't careful, he would own her heart as well.

Maybe he already did.

The realization washed over her, left her speechless as she stared into his impenetrable gaze.

Nathan didn't permit the silence to linger. Nor her touch either.

He pulled away. "It's late. I should go." He started to get up, then scowled and uttered a low curse. "Fuck . . . you're bleeding."

Jordana glanced down at the sheet beneath her. A faint pink stain wet the pristine white cotton where she'd lain with Nathan. Embarrassment flooded her face with heat. "Oh . . . no, it's nothing."

"Like hell it is." He grunted, his brow furrowing deeper. "Dammit, I didn't want to hurt you."

Awkwardly, she shook her head. "You didn't. It was just a little blood, and I'm not hurt. I've actually never felt better in my life."

"Christ, Jordana." He snarled under his breath. "You deserved someone who would've been more gentle with you. You still deserve that." Another curse boiled out of him, but with less venom now. He held out his hand to her. "Come with me."

Jordana slipped her fingers into his grasp, not that he had intended to wait for her agreement, of course. That dominating side of him was in full control of the situation—and her—before she could even utter a syllable.

He hauled her up from the bed. In the adjacent bathroom suite, the shower turned on with a sharp hiss, obeying his mental command.

Led by the hand, Jordana followed after him. As her bare feet padded softly on the hardwood a pace behind his long-legged strides, she tried not to gape at the lusciousness of his naked body. Six and a half feet of muscle and gorgeous, *glyph*-adorned skin, all of it moving in catlike fluidity as he prowled across the room with her in tow.

Her blood warmed in her veins, and that molten pool in the center of her began to simmer all over again.

God, she really had it bad for this man.

Nathan brought her into the steam-filled bathroom, his fingers yet clamped around hers. When he opened the tall glass door of the shower, she half expected him to toss her inside and order her to attend herself.

Instead, he led her inside, bringing her under the hot spray with him.

He didn't speak, didn't explain. Nor did Jordana need his words. Not when his hands were tender as he began to wash her, handling her with utmost care and gentle attention.

She needed nothing more than this.

This moment.

This man.

Jordana closed her eyes as Nathan's cleansing touch eventually turned sensual and his mouth found hers through the steam of their surroundings.

Heaven help her, she was on unsteady ground here.

She was stepping off that ledge tonight, falling too fast.

Falling too hard for a lethal, untouchable Breed male who'd promised her nothing.

She knew this, the same way she understood that if reality waited for her at the bottom of this mad leap, it was certain to break her.

17

AS THE NIGHT CREPT PERILOUSLY CLOSE TO DAWN, NATHAN REAL-
ized he had never been further outside of his element.

When he'd shown up at Jordana's apartment, he hadn't intended a
full-scale seduction.

Nor had he intended to use their time in the shower together as a
prelude to still another round of mind-blowing, incredible sex.

He sure as hell had not intended to find himself seated in a chair in
her bedroom sometime afterward, watching over her as she slept curled
up like a kitten in a nest of fluffy sheets and coverlets.

When he'd crawled out of her bed to get dressed so he could head
back to the command center, he told himself it was only reasonable for
him to stay awhile to ensure she was safe for the night. Once she was
comfortable and resting, he would go back where he belonged.

That was hours ago now.

Night was ending soon, and if his own free will wouldn't drag him
away from her, the coming daybreak would.

Damn, how had he allowed himself to get so entangled with this
woman?

When had she slipped through his defenses to become something
more than a sexual itch he needed to scratch?

How did he imagine this whole thing would continue—worse, how
would it ultimately end—when he had nothing to offer a woman like
Jordana?

It hadn't been empty flattery when he told her she deserved something more, someone better, than him. It had been a warning. One of many he'd issued that didn't seem to sway her. His dark look or growled threat had always been enough to cower man and Breed alike, but not her.

Jordana Gates was nowhere near as delicate or conservative as she looked. Nothing like the pampered, fawned-upon Darkhaven female he'd often guessed her to be. Right now, he wished like hell she was.

Instead, he'd found her to be strong, unshakable. There was a roaring warrior inside her, buried deep but clawing to get out. She was unlike any woman he'd ever encountered, with her sharp, curious mind and sensitive artist's soul. It didn't help that she also had the face of an angel and the all-too-tempting body of a goddess.

He'd never known a need as consuming as the one he felt for this woman. And if it had been confined to purely physical hunger, that would be bad enough.

No, what Jordana stirred in him was something deeper.

She intrigued him. She confronted him, challenged him.

She gentled him, when his entire existence had been built on violence and cold detachment.

Jordana was, in a word, extraordinary.

Nathan's veins thrummed in agreement, his blood still running hot for her.

He had no right to be the one she gave herself to for the first time. But looking at her sleep so trustingly under his watch, recalling the fevered way she'd responded to him—the open, accepting way she'd submitted to his every desire and demand—made something possessive and primal churn deep inside him.

For a moment, he let himself imagine what it might be like to be one of the golden, privileged males of her world, not the rough enforcer he was now. Not the assassin whose hands had been stained with death from the time he was a seven-year-old child.

He had never looked back in shame on where he'd come from or on what his past had done to him. But as he considered Jordana and the way he still craved more of her, a cold hollow opened in his chest. Regret for the choices that had been taken from him.

Anger and, *dammit*, a sudden, fierce longing for the future that had been denied him even before he'd been conceived in Dragos's lab.

Useless feelings.

Weakness he'd been disciplined never to let manifest.

He'd allowed Jordana more than most tonight. Intimacy he'd never granted anyone. Insight into his bleak beginnings and how they shaped him.

He'd let her past a threshold all her own tonight, but she hadn't seen everything.

He could never permit that.

There were things no one knew, not even the few of his closest friends and squad members in the Order. Not his tenderhearted Breedmate mother, Corinne, or her devoted warrior mate, a formidable Gen One Breed male who'd been a product of the Hunter program decades before Nathan had been born into it.

Nathan had endured things, done things, that were better left inside him.

Locked away.

Memories best held to the dark, which he managed with the same iron control he employed in every other aspect of his life.

Just thinking on the days and nights—the decade and more—of his enslavement under Dragos's command and his torture at the hands of the Minion assigned as his keeper made Nathan's skin go taut.

He could still hear the crack of the lash, the jangle of chains . . . the sharp, olfactory punch of his own spilled blood and viscera.

Even worse was the recollection of the suffering inflicted on others.

Because of him and, ultimately, by him.

Absently, his fingers grazed his throat in search of the ultraviolet collar that had been every Hunter's shackle from the time he was old enough to crawl. It wasn't there, of course. It had been gone since the night his mother and her mate tracked him down and rescued him at the age of thirteen.

Christ.

Twenty years away from his past, yet it still surprised him to reach up and find his neck bare.

And this was what he'd brought into Jordana's bed, into her life.

If he were a better man, he'd wake her with an apology and hope she could eventually forgive him for taking the gift of her innocence and her trust. No, if he were a better man, he'd have never let her kiss him those few nights ago. A better man would have never let himself crave her the way he did.

Too late.

True to his born-and-bred nature, he'd lived up to the warning he gave Jordana tonight: He pursued. He conquered. And if he were a better man, he'd carry out the rest of his warning and walk out now, never looking back.

Nathan stood up on a low curse, bewildered that his discipline had failed him so badly when it came to Jordana.

The sight of her drew him toward the bed when he tried to command his feet to leave the room. The scent of her pulled a ragged moan out of him, the intoxicating combination of warm skin and soft, sensual woman proving almost too much for him to bear.

Jordana's bloodscent lingered faintly on the air as well. Nathan's Breed senses seized upon the elusive fragrance, which called to both the man in him and the beast.

Every Breedmate's veins carried a unique scent, but Jordana's natural perfume was beyond unique. It was unearthly, addictive. He found it impossible to describe the mix of exotic spice and crisp, delicate citrus that tickled the back of his throat and made his gums tingle with the presence of his emerging fangs.

All he knew was that he wanted her.

Again.

Still.

Nathan leaned over her in the dark, watching as the banked but burning embers of his transforming eyes illuminated her face. She must have sensed him in her sleep, just enough to coax a quiet little sigh from between her parted lips.

Nathan wanted to taste those lips again. He couldn't resist sweeping aside an errant tangle of her platinum hair that snaked across the smooth column of her throat. He wanted to press his mouth to the fluttering pulse point below her ear.

He wanted to do more . . . much more.

He likely would have, if a faint noise outside the bedroom hadn't jolted him to full attention.

Someone was entering the apartment.

In an instant, desire was doused with concern for Jordana's safety. Nathan moved with lightning speed, battle instincts switched on and lethal as he flashed out of the bedroom.

He rushed the opening elevator doors, total stealth and menace, prepared to kill.

Carys Chase stood in the center of the lift. She gaped, her eyes going wide.

"Shit," Nathan hissed. "What the fuck are you doing here at this hour?"

Her brows hiked upward. "I live here. Rune just dropped me off. What the fuck are *you* doing here at this hour, Nathan?"

Damned good question. He backed off on a snarl and raked a hand over his scalp. "I came to check in on Jordana earlier tonight. I had questions about what she and Cassian Gray discussed before he was killed."

Questions he'd all but neglected to ask, because he was too busy getting naked with her.

Carys's narrowed look said she suspected as much.

She stepped off the elevator to jab a finger in his chest, her voice a sharp whisper. "You asshole. I can't believe you would come back here like this. I can't believe she even let you in, after what you did to her the other night."

"After what I—" *Fuck. Of course.* Carys had almost certainly been with Jordana at La Notte when he'd come out of the private room with the human female.

Jordana had probably confided the evening's entire chain of events to her best friend, starting with his near seduction of her in the elevator. A seduction that would have been a certainty if running into Bentley-Squire hadn't put a damper on Nathan's plans.

And Jordana hadn't exactly let Nathan in tonight, but somehow he didn't think Carys needed to hear that. The Breed female was furious enough with him already. She glared, her blue eyes crackling with sparks of amber outrage.

"We've worked things out," he said, all the explanation he intended to give. What happened between Jordana and him tonight was their business. Not that Carys didn't have a pretty good idea anyway. "It's not what you think. I don't want to see her get hurt. Not by anyone." He paused, trying to find the words to summarize all the things he felt where Jordana was concerned. "She's become . . . important to me. I care about her."

Carys stared at him for a long moment. "My God. I believe you actually mean that."

He stepped around the daywalker without further comment. "It'll be morning soon. I have to go. Look out for her today," he added. "I'm not convinced she's safe so long as whoever killed Cass is out there."

"You think his death could be linked to Reginald Crowe and Opus Nostrum?"

"Could be," Nathan replied, unable to keep the gravity from his tone.

In his gut, he dreaded that the truth might prove to be something even worse. Until further word came in from the Order in D.C. about Crowe's apparent mistress and any useful intel she might provide, Nathan wasn't ruling out anything.

"I will protect Jordana with my life, Carys. No one will do her harm so long as I'm able to keep her safe. But during the daylight hours—"

"Of course." Her gaze softened with understanding now. "She's important to me too, Nathan. I'll make sure she's all right."

He inclined his head in acknowledgment. "Tell her I'll be back tonight at sundown to look in on her again. We'll talk more about Cassian Gray then."

Carys shook her head. "She won't be home. The exhibit opens this evening," she reminded him. "We'll both be at the museum reception tonight, along with a couple hundred invited guests and visitors."

Shit. He didn't want Jordana out of his sight tonight, let alone out of reach entirely and surrounded by a museum packed to the gills with the general public.

"You could always come as her date," Carys suggested, a teasing glimmer in her eyes. "Might do you some good to take a night off for once. You might even have fun."

Fun? He scoffed at the idea. Even if he did decide to attend the event, fun would be the last thing on his mind. He'd be there for the sole purpose of ensuring Jordana's safety, making certain every person in the vicinity understood that if they intended harm toward her, they would have to come through him first.

Not that Jordana needed him showing up to disrupt everyone else's good time. He'd already done that once this week with his team and Carys's brother. None of the Darkhaven and human elite of Jordana's social circle would appreciate having the Order present in the room—no doubt that sentiment would be doubled for the soulless killer Nathan's past had branded him in the public's eye.

Not gonna happen.

Jordana didn't need him barging into every aspect of her life, least of all an event she'd obviously poured her heart into for weeks or months. It was her moment to shine; he owed it to her to let her have it without him distracting from her accomplishment.

"Keep your eye on her, Carys. Let me know if you have any cause for concern. Anything seems off, you call me at once. Agreed?"

She gave him a nod. "Yes, of course. But I still say you should come to the museum tonight and look after her yourself."

Nathan dismissed the idea with a curse as he strode for the waiting elevator car.

At the Order's global headquarters in Washington, D.C., Lucan Thorne leaned back in his chair in the war room, listening in displeased silence as Sterling Chase briefed him via video feed early that morning on the night's patrol report out of Boston.

It wasn't good news.

Then again, good news was something the Order had been coming up short on for too many months to count now. Years, in fact. Hell, more than a couple of decades, if he really wanted to do the math.

Lucan felt a dark rage building in him as he received the details of Cassian Gray's slaying. A crucial lead lost. Possibly their only viable lead on the race of immortals reputed to be plotting war against the Order and the rest of the planet.

And now that lead had been severed on the edge of a hidden enemy's blade. An enemy with unknown motives, and still at large.

Damn it all to bloody hell.

Before his fury had a chance to explode out of him in a roar that would bring his mate, Gabrielle, flying into the room in alarm, Lucan vaulted out of his seat.

He began an agitated pace behind the conference table where Gideon and two of the Order's district commanders had assembled with Lucan to review current missions and organize further operations. Tegan, chief of the New York City operation, and Hunter, who oversaw the Order's presence in New Orleans, had remained in D.C. with their mates since the Global Nations Council summit last week.

A peace summit that had nearly resulted in catastrophe.

"I'm sure I don't need to tell you that this was not what I wanted to hear right now," Lucan said, glancing at Chase's grim expression on the screen. "We had slim prospects to begin with—just two potential sources of intel on this operation—and now we're down one before we even get out of the gate. As for the other, the way things are going in

Ireland with Mathias Rowan and his team, we may end up holding nothing but our dicks before this whole thing is over."

"It could be worse," Gideon said without looking up from the array of 3D touch-screen monitors laid out before him and illuminated with countless servers' worth of data, which he swept through and resequenced like a deranged symphony composer. "A few nights ago at the summit, if we hadn't stopped Reginald Crowe and Opus Nostrum's Morningstar bomb, today we'd be engulfed in certain world war between the humans and the Breed."

Lucan grunted. "Don't think that's off the table yet. If what Crowe promised—that Opus Nostrum and their plans are nothing compared to what the Atlanteans mean to do—then we stand on the brink of war every second of every day that we let Crowe's kind elude us."

On the video screen, Chase's face remained sober. Lucan knew the serious warrior long enough to realize that failure didn't sit well with him either. "Nothing to report out of Dublin yet, I take it?"

Lucan shook his head. "Rowan's got a full squad on the ground in that city and outlying areas, searching for anything they can find on Crowe's purported mistress. Without a name or physical description, they're getting nowhere fast." Lucan blew out a low curse. "It doesn't help that Rowan's had his hands full with JUSTIS in London recently as well."

"How so?" Chase asked.

"They've been dealing with a rash of unsolved murders in that city recently. Human and Breed victims, a few of them high profile. Joint Urban Security finally got so desperate to make the killings stop, they extended an olive branch to the Order in exchange for an unofficial assist on the investigation."

Tegan grunted. "'Unofficial assist' meaning handle it for them quietly and by any means necessary, so long as they don't have to get their hands dirty."

"It's the old Enforcement Agency all over again," Gideon said, his hands flying from one large display to another. "Except now it's got a shiny new, politically correct name. Same old shit, but someone else is doing the shoveling."

A onetime career Enforcement Agent himself, Chase arched a golden brow. "And there's twice as much of it, now that the bureaucracy has been extended into both Breed and human law enforcement combined under the JUSTIS banner."

"Their inefficacy is our advantage right now," Hunter said, his deep voice unnervingly level, his input logical as always. "If local law enforcement decides to wash their hands of Cass's slaying too, then the Order can investigate unimpeded by JUSTIS red tape."

"We'd better hope for that," Lucan said. "Hell, we'd better do more than hope. We need to run this thing down with every resource at our disposal. If Nathan and his team are right about this killing—this immortal-style execution in the middle of a city street—then we need answers, and we need them yesterday."

"Understood and agreed," Chase replied. He hesitated for a moment, then pointedly cleared his throat. "There was a witness . . . not on scene at the time of the killing, but someone who saw Cass—spoke to him—within hours of his murder."

Lucan frowned. "You didn't mention that a witness had been identified in the team's reports."

Another pause, and Chase's mouth flattened. "Because she wasn't included in any of the field reports that Nathan or his team filed. Rafe came to me a short while ago and personally informed me about the female. She's a Breedmate from one of the Back Bay Darkhavens. Actually, she's Carys's best friend and roommate as well."

Hunter cocked his head, eyes narrowed on Chase. "You're saying Nathan overlooked a key detail of his investigation? He doesn't make mistakes. That's impossible."

"No," the Boston commander said carefully. "I'm saying Nathan deliberately omitted a key detail of his investigation when he sent in his report this morning."

Lucan practically snarled his response. "Why the hell would he do something that stupid?"

Chase's look said it all.

"Ah, Christ." Lucan ran a hand over his jaw and barked out a humorless laugh. "He's fucking her?"

"Nathan didn't report back to base from patrol until just before sunrise," Chase explained. "I don't suppose he was out taking a long stroll."

Lucan shot a hard look at Hunter. "You and Corinne don't know anything about this?"

The former assassin who'd taken Nathan's mother as his mate some twenty years ago gave a shake of his head, looking every bit as displeased as Lucan was. "Nathan is our son, but he came to us as a man, even at his young age. He keeps his private life private. That wall has been in place for a very long time. That said, Nathan would never allow his physical urges to overrule his duty. Or his training."

"I suspect this could be something more than just a physical urge," Chase interjected. "He's distracted. Maybe even a bit obsessed. He thinks he's keeping a lid on it, but the only one he's fooling is himself."

Tegan chuckled darkly. "He's hardly the first of us to fit that description."

"No, he's not," Chase agreed. "But if he doesn't watch his step, he's going to leave me no choice but to pull him off the mission."

"Chase is right," Lucan said. "This shit is too critical. We need every team working as a unit—no exceptions. If Nathan can't get on board with that, then we regroup and keep moving without him." Lucan glanced back at Chase on the video screen. "What else do we know about this witness?"

"Her name is Jordana Gates. Her father, Martin Gates, is one of Boston's most prominent residents. Gates is unmated. He adopted Jordana as an infant."

Lucan grunted. "Not a typical arrangement, for a single Breed male to take in a Breedmate as his child."

"Not typical, but not unheard of," Chase said. "My family has been friendly with Martin Gates since his arrival in Boston from Vancouver a few years before First Dawn. His reputation over those twenty-plus years has been spotless. He made his fortune in the stock market and investments in fine art. As for taking in an orphaned infant to raise on his own, I've personally heard Gates say more than once that without blood heirs or family to look after, he felt it a shame to have acquired so much and have no one to share it with. The man is as charitable as he is wealthy. And Martin Gates is very, very wealthy."

"And Jordana?" Lucan asked.

"A nice girl," Chase said. "A bright, beautiful woman. She could probably have her pick of any man in the city, Breed or human. For some time, there were rumors that she was involved with a vampire named Elliott Bentley-Squire, Martin Gates's prominent, longtime attorney and friend. To hear Bentley-Squire talk, it was only a matter of time before they would be mated. Back Bay society rags have been speculating on the match for years."

"Nothing like dragging a high-profile civilian into the middle of covert Order business," Lucan muttered under his breath. He crossed his arms over his chest. "I don't know what Nathan thinks he's doing with this female, or what his intentions might be where she's concerned. So long as she's a potential intelligence source, I don't give a damn about any of that. Our mission is all that matters. We fuck that up, people die, wars happen."

Lucan glanced to Hunter, who met his comment with a concurring nod. The former assassin's tone was steady, coolly logical. "Nathan pledged himself in duty to the Order. If he can't uphold that promise, he will expect nothing less than to have it taken from him."

"Yeah, that ought to go over well," Gideon remarked, furiously sifting through what looked to be thousands of digital files and sweeping them off the screen one after another. He slowed after a moment and raked his fingers through the short blond spikes of his hair.

"Holy shit." He glanced at Lucan and the other warriors over the rims of his ever-present pale blue glasses. "My packet sniffer just encountered a remote back door on one of La Notte's commerce account firewalls."

Lucan, along with Chase on video and the other warriors seated in the room, all stared at Gideon in questioning silence.

A grin spread over the vampire hacker's face. "I found a way in. Once I machete through a few more layers of tangled security and subterfuge, I'll have all of Cassian Gray's secrets cracked open like a walnut."

18

JORDANA HAD BEEN AWAKE SINCE DAWN.

Her head was buzzing with a thousand thoughts and minutiae about the exhibit opening that evening, but it was the deep, blissful thrumming of her body that roused her from sleep hours ago.

That enlivened vibration of her limbs and core—of her very blood—was also to blame for the secret, irrepressible smile she couldn't seem to wipe from her face no matter how hard she tried.

Making love with Nathan last night had been nothing short of spectacular.

Even now, when she closed her eyes, she could still feel his strong hands on her, his hot mouth on her. His hard body moving over her, inside her . . .

Jordana groaned into her teacup as she took a sip of her favorite morning blend. She'd showered a while ago and now sat in her robe on her bed, answering emails before she and Carys needed to head in to the museum for the day.

"Someone's up early." Carys stood in the open doorway of Jordana's bedroom, leaning against the jamb. Her caramel-brown hair was swept up into a ponytail, baggy gray sweats hanging loosely on her athletic figure. "Everything all right?"

"Yeah." Jordana nodded, wondering if she looked any different to her friend today. God knew she felt different. Everything seemed different today. "Just getting a jump on a few things since I couldn't sleep."

"No wonder," Carys replied. "Quite a night you had."

The ghost of a smile played at the corners of her mouth, and Jordana realized instantly that her friend wasn't referring to the awful incident at La Notte. "You know Nathan was here?"

"I ran into him before sunrise here in the apartment. He was trying to slip out just as I was coming home."

Jordana hadn't really expected Nathan to be next to her when she woke up, but she couldn't deny the pang of disappointment she'd felt when she opened her eyes earlier and found him gone.

And she had to admit, at least to herself, that she'd been hoping to hear from him by now. All she needed was some small indication that last night meant something to him too.

"How did he seem to you?" she asked, setting her tea on the nightstand to give Carys her full attention. She was hungry for every last detail her friend could provide. "What did he tell you? Did he say anything about me?"

Carys arched a slender brow. "You mean after he realized I wasn't someone he needed to attack for coming in to harm his woman?"

"Did he say that—those exact words?" Jordana's heart skipped a beat. "How did he say it? Did he specifically call me his woman?"

Laughing softly, Carys entered the room and took a seat on the edge of the bed. "I see this is even worse than I first suspected." She leaned in and whispered, "If you want to write him a note, I'll ask Rune to pass it to him after school."

"Tell me what he said!" Jordana gave her friend's shoulder a light shove, giggling with her now. "Come on, Car. I need details. I'm serious."

"I know you are," Carys relented. "And so is Nathan, I think. More serious than I've ever known him to be."

Without saying any more, Carys got up from the bed and strode into Jordana's walk-in closet. "Did you decide what you're wearing tonight?"

Jordana hurried after her. "I've narrowed it down to the black tea-length or the pale rose silk cocktail dress." It was hard to think about clothing choices, let alone discuss them when her breath had suddenly caught in her lungs. "What do you mean, Nathan is more serious than you've ever known him? Serious . . . about me?"

Carys found the two dresses Jordana mentioned and was now pulling them out of the wardrobe. She held them up, one in each hand. "I'd have to see these on you before I could decide which one is best. Here. Try the black one first."

Jordana grabbed the dress her friend pushed toward her. "Did Nathan say he was serious about me?"

Carys waggled her hand dismissively. "Let me see the dress, then we'll talk."

On a grumble, Jordana twisted her long blond hair into a makeshift knot on top of her head, then shucked her robe and bra and slipped into the fitted black dress. It was her original choice, a purchase she'd been saving for months specifically for the exhibit opening. Classic, conservative, perfect.

Carys cocked her head to the side, then feigned a yawn. "Next."

"You don't like this one at all?" Jordana turned to one of the full-length mirrors in the massive walk-in. The portrait-collared, mid-calf-length dress was lovely.

It would have been an excellent choice for any social event . . . particularly if Jordana was officiating at a funeral instead of an art exhibit.

She slanted her friend's reflection a conceding look, then crossed her arms over her breasts. "Tell me what he said."

"He said he didn't want anything to happen to you. He doesn't want to see you get hurt."

Not exactly a love song, but it made Jordana's heart pound heavy and hopeful in her breast. "That's it? He didn't say anything more than that?"

Carys gestured for her to continue with the fashion show. Jordana frowned but quickly took off the black frock. When she reached for the equally uninspired rose silk dress, Carys snatched it away and pulled a different one from out of the sea of elegant attire. "Try this instead."

"Oh," Jordana said, already beginning to shake her head. "No, that's not appropriate for tonight, and I—"

"I thought you wanted to know what else he said," Carys teased. "So put it on."

Given little choice, Jordana accepted the red cocktail dress from Carys's outstretched hand. The silken fabric was sleek and soft in her fingers, if somewhat shapeless on its hanger.

Jordana recalled the impulse buy with alarming clarity now. She'd bought this dress the day after she'd so recklessly—insanely—forced a kiss on Nathan in the other room of this very apartment.

It wasn't the kind of dress she'd ever have chosen for herself normally, and she had no idea why she hadn't immediately returned it.

She gathered the light bundle of fiery fabric over her head and let it settle down over her body. It felt like liquid skating along her skin, decadent, luxurious. Deliciously sinful.

"Tell me what else Nathan said," she ordered her friend as the red dress smoothed into place.

"He told me that you're important to him," Carys replied from behind her. "He said he cares about you."

Jordana pivoted around. Cool air caressed her spine where the swooping, low-cut back of the knee-length cocktail dress plunged daringly low. "He really said that? He said I'm important. That he cares about me?"

"Yeah." Carys looked her up and down, then a broad, slow smile broke across her face. "Damn, Jordana. You just found your dress."

Dubious, she turned to face the long mirrors again.

She hardly recognized the woman staring back at her. The sleeveless red dress clung in all the right places and showed just enough leg, yet still managed to look tasteful and sophisticated. In front, its draped neckline only hinted at her curves and cleavage, while the real show was in the back.

"My father will choke on his tongue if I walk into the exhibit opening in this dress," Jordana mused. She shook her head and could hardly bite back her giggle when she pictured all of the stunned reactions she would stir. "Elliott will be completely scandalized—possibly apoplectic."

Carys shrugged. "That'll be their problem. You look amazing."

Jordana studied her reflection, wondering if it was merely the powerful hue of the fabric that intensified the ice-blue color of her eyes and made her features seem somehow bolder, indomitable. Not the good girl held back by propriety and expectation but a fearless woman ready to take on the world.

Or maybe that fierce look came from the way thoughts of Nathan had her blood running hot and quick through her veins.

She felt different. Not simply because of her lost virginity and the incredible passion she experienced last night.

She *was* different.

Changed in a way she couldn't quite define. It was as if she were evolving into a new skin, into a new sense of herself, and doing it at an accelerating pace that should have frightened her.

Yet it didn't. She felt strong and alive. And all she knew was, regardless of where she was headed with Nathan, her life now could never go back to what it was before.

"Carys," she murmured, "do you remember when I told you how Nathan makes me feel?"

"Of course I do." Carys stared at her with clear-eyed understanding. "Like you're on the edge of a cliff and he's a storm about to sweep you over."

"Yeah, like that. Well, last night . . . I did it. I stepped off." Jordana sighed. "I stepped off with my eyes wide open and now I'm falling. What if no one's there to catch me? What if what I'm feeling for Nathan is sheer, heedless stupidity and I end up crashing and burning on the ground?"

Carys smiled at her in the mirror. "Sweetheart, if Nathan sees you in this dress, the only one in danger of crashing and burning will be him."

Nathan's comm device vibrated just as he was about to drop his knuckles on Commander Chase's study door at the Boston compound. Paused there, he frowned and glanced at the incoming message. Probably Rafe or another member of his team, wondering why he wasn't down in the weapons room with them, putting the crew through their daily paces.

He stared at the number on the display.

It wasn't any of the warriors.

Jordana.

How the hell did she know his private call code?

Curious now, and more intrigued than he cared to admit, Nathan tapped the message open.

Hi. Carys gave me your number. Hope you don't mind.

Fuck.

Yes, he did mind, but that didn't keep him from scanning to the next short message, his veins going suddenly electric.

Can't stop thinking about last night. About us.

Neither could he, and the distraction was driving him out of his damned mind.

I can't stop thinking about you, inside me.

Holy fuck.

Now that hot current racing through him arced sharply south, rendering him instantly hard. He shifted his stance, for all the good that did.

He had a crystal-clear mental image of Jordana lying naked and open beneath him, and there was no way to relieve the pressure of his huge erection, which strained full and heavy in his fatigues.

Scowling furiously, he glanced to the next line.

I'll be thinking of you at the exhibit party tonight too. Join me, maybe?

He didn't miss the real invitation she was extending. Neither did his cock. Every blood vessel in his body lit up with eager agreement. As tempting as it was to pick up again where he and Jordana left off, Nathan growled and tried to push the idea out of his head.

He'd already let his hunger for her trump his good judgment. He may have jeopardized his team's entire mission by taking Jordana's virginity last night instead of bringing her in to take her statement as he would any other witness.

That was the reason he now stood outside Chase's office, fully prepared to take whatever punishment he was due.

He'd placed his own selfish wants above his greater responsibility to his brethren last night. He couldn't regret a moment of the hours he'd spent in Jordana's bed, but the fact he'd done it in spite of the hard-won discipline he prided himself on—worse, that he pursued Jordana at the expense of his duty to his teammates—was a failure he intended to rectify by any means possible.

He read Jordana's message again and groaned at his loss.

He would call her after his meeting with Chase and tell her not to expect him.

Dammit. He was going to have to try to explain to her that the next time she saw him, it would likely be on instructions to collect her and hold her at the command center as a witness until the Order felt she was of no further use in their investigation.

He could only hope she wouldn't despise him for not having that conversation with her before she surrendered to him so openly last night.

As he berated himself for that further failure, his comm vibrated with another incoming transmission.

No message this time. Just an image.

Jordana, in a red dress.

A sexy, back-baring, curve-hugging, stupefyingly hot red dress.

And she had to know how incredible she looked in it. Posed from behind in front of a full-length mirror inside her dressing room, she looked over her shoulder at the camera with an expression that was confident, provocative, utterly sensual.

And meant just for him.

Nathan's fangs punched out of his gums and his already uncomfortable hard-on became unbearable. He stared at her photo in abject lust, his fingers clamped so tight around his comm unit, it was a wonder the device didn't shatter. All the air left his lungs on a ragged exhalation.

"Holy. Fucking. Hell."

Without warning, the door to Commander Chase's study opened.

"Shit." Nathan jerked his head up, at the same time casually but quickly stowing his comm unit in the pocket of his fatigues. As an afterthought, he shoved his hands into both pockets too, hoping the added bulk would conceal the very obvious evidence of his arousal.

His fangs and amber-flecked irises were equally difficult to hide.

"Nathan." Sterling Chase's shrewd blue eyes hit him like twin-focused laser beams, missing nothing. The commander's deep voice was low, his mouth grave and unsmiling. "I reviewed the reports from your team's patrol last night. I was just about to call you in here to discuss them."

Nathan gave a grim nod. "I thought you might, sir."

"Come in." Chase turned and strode back to his desk inside the spacious office. "Close the door and sit down."

Nathan did as instructed, taking a seat in one of a pair of leather chairs on the opposite side of Chase's desk. Even though he'd arrived there of his own volition, he knew full well that this was a reprimand waiting to happen.

More than likely, Chase had already spoken with Lucan and the two Order elders had discussed his failing . . . and his fate.

Nathan waited in respectful silence for his commander to address him. And he was glad for the opportunity to wrestle his libido into submission—no easy feat when that image of Jordana dressed in flame red silk was burned indelibly into his mind.

Chase put his elbows on the surface of his desk and studied Nathan for a long moment. "We'll talk about what the hell you think you're doing with her—and why she's messaging you on a secure comm port—after we cover our other business this morning."

With that, Chase leaned back and pulled up Nathan's patrol report on the touch-screen monitor perched on the edge of his desk. "As I said, I reviewed the team's reports on Cassian Gray's slaying last night. Disappointing, to say the least. Not only did he manage to elude our sweeps and shakedowns these past several nights, but his death provides the public with a story they'll be talking about for years. A beheading in the middle of the goddamned city of Boston?" Chase's eyes crackled with angry sparks. "Fortunately, JUSTIS is operating in typical head-up-the-ass fashion, so they've officially declared it a random homicide, subject and motive undetermined. We know that kind of killing, not to mention the victim, was anything but random."

Nathan inclined his head in agreement. "Whoever killed Cass knew what it would take to end him. They had to understand what he was."

Chase's mouth pressed flat. "Or they are the same as he was. Atlantean."

"That would be my guess," Nathan said. "The question remains, why would someone—particularly one of Cass's own kind—want him dead?"

Chase grunted, his stare unwavering. "I'm informed there is a witness who saw Cassian Gray just hours before his death was discovered. A witness who did not seem to warrant a mention in any of the patrol reports. I wouldn't have heard about this at all if Rafe hadn't come to me with the information earlier this morning. Seems he wanted to shield a friend, so he omitted this crucial detail from his findings."

Nathan struggled to keep his face neutral, but inside he was kicking himself. Damn Rafe for trying to protect him. Nathan hadn't asked it of him; he would never have expected it.

"Fortunately for Rafe, his loyalty to the Order won out before the breach of trust was discovered on its own, or the consequences for him could be severe," Chase said. He glanced over at the patrol report still displayed on the monitor. "I'll deal with Rafe later. Right now, I want to know why this same witness isn't noted on my patrol team captain's report—which also wasn't filed until daybreak this morning. I want to know why one of my best men, a warrior who's served this unit faithfully, flawlessly, for more than a decade, suddenly decides to defy protocol." Chase slammed his fist on the desk. "Dammit, I want to know why you're practically forcing me to remove you from your command of the team."

Nathan remained calm, knowing he had earned every bit of Chase's fury. "I can offer no excuse. I failed my team and you. I can only give my word that it won't happen again."

Chase studied him silently with a long, measuring look. Then he blew out a harsh sigh. "What the hell are you doing, Nathan? Forgetting for the moment that Jordana Gates is currently a lead in an ongoing investigation for the Order, she's also a Breedmate, for crissake. How far do you intend to take things with her? You've already slept with her. What's next? Am I going to find out you've blood-bonded to this female?"

Now Nathan's schooled calm faltered slightly. His lip curled, the barest hint of a snarl. "All due respect, sir, but that's none of your damned business."

"The hell it isn't." Chase got up. He walked around the desk and sat on its edge, directly in front of Nathan. "This won't do. You know that. The stakes are too high. If we're soon to face another rising war—this time against an entire other race of immortals—then we can't afford distractions. And Jordana Gates is a very big distraction for you. There's too much at risk for you to allow an emotional entanglement to hamper your effectiveness."

Although Chase couldn't have known, the charge he leveled now was a direct hit to Nathan's soul. Like a tide of black water, memories from his past swelled up around him.

The shattering impact of thick chains striking his back. The threat of sunlight breaking in through the weathered slats of the old barn's roof where he and the other young Hunters were brought after lessons in obedience and duty had failed to teach them who—and what—they were meant to be.

You are a weapon.

Crack!

Effective weapons do not feel.

Crack!

Effective weapons do not bend. Not ever. Not for anyone.

Crack!

Nathan said nothing, silently working through the vivid, unexpected recollection of his conditioning. He reached for the part of him that was the detached Hunter. The survivor who endured his merciless training and lived to find a better life for himself outside of that other, brutal, bleak existence.

But there was a part of him that would always recall the stench of spilled blood and urine and other offending body fluids . . . and taste the salty tears of a terrified, brutalized little boy.

"Nothing will hamper my effectiveness," he murmured evenly.

Chase stared. "Do you love her?"

A quick, sharp denial sat on the tip of his tongue, but he couldn't seem to spit it out.

Whatever it was that he felt for Jordana, it surpassed simple desire or affection. It consumed him. Made his heart feel squeezed in a tight fist yet soaring free at the same time.

He glanced down, gave a mute shake of his head. "Maybe I do. Fuck, I don't know."

"You better figure it out," Chase replied. "Because anything less than that is a waste of our time here. Especially when it could cost you your rank under my command. Possibly even your place in the Order as a whole."

"I won't let that happen," Nathan assured him. "No matter what I have with Jordana, the Order is my family. My duty. I've got this under control."

Chase grunted. "Then prove it to me. Prove it to yourself, and bring her in, as you should've done last night."

Nathan pictured her in her stunning red dress, surrounded by half of Boston as she proudly unveiled her exhibit.

Then he imagined walking in there, just as he'd dreaded, not as the man she hoped to have at her side for that important moment but the warrior sent to ruin her night and likely earn her hatred.

He swore roundly under his breath. "I can't do that. Not tonight. She's got this event at the museum. She's been planning it for months—"

Chase rose to his feet on a snarl. He scrubbed his hand over his brow, then leveled a hard look on Nathan. "Listen, I didn't live nearly two hundred years without more than a few fuckups and near disasters to my credit. You know my history; it's far from spotless. I'm hardly the one to lecture you on duty or how you should live your life. But I'm your commander. I'm taking you off patrol for the night. Tell Elijah he'll captain in your place."

Nathan absorbed the edict with a conceding nod. "I understand."

"Do you?" Chase challenged. He motioned for Nathan to stand up. "Consider this a chance to figure your shit out with Jordana. I need to know if you can come back and continue your mission as captain of your squad. I'll expect your answer first thing tomorrow morning."

Nathan gave him another nod. "Yes, sir."

Chase slanted him a thoughtful but frustrated look. "Now get the fuck out of here."

Nathan left and headed down the corridor.

Rafe rounded a corner up ahead and immediately jogged forward to meet him. Worry etched his face.

"Have you seen Commander Chase yet today?"

"Yeah. He just finished chewing me a new asshole."

"Shit." Rafe looked at him, contrite. He fell in alongside Nathan and walked with him toward the warriors' wing of the compound. "I had to name Jordana as a witness, man. I left her out of the patrol report because I didn't want to make things hard for you, but—"

"It's nothing," Nathan replied. He could hardly be upset with his friend for simply carrying out his duty. "You had to report. I would've done the same thing."

"So what'd he say?"

Nathan shrugged. "Nothing I didn't deserve to hear. Then he yanked me off patrol for tonight. I need to let Eli know he'll be heading things up in my place."

"Jesus, Nathan." Rafe frowned, gave a slow shake of his head. "This is serious shit."

Yes, it was. But what he felt for Jordana was serious too.

And Chase was right, he needed to sort it out. He needed to see if there was any way for both the Order and her to fit into his life.

"What are you going to do?" Rafe asked.

Nathan chuckled. "I guess I'm going to go to Jordana's exhibit opening at the museum tonight."

Rafe gaped. "What? You mean, like some kind of date? You've got to be joking."

"I'm not." When Rafe paused outside the weapons room, Nathan kept walking, heading for his quarters.

"I hope you don't plan to go there in full patrol gear," Rafe called out from behind him, laughing now.

Shit. Nathan hadn't considered things that far. He, the consummate tactician. The expert at weaponry and warfare didn't have the first clue how to present himself as anything even remotely resembling a man going to be with his woman in a social gathering.

A date, for crissake.

Nathan pivoted and strode back to find Rafe. He pulled him outside the weapons room and lowered his voice. "What the fuck does someone wear to a museum party?"

19

JORDANA STOOD IN THE GALLERY OUTSIDE THE EXHIBIT HALL of the museum, feeling a sense of relief—a sense of pride and accomplishment—as she looked out over the packed house at the grand opening that evening.

She had been hoping the event would be well attended, but the sea of benefactors, society elite, museum members and general public arriving to fill the space far exceeded anything she'd dared to imagine.

Everyone was there tonight, her father included. Martin Gates mingled easily among his Darkhaven peers and the other upper-class citizens of Boston. Dressed in a conservative charcoal gray suit, pristine white shirt, and perfectly knotted silk tie, the handsome, staid, dark-haired Breed male looked every bit the wealthy investor and businessman that he was.

It was hard even for Jordana sometimes to remember that her father wasn't a Brahmin product of this city but a self-made man who'd established himself in Vancouver before relocating to Boston with Jordana almost twenty-five years ago.

She'd been just a newborn then, an orphaned Breedmate adopted by Martin Gates only days after her birth. She could never repay her father for the life he'd provided her, and it warmed her heart to see him there to support her tonight.

Hundreds of people strolled the exhibit, conversing with one another, admiring the art and sculptures, enjoying the canapés and champagne being served by catering staff in tuxedoes while a small orchestra played softly in the background. The exhibit hummed with conversation, laughter, and enthusiastic energy.

Even Elliott had come, despite the graceless way she'd ended their nonrelationship. But that was Elliott—dutiful, political, in all things. Then again, watching him blithely chat up a couple of Back Bay socialites in front of the French tapestry collection, she had to wonder if his prior interest in her had been more about pleasing her father than any kind of true affection he may have felt for her.

It certainly hadn't been desire, not even during Elliott's most ardent moods. Jordana knew true desire now—scorching, insatiable, consuming desire. What she and Elliott had was little more than a tepid, companionable regard for each other.

Nothing like what she'd experienced the past few nights with Nathan.

Jordana scanned the exhibit hall again, looking for the one face in the crowd she longed to see above all others.

She knew better than to think Nathan would actually come. This wasn't his kind of place, not his kind of event at all. He had far more important things to do. She knew that even when she'd sent him those impulsive messages earlier in the day.

God, what did he think of her now? She was sure she wouldn't want to know.

If only she could erase those messages, take back the photo she'd sent him. He hadn't responded, so there was a chance he hadn't seen her messages. Maybe Carys had given her the wrong number.

She could only hope to be that lucky.

"Old Mr. Bonneville sends his regards," Carys said with a wry grin, emerging now from inside the exhibit hall to join Jordana in the quiet of the adjacent gallery. "As do Mr. Delano, Mr. Putnam, and Mr. Forbes. I told you that dress was amazing. Every man in that room who still has a pulse is waiting to get another glimpse of you. What are you doing hiding out here?"

"I'm not hiding, I'm—"

"Waiting," Carys gently finished for her. She strolled over, catlike and graceful in a pair of strappy, stiletto sandals that perfectly complemented the midnight hue of her body-hugging cobalt blue dress. "Come on. Rune won't be here either, and we both look much too hot to be flying solo." Carys looped her arm around Jordana's elbow and gave her a bolstering smile. "Let me be your date tonight."

They walked into the noise and bustle of the party, offering greetings to clusters of happy patrons and supporters who sought Jordana out as soon as she entered the hall.

It didn't take long for her to put aside her disappointment that Nathan hadn't come. There were too many people to welcome, endless hands to shake, one conversation after another to attend to as she slowly circulated through the crowd. Carys drifted away as the attendees converged on Jordana.

"An exquisite collection, my dear," enthused the jewel-draped Breedmate of a prominent Darkhaven leader from within her circle of elegant society companions. The ladies all nodded in agreement. "Each display offers something to delight or intrigue."

"Just lovely," added the petite, silver-haired human of the group as she wrapped cool fingers around Jordana's hands. "If the museum doesn't take care of you properly, tell your director I may have to steal you away to curate our family's private collection."

Jordana accepted the praise with a polite smile to the elderly matriarch who'd raised a powerful Boston political clan the likes of which hadn't been seen since the middle of the twentieth century.

"That's very kind of you to say, Mrs. Amory," Jordana demurred. "I'm so pleased you're all enjoying the exhibit."

The old woman winked and leaned in close. "If any of my unwed sons were here tonight, I might attempt to convince you to join our family in a more permanent capacity. Not that they would complain. Have you met my youngest, Peyton? He's quite the charmer."

"I, um . . ." Jordana stammered, eager to make her excuses and move on, but then her father stepped in to do it for her.

"I'm afraid you'll find my daughter is immune to matchmaking, Mrs. Amory," Martin Gates replied smoothly, placing a light, sheltering arm around her shoulders. He offered a gracious smile to the now-giggling ladies before turning a warm, if less jovial, look on Jordana. "Take it from someone who knows."

She winced inwardly at the private chastisement. So much for hoping she might delay having to explain about her abrupt breakup with Elliott.

"May a proud father steal his daughter away for a moment?" he asked the women, to a collective round of approval. As he guided Jordana away from the well-meaning society hens, he murmured quietly, "An interesting choice of dress tonight. You look . . ."

She waited for him to disapprove, to tell her it was too provocative, drawing too much attention. Or maybe her father would say no more than he had, merely give her the silent, pensive look that always made her worry she was letting him down by not doing what he expected of his only child.

He paused and affectionately smoothed his hand over her hair. "You look beautiful, Jordana. And what you've done here tonight is remarkable. I'm very impressed."

His praise was heartfelt; she could see as much in his caring expression. That he approved meant more to her than all of the other attendees' compliments combined.

Jordana reached up and squeezed his hand. "Thank you, Father."

"I want you to know that I'm pleased that you've found something that gives you so much obvious satisfaction—"

"But," she prompted, noting the faint crease forming between his dark brows. He was trying to be supportive, but it was obvious he couldn't turn off the part of him that seemed determined to direct the way she lived her life.

His frown deepened, and he shifted his weight from one foot to the other. "Jordana, this is hardly the best time or place—"

"Say it," she said without venom or dread. "It's okay. I've been avoiding this conversation long enough. I've got a few minutes before I need to make my welcome speech. We might as well have this talk right here and now."

Although he didn't seem to agree, Martin Gates lowered his voice to a private tone. His features were pinched with genuine concern. "I've always been proud of your accomplishments, Jordana. You've given me so much reason to be proud that you're my daughter. But when I took you in as my own, I made a promise—to myself, and to you. I made a promise to the parents you would never know. I vowed to do the best for you, to provide everything you could ever possibly need."

"And you have."

Unmated and without heirs of his own, it was common knowledge that Martin Gates, the Vancouver hospital's most generous benefactor, had stepped in to take personal responsibility for Jordana after learning that a Breedmate had been orphaned there by a penniless, unwed mother who died giving birth to her.

"No." He slowly shook his head and muttered a low curse. "I made a vow that I would see your future was secured. It's all that matters to me, and I'm failing you in that, Jordana."

Seeing his genuine distress, she reached up to touch the tense jaw of the Breed male who had always been her father, her only family. "Elliott Bentley-Squire was never my future. I know you hoped he would be. That wasn't your failing, Father. It wasn't even Elliott's. It was mine."

"It doesn't matter who's at fault now. We must fix it," he argued quietly but firmly as he took her hand in his. Idly, his thumb moved over her Breedmate mark on the inside of her wrist. "It's important that you find a suitable mate. Time is running out, Jordana. You must do this— for me, if you won't do it for yourself."

His grip tightened, desperation filtering into his stern gaze as he spoke. Jordana's veins jangled at the urgency in his voice. She'd seen him argue this point before, but never with such intensity. "I'm a grown woman. You worry about me too much."

"No," he snapped, giving a taut shake of his head. "Jordana, we must talk this through. When this event is over tonight, I want you to come home with me to the Darkhaven. I'll tell Elliott to stop by—"

"I can't," she said. "Father, I won't. I don't want Elliott."

Her father's mouth flattened, but his tone was tender with concern. "He's a good man. Can't you understand, I only want what's best for you. Someone worthy. Someone decent."

"Someone of your choosing?" she asked gently.

His gaze sharpened a bit, intense with purpose. "Someone I trust implicitly to have your best interests in mind, yes."

"What about my happiness? What about love?" She stared up at him. "What about the things I need?"

Clearly taken aback, he went silent for a long moment, regret creeping into his features. "Have you ever felt unloved or unhappy as my daughter?"

"No," she assured him. "I've never wanted for anything, Father. You've given me more than I ever could've hoped for." She smiled sadly. "Except the freedom to become an adult woman with my own mind, my own dreams . . . my own plans for my future."

He said nothing, not for several endless seconds. "Please come home, Jordana. Let me fix this . . . before it's too late."

She shook her head. "I don't love Elliott. I never did, no matter how much you seemed to wish it were so. And now there's someone else—"

The words seized up in her throat as her senses prickled to attention. A shiver of awareness traveled through her bloodstream, making her veins sizzle and her palms tingle with the dancing of a thousand needles.

He was here.

Nathan.

Jordana felt him even before she turned around to confirm it with her eyes. The entire room seemed aware of his powerful presence too. She watched as a clearing began to form down the center of the exhibit hall.

Bit by bit, a path opened between Jordana's place in the room and Nathan, standing just inside the doors.

He came after all.

And, God, he looked good.

Tall and dark and dangerously handsome in a basic black suit that looked anything but basic on him. He wore an ebony silk shirt, unbuttoned below his throat, exposing just the sexiest hint of the Gen One *dermaglyphs* beneath his clothing.

Glyphs Jordana was now intimately familiar with and couldn't wait to see in their full, naked glory once again. Along with the gorgeous Breed male they belonged to.

Her mouth watered just thinking about it, and her heart rate kicked into a faster, heavier tempo.

Without a word of excuse to her father or anyone else who had stopped to gape, Jordana waded into the parting crowd and headed straight toward Nathan. She could hardly keep from running to him, and there was no curbing the smile that spread across her face as she came to a halt in front of him.

"I didn't think you'd be here."

His stormy eyes took a long, slow trip from her face to her toes. When he met her gaze again, amber sparks glowed in his irises. "How could I refuse such an enticing invitation?"

She felt warmth flood her cheeks. It had nothing to do with shyness, but an eager reaction to the hunger she saw written so plainly on Nathan's face. It was written on his skin too. The tawny-hued *glyphs* at his throat surged with deeper saturation, and she knew the rest of his Breed markings would be livid with wild, waking colors underneath the urbane dark suit.

She smiled, barely resisting the urge to touch him. To kiss him and press herself against him, even in front of hundreds of observing eyes.

"I'm glad you came," she murmured. "I realize you probably can't stay long. Your patrols—"

"My patrols will wait. For tonight, anyway."

Hope flared in her belly. "You have the night off?"

"More or less," he replied, his sensual lips flattening slightly. "I was instructed to take the night off."

"Because of me?" She frowned, reading the meaning in what he didn't say. "Because you stayed with me last night. Oh, God . . . not because of the messages I sent you today? I never should've done that. I overstepped—"

"You did nothing wrong."

His hand lighted gently along the side of her face, an unexpected touch Jordana savored. She tilted her head into his palm, greedy for the brief contact.

"I chose to be with you," he said, bringing his hand back down to his side. "I knew what I risked last night." Nathan's voice was a rumble in the back of his throat, low and deep, as his heated gaze drank her in once more. "As for the messages you sent, I haven't been able to focus on anything else since I saw the photo of you in this dress. You look even more incredible in the flesh." His mouth curved wickedly. "But then, I already knew that."

Her veins thrummed in response to his innuendo. All it took was his dangerous smile and her core bloomed with liquid heat at the remembrance of their night together.

She wanted him now, again . . . always, she was certain.

"I'm glad you're here," she murmured, wishing he'd touch her again. "But I don't want to cause problems for you with the Order."

"Any problems there are mine to deal with." That devastating smile faded as he sent a dark glance around the gathering. When his eyes came back to her, they glittered as bright as embers. "And there was no way in hell I was going to let you wear this dress for anyone but me. Even if I had to put on a monkey suit and try to play nice with the natives."

"It's a very nice monkey suit," she said, melting under his possessive stare. "Oddly enough, seeing you in it only makes me want to sneak away somewhere and tear it off you."

Nathan's answering growl vibrated all the way to her bones. "Don't tempt me, female."

Oh, but she wanted to tempt him. She wanted to be the one in control, the one making him crazy with pleasure and need, until she was certain she owned his body the same way he had mastered hers.

She wanted to kiss him. She wanted to be naked with him again, feel him crashing into her, filling her.

The urge swamped her, feral and fierce.

"Keep looking at me like that and watch this civilized facade turn to ash right where we stand."

Jordana grinned. "Is that a promise?"

Another growl, this one darker, accompanied by a flash of his fangs. "What do you think?"

She gazed up at him for a long moment, surprised by the current of interest that lit up her veins. She felt daring with him, fearless. Too aroused by him to let inhibition put any limits on what they could share together.

"I think we should definitely explore the idea," she said, but it was a knowing tease when she was already late for the podium. She gestured vaguely behind her. "I have a little speech to give right now. It shouldn't take very long." Jordana stepped in closer to him, putting her lips almost against his ear. "So, whatever wicked thoughts you have, hold them until I get back."

At his rumble of interest, she drew back, out of his reach. Then she slowly pivoted to give him time to watch her stroll away from him.

She didn't have to glance back to check if he was watching her, but she did anyway.

Oh, yes, he was watching.

His smoldering eyes threw off a palpable heat, desire so intense it nearly burned everything in its path. And all of it trained on her.

Jordana tossed him a flirty smile, then headed for the dais at the front of the crowded exhibit hall.

20

EVERY BLOOD VESSEL IN HIS BODY SEEMED TO HAVE MIGRATED south as Nathan watched Jordana walk away from him to take her place at the raised podium. His ear was still warm from her whispered suggestion—a suggestion he had every intention of holding her to as soon as she finished greeting her event's guests.

Damn, he wanted her naked beneath him now. How he was going to survive the rest of the night without burying himself inside her, he had no idea.

Nathan shifted his stance and tugged at the jacket he'd borrowed from Rafe. For all the good it did. Nothing was going to ease his ache except the sheath of Jordana's hot, wet body.

And her hands.

Or her pretty, pink mouth.

Had he actually believed at one point that a taste of this woman would be enough to satisfy his need for her?

Christ, what an idiot he'd been.

Now he craved her more than ever. She captivated him completely, held the power to render him hard as steel with just a few simple words.

He tried to tell himself he didn't like the feeling. He'd kept such a merciless grip on his needs and desires for so long, it should chafe more to realize he was losing his hold so easily where she was concerned.

Jordana was magnetic, her blond hair and flame-colored dress a beacon across the sea of darkly attired men and women. Watching her smooth command of the room and everyone in it filled Nathan with a possessive, selfish pride.

How had such an extraordinary woman become part of his life? Why choose him, when she had her pick of a hundred other more worthy males in this room alone?

But she had chosen.

The private glance she sent him through the thick crowd as she delivered her welcome would have erased any doubt. The instant their eyes connected, Nathan's blood simmered with added fire. His veins throbbed, and the erection he'd been sporting when she left him a minute ago now worsened to near agony.

He felt his *glyphs* surge with heat and knew his desire would be plain in the deepening colors that were blooming at his collar and up the sides of his neck. His fangs pricked his tongue, sent saliva surging into his mouth.

Jordana belonged to him.

And whether he wanted to admit it or not, he belonged to her too.

A throat cleared pointedly from beside him. "Remarkable, isn't she?"

Nathan swung a hard look over his shoulder at the Breed male who'd moved in from the surrounding crowd without his notice.

Son of a bitch.

"Yes, she is," he replied stiffly, then extended his hand to the Darkhaven leader. "Mr. Gates. I'm Nathan—"

"I know who you are." Gates kept his arms folded over his tuxedoed chest, his gaze trained on the podium across the wide hall. "What I don't know is what interest you have in my daughter." Now he turned his head in pointed observation of Nathan's ember-flecked eyes and churning *dermaglyphs.* "Aside from the obvious, that is."

Nathan bristled but could hardly take offense at her father's disapproval. "My interests are no different than yours, sir."

Gates scoffed. "I'm sure they couldn't be any more different." His cutting stare narrowed. "I suppose you're the reason she cast Elliott aside?"

Nathan glanced toward the dais, where Jordana had just finished her speech to a round of enthusiastic applause, and was now being swamped by adoring party guests. "Maybe you should ask her that question instead."

"There's no need," Gates replied. "I saw the way she looks at you, the way she's acting . . . the way she's dressed tonight. It's all because of you, isn't it?"

Nathan met the elder vampire's accusing gaze. There was something more than suspicion or disapproval in the male's eyes. A protectiveness that verged on desperation.

"Jordana has her own mind," Nathan said. "She has her own will. How she acts or thinks or behaves is up to her."

Gates grunted. "Well, I don't like it. I want this to stop. Immediately, do you understand?"

"I'm not sure I do," Nathan challenged. He had no wish to make an enemy out of her father, but if Gates thought he had anything to say about Nathan's relationship with Jordana, he was sorely mistaken.

"Jordana means the world to me," Gates said. "She's a very special young woman. I don't expect someone like you to comprehend that, or to care—"

"Someone like me." Nathan all but growled the words.

"Stay away from her," Gates ordered tightly. "As a man—as a fellow Breed male—I am asking you to leave my daughter alone."

Nathan thought back to a mere week ago, to who he was before the night Jordana crashed into his life with one impulsive, unforgettable kiss.

That man—the street warrior whose nights were filled with ugliness and violence—would have never imagined himself standing in the middle of a glittering society event in a borrowed suit, waiting to be reunited with the most exquisite, extraordinary woman in the room.

He would have never imagined a time or place where he would want to belong to that kind of world, or wish that he had all along, if only to be part of it with her.

To be worthy of her.

To have some kind of future to offer her that didn't consist of darkness and war and bloodshed.

As the Hunter bred and trained for destruction, he never would have dared permit himself to care for someone as he did for Jordana.

There was no turning back.

Now that he had let her in, no one was going to tell him to let her go.

"No," he said finally. He gave a solemn shake of his head. "I don't think I can do that."

Martin Gates studied him in a searching, scrutinizing glare. Resignation bled into his face and he huffed out a brittle sigh. "Very well. How much will it take for you to comply?"

"A bribe?" Nathan's voice was cold and level, even while his outrage spiked. "You can't be serious."

But Gates was unswayed. "Name your price and it's yours. She need never know."

Nathan's answering curse was ripe with outrage. Dark with fury. "There isn't enough goddamn money in the world. If you really love Jordana as much as I do, you'd know that."

Gates reeled back, his head snapping up as if he'd taken a physical blow.

Only then did Nathan realize what he'd said.

He loved her.

He couldn't bite the words back, not because he'd already let them out, but because they were the truth.

Holy hell . . . he meant it. He was in love with Jordana.

Gates said nothing, not for a long time. Then, face blanched, hands visibly shaking at his sides, he lowered his voice to a savage whisper. "Stay away from Jordana. Or you will leave me no choice but to make deadly certain that you do."

A threat? Nathan saw the menace—and the abject alarm—in the Breed male's dark eyes.

Martin Gates would have Nathan's head before he allowed him to continue with Jordana. Or, rather, he would try.

Nathan didn't want to think about a confrontation between the elder vampire and himself. And Gates had to know that taking on one of the Order, particularly a Gen One Hunter like Nathan, would be tantamount to suicide.

Yet that was his intent. Gates would risk anything, including his own life, to keep his daughter away from Nathan.

"Leave my daughter alone," Gates ground out. Then, as quickly as the threat had been thrown down, he flashed away, vanishing into the thick crowd.

Nathan understood why in that next instant. Jordana was approaching from behind.

Nathan sensed her like a current in his blood. The air stirred with her bright energy. Her voice drifted to him, vibrant and rich, as she accepted praise and offered thanks to the patrons and museum guests who vied for her attention as she made her way through the throng.

He turned toward her, prepared to explain what had happened with her father. But Jordana's beaming expression stopped him short.

She didn't know. She must not have seen them talking while she was at the dais.

And Nathan wasn't going to be the one to ruin her night. Not when she was looking at him with such exuberance and satisfaction. Despite all the eyes on her, she looked at him as though he were the only other person in the room.

"Still want to make good on that promise?" She reached up and touched his face, just the briefest contact.

Old, battered instincts clenched inside him, but newer ones—the ones she'd awakened in him—responded to her fleeting caress with heat and hunger for more.

Mischief danced in Jordana's ice blue eyes. Her smile broke slowly, seductively. "Come with me."

She breezed past him, the sight of her bare back in that red dress, her hips swaying with each fluid stride of her long legs, leaving him no choice but to obey. Nathan stalked after her, out of the exhibit hall and into a gallery outside. She kept going, leading him farther away from the buzz and activity of the party.

He was enjoying the view so much he hardly realized what she was doing until she disappeared into the gloom of a nearby office. When he reached the open doorway, she yanked him inside by the lapel of his suit coat and shut the door behind him.

Her mouth came down hard on his as she pushed him backward against a desk.

No warning.

No waiting for him to make the first move.

Not the slightest trace of uncertainty as she pressed her body against his and pushed his lips apart with her demanding little tongue.

And fuck if that didn't shoot molten fire into his veins.

Outside the closed door of the office, the drone of conversation and soft music carried from the exhibit hall several yards away. Low light from the gallery filtered through the shuttered blinds of the window behind the desk. A bark of laughter sounded from just outside as a small group of party guests walked the promenade that led to the museum lobby.

He and Jordana were secluded enough in the private office, but there was no escaping the knowledge that the risk of discovery lurked just beyond its four walls.

She didn't seem to mind.

Hell, she seemed to revel in the risk. As she kissed him, he felt her hands at the collar of his shirt. His mind was slipping, getting pulled under the more powerful force of his need.

He only vaguely registered that his shirt was open, his chest bared to her gaze, to her touch. When she dragged her mouth down along his throat to the *glyphs* that rode his pectorals, he wrenched up off the desk on a lust-filled groan.

"Shh," she admonished him with a playful smile and a daring glimmer in her eyes. Her pretty pink tongue followed the arc and flourish of his *dermaglyphs*, making them flush with darkening colors. "I've been wanting to do this all night."

Ah, Christ. Nathan watched, entranced, hard as granite, as she licked and suckled him, each wet kiss igniting a dangerous fire in his veins. She drew his nipple into her mouth, grazing the tight peak with her teeth.

Her touch shouldn't have been so welcome, so easily accepted. It didn't fit into the way he lived his life. It went against everything he'd been taught. Defied the years of training and hard lessons that still haunted his dreams, all too often left him soaked in cold sweat, stomach pitching with nausea for what he'd witnessed. What he'd been made to do.

But those nightmares and horrors had no hold on him when Jordana's lips were warm and questing on his skin. All he knew was the ecstasy of her mouth and his yearning for everything she would give him.

Nathan growled with pleasure, his cock straining with unbearable demand. He brought his arms around her and urged her up to his mouth once more, leaning back onto the desk as he took her in a scorchingly deep kiss.

Her skin was hot beneath his palms, her bare back like velvet under his fingertips. She moved against him as their tongues tangled together, their bodies creating a friction that drove him swiftly to the edge of his need.

He moaned as his cock surged against the warmth of her abdomen. Greedy for more, he smoothed his hands down over her dress and onto her ass. Gripping her firmly, he ground deeper into her heat, angling his pelvis to meet every sinuous movement of her body.

It was torture, plain and simple. All it did was ratchet him tighter, harder.

Made the tether of his self-control stretch taut, near to breaking.

If they didn't stop soon, nothing was going to keep him from taking her right there on the desk. Shit, he was already past that point of no return. And if anyone from the party had the bad judgment to come looking for Jordana—if anyone walked in on them now or in the next few minutes—he wasn't sure he'd be able to reel in his urge to kill.

"Christ, you feel good, Jordana," he muttered through gritted teeth and fangs. "Just the sight of you makes me wild to fuck you. To feel you on me like this, knowing how sweet your body is going to be when I get you naked and drive into you—" He sucked in a sharp breath and moved against her in a more fervent rhythm, astonished that their combined heat didn't incinerate their clothing. He stared into her eyes, the dim light from of his transformed irises gilding her in an ember glow. "If you think you can tease me like this then walk away, you've got a hard lesson coming."

A snarl rumbled out of him as she drew out of his embrace to stand between his legs. "Who says I'm teasing?"

Her mouth was kiss-bruised and glossy, her eyelids heavy over the now dusky blue of her eyes. Without further words, she reached for his hand and urged him to his feet. He stood, breath caught in his lungs as she began to unfasten his belt. It jangled softly as it fell loose, the only other sound besides her soft, shallow panting as she undid the button on his pants, then let down the zipper.

Her hand slipped inside, cupped his rigid shaft. Nathan hissed, steeling himself to the bliss of her gentle touch.

He'd been raised not to require touch or comfort, feeling or emotion . . . least of all pleasure. He had been brutally conditioned to reject all these things, and so he had.

But he'd never known Jordana's touch. He'd never known her kiss, or how silky and hot—how utterly perfect—it could feel to lose himself in the one woman he wanted above all others.

The only one he would ever want again.

Jordana stroked him briefly, catching her lower lip between her teeth as she palmed the head of his cock, smoothing the bead of slick moisture along his length. He groaned when she released him, but then her hands went to the slack waistband of his opened pants and his throat suddenly went dry.

With her gaze locked on his, she freed him in agonizing increments, until the fabric slid down his legs to pool at his feet. His cock jutted out, thick and heavy, dripping with need. The *glyphs* that encircled its base and tracked onto his shaft throbbed with furious hues of darkest indigo and bloodred wine, the colors of extreme desire.

Jordana stepped forward and wrapped her hand around his nape, dragged him down for another deep, unhurried kiss. He obliged, parting his lips to let her in, savoring the sweetness of her tongue and the hunger of her mouth.

His heart was hammering, his fangs filling his mouth by the time she released him. Jordana ran her fingers along the underside of his swollen shaft, wringing a hiss from him as she squeezed the head and slicked him with his own juices.

"Fuck," he whispered raggedly. Her touch would be the death of him. A death he'd gladly welcome.

Through blazing eyes, he watched her lower her head and place tender kisses across his chest. She stroked him some more, then began a downward trail of warm, wet heat with her mouth.

"Ah, fuck," he snarled again, incapable of anything more.

Her lips and tongue skimmed down his abdomen, over every hard ridge and muscle, along one path of churning *dermaglyphs* to another. Sensation electrified him, left him shuddering with fevered anticipation. All centered on her.

He speared his fingers into her pale blond hair, needing something to hold on to as she slowly sank to her knees before him.

She tilted her head and gazed up at him, her dusky blue eyes holding his searing amber gaze as she moved forward and took him into her mouth.

"Jordana . . . holy fuck," he rasped out savagely as her lips and tongue closed around his cock.

21

JORDANA HAD NEVER FELT MORE AROUSED, OR MORE ALIVE, THAN in that moment as she watched Nathan's pleasure mount while she suckled him deep into her mouth.

He dropped his head back on his shoulders and moaned, his muscled thighs braced apart and trembling as she worked her lips and tongue along the entire delicious length of him. His fingers lightly caressed her skull where they'd sunk deep into her hair, his broad palm curved along the back of her head as she took him deeper with each stroke of her mouth.

With the slightest change of tempo or flick of her tongue, she quickly learned how to make him growl in sensual agony or shudder in passion.

Nathan, the lethal warrior. The remote, unreadable Hunter. The Breed male who so easily assumed the lead in any situation, who dominated in everything he did.

The solitary man who'd stormed into her world and changed everything.

Changed *her*.

Here and now, Jordana had absolute control over him, and something about that knowledge made her feel both humbled and drunk with power.

She held him in her hands, stroking his velvety shaft as she drew him deeper into her mouth. He gasped as she leaned in and took all of him, hissed when she slowly withdrew all the way to the smooth, plum-shaped crown.

"You taste good," she murmured, running the tip of her tongue through the hot, silky fluid that coated the engorged head of his cock. His hips bucked when she enveloped him in her mouth again. His curse was raw, ragged, as she abraded him lightly with her teeth. She smiled, pleased with this newfound power. "You taste good enough to eat."

"Damn, Jordana," he bit off harshly, his already visible fangs elongating like bone-white daggers behind his parted lips as she sucked him even harder. "Gonna make me fucking lose it . . ."

His voice was gravel, little more than a coarse rumble in his throat. Just hearing him so close to the edge made wet heat boil in her core.

He grunted, his pelvis knocking forward in a spasm she knew he couldn't control. "Christ, that sweet mouth of yours . . ."

She moaned around his girth, thrilling in his response and taking far too much satisfaction in the torment she was delivering.

As she rode his length with her mouth, he clutched at her, tremors raking his immense body. His gorgeous face became something darker, otherworldly. His stormy eyes went volcanic, nothing but pools of amber swallowing up the catlike slits of his pupils.

His full lips peeled back on a feral snarl, his angular cheekbones sharpening to bladelike slashes as he stared down at her. His pulse drummed against her tongue and the roof of her mouth as he slid in and out of her lips, making her own heartbeat spike into the same hard tempo. Between her legs, she was drenched, aching to be filled.

Fueled by her own rising need, she dragged his cock deep, suckled him mercilessly, until at last he tore her away from him on a strangled growl.

No words, no gentle touches. He grabbed her under the arms and lifted her to her feet. Spun her around in front of him, then put one strong hand around the back of her neck and pressed her facedown onto the desk.

It was a primal move, his fingers like heated iron against her nape. With a low growl, he put his bare thigh between her legs, nudged them wider apart.

Jordana couldn't move, even if she wanted to.

She'd pushed him to the brink, but now he was back in control. And she could hardly breathe for how totally that turned her on.

Nathan held her down with one hand, while his other lifted the skirt of her dress up over her backside. She knew the precise moment when he saw her skimpy black thong. He stilled, sucked in a short gust of air.

"So pretty," he rasped thickly. His fingers skimmed up the inside of her legs, to where her soaked crotch throbbed.

He brushed her sensitive flesh, then she felt the thin excuse for underwear pull tight in his grasp. It snapped and fell away.

"Mm," Nathan grunted. "That's even better."

She trembled, every nerve ending lit up with anticipation. Outside her office window, shadows passed by the closed blinds as people strolled through the museum, conversations muffled, but not entirely muted, by the walls and glass.

Nathan's hand slid between her drenched folds. He penetrated her slowly, his fingers caressing the inside of her walls and wringing a strangled cry from the back of her throat. She wanted more. Needed more. Had to have all of him now.

"Should I make you scream when you come for me, Jordana?" Nathan's voice was a low murmur behind her, his breath fanning hotly across her naked spine as he leaned over her prone body.

His mouth came down between her shoulder blades. She shivered, then panted softly as his open lips and tongue followed the shallow valley of her spine.

"Yeah, maybe I should make you scream for me," he uttered against her skin. "I want every male in this building to know that you belong to me. Only me."

She moaned, ready to give him anything he demanded if only to ease the fierce ache roiling within her. He stroked her until she was squirming helplessly, her lip caught tightly in her teeth to bite back the sounds of her pleasure and her need.

Each wicked thrust of his fingers made her arch to receive more, her body totally exposed to him, her sex inflamed, juices trickling along her cleft.

"So greedy," he admonished, dark amusement in his voice.

"Nathan," she gasped as he teased her swollen petals, making her legs quake beneath her. "Please . . ."

"Stay there," he commanded. "Stay just like that."

He moved off her, leaving chill air in his wake. But then she felt his bulky shoulders between her parted thighs. Felt his breath rush against her wet core in the instant before he buried his face in her sex. Heat blasted her as he licked a slow, fiery trail from her clit to her ass.

"Oh, God." Jordana's voice was threadbare, choked with pleasure as he cleaved her slit with his tongue. She had no voice at all when he returned to the pulsing little nub and suckled it ruthlessly, the quivering seam of her body pressed tight to his face with nowhere to escape.

Not that she wanted to. There wasn't anywhere else she'd rather be. The world could go on without her on the other side of her office walls. Everything could float away and she'd be happy, so long as Nathan didn't stop touching her, tasting her, making her mad with pleasure.

She started to come, orgasm roaring up on her in a powerful wave of sensation.

"Not yet," Nathan ordered her, nipping her just enough to bring her back to earth.

He kissed her shamelessly, relentlessly, until her bones felt liquefied and her blood seemed made of lava. Only then did he release her, rising to his feet behind her. The head of his cock was a blunt, demanding presence in the slickness at her core.

"You're mine," Nathan growled savagely. "I can't stay away from you. Fuck, Jordana . . . I will never have enough of you."

And with that, he thrust deep, impaling her to the hilt.

Nathan couldn't slow down and sure as hell couldn't stop. He couldn't curb the ferocious need that wracked him as he pumped hard and deep into Jordana's slick, tight sheath.

He couldn't hold back the primal drum of his pulse, his blood running hot and molten through his veins.

She was his.

No one could tell him otherwise. No plea or command or lethal threat would change how he felt about her.

Jordana belonged to him.

Her body, her pleasure, her heart. Maybe one day, her blood bond.

Just the thought of taking her vein as he claimed her body made his fangs erupt farther from his gums. The recollection of her bloodscent, that ethereal, delicately elusive mix of citrus and spice, made his mouth water with the thirst to make her his in the one way no worldly force could ever break.

But not here.

Not like this.

He'd already taken more than he deserved from her.

She had driven him to the razor's edge of his control tonight, but he still had some sanity left.

Admittedly, too damned little, when she looked so sexy for him to-night and tasted so sweet. When she felt so incredibly perfect as he held her pinned beneath him and crashed into her welcoming heat with an abandon he'd never known.

All he knew in that moment was her. She consumed his senses, obliterating everything but the pleasure of their joining, the erotic sounds of their bodies moving together in slick and frenzied rhythm.

He wasn't going to last long.

Each thrust of his hips sent him deeper, jolted him further away from reason and control and discipline. His veins were lit up, sizzling. Tension coiled deep inside him, pressure that turned every tendon and sinew to the breaking point. His cock had never been harder, ready to explode.

"Come for me now, Jordana," he muttered fiercely beside her head as he leaned forward and angled himself even tighter into the milking tightness of her womb. "I want to feel it. I need to feel it right now."

Her response was immediate, her release a sudden, violent shudder that vibrated all along his shaft and down into his marrow. She cried his name on a broken gasp, arching into his thrusts as his own release roared up to overtake him.

He was gone in that same instant. He came hard and fast, blinded by pure, white-hot ecstasy as his seed shot loose into the contracting glove of her sex.

He didn't know how long they remained there, Jordana panting softly beneath him, splayed over the desk; he braced above her on locked elbows and fists, unmoving, unwilling to break the sexual connection of their bodies.

He was hard again. More accurately, still hard.

Jordana's pulse was a heavy, seductive thrum against his shaft. Her delicate muscles gripped him snugly, even now. When she shifted her hips in tempting invitation, Nathan groaned.

"Keep that up, and I'll never let you out of this room."

She turned her head and regarded him over her shoulder, her lips curved in a satisfied smile. "I think I might like that."

So would he, but they couldn't stay there much longer and expect her not to be missed. Exercising more self-control than he'd been able to claim since he met her, Nathan slowly eased out of her. Her disappointed moan nearly undid him.

"Give me your hand," he said, and reached down to help her rise up off the desk.

She turned around to face him, her light blue eyes dusky below the thick fringe of her lashes. Her cheeks were flushed, her lips cherry red and glistening.

He drew her close, brushed his fingers over her moist, tantalizing mouth. "You make me hard as stone, just thinking about how good your lips felt on me tonight." His cock twitched in agreement, ready to start all over again. "I can't wait to get you out of here and into bed with me. I've got some very creative ideas for how I'm gonna pay you back."

She grinned up at him. "Mm, I can't wait to hold you to that."

Tilting her face, she caught the tip of his finger between her teeth. Her tongue played him the same way she'd tormented his cock, maddening little flicks combined with ruthlessly intense suction.

Nathan grunted, a spasm shooting up his spine and straight into his rigid shaft. "Holy hell . . . on second thought, who needs a bed?"

She laughed softly as she released him. Nathan grabbed for her, but she ducked away, playful. The sexiest damned woman he'd ever seen. He wanted her badly, and he wanted her now.

She smoothed the hem of her red dress down over her fine bare ass and long legs, shimmying to adjust the silky fabric back into place. "I should get back out there, don't you think?"

He shook his head, eyes hot on her. "I think you belong right here, with me."

"Now who's the greedy one?" she tossed back at him, arching one delicate brow. Bending down, she retrieved the tattered remains of her thong from near his discarded pants. "I'm going to go freshen up, and, ah, destroy the evidence."

The scrap of black silk dangled from her fingers, and the understanding that she would be naked under the dress for the remainder of the night sent another shock wave of lust into his bloodstream. How he was going to survive the next few minutes, let alone potentially another couple of hours, in public without pouncing on her again, he didn't know.

As he contemplated all the things he wanted to do to her, a low buzz sounded from somewhere near his feet. Despite his preternatural senses, he could hardly hear the faint hum over the roar of his pulse in his ears.

Shit. His comm unit.

Jordana gestured toward the floor where the device lay forgotten in his pants pocket. "You take care of your business," she said lightly. "I'll go take care of mine."

Nathan stooped to pick up the comm, bringing his pants up at the same time. He fastened them hastily, unable to tear his eyes away from her as she strode for the door.

"See you back inside the exhibit hall in a few minutes," she said, beaming as she opened the door and slipped out.

Nathan glanced down at the comm unit buzzing again in his palm.

"Yeah," he said into the receiver, struggling to wrench his attention away from thoughts of Jordana as he took the call from the Boston headquarters.

"Nathan." Chase's deep voice held a grim edge. "We just got intel from Gideon in D.C."

Nathan's combat instincts went on immediate full alert. "What is it?"

"Are you with Jordana?"

Fuck. This couldn't be good. "She was just here with me a minute ago." Nathan gripped the comm device harder in his fist, started stalking toward the office door. "Tell me what's going on."

"It's Gates," Chase said. "He's been allied with Cassian Gray this whole time, partnered with him in the club. Gates isn't who he's pretending to be. The son of a bitch is dirty."

Ah, Christ. No.

"Do you think he's part of Opus Nostrum?"

"We don't know that yet," Chase said. "We're digging deeper. If it turns out Gates is involved with Opus . . ."

The commander let the statement trail off, but Nathan knew well enough what it meant. If Gates's partnership with Cassian Gray tied back to Opus Nostrum in any way, the Order would have no choice but to deal with him as an enemy and terminate him.

Nathan didn't even want to consider what all of this would do to Jordana.

He exited to the gallery outside, swiveling his head to ascertain which direction she might have gone.

"In light of this new intelligence," Chase said, a carefulness to his tone, "it makes Cass's visit to Jordana at the museum the day he was killed more than a bit troubling. Is it possible she's aware of the link between her father and Cassian Gray?"

"She doesn't know any of this," Nathan blurted. He would stake his life on it.

Jordana couldn't have been keeping a secret like that. She was too open, too innocent. She couldn't have been playing Nathan for a fool this whole time.

"The team and I are en route to the museum now," the commander said. "We know Gates is there tonight. We have to take him in for questioning. No delays. No warnings."

Goddammit.

"I understand," Nathan replied, his cold warrior's logic instantly at war with the man who dreaded the heartbreak about to visit the woman he loved.

"Don't let him leave," Chase ordered. "We're two minutes out at most. I need you to do whatever you must to hold him until we arrive."

"I understand," Nathan confirmed woodenly, ending the communication on a harsh curse.

Outside the open entryway of the exhibit hall, he spotted Carys chatting pleasantly with a small group of ladies. He motioned her toward him as he marched at a soldier's clip across the marble floor. "Find Jordana. Now. Keep her out of the exhibit hall."

The Breed female's face blanched. "What's happened?"

"Find her," he barked sharply. "Take her home. Don't leave her side, do you understand? And tell her . . . ah, fuck. Tell her I'm sorry."

"Nathan?" Carys called from behind him, but he didn't answer.

His heart as heavy as his feet, he strode into the glittering society event like a wraith, his ruthless Hunter's gaze searching out his quarry through the crowds.

STANDING IN FRONT OF THE RESTROOM MIRROR, JORDANA finger-combed her hair back into some semblance of order and checked her appearance one last time after freshening up.

Aside from the cat-in-the-cream grin she couldn't seem to suppress, she supposed she looked presentable enough. Although no one in the exhibit hall would detect what she'd been up to, Jordana wasn't sure how she was going to manage to look anyone in the eye without blushing from head to toe over the knowledge of where she'd been and with whom—or the fact that her shredded thong now lay in the bottom of the ladies' room waste bin.

She didn't know how she'd be able to pretend as if she hadn't just been thoroughly, magnificently fucked just a few scant yards and one closed door away from hundreds of Boston's most affluent, important citizens.

Not to mention her father.

She'd intended to seek him out after her welcome speech and introduce him to Nathan. So much for that plan. Her libido had other ideas.

Very good ideas, as it turned out.

She would just have to introduce the two men later in the evening—

Someone let out a scream in the exhibit hall outside. There was a crash of glassware and china, then a loud, discordant note from the orchestra before the music cut off abruptly.

Jordana's stomach dropped like a stone. "What on earth?"

The restroom door swung open and there was Carys. "Jordana," she said gently. Her friend's face was drawn and sober, her tawny brows pinched over anxious eyes. "Nathan wanted me to come find you—"

"What's wrong?" Now Jordana's stomach plummeted even further. A cold pit opened up in her gut. "Where is he? What the hell just happened out there?"

Jordana lunged for the exit, but Carys held her back. "He told me to keep you out of the exhibit hall."

"What? Why would he do that?" Confusion, incredulity, a barrage of disorienting emotions collided inside her as she tried to process what was going on.

She shook it all off and tried to step around her friend.

Tried, and failed.

Carys's halting grasp was Breed strong, and so was the female's determination. "I don't think you should go out there—"

Outrage spiked through Jordana's haze of confusion. "Let go of me."

Wrenching out of her friend's hold, she pushed out to the hallway. People were pouring out of the exhibit hall and adjacent gallery, faces awash in alarm.

A growing crowd gathered at the railing of the promenade that overlooked the museum's lobby, where the sounds of a struggle—the shouts of a furious man, the rapid drum of boots traveling over polished marble tiles—carried up from below.

Someone was being physically dragged out of the party, fighting and cursing every inch of the way.

Jordana raced to the balcony edge and her heart stopped.

"Father?"

He was fighting madly, fangs bared, head thrashing.

Bucking and twisting, Martin Gates tried desperately to get loose of the larger Breed male who held his arms behind his back like a criminal, ushering him swiftly across the lobby toward the main exit.

"Father!" Jordana cried. She ran to the wide staircase leading to the lobby, panic beating in her breast like a caged bird.

Cool night air gusted in as the glass doors opened to admit a team of warriors from the Order. They swarmed in to assist, garbed in black combat gear, bristling with deadly weapons.

"Unhand me!" her father shouted. "You have no right to treat me this way!"

Distantly, as though caught up in the slow-motion horror of a terrible dream, Jordana could hear herself screaming.

She could feel the hard marble floor beneath her tall heels as she ran down the stairs, yet each step seemed mired in quicksand, agonizingly slow.

She saw the grim faces of the Boston warriors positioned at the door as her father was pushed toward them in unyielding, merciless purpose.

And, with terrible dawning, she finally caught a glimpse of the immense Breed male whose hands were gripped so punishingly on her father. Hands that had only minutes ago been hot and pleasurable on every inch of her naked body.

"Nathan. Why are you doing this?" she gasped brokenly, stricken with shock. It took him a long moment before he turned his head at her approach into the lobby. "What's going on here? Where are you taking my father?"

She couldn't read the flat expression that Nathan held on her. His storm-cloud eyes were emotionless, chillingly so.

Gone was the passionate lover she'd left behind in her office. In his place stood the cold Breed warrior.

The merciless Hunter.

"Carys." Nathan's impenetrable gaze was looking past Jordana now. His voice was airless, a low command. "For fuck's sake, I told you to keep her out of here."

Gentle hands came down on Jordana's shoulders. She jerked out of the comforting hold on a strangled cry. Jordana shook her head mutely, blindsided and lost for words under the weight of her confusion.

Nathan gave her one last glance—this time, a note of regret shadowing his gaze. Then he shoved her father forward and the rest of the Order closed in to surround them.

In moments, they were all gone, swallowed up into a waiting black SUV at the curb, then vanished into the night in a squeal of tires on pavement as they sped away.

Most of Gates's fury and venom had left him by the time Nathan and the Order brought the Darkhaven leader into the command center for questioning. He'd roared and protested for most of the quick drive across town, but once seated in the interrogation room, the Breed male's broad shoulders sagged in his rumpled tuxedo.

His gaze was no longer simmering with anger but cautious. Cagey and wary, as he eyed Nathan and the other warriors from beneath the dark brown slashes of his brows. "I demand to know what this is about," he grumbled. "This is an outrage! I am a private citizen. The Order has no right—"

"We have every right," Sterling Chase informed him. The Boston commander leaned against the back wall of the closed room, his arms crossed over his chest. "We have evidence linking you to criminal activity in this city—"

"Criminal activity?" Gates scoffed. "Don't be ridiculous. You have no cause to believe that, let alone evidence."

"I assure you, we do," Chase said. "And I'm sure JUSTIS would be very interested to hear how one of Boston's most upstanding pillars of polite society has secretly been involved in illegal sport and various other unsavory pursuits."

"That's insane," Gates refuted with a scowl and a dismissive shake of his head. Then he turned a pointed glower solely on Nathan. "If you think humiliating me in front of my daughter and my peers will change my promise to you tonight, you're sorely mistaken."

At Chase's questioning look, Nathan grunted. "Mr. Gates made it clear to me that he does not approve of my interest in Jordana and won't permit it."

"He threatened you?"

Nathan shrugged. It hadn't fazed him then and hardly mattered now. After the way things went down tonight—the way Jordana looked at him, so hurt and betrayed—he doubted Gates had anything more to worry about when it came to Nathan's intentions with her.

She might never want to speak to him again, would most likely never forgive him for taking her father away from her. She might despise Nathan forever for breaking her heart.

And he wouldn't blame her.

He had never deserved her. Their worlds had been too different from the start, and tonight had proven that.

Bitter truth, and it didn't make the cold hollow in his chest ache any less.

He wanted nothing more than to go to her now and offer comfort, explanations. Reassurances that everything would be all right.

But as he watched her father protest and begin to squirm under his interrogation, Nathan knew he couldn't give Jordana any of those things.

Martin Gates's guilt was written all over him. He was a man with deep secrets, secrets he'd apparently kept hidden for many years. His darting, anxious gaze said he knew the respectable mask he'd worn for so long was about to be ripped away. Gates had been living a lie that was suddenly about to be exposed.

And when it was, nothing in Jordana's life would ever be the same.

"I have no intention of putting up with this thuggery for a moment longer," Gates announced, one final, obvious bid to halt the disturbing conversation before it went any further. "I demand you release me at once, or I'll—"

"Or you'll what, Mr. Gates?" Chase interjected calmly. "Go running to law enforcement? Complain to your Darkhaven cronies and country club colleagues? Or maybe you have other alliances you think you can lean on. The kind of alliances you and Cassian Gray thought you could keep in the shadows, along with your other less-than-respectable business dealings?"

Gates's expression went slack. "I have no idea what you're talking about."

Chase stared at him in dangerous silence. Gates endured the prolonged quiet for a few moments, his gaze flicking from Chase and Nathan standing before him to Jax, Eli, and Rafe positioned near the door of the interrogation room.

Abruptly, he bit off a curse and vaulted to his feet. "I don't have to sit here and listen to this bullshit. I'm leaving. You can expect to hear from my lawyer—"

Nathan took a half pace forward, subtly blocking Gates's path. There was no need for words or physical persuasion. Gates took one look at the flat intent in Nathan's eyes and immediately backed down.

As Gates dropped into his seat again, the last of his bravado fled and he peered up at Nathan, studying him nervously. There was defeat in the male's face, the kind of look that told of a crushing burden carried for far too long.

Gates lowered his head. When he spoke, his voice was subdued, reduced to a thready murmur. "Have you known all along, then?"

"You and Cass covered your tracks very well," Chase answered. "It took us a while to unravel it all, but you couldn't hide forever. We know you own La Notte. Cass may have run the place, but the club and all its profits—illegal and otherwise—belong to you. Now we need you to tell us about any other dealings you've had with him."

Gates looked up, eyes narrowed. "Since when does the Order have the license to police a citizen's private or business affairs?"

Chase wheeled on the vampire with a snarl. "Since the night last week when Opus Nostrum tried to blow up a global peace summit."

"Opus Nostrum," Gates replied, genuinely taken aback. "Are you saying you suspect that I—or Cassian Gray—had anything to do with that?"

Chase lifted a shoulder. "I haven't heard you say you didn't."

"Well, I didn't. Neither did Cass, I promise you that," Gates said. Then he exhaled a sigh and leaned back in his seat. "I should hope the Order has better leads on the attack last week than whatever supposed evidence you seem to think you have linking me, or Cassian Gray, to those terrorists of Opus Nostrum." Gates paused, pointedly cleared his throat. "If there is nothing further—"

"He's not telling us everything." Nathan approached him, taking in the look of relief on the Darkhaven male's face. "The club isn't the only thing he's invested in with Cassian Gray. What else are you trying to hide?"

Gates scoffed. "Cassian Gray is my friend. Our business dealings are between us. We may not run in the same social circles, but last time I checked, that wasn't a crime."

Nathan grunted. "Do you have many Atlantean friends?"

Gates stared, unspeaking for a long moment. "If you have questions about Cass, maybe you should ask him, not me."

"I would," Nathan said. "But unfortunately, someone took his head last night."

Gates's mouth moved soundlessly. He swallowed then. "Wha—what are you saying?"

"Cassian Gray is dead. He was attacked and killed outside La Notte."

"Dead." Gates's face went white. "He worried that he'd risked too much. Stayed in the city too long. He was fearful when I saw him the other day. That didn't seem like Cass."

There was shock in the Breed male's voice, and true grief as well. He'd lost a friend, and it took him a moment to process what he'd just heard.

Then a new shock seemed to overtake him. There was an even greater hush to the Darkhaven vampire's voice. "Ah, Christ . . . Jordana. I must see Jordana right away. Cass made me promise, should this day ever come . . ."

Nathan exchanged a look with Sterling Chase. "What about Jordana?"

"Where is she?" Gates asked, a franticness creeping into his voice. "Dammit, I have to get out of here." Gates rose, his muscles tensing as if he were about to bolt for the door. "I have to talk to Jordana right now. I need to make sure she's safe."

Chase stepped in, scowling as he faced Gates. "What the hell does any of this have to do with her?"

The Darkhaven male turned a troubled look on them. "My God," he breathed. "You really had no idea, did you? My friendship with Cass, the business partnership. It was all about her. Jordana is Cassian Gray's child."

23

JORDANA STOOD IN THE CENTER OF THE MUSEUM LOBBY, PARA-
lyzed, watching in a state of numbed detachment—of staggering, sur-
real shock—as her father was taken away and the exhibit party abruptly
ended, all of her guests scattering in the Order's wake.

There were whispers and curious, pitying glances as people hurried
out. A few murmured reassurances that it must be some kind of mistake, just a terrible misunderstanding that Martin Gates could have
somehow run afoul of Lucan Thorne and his warriors.

Jordana wanted to believe that.

She wanted to believe Nathan would come back any moment and tell
her it was a joke or a bad dream—anything to alleviate the ragged hurt
inside her.

A hurt that told her this was no mistake.

Her father hadn't acted like an innocent man. He'd fought and fumed
with a desperation that had made Jordana's heart quake as she watched
Nathan take him away.

Jordana had never seen him like that before, so terrified and combat-
ive. As though he knew he had something awful to hide.

As for Nathan . . . the hurt Jordana felt tonight was all the worse
when she thought of him.

Had she been wrong to get so close to him?

Could her father have been the reason Nathan had shown any interest in her?

Nathan told her from the start that he wasn't the kind of man she might have wanted him to be. He'd told her that as recently as last night.

By his own description, once locked on a target, he pursued, he conquered. Then he moved on, never looking back.

Oh, God.

Jordana felt physically ill. Had he used her to buy the Order necessary time or opportunity to go after her father?

Was that all she'd been to Nathan—a means to an end?

He hadn't pretended to be anything other than what he said he was: a warrior, a Hunter. Jordana had fallen in love with him anyway.

Last night she thought she'd seen a different side of him. A tender side, as though he'd let down some of his armor and shown her the wounded, noble man behind the forbidding wall of impenetrable stone and cold, cutting steel he reserved for the rest of the world.

At the party tonight, and during their stolen passion in her office, Jordana had felt as if she were seeing Nathan in a way no one else ever had. He'd made her feel special, as though she meant something to him.

As though he might even have loved her too.

Had it all been a facade meant to lull her into trusting him further?

Could he and the Order have been plotting to spring some kind of trap for her father with her as the unwitting bait?

It staggered her to think so.

Her heart wanted to reject the idea outright, but doubt ran like oil in her veins.

"How are you doing, sweetie?" Carys's heels clicked lightly on the marble as she came out to the lobby, turning off the museum lights behind her as she approached. "Everyone's gone now, and I've closed up. Come on, let's get you home."

"No." Jordana numbly shook her head. "No, I don't want to go home. I want to see my father. I want to see Nathan. I need to know if what happened tonight was his plan all along."

Carys's brows pinched in a mild frown. "Jordana, you have to know Nathan would never—"

"I don't know anything anymore," she replied hotly, hurting so badly she thought her chest might crack open. "I need my father to tell me what he's done. I need Nathan to tell me that he hasn't been using me, playing me as part of his mission for the Order. I need to know if the two men I care most about in this world have been lying to me this whole time."

When Carys reached out with a touch meant to soothe, Jordana wrenched away from her. "I'm going there now. I can't stand by another minute without knowing the truth."

"Jordana, wait."

Ignoring her friend's plea, she started across the lobby, heading for the exit at a brisk pace.

She didn't get far.

From behind her, Jordana felt a disturbance in the air. Carys sucked in a sharp gasp, then went utterly silent.

Jordana spun around—just in time to see her friend's legs crumble beneath her.

A large, hooded figure dressed in a black trench coat stood over the fallen Breed female. As he released Carys's limp body to the floor, the man lifted his head, his face obscured in deep shadows.

He bore no weapon, but his palms were bright with an unearthly glow as he stepped away from Carys to stalk toward Jordana.

She screamed.

Panic exploding in her breast, she lunged for the exit.

She pushed the glass door open, inhaling a breath of chill night air as another scream built in her throat.

No sound left her lips.

Her feet simply stopped moving. All her fear—all conscious thought—went softly, swiftly silent as her skull filled with sudden heat and light . . .

Then all went dark.

"Cass made me keep his secret," Martin Gates said, misery in his voice and in the droop of his mouth as he spoke. "He made me vow she would never know he was her father—not unless the worst should occur and his enemies caught up to him."

Nathan had to admit, there was a part of him that wasn't completely shocked to hear that Jordana's true father was Cassian Gray. Aside from a passing similarity in their fair coloring, in hindsight Cass's visit to Jordana at the museum the day of his death had been more telling. Had he gone there because he feared his enemies were closing in, and he wanted to see his child one more time?

As for the fact of Jordana being the child of an Atlantean father, that in itself was hardly a revelation. Although the truth had been unknown for many centuries, and was still kept secret from the public at large, a couple of decades ago the Order had discovered the link between the Breed and the immortal race that had fathered the rare females born Breedmates.

"If Cass wanted to keep her safe from enemies among his own kind," Nathan said, "he would've done better to leave Jordana in your care and stay far away from Boston."

Gates nodded. "He tried. And he never stayed in the city more than a few weeks at a time, just in case he might be found out. But Jordana meant everything to him. Cass loved her just as much as I do. I think that's why he understood when I couldn't make good on the other part of my original promise to him."

"What promise was that?" Chase interjected, narrowing a hard look on the Darkhaven leader.

"That I take Jordana as my mate before her twenty-fifth birthday."

Nathan recoiled at the idea, confused and suspicious. "Why the hell would he ask that of you?"

"Cass wanted her blood-bonded to someone he trusted. Someone he knew would keep her safe." Gates gave a slow shake of his head. "I couldn't be that man. I raised her as my own child. Jordana was my daughter every bit as much as she was Cass's. No matter what I promised all those years ago, I couldn't force my blood onto her. As she got older, I knew I had to safeguard her some other way. I had to find someone else I could trust with her secret."

Something still wasn't making sense. Nathan failed to find the logic in Cass's plan.

And deep down, a possessive, protective brand of fury sparked to life in him when he thought of Jordana with any male other than him.

"Why not let her choose who she wants to take as her mate? The blood bond is sacred. It's unbreakable." Nathan nearly spat the words, recalling how easily Gates would have pushed Jordana onto his crony, Elliott Bentley-Squire. A decent man, maybe, but a man who didn't love her.

Not like Nathan did, fiercely and with his whole heart.

"You would've locked her into an irrevocable union, all for the sake of a promise made without her consent?" Nathan blew out a violent curse. "Jordana is an extraordinary woman. You raised her; you ought to know that. She deserves more than you or anyone else of your choosing could give her as her mate. God knows she sure as hell deserves more than I could ever give her."

Gates lifted his chin, understanding flickering across his features. "You really do love her."

Nathan gave a firm nod, his chest heaving with the intensity of everything he felt for Jordana. "I do," he answered solemnly. "But even if I didn't—even if I'd never met her—I would tell you that no Breedmate should be forced into a bond she doesn't want. Not for any reason."

Gates stared at him. "I never said Jordana was a Breedmate."

A sound of disbelief went up, though whether it came from Chase or one of Nathan's team members in the room, he wasn't sure.

Nathan could count on one hand the number of times he'd been struck silent for any reason. Never like this. Never with the sense that the floor had opened up beneath him and left him dangling over an abyss of uncharted terrain.

Chase spoke where Nathan was unable. "What do you mean, she's not a Breedmate?"

"Jordana's mother wasn't human," Gates said. "She was one of Cass's kind."

"Are you saying Jordana is fully immortal?" Chase pressed.

Gates nodded. "She is Atlantean, as were both her parents."

Finally, Nathan found his voice. "She has the Breedmate mark." He could see the small, scarlet-colored teardrop and crescent moon symbol in his mind. He'd stroked it more than once as they'd made love. "It's on the inside of Jordana's left wrist."

"A tattoo in the shape of the mark," Gates clarified. "Cass inked it on her himself when she was an infant, soon after he took her out of the Atlantean realm."

"Jesus Christ," Rafe murmured from his position across the small interrogation room. "What for? Why try to pretend she was something other than what she truly was?"

Nathan knew. "To hide his child among the Breed," he said, the pieces beginning to fall into some logical pattern now. "Cass wanted to hide Jordana where he thought she'd be safest. In plain sight."

Chase looked at Gates narrowly. "How was he so certain you'd keep his secret, or that you could be trusted with raising his child?"

"Because I'd already proven myself to him the night I found Cass hiding with an infant in my barn outside Vancouver. He'd been on the run for days. He was bleeding, gravely wounded, even for an immortal," Gates explained. "Naturally, the scent of so much blood drew me to the barn. But when he pleaded with me to help him and I saw the baby girl in his arms, I put aside my thirst and allowed him to recuperate in my home."

Nathan pictured the scene, imagining what he might have done, had he been in Martin Gates's place.

Having been raised not to feel mercy or compassion—to have been conditioned as a Hunter to exploit weakness and punish kindness—Nathan couldn't deny that he was humbled by Gates's actions and his honor. He was grateful to the man as well.

"Cass was fortunate to have ended up in your care. There aren't many who would've been so charitable with their trust."

Gates shrugged in mild dismissal of the praise. "I was fortunate too. Back then, I was alone, with no mate or kin of my own. All I had was a meager farm in the middle of nowhere." Gates's expression softened in remembrance. "It's because of Cass that I live in luxury now. It was his wealth that allowed me to start a new life here in Boston. He made me who I am today. And he gave me the most precious gift of all, my daughter."

"She knows nothing of this?" Nathan asked. "Jordana has no idea that she's not a Breedmate but full-blooded Atlantean?"

"No. But soon enough, she'll know." Gates leveled a sober look on Nathan and the other warriors in the room. "When Jordana turns twenty-five, her Atlantean powers will mature. In addition to extrasensory gifts a Breedmate might have, she will become stronger both physically and psychically. Her aging will stop, and she'll be impervious to all but the most severe injuries. She will know that I've been deceiving her all along about who she is. But even worse, Cass warned that unless she's shielded by a blood bond, the enemies who hunted him will now be able to sense her as one of their own kind."

The thought of Jordana being pursued by the same killers who caught up with Cass made Nathan's veins go icy with dread. If he had to take on the entire Atlantean race to protect her, he would. There wasn't anything he wouldn't do for her, and if he'd known his blood might keep her safe, he would have already begged her to accept his bond.

Hell, he wanted that connection to her regardless of anything he'd heard here just now.

And he could only hope she would let him make it up to her for how things had gone so wrong tonight.

"She has to be told." Nathan pulled out his comm unit and hit Carys's number. As it started to ring, he stalked for the door. "Jordana should have been told all of this long before now."

And she needed to be told how he felt about her. That he loved her. That he was sorry if he hurt her tonight. She needed to hear that she was the only woman he would ever want, if she would have him.

Carys wasn't picking up.

The realization seeped into him like acid. Something wasn't right.

Nathan knew it in his marrow.

He was already bolting into the corridor outside the interrogation room before he heard the rise of panicked female voices carrying from the other end of the long hallway.

Tavia Chase had her arm around her Breed daughter, Carys staggering alongside her mother. When she saw Nathan heading toward them, Carys let out a ragged sob.

"I didn't see him until it was too late," she murmured. "He did something to my head. Bright light in my skull. Too much power—I couldn't fight it. I'm so sorry, Nathan. I couldn't do anything. It just happened so fast."

All the blood in Nathan's body seemed to halt. Froze solid in his veins. "Where is Jordana?"

"He took her." Carys shook her head weakly, her face wrenched with anguish and worry. "When I came to in the museum lobby a few minutes ago, there was no trace of her. Oh, God, Nathan . . . Jordana is gone."

24

THE SUDDEN, BRIGHT TWITTER OF A SONGBIRD PIERCED THE FOG
of Jordana's waking senses. A soft, warm breeze blew in from somewhere, carrying the fragrance of a nearby garden—flowers and lemons
and rich, fertile earth. Farther away, quiet thunder rolled, its rhythm
drawing her out of a deep, dreamless sleep.

No, not thunder, she realized.

Waves.

The sea.

Where was she?

With a jolt of alarm, she recalled the dark intruder in the museum.
The attack that came out of nowhere. Carys lying motionless on the
lobby floor, the hooded man standing over her unconscious body.

Then a blinding, powerful light exploded inside Jordana's skull before everything around her went black . . .

Oh, God.

What happened?

Where had he taken her?

Jordana opened her eyes, expecting to meet the horror of her impris-
onment. She expected to feel pain. She braced herself to feel the cold
bite of restraints or any number of other abuses dealt to her by her captor.

But she felt no discomfort. Her limbs moved freely as she gingerly
tested her muscles. Nothing but velvety bedding beneath her on a pil-
lowy, decadent mattress.

And the room she awoke in was nothing remotely close to a prison cell.

Spacious and inviting, it was elegantly furnished with antiques and the king-size bed she lay in, which was canopied with sumptuous white silk and flanked by a pair of delicate, French Provincial nightstands. Creamy, lacquered millwork festooned every wall; snowy, polished marble covered the floors, luxury that extended into the adjacent palatial bathroom suite.

Jordana cautiously sat up to better take in her surroundings.

The place was quiet, all was still, except for the gentle stirring of the airy silk drapes drawn over the open window across from the bed. Where was her abductor?

Jordana scooted carefully to the edge of the mattress and put her bare feet down on the cool marble. She was still wearing her red dress from the museum event, her high heels placed neatly beside what appeared to be a Louis XV bureau. Atop the expensive piece was a vase full of cheery, fresh-cut flowers. A vase that appeared to be museum-quality Italian porcelain.

Good Lord, that Renaissance-era painting hanging behind the bouquet couldn't be an original Raphael, could it?

She might have been tempted to look closer, but she reminded herself that despite the impressiveness of the place, she had still been taken there against her will.

By someone who had not only disabled a Breed female with his bare hands but had also knocked out Jordana and apparently spirited her far, far away from everything she knew in Boston.

Why? What the hell was going on?

She stood up and took a few hesitant, soundless steps. Peering out toward the larger, equally luxurious living area outside the bedroom, she searched for signs of her abductor.

She saw no one in that room or elsewhere in the sunny, beautifully appointed villa. Jordana crept closer to the open bedroom door, then into the living room, where the scents of the gardens and ocean beyond were stronger, more enticing.

French doors stood open onto a terrace patio perched on a high hillside overlooking a craggy, green mountain coastline. Early morning sun-dappled blue water stretched as far as the eye could see.

Lush vegetation, much of it laden with exotic blooms and large yellow lemons, provided fragrant shade for the large terra cotta patio tiles and a charming little cafe table set with breakfast service for two—complete with crisply pressed white linens and gleaming, polished silverware. Jordana eyed the delicious-looking pastries, fruits, and thin-shaved meats with a frown.

Was this some kind of joke?

Or had she been kidnapped by the most gentlemanly psychopath on the planet?

Jordana spotted him out on the terrace as she ventured a few more paces into the main room of the villa. Every bit as big and tall as she remembered, except now he wasn't garbed in black or hooded.

He stood at the railing overlooking the sea beyond, wearing a gauzy linen tunic and loose-fitting linen pants. His back to the villa, he held his arms spread wide, palms turned up. On one of his wrists, he wore a brown leather thong, from which a small silver emblem glinted under the rising sun.

As she watched, the man tipped his golden blond head back on his shoulders to put his face full in the morning light.

It was a worshipful pose, a peaceful pose.

Yet there could be no mistaking the immense power that radiated from every inch and muscle of his body.

He wasn't human.

Obviously not Breed either. Not even a daywalker like Carys or her brother, Aric, would risk such intense UV exposure.

This man seemed to relish it. He seemed to need it.

Hopefully he was so deep in meditation he wouldn't notice she'd escaped until she was long gone.

Jordana turned her attention away from him and took a step forward.

"Good morning." The golden man from the terrace now stood directly in front of her.

A startled cry caught in her throat. Jordana threw a wild glance over her shoulder to the balcony outside, just to confirm what she was seeing.

He wasn't there anymore.

No, he'd vanished from his position several dozen feet away and had materialized barely an inch from where she stood. Shoulder-length blond hair shot with burnished shades of copper haloed a face blessed with perfect angles, flawless bronzed skin, and arresting, tropical blue eyes.

So the psycho who kidnapped her was not only gentlemanly and an art connoisseur but gorgeous besides. That didn't make him any less of a threat.

He reached for her, and Jordana screamed in earnest now. Fear and fury swelled inside her like a rising fire until it exploded out of her on a sharp, terrified yell. At the same time, she gave her abductor's massive body a hard shove and tried to dodge left to get around him.

To her amazement, he stumbled backward half a pace before righting himself and catching her around her upper arms. He actually seemed pleased.

"Impressive. Your powers are still young, of course, but they're already strong. They're manifesting quickly now."

Jordana's hands tingled with the pricks of a thousand tiny needles. She'd felt the odd sensation before—most recently while making love with Nathan, a memory, and a longing, that made her heart ache sharply in her breast.

Now she glanced down at her palms and was astonished to find them imbued with warm, glowing light. Faint, but unmistakable.

And not a little disturbing.

"Oh, my God," she gasped at her captor. "What's going on? Who are you? What have you done to me?"

"Shit." He let go of her and gave a mild shake of his head. "I'm scaring you. I'm sorry, Jordana."

"How do you know my name?" Her panic climbed. "Where are we? What is this place? How the hell did you get me here? What did you do to my friend Carys?"

"So many questions," he murmured. "It's understandable. Your friend is fine, I didn't harm her. I won't harm you either. I only wish to help. That's why your father called me—"

"My father?" She hardly dared hope he was telling her the truth, but it was all she had. "When did you talk to him? Did the Order let him go? I want to see him, right now. Please. You must take me to him."

As her words spilled out of her, the golden man looked at her in sympathetic, gentle silence. "I wish there had been an easier way to explain all of this to you. There wasn't time. If I hadn't taken you out of Boston, they would've gotten to you first. They were already closing in on you, Jordana."

"What are you talking about? Who was after me?"

"Your father's enemies. The soldiers who once served under his command—as I did, a very long time ago. I was your father's friend. My name is Ekizael."

Jordana shook her head. This guy may look like a fallen angel, but he was obviously very disturbed. "Look, Eh-kee-zayel—"

"Zael," he said, offering her a courtly bow of his head.

She stared at him. "Whoever you are, you don't know my father. His name is Martin Gates. He's a businessman. A Darkhaven leader. He was never a soldier and he doesn't have any enemies."

"No, Jordana," he said quietly. "I'm not talking about the Breed male who raised you. Your true father was a royal guard. He was once the most decorated warrior in the queen's legion."

"The queen's legion? Oh, right, of course." She couldn't bite back the small, nearly hysterical laugh that bubbled up from her throat. "And which one would that be—the Queen of England or the Queen of Sheba?"

The golden man—Zael, she mentally amended—remained sober, utterly serious. "Her name is Selene. She's been my people's queen for many thousands of years. Your people, Jordana."

She wanted to scoff at this insane statement too, but as her captor spoke, his hands began to emit the same soft light that hers had just a moment ago.

Even more unsettling, in the center of his broad palms glowed a symbol she recognized all too well: the teardrop-and-crescent-moon mark she bore on the underside of her left wrist.

"You have the Breedmate mark," she murmured. "I don't understand. How can you—"

"It is our symbol, Jordana. The symbol of the Atlantean race. The one on your wrist was put there as a decoy. Your father hoped the tattoo would help you fit in among the Breed and the halfling daughters of our kind born outside our realm."

"I was born with this mark," she argued. "The same as any other Breedmate."

"No. You, Jordana, are something different from them." Zael's deep voice was unnervingly rational as he spoke. "You're no halfling, not even close. You are full immortal. A pureblood Atlantean."

She looked at her symbol with fresh eyes, realizing only now that it might not be a birthmark after all, but crimson ink embedded meticulously under her skin.

Confusion swirled inside her. She wanted to deny what she was seeing—she wanted to deny everything she was hearing—but the evidence was too compelling to dismiss.

She already lived in a world where vampires and humans coexisted. Why did it terrify her so deeply to think she might be something *other* too?

Because it would mean accepting the fact that her entire life had been a lie.

"Did he know all of this? Martin Gates, I mean. Does he know?"

Zael gave a mild nod. "He agreed to raise you and keep you safe as his child, as a Breedmate. For your protection, you were never to be told that you were different. Cass trusted him with that secret implicitly—"

"Cass," Jordana whispered, her breath drying up in her lungs. "Cassian Gray."

She closed her eyes as the realization sank in, a wave of shock washing over her. Then sorrow, when she recalled Cass's strange visit to the museum.

The enjoyable, far-too-brief time she'd spent talking with him. And the unthinkable way he died, just a short while later.

"His true name was Cassianus," Zael said. "He adopted a simpler one—an entirely new identity as well—to help him blend in with the mortal world after he left the Atlantean realm."

"Is that where we are now?" Her new reality settling over her, she glanced out at the breathtaking coastal paradise beyond the open French doors and couldn't help but wonder . . . "Is this Atlantis?"

"No." Chuckling quietly, Zael lowered his head. "Atlantis was destroyed long ago by our oldest enemies, the Ancient fathers of the Breed. There are some similarities between this place and Atlantis, but this is Amalfi, on the coast of Italy. This villa was a private sanctuary of Cass's for a long time, although it's been many years since he was last here."

Jordana could hardly speak. She glanced around at the sophisticated villa with its priceless antiques and masterpiece paintings. At least that part made sense now: Cass's unexpected, uncanny knowledge of art. He had apparently loved it as much as she did.

Cassian Gray was her father.

The news staggered her, perhaps even more so than any of Zael's other incredible revelations. To say nothing of the fact that she was hearing all of this not in the comfort of her home in Boston but evidently a continent away, and from the mouth of a man who'd brought her there through means she still hadn't determined and was almost afraid to guess at.

Her head spun with a hundred questions—so many, she wasn't sure where to start.

"You said Cass had enemies," she murmured. "Soldiers from the queen's legion who are also after me. You mean Atlantean soldiers. That's who killed him?"

"Yes." Zael's face was grim. "Their method left little doubt. They had been pursuing him for a long time on Selene's orders."

"Why?" Jordana struggled to keep the memory of the savagery from forming in her mind. "What did he do to her that she would hate him enough to want him killed?"

"For starters, he fell in love with a member of her court. It was forbidden, even for a legion soldier of Cassianus's renown. But Soraya loved him too," Zael explained. "For a while, they carried on in secret, meeting anywhere they could. They even risked time together outside the realm, coming here, to this villa."

It didn't take much for Jordana to imagine loving someone in defiance of what anyone else wished or expected. When it came to love, she'd learned firsthand that the heart gave itself freely, openly, completely.

Sometimes foolishly.

She met Zael's solemn look and knew the story he was telling her would not end well for the forbidden lovers.

"So, Cassianus and Soraya . . . they were my parents?" At his grave nod, she had to ask the other question that sat like a jagged pill on her tongue. "What happened to my mother?"

"She died," Zael said. "Soraya had you in secret, here in this villa. Cass thought the three of you could be a family together, stay on the run, never go back to the realm. But Raya missed the Atlantean way of life. She missed her home. To please her, Cass returned with Raya and you. Selene was furious. She called for his immediate execution. Raya pleaded for mercy. Selene finally granted it, but at a price."

Jordana listened, rapt yet heartsick for what her parents had endured. "What did the queen ask in exchange for Cass's life?"

"She made Raya agree to take a mate of Selene's choosing and exile with you until you turned twenty-five and your powers came of age. Once that occurred, Raya would be free to return, and you were to take your place as a member of the royal court."

"But Soraya didn't accept the queen's terms?" Jordana guessed.

If she had, Jordana would have never been raised as Martin Gates's daughter.

She would have never met Nathan.

As much as it hurt to think she'd meant nothing to him, the thought of having never known his touch, or his kiss, or the pleasure they shared, was too bleak to imagine.

Zael shook his head, his voice low. "Raya could not promise to give herself to another man. She begged for a different punishment, but Selene would not be swayed. Finally, on the day Raya and you were to leave the court for your new home, she took a drastic, irrevocable step."

"What happened?" Jordana whispered, her heart in her throat.

"Raya put you in the palace nursery. Then she went to her chambers, locked herself in, and set the place ablaze. By the time the fire was discovered, it was too late. Even an immortal could not heal from the wounds Raya inflicted on herself."

Jordana choked on a ragged breath. "And Cassianus? What did he do?"

Zael smiled sadly, proudly. "He did what any loving parent would do. Risked everything to take you away from there and ensure that you had a new life—a better life. One where Selene's guards wouldn't find you. Cass wanted you to have a life of your own choosing."

Except the irony was, as good as her life had been living with Martin Gates as his child, it hadn't been authentic. She'd lived under the cloak of secrets and half-truths, never really knowing who—or what—she was. She'd never been given the chance to know the two people who brought her into the world and gave up everything, including their lives, because of her.

Two people she missed keenly now, despite having had them in her life so briefly.

"Why did she do it?" Jordana murmured. "Why couldn't the queen just let them be happy together? Why chase Cass down and kill him after all this time? Why keep her guards searching for me?"

Zael's tropical blue eyes were steady on her. "Because Soraya was her only child."

Jordana went still. She shook her head slowly, at a complete and sudden loss for words.

When she couldn't speak, Zael did it for her. "You, Jordana, are Selene's granddaughter. You are her only living heir to the Atlantean throne."

25

IN THE HOUR FOLLOWING CARYS'S ARRIVAL, THE BOSTON COMmand center buzzed with sober conversation and urgent preparation for a do-or-die sweep of the city.

Gathered in the weapons room along with Nathan, Rafe and Eli and Jax rehashed the team's game plan for turning the city upside down in their search for the Atlantean bastard who had Jordana. In the corridor outside the war room, Sterling Chase and his mate, Tavia, were attempting to reassure a shattered, sobbing Martin Gates that the Order would do everything in its power to find Jordana quickly and bring her back, safe and sound.

Nathan had no words for anyone. He had no energy to expend on talking or hoping or wishing. He had no patience for consolation or promises that morning wouldn't be allowed to break without Jordana returned home.

All he had was his determination, his ruthless discipline.

With robotic efficiency, Nathan suited up in his patrol gear. In utter silence—with deadly calm purpose—he zipped and cinched, buckled and tied his black fatigues and combat boots, then strapped on his weapons belt and holsters for multiple firearms.

He *would* find Jordana.

There would be no failing that mission.

There would be no failing her, not ever again.

He had never been more committed to any goal in all his life. Jordana was all that mattered to him. If she were found harmed—if the man who took her tonight inflicted even the smallest pain on her—Nathan would eviscerate the son of a bitch.

Slowly.

He knew countless ways to kill, incrementally when necessary. If Jordana was hurt in any way, her abductor was going to suffer the full, merciless force of Nathan's wrath.

He readied the last of his weapons and threw a hard look on his team. "Let's go."

Leading the way, he stalked out to the corridor with Rafe, Jax, and Eli.

They were halfway up the winding hallway when Carys came rushing around a corner, her face stricken and grave. She clutched her comm unit in a white-knuckled grasp. "Nathan, wait. Something's happened."

The female's fearful voice just about stopped his heart. He was almost afraid to guess at this new, obviously bad news. "Jordana?"

Carys shook her head. "There was an attack at La Notte a few minutes ago. Syn's been killed. Rune wants to talk to you."

Normally, the death of a Breed cage fighter would be the last of the Order's concern. And neither Syn nor Rune had many friends among the warriors. But this was a night unlike any other, and a deadly attack on Cassian Gray's club within hours of Jordana having gone missing was far from coincidental.

Without slowing down, Nathan grabbed the comm unit and put it to his ear. "What happened?"

"That's what I wanna know." Rune's breath was tight, shallow. His deep, growling voice held an edge of wariness that Nathan had never heard before. "We just took a bad hit down here at the club. Couple of thugs tossed Cass's office. They fucking killed Syn, broke every bone in his body."

Like Rune, Syn was a proven champion in the cages. It would take a hell of an opponent to knock him down. "You see who did it?" Almost too much to hope.

Rune grunted. "Yeah, I saw them. Heard a ruckus in the office above the arena, then I smelled blood. Lots of blood. Found three men tearing the place up. Syn was already in bad shape, no more fight left in him. I dropped one of the bastards, but the other two got away." Rune paused. "The one I killed? He didn't go down easy, man. Not until I took his fucking head from his shoulders. Then the whole damn place lit up with the glow he threw off as he died. Sure as hell wasn't human, but he wasn't Breed either."

No, Nathan thought, grave with understanding. *They were Atlanteans.*

"Any idea what they were looking for?"

"Yeah," Rune replied. "When I found the fuckers hammering on Syn, they kept demanding that he tell them where Cass's daughter was."

Nathan cursed and drew up short in the corridor.

"Syn kept telling them Cass didn't have any family, but they wouldn't believe him."

Nathan stood there, frozen, his mind racing to process everything he was hearing. "This just happened, you say? These men—they were there just now?"

"Aye," Rune said. "The corpse of the one I killed is still warm."

Rafe drew up next to Nathan, the blond warrior frowning in question. "What is it?"

"You're certain they were looking for Cass's daughter?"

"Dead certain." The fighter was quiet for a moment, menace radiating through the comm. "Carys just told me what happened to her and Jordana a little while ago. Goddamn it, Nathan. I'm sorry about Jordana. And I hate like hell that Syn is gone. But these fucks—whoever, *whatever,* they are—put their hands on my woman tonight. This shit just got personal."

"Tell me about it," Nathan replied grimly.

With a murmured end to the conversation, he handed the comm unit back to Carys. She pivoted away, speaking to her lover in hushed, private tones.

Outside the war room, Nathan and his team were joined by Sterling Chase and Tavia, their expressions indicating they knew the weight of the information he'd just received.

Martin Gates drifted over too. "What is it? Has there been news about Jordana?"

Nathan glanced grimly from his commander and teammates to Jordana's distraught father. "Three men just broke into Cass's office at La Notte. They killed one of the fighters. Rune said they're looking for Jordana."

"Atlanteans," Gates murmured woodenly.

Nathan gave a sober nod but turned a look on Chase and the other warriors. "So, if Cass's enemies don't already have Jordana . . ."

"Then who took her?" Tavia asked.

Nathan glanced back at Gates. "Was there anyone else Cass might have trusted to know about Jordana living in Boston? One of his own kind?"

Martin Gates considered for a moment, then gave a shaky nod. "Yes, there is one other person who knew. Oh, my God. Dare I hope she's with him?"

"It may be all we've got," Chase replied.

Gates met Nathan's unblinking stare. "If she's been taken somewhere safe, I believe I know where you'll find her."

Jordana wiped some of the steam from her shower off the large mirror in the villa's master bathroom suite. She stared at her reflection for a moment, trying to understand how the pale blue eyes and familiar face looking back at her could feel so much a stranger now.

It had been only a few hours since her conversation that morning with Zael. A few hours since everything she thought she knew about herself had been peeled away.

Now, with the sun soon to set outside the villa where she'd been born, Jordana was looking at a new face. A new reality.

She was Atlantean.

Immortal.

The orphaned granddaughter of the race's vengeful queen.

It all felt so foreign to her, so incredible. And yet it also seemed as if the missing pieces of a puzzle had finally dropped into place. Her restlessness, her sense that she'd been sleepwalking through her own existence, living someone else's vision for what her life was supposed to be.

Because she hadn't been living her own life. She'd been living a fantasy conjured for her protection by parents she would never know and by a beloved adoptive father who'd sacrificed the past twenty-five years to the promise he'd made to keep her safe. To keep her hidden from enemies she'd never even realized had existed.

Enemies who were seeking her out even now.

After the initial shock of it all had worn off a bit, Zael had done his best to explain to her about his people—*their people*—and about Cassianus and Soraya and the Atlantean realm. He'd been patient and kind, forthcoming with everything she wanted to know. But she still had so many questions.

In particular, how long before she could get back home to Boston and resume her life.

Refreshed from sleep and a long shower, and dressed in comfortable, soft white linen palazzo pants and a sleeveless tank of the same fabric, Jordana braided her damp hair and let the long plait fall down the center of her back.

She heard Zael in the villa's kitchen, the aromas of roasting meat, wine and spices, and warm, baked breads wafting through the place. The dinner smelled wonderful, but her stomach seemed to have other ideas. It rolled and twisted, making each step a delicate, careful effort.

Her veins seemed charged with a low-level current. Her palms felt prickly and warm again, the way they sometimes had when she was making love with Nathan, only more intense now. More persistently heated and tingling.

"How do you feel?" Zael asked as she entered the open-concept gourmet kitchen.

"The rest and the shower were just what I needed, but now I'm kind of woozy." Her knees started to buckle beneath her, as wobbly as a new fawn's.

In an instant, Zael came around and helped her to one of the tall counter stools at the center island. "Better?"

She gave a weak nod, then crossed her arms on the snowy marble countertop and laid her head down. No doubt she had to look more than a little green around the gills. "Some immortal princess I make, huh?"

He chuckled. "It's par for the course. We all go through this—call them Atlantean growing pains. Your system will mature and stabilize after you turn twenty-five."

"That's next week." Zael nodded and she took the glass of water he handed her. "What's going to happen to me then?"

She sat up and sipped the water while he went back to chopping and sautéing a pan of fresh vegetables. "Your body stops aging completely. You'll become stronger, your senses keener. You'll be able to tap into an energy that connects all of our people—you've already experienced that when I frightened you earlier and you used your power to push me away."

"My hands were glowing," Jordana said as she glanced down at her palms, which still tingled but held no light. "Yours glowed too, but I could also see the teardrop-and-crescent-moon symbol in them."

"Yes," he said. "Your symbol will manifest eventually too. As a member of the royal bloodline, it will happen sooner for you than most. Others of our kind have to be much older before the symbol appears."

"How old?"

He lifted a bulky shoulder. "A hundred years, give or take."

"So, you're—"

"Older than that," he replied, his mouth quirked in a grin.

She shook her head, unable to believe the youthful, golden man could be even a day out of his twenties. "How old can you—or any of us—get?"

"Atlanteans don't keep count of years the way humans do, or even the Breed. We can live for many millennia, and have. Selene herself is one of the longest lived of our kind. When we mature, we develop the ability to heal from within, and nothing but catastrophic injury can kill one of us."

"Like beheading," Jordana murmured quietly. "Or self-immolation."

Zael gave a sober nod.

"Would he ever have told me? Would Cass ever have explained any of this to me—who I was, who he was . . . who my mother was?"

"No," Zael replied gently. "He wouldn't have. You have to understand, he did what he thought was right for you. He manufactured a completely new identity in Boston, an unsavory facade meant to keep him under Selene's radar. He was a soldier; he wasn't afraid of dark work. But he never would've wanted that part of his life to brush up too closely against you."

"Are you saying La Notte was just a front for him?"

Zael inclined his head. "A lucrative one, but yes. The club provided a deep cover for Cassianus in Boston. As for you, he thought you'd have a better life outside the Atlantean realm, in this world. He thought you could blend in if you were brought up as a Breedmate. Cass felt you'd be safest if he hid you in plain sight."

"How could my secret stay hidden from everyone? How could it stay hidden from *me*?" She thought about the energy she felt coursing through her, building in her, even now. "I would've known I was different. I've had a feeling all my life that *something* about me was different, that some piece of me was missing."

"Yes," Zael said. "That's why Cass wanted you blood-bonded to one of the Breed before the age of twenty-five. A bond would have eased the changes in you. It would've explained your lack of aging. Most important, it would've shielded you from Selene's legion by making your energy harder for our kind to detect."

Jordana considered the certainty she heard in the immortal's voice. "You say that as if it's proven fact. Has it been done before—an Atlantean mating with one of the Breed?"

Zael nodded. "There have been pairings between our races over time. But they're rare, and the blood-bonded couples living their secret are known only to a chosen, trusted few."

"That's why my father—Martin Gates—tried so desperately to match me up with someone."

Zael gave an affirmative dip on his head. "He and Cass had agreed that you would be blood-bonded before your twenty-fifth year."

She sat back in her seat on a long, heavy sigh. "It staggers me to think of all the promises made with me in mind, all the sacrifices. And I understand it was all done out of love—the purest kind of love, that of parents wanting the best for a child." Jordana met Zael's gaze across the kitchen. "But when everyone was coming up with these promises, all these secret plans, there was one thing they all overlooked. It was *my* life they were manipulating, my future. It was my heart."

They would have locked her into a bond with someone she didn't desire and would never love.

Not the way she wanted Nathan.

Not the way she loved him.

There was a heartbroken, desperate part of her that hoped this was all just a dream and she might wake up and discover she was still in Boston. That none of this was real.

She closed her eyes, wishing that when she opened them she would find herself curled up next to Nathan in her bed.

If she sent up a silent, pleading prayer, could this all turn out to be just some cosmic mistake? Maybe the exhibit opening hadn't yet occurred, and she hadn't felt her whole world crumble as Nathan stoically, mercilessly led her father away like a criminal.

Maybe Nathan hadn't simply seduced her as a means of closing in on her father.

Maybe she had actually meant something more to him.

Maybe he really did want her, love her, even just a little.

And maybe the only dreaming or wishing she was doing was in trying to shape Nathan into someone he would never be.

He'd warned her away from him, but fool that she was, she hadn't listened. He'd been the wild, dangerous storm she feared—the one she'd leapt into from atop her high ledge, knowing full well she might get tossed onto the rocks below.

Now, with her heart lying in broken pieces on the ground, she could only blame herself for jumping off.

Zael was staring at her. Studying her in thoughtful silence. "Who is he?"

She glanced down, shook her head. "I'm not sure it matters anymore. Not to him, anyway." But thinking about Nathan and the way things had ended renewed her concern for her father. "I need to get back home now. It's very important. Last night the Order arrested my father, and I—" She paused to think, suddenly unsure. "*Was* it last night? How long have we been gone? And exactly how did we get here?"

"I took you from Boston last night, around nine in the evening," he said. "You've been gone from there not quite fifteen hours now." As she worked to make sense of how that could possibly be, considering travel distance and time zone differences, Zael gently cleared his throat. "As for how we got here . . ."

He held up his wrist, the one with the leather thong and the silver emblem dangling from it. Jordana saw now that the emblem was in the shape of the Breedmate—or, rather, the Atlantean—symbol.

And the charm wasn't made of silver at all but an unusual crystal that somewhat resembled mercury glass.

She blinked at him. "I don't understand."

"The crystal this is made from is an energy source belonging to our people. It generates power, provides protection . . . it's useful for many things, both good and bad. It also allows our kind to travel great distances, or small ones, in the blink of an eye."

Jordana gaped. "Are you saying this bracelet brought us here?"

"It will take us anywhere, so long as the place can be imagined accurately in the traveler's mind." Zael's voice became more serious now. "It can take you to asylum, Jordana. Somewhere Selene and her soldiers will never find you. There are others living in exile from the realm, some for many hundreds of years. Cass wanted me to offer that choice to you, should the worst occur and the legion finally caught up to him. That's why he summoned me. He wanted me to give you the option to escape to a protected colony with those of your own kind."

"Leave Boston?" she asked. "You mean here and now. You mean forever."

He gave a grim nod. "For obvious reasons, you could tell no one about this. For the safety of all, no one in the colony is permitted to leave. No outsiders are allowed in, except in the most extreme of circumstances, like my mission to contact you. This would be a permanent decision. And one you don't have much time to make. With your powers manifesting already, every minute we spend here risks your being located by the queen's guards."

It was tempting to think there was somewhere she could go. It was a relief to think there was a place for her to get away from the kind of enemies who had killed Cass and were now on the hunt for her.

A place where she could be with others of her kind—her *true* kind. Somewhere she wouldn't have to hide who and what she was. Where her very existence wouldn't jeopardize the lives of the people who loved her and wanted to protect her.

Selfishly, there was a part of her that craved the asylum Zael described.

But could she really go without even a word of good-bye?

Could she leave her father? Could she leave Carys or her other friends? Could she abandon the job she adored and the colleagues and community she'd worked with for years?

And what about Nathan? Could she imagine any kind of life that didn't somehow include him in it?

Of all the people she loved and would miss so terribly, it was this last thought that twisted her heart the most.

And she had to face the fact that whatever she thought she had with Nathan might already be gone.

But could she really walk away without knowing for certain?

"I realize this is an impossible choice, Jordana."

She slowly shook her head. "No, you can't know that. You're asking me to walk away from the only home I've ever known. To never see the people I love most in this world ever again. Is my safety worth that? Is anything worth all of that?"

Zael's handsome face was solemn, a dark, private pain swirling in the depths of his Caribbean blue eyes. "I will need your answer soon. If we mean to leave before you're discovered, we must do it tonight. Make no mistake, Selene's soldiers will come for you here. It's not a question of if, Jordana, but when."

26

NATHAN SAT BEHIND A PANE OF UV-BLOCKING GLASS IN THE BACK-seat of a dark sedan that idled in the dusk on a narrow street in the coastal village of Amalfi. The driver, Salvatore, was human, a discreet, proven ally, hired to meet Nathan's flight earlier that afternoon by the Order's district commander in Rome, Lazaro Archer.

Nathan had been airborne from Boston within three hours of Jordana's disappearance. The fly time on the Order's private jet and the wait for sundown once he arrived in Italy had been maddening. Each second had crawled by in agonizing slowness. He wasn't sure how he would have endured any of it if Martin Gates hadn't been certain Jordana was in friendly hands, in a place that had once been a private sanctuary for Cass.

Knowing that Jordana was in any other man's hands, particularly those of an Atlantean, hadn't made the delay in reaching her any less torturous.

Now, finally, Nathan found himself looking up the steep, tree-choked hillside, to the secluded villa perched high above the serpentine little street.

He opened the door and got out. A quiet rap on the roof of the car sent Salvatore on his way back down the road. Nathan had no idea what he was walking into, and he and Lazaro Archer agreed that discreet or not, the farther they kept humans out of Order business, the better.

That went double when it came to Order business involving the race of immortals who were evidently hunting down and slaying their own kind while purportedly plotting war against the Breed and humans both.

A race of immortals that claimed Jordana as one of their own.

Part of him still couldn't reconcile the idea that she belonged to a different people, a different world. He'd felt from the beginning that she deserved someone better, more worthy of her. That she was destined for greater things than he could ever hope to offer her. He just hadn't realized how true his sense would actually turn out to be.

Movement on the terrace patio high above him drew his attention up to the villa.

As if conjured by his thoughts, Jordana appeared at the railing overlooking the hillside and coast below. Relief poured over him the instant he saw her.

She was safe.

Thank God, she was safe.

And she was more beautiful than ever, the sight of her so welcome he could hardly breathe for the way his heart was jackhammering in his chest.

Nathan stood motionless, arrested by the sight of her in the indigo wash of evening.

She looked different to him tonight. Changed, somehow. Stronger, more vibrant.

She wore a loose, white linen tank and gauzy pants, simple clothing that couldn't quite hide the enticing curves and lean, graceful lines of Jordana's body. Her long, platinum blond hair was gathered off her delicate face and braided in a thick rope that snaked down her spine.

Willowy and ethereal, she glowed as pale as moonlight and as breathtaking as a goddess.

Fitting, he thought, that she should look so enchanting, like a being from another realm.

As for Nathan, he had never felt more out of place than he did just then, staring up at her from the shadows in his warrior's gear, bristling with all the ugly, brutal weapons of his trade.

He'd come to find her, to bring her home. He'd come to tell her what she meant to him, to say the things he should have told her when he'd had the chance—before everything went so wrong last night.

He'd come to rescue her on behalf of her father and the Order, but in his heart, he knew he'd come here with the hope he'd bring Jordana home as his mate.

Now he had to wonder if she wasn't already on the path that she truly belonged on.

Not certain how he would be received, or even if she would want to see him again, Nathan took a step out of the gloom on the street. He lifted his hand, about to call out to her and let her know he was there.

Before he could speak, a man walked up beside her on the terrace balcony. Nathan's chest went hot and tight at the tender smile and nod Jordana gave this stranger. Tall, golden-haired, too handsome to be merely mortal, the man wrapped a protective arm around Jordana's shoulders.

Then her Atlantean guardian gently guided her away from the railing, and the two of them disappeared inside the villa.

Jordana rubbed a sudden chill from her bare arms as she reluctantly walked back inside the villa with Zael. She didn't want to leave the terrace, or the warm night air that had drawn her out to the railing while Zael was serving the dinner he'd prepared.

She'd gone outside for answers, for comfort.

For some much-needed space to think about the choice she'd made a short while ago.

She would be leaving with Zael soon. Whether she was making the best decision, or one that she would eventually regret for the rest of her life—forever, in that case—Jordana couldn't be sure.

Whatever she chose, Zael had made it clear there could be no reversing it. Once she left the villa with him, her course would be set and final.

"Wine or water with your coq au vin?" he asked, waiting politely as she took her seat at the table. The meal smelled delicious, and looked even more incredible.

Not that she was hungry in the least.

"Water, please." Her head was still a little woozy, and the electrical buzz that had been with her all day was only intensifying. She put her prickly hands on her lap under the table and tried to ignore the warm tingling of her palms. "How soon will we be going?"

"As soon as you're ready." Zael retrieved a bottle of San Pellegrino and poured some in her glass. He gave her a sober look that said she hadn't fooled him by trying to hide that the power within her was getting stronger by the moment. "It's not too late to change your mind. But we don't have long."

"Do you think I'm making the right choice?"

Zael's expression was mild, deliberately neutral. "Only you can answer that."

She nodded and took a sip of the sparkling water. Zael seated himself across from her at the dining table, then attacked his culinary masterpiece with abandon.

He seemed relaxed, confident, and unrushed, but Jordana hadn't missed the fact that at some point that day, he'd acquired a slender, gleaming sword from somewhere in the villa.

The long blade leaned against the table at his right, easily within his reach.

It didn't look like any other kind of blade she'd seen before. The steel was inscribed with some kind of ancient-looking lettering and symbols. And the pommel bore the symbol Jordana now recognized as the Atlantean mark.

"You don't really think you'll need that, do you?"

Zael lifted one bulky shoulder as he shoveled another mouthful of food to his mouth. The corner of his lips quirked with unrepentant male pride. "If I do, don't worry. I know how to use it."

As he finished speaking, the joviality faded from his eyes. He dropped his fork, face turning lethal in an instant.

Jordana glanced behind her to the open French doors to the terrace. A man stood there, dark and grim in his black combat fatigues. Shock and disbelief—along with a piercing, desperate hope—sprang to life inside her.

She pivoted and started to rise. "Nathan?"

She had barely gasped his name before Zael was in motion.

One second, he was seated across from her at the table; the next, gone and materialized again to stand in front of her like a full-body shield. He held his Atlantean sword in a defensive angle in front of them, poised to kill.

While Zael squared off at Nathan, Nathan stood unarmed, all of his weapons holstered and sheathed, his hands held loosely at his sides.

"No." She put her palms briefly on the Atlantean male's shoulders, her eyes locked on Nathan in tentative, uneasy question. "It's okay, Zael. Nathan is my . . . he's with the Order."

The tension in Zael's big body relaxed only slightly. He didn't lower his blade, but he didn't move to attack either.

Nathan said nothing, his thundercloud eyes moving away from Jordana's protector to her, standing behind Zael. His gaze was unreadable in the shadows of the terrace patio. His face remained impassive, emotionless and schooled.

More than anything, Jordana wanted to move around Zael and rush into Nathan's arms.

Instead, she stayed the impulse, terrified of his rejection. And she was still too wounded by the way things had ended between them last night to risk another heartbreak.

In the heavy silence, Zael took a step away from Jordana. The look he turned on her said he understood that Nathan was the man she'd been thinking of earlier today. The man she'd been longing for when she spoke of the way few had considered how she wanted to live her life or where her heart might be the happiest.

Zael's wise, ageless gaze said he recognized that this was the man she loved.

He gave her a faint, almost reverent, bow of his head. "You'll want some privacy, no doubt. I'll be just in the other room, if there is anything you need."

"No," Jordana murmured. As relieved and hopeful as she was to see Nathan standing there, she was afraid of what she might hear. Afraid for what the Order might have done to her father.

Afraid for herself, and the heart that was beating so frantically in her breast, a heedless organ that wanted to forgive Nathan and believe she meant something to him simply because he was there.

But she didn't know why he had come, and she refused to be the trusting, naive fool after everything that had happened since she last saw him.

"No, Zael. I want you to stay," she told him. "Anything the Order has to say to me can be said in front of you."

Nathan exhaled a short sigh, the first crack in his iron-clad composure. "I guess I deserve that."

Jordana held tight to her resolve, but his low voice still had the power to make something inside her melt. He glanced at Zael briefly as the Atlantean relaxed his stance with his blade, then settled back on his heels to remain, at Jordana's request.

"Are you all right?" Nathan took a step toward her, emerging into the light of the villa's living room. "You haven't been hurt?"

"No. Not by Zael." Sharp words, but she couldn't bite them back. She steeled herself as Nathan took another few steps inside. "Where's my father? What have you and the Order done to Martin Gates?"

"He's at the command center in Boston. He's worried about you, Jordana. The Order is very concerned for you as well. So is Carys." Nathan's cool gaze slid to Zael in unspoken warning. "Everyone wants you returned home safe. I mean to ensure that happens. And make no mistake, I'm not leaving without you."

She bristled at the idea that he expected to dictate any aspect of her life. Especially when he was doing it on behalf of a committee: her father, her friend, the Order.

Everyone except him.

She raised her chin, hoping he wouldn't see through her to the sting she was feeling all over again. "And if I decide I don't want to go with you? What then? Do you mean to physically force me into custody, the way you did my father?"

Beside her, Zael tensed with palpable menace. Nathan's brows furrowed as he looked at her and gave a slow shake of his head.

"Jesus." He uttered the low, ripe curse. "Do you think I would do that to you?"

"I don't know what to think, Nathan. Last night, I thought I knew you. Not the warrior or the Hunter—I thought I knew *you*. I thought I could trust you. I thought that you and I—" She stopped herself before the confession—the dashed hope—could escape her. "It doesn't matter what I thought last night. Today nothing is the same."

"That's right. Today everything is different," Nathan agreed. "Last night, we took Martin Gates into custody because we discovered he'd secretly been in business for years with Cassian Gray."

"In business with him? How?"

"La Notte belongs to Martin Gates, not Cass."

The news came as a surprise, but she was beyond the capacity to be shocked. A club like that, with its illegal sporting arena and gambling operation, to say nothing of the BDSM dens, would be the last kind of business her father would be involved in. Then again, if it had been a front for Cass, what was to say her father hadn't been secretly holding the club as some further means of protecting Cass and his secret?

"We had to assume that as Cass's longtime business partner, Gates knew he wasn't human. We needed to know why they were keeping those kinds of secrets, Jordana. And more urgently, we needed to determine whether Martin Gates and Cass could also have ties to Opus Nostrum."

"No. That's impossible." As incredible as it was to her to imagine Martin Gates having anything to do with Cass's notorious club, she refused to believe her father—either of them, for any reason—would ever be part of the terrorist group responsible for multiple assassinations and the recent attack on the global peace summit in D.C.

Nathan nodded. "We realized soon enough that wasn't the case. Martin Gates and Cassian Gray were keeping a very big secret, but it wasn't Opus Nostrum. It was you."

He stepped closer, but she retreated a pace. "How long did you know the Order would be coming after my father? Did you know the whole time last night?" Jordana's voice sounded broken, even to her own ears. "Were you planning for his arrest even while you and I were alone together in my office? Did you use me, Nathan?"

Now Zael growled, low under his breath.

Nathan's scowl deepened. "Did I use you? Fuck no. Never, Jordana." He gave a sharp shake of his head. "But understand I also had to do my job."

She scoffed quietly, even while her heart caved to him a little more. "Are you just doing your job now too? Is that why you're here—because of what I am? Because of who I am?"

"I came because as soon as we figured out where you might be, nothing would've kept me from finding you. *Nothing.*"

He stared at her, moved forward despite the further warning that curled up from the back of Zael's throat. "You need to come back with me, Jordana. Yes, because of everything we know about you now. You need to come back to Boston, where it will be my job and the Order's to keep you safe from Cass's enemies. Or anyone else who might think he has a claim on you," he added, slanting a challenging look on Zael.

"I have no claim," Zael said evenly. "But someone more powerful than any of us does. It was at her command that those soldiers tracked and killed my old friend Cassianus. And unless they're stopped—or unless they lose the trail they're most certainly on now—those same men will continue to look for Jordana by order of their queen."

"Their queen," Nathan murmured, clearly suspicious. "What are you talking about?"

"Jordana is her granddaughter."

Nathan's answering curse was rough, disbelieving. But Zael continued, undaunted. "The soldiers were closing in on Jordana last night in Boston."

"Closing in on her," Nathan said, then he seemed to understand. "Because her latent powers are maturing. Her Atlantean nature is leading them to her like some kind of beacon?"

Zael gave a grim nod. "They will track her to the ends of the earth unless steps are taken. They were in Boston since the night they located Cass. They would've found Jordana. If I hadn't reached her first, they would've already taken her back to the realm."

"Ah, Christ." Nathan turned a stricken look on her. "And I had left you alone. They might've come for you, and I wasn't there."

Anger flared in her. "It's not your job to protect me, Nathan. Dammit, it's not anyone's job to protect me!"

As her voice rose, the prickling in her hands intensified. The buzzing in her veins grew deeper, a pulsating thrum that filled her ears.

She swung a furious look between Nathan and Zael. "I'm not made of glass. I'm not a child. I'm a grown woman, and I'm tired of being treated as if everyone else knows what's best for me."

She didn't realize how strong the sensation of heat and energy had gotten in her hands until she noticed both Zael and Nathan staring at her. Only then did she look down at her palms.

At the fiery glow that emanated from their centers.

And in the midst of that ember-bright light was the outline of a crescent moon and teardrop.

The Atlantean mark.

"Holy hell," Nathan gasped. His stormy eyes lifted to her gaze and he seemed speechless for a long moment, awestruck. "My God . . . Jordana."

Zael's response was less amazed than it was grim. "Son of a bitch." He cocked his head, then shot a grave look at Jordana. "We delayed too long. They're here."

27

EVERY MUSCLE IN NATHAN'S BODY SNAPPED TO ATTENTION ON Zael's warning.

There was no time to process the astonishing change he'd seen in Jordana. No opportunity to assess the newly arrived danger, or to catalog the numerous vulnerabilities of their surroundings in preparation for the battle to come.

"We cannot let Jordana be taken." Zael looked to Nathan, gravity in his face and his words. As he spoke, Nathan noticed the leather thong looped around Zael's wrist. The silvery emblem that dangled from the cord was lit with unearthly fire. "This crystal can transport her far from the queen's reach, but I must take her now."

Nathan gave the Atlantean warrior a nod. He looked at Jordana, his heart choking as though it were caught in a vise. "Go with him. I need to know you're somewhere safe."

"What about you?" Panic bled into her face, into the ice-blue eyes that had looked at him with so much pain and mistrust tonight. "Zael," she said, an urgency—a clipped, regal demand—in her voice. "What about Nathan?"

The Atlantean shook his head in faint denial. "I'm sorry, Jordana. The crystal will only work for our kind. And besides, he can't go where I must take you."

His sword in one hand, Zael reached out for her with the other, the crystal's light building.

"No. I'm not going anywhere. Don't touch me, Zael." Jordana

snatched her hand away from him. She swung a tormented look on Nathan. "How could you think I would leave you behind only to save myself? Don't you realize what that would do to me?"

Nathan cursed. If anything happened to her, it would be worse than any abuse he'd ever suffered. He would never forgive himself. "Jordana, I don't matter. I want you to go—"

"Dammit, Nathan, don't you realize that I love you?"

She had no sooner said the words than the air stirred outside the open French doors to the terrace.

In the blink of an eye, a pair of immense males materialized there. It was apparent they were soldiers. Obvious they had come for her, just as Zael said they would.

Each man held a long, gleaming blade much like the one Zael now raised in front of him, as he swiftly ushered Jordana behind him.

Nathan wasted no time waiting for the attack to come. He drew one of his guns and opened fire on the two Atlanteans.

The larger of the two, dark-haired and snarling, staggered back on his heels under the sudden barrage of bullets that ripped into his chest and skull. His companion, a copper-haired warrior with piercing, determined green eyes, took a couple of rounds in his torso before vanishing into thin air.

Nathan kept firing on the big male, blasting holes into the bastard until his tattered, unmoving weight tumbled right over the railing of the balcony.

Jordana's scream jerked Nathan's head around. The other soldier had reappeared farther inside the villa and was now bearing down on her and Zael.

Zael put his body between Jordana and their attacker, raising his blade as the other male's sword came slashing toward him. The Atlantean weapons clashed in a screech of metal and a brief shower of blue and green sparks. Zael went down on one knee, driven low by the sudden, wrenching thrust of his opponent's arm.

Nathan dropped his empty pistol. Using the speed of his Breed genetics, he flashed across the room and came up behind the copper-haired soldier. He grabbed the Atlantean's head in both his hands and gave a violent twist. Vertebrae popped like firecrackers. The soldier let go of his blade and slumped to the floor in a lifeless heap.

As the body fell away, Zael opened his mouth in a shout of warning.

Too late.

Nathan felt a sharp length of ice impale his torso from behind.

The blade withdrew and he wheeled around on his heel, astonished to find the dark-haired Atlantean standing there. Blood was all over the soldier, but not a single bullet wound remained.

The immortal had come back from the gunfire and the fall. His gleaming sword was dripping, stained scarlet from the hole that now bled from Nathan's back and abdomen.

The wound was bad, but it wouldn't kill Nathan. It did, however, severely piss him off.

And before he could regroup and retaliate, Jordana's terrified cry rent the air.

"Oh, my God. Nathan!" She lunged from behind Zael.

The dark-haired Atlantean's hand shot out and grabbed hold of her, merciless, unrelenting. His long fingers wrapped tightly around her arm. Nathan saw that he wore a thong around his wrist similar to Zael's. The crystal emblem affixed to it now began to throw off powerful, fiery light.

He was going to take her away. Back to their realm. Back to their queen.

Jordana's wild, terrified gaze shot to Nathan.

No. He couldn't lose her.

"Goddamn it, no!" Nathan shouted.

He reached for her other hand and held on tight. He couldn't bear to let her go.

And at that same moment, in no time at all, he felt a heat begin to surge through Jordana's fingers. The energy was immense, awesome.

Not of this world.

"Release me," she growled at the soldier who captured her. The power within her expanded, growing swiftly. In a blinding flash, it erupted out of her as she roared the command again. *"Release me!"*

The Atlantean guard flew off her as if torn away by an unseen force. Nathan too was staggered by the sudden blast of light and power that surged through Jordana's hands.

He let go, only because he noticed that the dark-haired male had dropped his sword in that moment. Nathan grabbed for it, at the same time Zael hurled himself at the soldier, tackling the guard while his reflexes were dazed from Jordana's defensive strike.

But now the second of the Atlantean soldiers had come back from his injuries.

Although Nathan had broken the male's neck, the copper-haired immortal shook it off with a menacing chuckle as he got to his feet. He swiveled his head, popping his spinal column back into alignment.

Nathan vaulted up from the floor, pivoting around at the same time. The dark-haired immortal's sword held in his hands, he swung it around as the second guard charged at him.

Steel met flesh and cleaved in deep, sweeping the immortal's head off in one sure, lethal blow.

Behind him, Zael's sword was also biting into muscle and bone, the head of the other Atlantean hitting the floor with a wet, final thud.

"Nathan!" Jordana flew across the carnage toward him.

Her heart lodged in her throat, panic and relief swamping her at the same time, Jordana raced to Nathan's side and threw her arms around him.

He was wounded and bleeding, but still standing. He was alive.

He had saved her—he'd likely saved Zael as well—and nothing could have kept Jordana from embracing Nathan and burying her face in the living, breathing warmth of him.

"Oh, God," she murmured against his chest. She clung to him, needing to feel his body against hers, whole and hale. "I've never been so scared, Nathan. When that soldier ran his blade through you, I thought he'd killed you—"

"Shh," he soothed, his palm stroking her back as he dropped a kiss on top of her bent head. He held her close, his pulse drumming beneath her ear. So strong and steady, so comforting. "I'll heal soon enough. I've survived worse than this before."

He lifted her chin, both his fingers and his gaze tender on her. "It would've taken a hell of a lot more than that blade to stop me. I wasn't about to let them have you. I don't give a fuck if the Atlantean queen and her entire army think they have any claim on you. They'll all have to come through me first."

He lowered his head and kissed her. Not a tentative kiss but a fierce, possessive one.

Jordana melted into it, savoring the taste of him, the feel of him. The unearthly energy that had poured through her veins during the battle stirred again, but with a different power, as Nathan's mouth moved over hers in a deep, passionate joining.

Would she always respond so easily to his touch, his kiss?

Or now that her Atlantean genetics were awakening, becoming part of her, would she crave him with an even greater need?

She hoped she'd have the chance to find that out.

She hoped she'd have an entire future ahead of her with Nathan to find that out.

But right now, his injury needed tending, and across the room, Zael was standing over the corpses of the two Atlantean warriors.

Nathan broke contact on a low moan. As he raised his head to regard Zael, he brought Jordana under his arm in a protective stance. "Will more soldiers come?"

Zael gave a sober nod. "Once it's determined these men have failed and are lost to her, Selene will send out more. She'll keep sending out more. The queen does not accept defeat easily. She forgives even less." Zael's gaze slid to Jordana. "The best place to elude her is in the colony."

"Or through a blood bond," Jordana pointed out.

"If you remain in the mortal world, that's all that would protect you. But only if Selene's legion doesn't find you first."

"And she has me." Nathan said it like a vow: firm, unwavering.

"True," Zael acknowledged with a level glance, but his grave tone stopped short of encouragement. "Unfortunately, nothing can be as certain as the asylum the colony can provide. It's hidden, known only by a small few outside the realm. I am one of only a handful trusted with its location, aside from the exiles who live there in seclusion under the colony's protection."

"What kind of protection?" Nathan asked.

Zael indicated the silvery crystal he wore on the leather thong at his wrist. "This is crafted from a larger source of energy belonging to our people. The colony has one, and so does Selene. At one time, very long ago, the realm had five of these crystals, much larger than this small, harvested piece. The crystals are sacred to the Atlantean people. They shielded us from the world outside and kept the realm safe from enemies who would want to destroy us."

Beside Jordana, Nathan studied Zael's bracelet with narrowed scrutiny. "That material's nothing found on this Earth."

"No," Zael said. "My people, like the Ancients who fathered your kind, the Breed, were from somewhere else. The two races were at war, in fact. Even before fate brought them here."

Nathan swore under his breath. "Is that why another of your kind, Reginald Crowe, recently boasted before he died that the Atlantean queen has been plotting a new war—one against both mankind and the Breed?"

"Selene is a bitter queen." Zael grunted. "Worse, she's a scorned woman. I can't say what she's plotting, but it's rare that she's not looking for reasons to fight or enemies to destroy. It wasn't always that way with her."

"What happened to make her that way?" As much as Jordana feared the woman who had driven her mother to suicide and ordered her soldiers to hunt down and execute Jordana's father, she felt compelled to try to understand something about the queen if she could.

"Selene changed after our first settlement was destroyed," Zael explained. "Two of the realm's crystals were stolen, and our enemies—your Ancient forebears," he said to Nathan, "used the crystals' power to annihilate us. Selene fled Atlantis with as many of our people as could escape the destruction of all we'd built and the giant wave that swallowed up the rest."

"Just like the myth," Jordana whispered. "That story has been in place for thousands of years."

Zael gave an acknowledging shrug. "More or less. And Selene's had little but mistrust or hatred for anyone since that day."

Nathan frowned. "So the colony has a crystal, and the queen has one also. Two were stolen before the attack by the Ancients. And the fifth?"

"No one knows for certain. It vanished about twenty-five years ago." Zael glanced at Jordana. "There were rumors Cassianus had taken it with him when he fled with you . . ."

"But you don't believe that?" she asked.

Zael's brows lifted in contemplation. "Cass would've had the balls, that's a given. But to make off with an object with that magnitude of power? To keep it hidden all this time would've been quite a feat. He'd have had to shield it somehow."

"The way he wanted to shield my power with a blood bond," Jordana said. "Would he have any reason to take something like that with him when he left the realm?"

"Anyone who understood how valuable the crystal was would have reason to want it for himself." Zael thought for a moment, then chuckled softly as he looked at Jordana. "Or for someone else, if he thought it might prove useful in some other way."

"A bargaining chip," Nathan suggested. "Leverage against the one other person who wanted it the most. Wanted it maybe more than anything else."

Zael grunted. "Well, even if Cass did take it, he can't tell anyone where to find it now. The missing crystal is most likely lost forever."

Regardless of whether Cassianus escaped with a valuable Atlantean treasure or not, and regardless of any motivation he may have had to do so, Jordana felt a wave of renewed sorrow for the father she never knew. She mourned her mother too, for the love she lost and the family she never had the opportunity to enjoy.

There was even a small part of Jordana that pitied her grandmother. After all, what kind of lasting emotional pain must it require to turn a woman into the kind of unfeeling, destructive monster Selene seemed to be?

Nathan looked to Zael in question. "If Cass worried so much about Jordana and her safety, why not take her to the colony as an infant and stay there with her? Why would he risk her future—Jesus, why risk her life—by leaving her to grow up among the Breed and mankind?"

"Because if he brought her to the colony, Cass understood that like the others who live there, she'd have to remain under its veil for her entire existence. He didn't want to make that choice for her. Exile to the colony was a last resort, only if the worst should happen and time was running out. Cass wanted to give his daughter the chance to find her own path."

Nathan's dark gaze settled on Jordana. He'd never seemed uncertain, not in all of the time she knew him. But now there was a hesitance in his eyes. A quiet dread in his voice. "If I hadn't come here to find you tonight, what would you choose?"

"She already had chosen," Zael interjected gently. "Jordana decided even before you arrived. We were preparing to leave around the same time you came in."

Nathan's head drew back slightly, doubt flickering across his typically cool, controlled features. "I came that close to losing you?"

She shook her head, emotion nearly choking her. "Zael was going to bring me back home to Boston. Everything that matters to me is there . . . and right here in front of me."

His exhalation sounded heavy with relief. "I came to find you because you're everything that matters to me."

On her tear-thickened, happy laugh, Nathan pulled her into his arms.

When he spoke next, his voice was reverent and solemn, his hands on her the tenderest they'd ever been. "I will protect you with my life, Jordana. Always. And I'll protect you with my blood bond, here and now, if it means men like the ones who came for you tonight will never find you again."

That he would make such a promise moved her deeply. She loved him for that alone.

God help her, she loved Nathan for that and a thousand other reasons.

Jordana could hardly summon her breath as he gently stroked her cheek, his stormy gaze flecked with a galaxy of amber stars.

"Don't think I'm offering this out of duty or anything half as noble. You know I'm a selfish bastard who demands things go his way. I don't settle for anything less than what I want. And what I want right now, forever, is you." His eyes glowed bright with tender emotion. He held her face in his hands, searching her gaze with an intensity that made her blood heat beneath her skin. "I'm offering my bond because I love you. Because I need you, Jordana, and I don't want to know what life without you will feel like ever again."

He kissed her hard and deep, so passionately she lost herself to the overwhelming power of the moment, unaware that Zael was even still in the room until the Atlantean awkwardly cleared his throat.

Nathan released her, only to utter a growl and take her mouth again in another hungered, but brief, kiss. She was laughing as they separated and both turned to face Zael.

While they'd been caught up in passion, he'd collected the soldiers' remains and now belted their sheathed blades around his waist. "I must go," he said. The crystal at his wrist was starting to glow. "I'll take the dead with me and scatter them far enough away from here or Boston to throw anyone else off their trail. Whoever Selene sends next will have to start all over again. And if you're blood-bonded by then—"

"She will be." The dark confidence in Nathan's voice sent a jolt of fire through Jordana's veins.

Zael smiled. He held out his hand to Jordana. In his palm was a leather thong like the one he wore. One of the dead guards was missing his. "For you, should you ever need it. If you're ever in trouble, it will take you anywhere you can picture in your mind."

"But only me," she said, recalling that he'd explained the crystal would only transport those of Atlantean blood. She glanced up at Nathan, before looking back to Zael and giving a shake of her head. "There's nowhere I'll ever need to go if not with Nathan."

She reached for Zael's strong golden fingers and curled them around the gift she wouldn't accept. "Thank you for being a friend to my father Cassianus. And to me."

Zael bowed his head low, reverently. "Godspeed and a very happy, long life to you, Princess Jordana."

Zael held out his hand to Nathan. The two immense males—one golden and godlike, one dark and dangerous as night itself—clasped each other's hands in a solid, if unspoken, gesture of friendship.

With that, Zael strode over to the fallen Atlanteans and knelt down beside the bodies. He took the wrist of each one in his hands as the crystal on his bracelet glowed brighter and brighter still.

Light exploded from it in all directions—a lightning-quick blast of pure energy.

When it went out an instant later, Zael and Selene's dead guards were gone.

28

NATHAN HELD ON TO JORDANA AS THE VILLA WENT QUIET IN THE wake of Zael's departure, leaving the two of them alone with the weight of all they'd just seen and done and heard.

The battle with the two immortal guards had been harrowing, hard won. Zael's many revelations before and after the fight had been astonishing, even mind-blowing.

But nothing had leveled Nathan so much as Jordana's declaration that she loved him.

That she would have given up a guaranteed asylum to return to Boston—return to him—even before he'd come to find her was a sacrifice he could hardly fathom.

Then again, yes, he could.

Because as he held her under the circle of his arm in that moment, he knew with a certainty deep down into his marrow that there was nothing he wouldn't give up if it meant forever with Jordana.

When he might have held her against him even longer, content simply to feel her beside him, Jordana drew back. "Your wound, Nathan." She glanced down at her hand, which had been resting against his abdomen. The palm was stained red. "It's still bleeding. Let me take care of you now."

The injury was already healing. He knew it would mend soon enough on its own, but he didn't resist as she took him by the hand and led him through the villa, into a lavish bathroom adjoining the large master bedroom suite.

"Sit there." She pointed to the white marble edge of a deep soaking tub. As he obeyed her soft command, she went about gathering a supply of clean washcloths and towels. When she returned, she set them down next to him, then carefully untucked his body-hugging black shirt from his pants. "Can you lift your arms?"

He did as she asked, realizing only now that this was the first time in his life that anyone had cared for him in such a way.

The only time he'd ever permitted anyone to care for him like this.

Or wanted it so fervently.

A dark memory tried to push through his subconscious as Jordana gently drew his ruined shirt away from the sticky mess of his injury. Her hands were so tender, so light on him after she laid the shirt aside and knelt down to inspect the wound.

She ran water onto one of the washcloths from the tub faucet, then wiped away the worst of the blood with aching care. The cloth was cool against his torn flesh, a balm almost as soothing as her sweet attention.

Yet in the back of his mind, Nathan felt the bite of a lash. He heard the clamor of chains. Smelled the oily stench of blood-soaked metal and stone.

He had to battle every instinct he had not to shove her touch away.

Jordana must have sensed the tension in him. Glancing up now, her lovely face was pinched with concern. "Am I hurting you?"

"No." The word came out strangled, thick with restraint.

She went back to her careful ministrations, hesitantly now. She watched him too closely. She had to feel the rigidity of his muscles, the torment in all of his senses, as he struggled to hold back the ugliness of his past while she touched him so lovingly.

"Nathan, if you don't want me to touch you . . . if you want me to stop—"

"No. Fuck, no. I'll never want that." He reached out to caress her face, gutted that she would think he'd reject any part of her now, after all they'd been through together. He uttered a harsh, low curse, hating that his ugly past had invaded here. "You're not doing anything wrong. It's just . . ."

He couldn't hold her innocent gaze. He didn't want her to see through him to the Hunter he'd never totally managed to leave behind.

He didn't want her to see the scars that had never fully healed, despite that his Breed genetics had hidden all outside traces of them.

Jordana reached up to grasp his fingers where they lay against her cheek. "You can tell me when you're ready . . . or not at all. I'll love you either way."

Her promise was so sweet, so patient, any words he might have offered just then got strangled in his tight throat.

What would she say if she knew what his handlers had done to him, how they'd eventually broken him?

What would she think if she knew what he'd done to survive?

As she went back to tending him, the memories flooded in. He couldn't stop them.

And he knew that if he didn't spit them out, his past would always stand in the way of the future he hoped to have with Jordana.

"In the program, they had tests to cull the most viable Hunters from the rest," he murmured, his voice sounding wooden in the quiet of the bathroom. "They tested things like physical strength, linear and abstract thinking, problem solving. They tested endurance, and the ability to withstand pain. All kinds of pain."

Jordana's hands stilled. Slowly, she sat back on her heels in front of him, listening in utter silence, a quiet dread in her eyes. "Nathan . . ."

He kept going. He knew he had to push through before her sympathy froze him up. "The beatings were easy enough to handle. Even the torture. Eventually you find a place to park your mind and you can separate yourself from what's being done to you. That was the lesson our handlers were trying to demonstrate. Except, when nothing seems to break you, it creates a temptation in some people to find something that will. They get creative. They get fucking sadistic."

She swallowed hard, staring at him as though bracing for a physical blow herself. "Oh, Nathan."

"They used clubs and chains," he recalled, still able to feel the crush of his flesh and bones when the strikes landed on him. "When that didn't make me beg for mercy, they used blades, sunlight, sometimes they used fire. They could've used any weapon on me and I would have endured it. It was only physical pain. My body healed as good as new every time, thanks to the Gen One DNA they bred into each of us."

He exhaled a tense breath, recalling the countless hours and days he spent huddled and shivering on the floor of his cell, enduring the anguish of broken bones and savage injuries that would have killed a Breed with less hardy genetics.

But death hadn't been the goal of the Hunter program. Dragos had been trying to create perfect killing machines. Soulless weapons to command at his whim. He wanted only the strongest.

Only the merciless.

"After some time, my handlers decided to test me in other ways. They started teaching me new lessons. Inflicting wounds that would leave scars on my mind, ones that no DNA could heal."

Jordana let out a soft, ragged sigh. "Nathan, don't. You don't have to tell me any more."

"I do." He bit off the words. "You're the last person I want to tell any of this to, but you're also the only one . . . ever. And you need to know, Jordana. Before you touch me and tell me you love me, before you let me promise you a future I'm not even sure I can deliver, you need to understand who I am. You need to know all of it."

As he continued, she held his stare, her light blue eyes unwavering.

"Instead of limiting the torture to me alone, one day they brought me into a cell with another Hunter. He was younger than me, and our handlers informed me this was his first training session. I could see he was afraid, even though he tried to hide it. I thought they would start abusing both of us. They spared him, only made him watch all the things they did to me. And their creativity that day was especially brutal." Nathan blew out a harsh breath. "I didn't realize the other Hunter's lesson would come later. We both would learn something different that day."

Jordana reached out for his hand. It took all his will to accept the kindness, to wrap his fingers around hers even as he relived the horror of what was done to him that day in the cell and the even worse lesson that followed.

"They left me on the floor in a pool of my own blood and vomit. I didn't realize the other Hunter was still in the cell until sometime later, when I felt his hands under me, helping me up. He moved me out of the puddle of filth, then used his shirt to clean the worst of it off my face. Neither one of us realized that our handlers were watching the whole time. Waiting for just this kind of failure. Eager to make both of us pay for it."

Jordana drew in a breath, her fingers squeezing his tighter. "Oh, no . . ."

It had been a long time since Nathan had thought about the young male whose compassion had cost him his life. He wasn't the last.

"I should've known what they would do. It was the same game my handlers played in the beginning. They'd beat me, brutalize me, then come back around after a while to offer a hand up or some other small consideration. If I accepted, there was always more pain. And much worse than any that came before."

He looked at Jordana, saw moisture gathering in her eyes. "After that incident, they brought more Hunters into the cell with me to observe my training. If my untrained comrades touched me afterward or showed me kindness or pity at any time, my handlers would torture and kill them. If I warned my comrades not to do those things, then my handlers made me mete out the torture and the killings instead."

Jordana covered her mouth with her free hand, mutely shaking her head. One of the tears that had been welling now spilled over her and rolled down her cheek.

"Finally, all of the training stopped," he said. "They deemed me ready, and sent me to live with the Minion assigned to watch over me while I awaited my first kill order from Dragos."

Jordana exhaled softly, her brows lowered over her tender gaze. "My God, Nathan. How long did this *training* go on?"

"It took me longer than some others to conform, to submit." He paused, considering. "I guess I was about seven when I left the labs for good."

She gasped. "You were just a child—a little boy."

"I never recall a time when I felt I was anything other than what they made me: a Hunter. A killer. A weapon at Dragos's disposal."

"You never tried to escape?"

He grunted. "There was no escape. I had a collar that made any disobedience punishable by death. Every Hunter had one. The ultraviolet collars were locked onto us from the time we could walk. Venture too far, defy an order, attempt to escape . . ." He shook his head. "I saw more than one Hunter ash himself when his collar detonated. Some deliberately."

Understanding filled her horrified gaze. "So, if you refused to do anything your handlers demanded . . ." At his grave nod, Jordana briefly closed her eyes. "They trained you to fear tenderness. You learned to hate anyone's touch. They taught you that."

"They taught me that control was the only way to survive," he said. "I learned to dominate every situation thrown at me. Or die."

"You're free now," she pointed out. "You don't have to let your past keep you in the prison they made for you, Nathan."

Slowly, but without waiting for his permission or approval, she leaned toward him and placed her mouth at the base of his throat, where the cold weight of the UV collar once chafed his skin. He braced himself as her warm lips closed on him.

Unrushed, impossibly sweet, she kissed a trail around either side of his neck. Tender empathy for what he'd been through, or undeserving absolution for all he'd done, he didn't know.

Nor did he know how he could ever be worthy of the affection—the love—Jordana gave him so openly. She had changed him. His old methods for coping, for surviving, were obliterated from the moment she first stepped into his life.

She'd captivated him with a kiss.

She'd challenged him, gentled him.

Now she owned him.

Nathan growled in pleasure as her mouth completed its slow circuit of his neck, her tongue following the lines of the *dermaglyphs* she found there. His blood was thrumming through his veins, breath coming harder as arousal ignited like a wildfire within him. He tilted his head back on a low, shuddering moan as her kiss traveled lower, down across his bare chest.

"I wish I were a better man for you," he murmured, taking her face gently in his hands and tipping her gaze up to his. He was so hungry for her, his voice was gravel, thick with desire. And tight with love for this woman. "I wish I could promise you a peaceful, normal life . . . a tranquil future. I can't give you those things, Jordana."

"No, you can't." She smiled and reached up to caress his face, her fingers tracing lightly over the furrow now creased in his brow. "But I don't want those things. I want you. I want the storm I see in your eyes when you look at me. I want the high cliff and the breathless leap into the dark, which is how I feel when I'm with you. All I want is you, Nathan. I love you."

His heart swelled in his chest. She knew everything now, his ugliest sins and pitiful, ignoble past. And she still wanted him.

She still loved him.

Swamped with emotion and need, he took her mouth in a fierce claiming. His fangs surged out of his gums. Amber light exploded behind his eyelids as his irises transformed.

Jordana wrapped her arms around him as he drew her up onto his lap on the edge of the large tub, their mouths still joined and hungry for each other.

On a low moan, Nathan pulled his head back and looked at her. "You're mine."

"Yes." She stroked his cheek, and he nuzzled deeper into her touch. She watched him, her smile softening. "And you're mine."

Nathan nodded. "Always."

"Then take me," she told him. "There's one more leap I'm ready to make with you."

His veins responded before he could find his voice. Kicking as though lit with a jolt of electricity, his pulse hammered, more than eager to seal the bond that would make Jordana his woman forever.

His eternal mate.

With his eyes locked on hers, Nathan brought his wrist to his mouth and bit into his flesh.

"Drink," he said, the word dry as sandpaper as he watched her lick her lips.

Jordana leaned forward and fastened her mouth over the punctures.

At first she was tentative, careful with her suckling. She moaned as the first swallow moved down her throat. Both her hands came up to hold on to his arm as she drew another, deeper pull from his vein.

Nathan was rock hard now, every muscle in his body rigid, all of his senses trained on the erotic suction of her mouth. He groaned a curse, his spine arching as if she were sucking his cock at the same time.

With his free hand, he petted her head as she drank more of him. His fevered gaze latched on to the pulse point throbbing frantically in the side of her delicate neck. He could hear her heart beating. Could practically feel the rapid tick of her carotid echoing in his own veins.

Jordana owned him, with or without the blood bond, but he couldn't wait another second to make her his completely.

He smoothed his palm over the graceful column of her neck. Jordana whimpered as he stroked her, then she angled her head to give him clearer access.

It was all the temptation he could take.

On a hungered snarl, Nathan lowered his mouth onto her pale skin. The points of his fangs sank in deep, then a rush of hot, intoxicating blood flowed over his tongue.

Ah, Christ.

She tasted like heaven. Citrus and elusive, exotic spices and purest, otherworldly light.

The first hot gush of her blood roared into him, nearly making his cock explode. Like liquid lightning, her blood coursed into his body, into his cells, into his soul.

He could feel her light envelop him, engulfing him from the inside. Heat flowed up the arteries in his neck, his limbs, every fiber of him infused, nourished—completed—by the heady power of Jordana's Atlantean blood.

Emotion erupted inside him, so intense it rocked him. It was overwhelming, a total flood of pleasure and sensation . . . of naked, boundless love.

Jordana felt it too.

He knew, because their emotions were now twined together through their bond.

She drew away from his wrist on a sigh, her face aglow with desire and something so much deeper.

"Make love to me." A soft but undeniable command. One he was desperate to obey. "Now, Nathan. I need to feel you inside me now."

He didn't know if he answered or not. He wasn't even sure he was capable of speech, for the intensity of his feelings for this woman.

His woman.

His mate.

Pausing only long enough to seal their bite wounds with quick sweeps of his tongue, he lifted her up into his arms.

She was on fire as he brought her out to the waiting bed in the other room. Every cell inside her was enflamed, enlivened. Supercharged with light and unearthly energy.

But running undercurrent of all that was a raw, dark power that was Nathan.

She'd felt his strength pour into her as she drank from him. The first taste had been a shock, a revelation. The second had been pure bliss. Heady, intoxicating.

And as she'd taken more and more, Jordana understood that her bond to him would be an addiction unlike any other.

She would always crave him, even without the connection of his blood joined with hers. But now she hungered for him in a new, deeper way.

A wild, demanding way that knew no patience. No mercy.

She couldn't tear her clothes off fast enough as he set her down on the bed. The linen tunic and loose pants were gone in an instant, cast aside on her throaty growl of need.

Jordana reached to unfasten Nathan's black fatigues and only then did she hesitate.

Because the blade wound that had pierced his torso was no longer bleeding. Not even a little.

"My God," she whispered. "Nathan, look."

He glanced down, and as they both watched in astonishment, his skin knitted back together. In seconds, nothing of the injury remained.

He uttered a quiet laugh and when he looked back at her, there was wonder in his stormy, amber-soaked eyes.

And love.

So much love, it drowned her. Swept her into a tide of emotion so swift and strong, she could barely breathe.

She could feel Nathan's love for her in her veins, in her marrow. In every thrumming fiber of her being.

No more doubt, no more hiding for either of them. They were entwined as one now.

This would be their bond forever.

"Forever," he growled fiercely, as though he understood the depth of her feeling.

As though he felt it as surely, as completely, as she did.

He quickly stripped out of his pants and boots, then prowled back up to her on the bed. Heat rolled off his naked body as he took up a position between her spread thighs.

He kissed every inch of her, then tongued her sex until she was trembling and gasping beneath him. His eyes were blazing as he crawled back up to loom over her. His lips were slick with her hot juices, his fangs enormous behind the pleased, seductive curve of his smile.

Jordana touched his face, his harsh, handsome face. She stroked his cheek and hard jaw, then gently traced her fingertips down his neck, where she'd tried to kiss away the memory of his punishing Hunter's collar.

He didn't stop her from touching him now. He didn't take his eyes off her, didn't flinch as she skimmed a tender caress over his strong shoulders and the bulky muscles of his arms.

Only when she reached lower, to where his thick cock jutted between them, velvety, warm, as firm as steel, did he close his eyes and emit a low hiss between his teeth and fangs. He groaned as she stroked his rigid shaft.

He growled as she squeezed him, then uttered her name like a curse and a prayer as she opened her legs wider to him and guided him through the slick cleft of her body.

Then he devoured her mouth in a consuming kiss, nothing gentle in him now. Only raw desire, fueled by the intensity of their bond.

Wet heat boiled in her core. She was ready, so ready.

"Yes," she hissed against his mouth. "Take me."

He sank in on a ragged snarl, plunging deep and hard and full. His hips bucked, thrusted, then kicked into a ravenous urgency that made her dizzy. He buried his head against her shoulder, driving into her with the sweetest frenzy, the hottest passion she would ever know. "Ah, Christ. Jordana, you feel too good. I can't be gentle. Jesus, fuck . . . I can't stop."

"I don't want gentle. Not right now." She wrapped her legs around him and dug her heels into his pumping ass as he rode her toward the crest of a shattering climax. "Oh, God, Nathan. Yes. Give me everything."

And so he did.

He gave her the storm and the cliff and the leap into a wild tempest. He gave her all of that and more, taking her senses to a height she never dreamed existed.

All she could do was hold on tight as he crashed into her, their gazes locked as passionately as their bodies.

It felt so right, the need they shared, the bond that joined them now, forever.

He shouted as he came, and Jordana followed him there at the same time, hurtling into a brilliant wave of release. She felt his pleasure, and knew he felt hers too. She shattered beneath the pleasing weight of him, all her nerve endings crackling with sensation, with pure pleasure, as her body slowly spiraled back down to earth.

Panting, shivering with a thousand little aftershocks, she exhaled a shaky laugh. "That was, ah . . . *wow.*" She sifted her fingers through his short dark hair, his forehead resting on her shoulder. "Do you think it's always going to be like this for us?"

He grunted, his breath hot against the side of her neck. "No, I don't."

Not the answer she expected. She was frowning when he lifted his head to look at her. But his dark, blue-green eyes didn't have a speck of doubt in them. They glittered with bright amber sparks. And deep inside her, his cock twitched, already hard again.

Nathan grinned, one black brow rising wickedly. "I have a feeling it's only going to get better."

Then, with no more warning than that, he rolled over onto his back, bringing her with him so that she was seated astride him, their bodies still joined.

"But why wait to find out," he said, and dragged her down for another hot, claiming kiss.

29

THEY MADE LOVE FOR ANOTHER COUPLE OF HOURS.

He'd been right; sex was only going to get better between them. Nathan had enjoyed watching Jordana's pleasure as she straddled his body and set the tempo for their next round.

He'd never seen anything so erotic as her insatiable enthusiasm—her relentless ferocity—while she chased a second, and then, God help him, a third and fourth explosive climax.

No doubt about it, his lovely mate was extraordinary.

But then, he'd known that all along.

And he knew it was going to take a lot longer than the years they would have together—eternity, if he had anything to say about it—before he would desire her any less than he did tonight.

It was desire that woke him from a brief, recharging doze. He wanted Jordana again, but when he moved his hand to find her, he felt nothing but cool, empty sheets.

Where was she?

He vaulted out of the bed, alarm shooting through him.

But only for an instant.

Then he felt her, safe and serene, in his blood.

Their bond reassured him. It led him out to the terrace, where he found Jordana, wrapped in a thin coverlet from the bed, standing beneath the moonlight.

She sensed him as well. Without turning around, she reached back to him, beckoning him out to join her. Nathan took her hand and walked up beside her. Then he gathered her into his arms and looked out with her at the dark, rippling water and shadowed cliffs below.

"It's so beautiful here," she said quietly. "I can see why this place was special to him. It must have broken his heart when my mother decided she couldn't stay here with him. With us."

Nathan kissed the top of her head and nestled her closer. She was talking about her parents, Cass and Soraya. Jordana had told him about them while Nathan and she had lain in bed a short while ago. She told him everything Zael had shared with her, including the fact that Jordana had been born in this very villa.

And he knew about her mother's punishment for falling in love with a man deemed beneath her. He knew about the suicide that had robbed Cassian Gray—Cassianus—of the woman he loved and sent him on the run with an infant daughter he was desperate to hide.

A daughter who would never know him.

A young woman who wouldn't find out just how loved she'd been by her father until it was too late to return that affection.

Nathan hugged her deeper into his arms. "Do you think you'll want to come back here sometime?"

She shook her head where it rested against his bare chest. "No. This was his place, their place. It belongs to them, not me." Her face tilted up to meet his gaze. "The only home I need is in Boston. With you."

They'd already discussed living arrangements, and although Nathan's quarters at the command center were nothing close to Jordana's lavish penthouse, she conceded to living with him as part of the Order.

Nathan was prepared to go anywhere she wanted. There was a part of him that wanted nothing more than to take her as far away as possible from Boston and this villa—all the places Selene's legion might begin to look for her again—but she refused to run. She refused to cower or hide.

She was stronger than either of her parents; Nathan recognized that easily enough.

Jordana was gentle and sweet, innocent in many ways, but she was also fierce and courageous. If the Atlantean queen was a force to be reckoned with, she would find her granddaughter every bit her equal in terms of tenacity and the refusal to let anyone intimidate her.

It would likely surprise few to learn that royal blood, immortal blood, ran through Jordana's veins.

And now Nathan's blood ran through her too.

He couldn't be more humbled by that fact. He had an entire future to make sure she never regretted giving herself to him as his mate.

A future he was eager to begin.

"We should go soon," he murmured against her brow. "Lazaro Archer can have the Order's private jet ready for us at any time. If I don't call him soon and make the arrangements, there's a very good chance I'll tie you to the bed and have my wicked way with you again."

She smiled, looking anything but worried. "I like your wicked ways. And I also liked being on top. So maybe I'll be the one to tie you to the bed sometime."

His cock responded instantly, evidence she could see plainly enough, not to mention feel. As if to let him know she had him precisely where she wanted him, Jordana reached down and stroked his erect shaft.

On a groan, he caught her hand and linked his fingers through hers. "Come on, let's go inside before I spread you beneath me on the tiles out here."

He led her back into the villa, past the blood from the battle they'd survived together and into the living area. Nathan hadn't realized until now how rich Cass's villa was with original art and other treasures.

And there was something else he hadn't noticed until now either.

A small, framed snapshot occupying a private place of honor on the far wall of the living area. It was a black-and-white photo of a young woman. A woman with long dark hair, dressed in a pale linen, ankle-length sheath. She stood on the same terrace Nathan and Jordana had just come in from, overlooking the same cliffside and coast, except she stood there under the full light of day, the sun glinting off the sheen of her hair.

Nathan frowned. "Is that a picture of—"

"My mother," Jordana murmured at nearly the same moment, shock and wonder in her quiet reply. "Oh, my God. That has to be her."

She broke away from Nathan and crossed the room for a closer look. He followed, taking in the details of the candid shot, which had been captured from inside the villa by someone who clearly adored the subject.

The woman stood half turned near the railing, her delicate face dipped down toward her shoulder, wistful, smiling with a private joy. Nathan knew the elegant profile well enough: One glance in Jordana's direction would have confirmed the same high cheekbones, the small, straight nose and regal, if stubborn, chin.

"That's Soraya," Jordana whispered. She pointed to the photo, where it was just possible to see from the woman's angle the hint of a rounded belly. "Oh, Nathan. That's my mother and me."

Jordana carefully reached out to take the frame off its fixture on the wall. It stuck a bit, then sprang free on a soft click, followed by a mechanical whir from somewhere within the wall on which the photo had hung.

The tall millwork panel began to slide open, revealing an alcove hidden behind the false wall.

Nathan stepped back, taking Jordana with him by the arm. "What the hell . . ."

He tried to sweep her behind him, but she stepped forward, unafraid. "Nothing in my father's house will hurt me," she reassured him.

Even so, as the panel slid all the way open, Nathan's muscles tensed for battle, his senses instantly on high alert. He realized right away his concerns were unfounded.

The panel hid another piece of Cass's art.

A sculpture, roughly a foot tall, depicting a handsome shepherd youth asleep beneath a crescent moon.

Nathan had seen this piece before.

It was on display in the exhibit Jordana had lovingly curated and unveiled to the public just the other night.

"*Sleeping Endymion,*" Jordana whispered, astonished to find the sculpture here, in her father's Amalfi villa. "How can this be?"

Nathan stood beside her as she gaped at the terra cotta work of art she knew so well.

Or, rather, thought she had.

Now she realized she'd made a mistake.

There were things she hadn't seen before. Not until this very moment.

"When Cass came to the museum that afternoon, we talked about art. He knew so much. Seeing this place, I understand why now," she said, trying to put the puzzle together in her mind. "He asked me what my favorite piece was in the exhibit. He seemed so pleased when I told him it was this one." She shook her head as understanding dawned. "Not this one precisely, but the one Cass donated to the museum anonymously twenty-some-odd years ago. It was *him.*"

"What are you saying? That this sculpture meant enough to Cass that he had a second one made for himself?"

"No." She shook her head, incredulous as she inspected the piece more carefully. "Oh, no, Nathan. I think this may be the original. In fact, I'm practically certain it is."

"This is the real one?" He glanced at her, scowling in question. "Then the one in your exhibit at the museum . . ."

She nodded, completely confident that Cass had fooled them all. "It's a fake. The one in Boston is a very good, flawless reproduction. So good, it got past everyone. Even the curators and art historians who handled it before me."

Nathan peered at the sculpture more closely and blew out a sigh. "Maybe he didn't know. Why give the museum anything at all, if he was knowingly giving them a fake?"

"I don't know. It doesn't make sense. It's not that important of a piece for any deliberate attempt to bait and switch. Unless—" She considered for a moment, then turned a look on Nathan. "Unless Cass had something he wanted to hide. Maybe something else he took from the Atlantean realm."

"Something he felt would be safest hidden in plain sight," Nathan said, finishing her thought. He ran a hand over his head. "Holy hell. You don't really think . . ."

Zael's recounting of the destruction of Atlantis came back to her in a rush.

She recalled his mention of the crystals that had once belonged to their people. The ones stolen by the enemy Ancients and used against the Atlanteans . . .

And the one rumored to have vanished around the same time Cassianus whisked his infant daughter away to live as something she wasn't.

To masquerade unknowingly among the general public, protected by the simple fact that no one had any cause to suspect a thing.

"We have to go," Jordana murmured. "I need to get back to Boston now. We need to know if my father has been hiding any other secrets all these years."

Nathan nodded. "I'll call Lazaro now."

Epilogue

Boston. Two days later.

Jordana's pleasured cry tore from her throat as she came, a sound that never failed to make Nathan grin with unrepentant male pride.

Hard as granite inside her tight, wet sheath, he was ready for the third climax certain to follow swiftly on the heels of this explosive second. He groaned as the tremors of her release rippled all along his cock, tempting him to spill. But he held steady for her. He knew what she liked, knew just how to please his insatiable, immortal mate.

His hands fisted where she'd tied them to the headboard, muscles straining but making no effort to break loose of his bonds. He was learning to enjoy letting Jordana be in control.

Enjoy it, because eventually it would be his turn, and he loved dealing pleasure to her as mercilessly as she did to him.

She'd already sucked him off once, so he was content to watch her ride him for now. Jordana rocked atop him, her breasts bouncing prettily, rosebud nipples still peaked and glistening from his kisses. She pinched them as she slid up and down his length with deliberate slowness, ruthlessly teasing him with all the fruits just outside his reach.

"You feel so good, Nathan. I think I may never let you out of this bed." She leaned down over him then, bracing her forearms on either side of his head while she kissed him.

Her tongue slid past his teeth and fangs, deep into his mouth. Her naked body pressed all along his length made him mad with need. She squirmed and flexed the tiny muscles of her sex, milking his already engorged shaft in the best kind of agony.

Finally, he couldn't take another second more.

Ripping free of his silken restraints, he caught her in his arms and tumbled her around beneath him on the bed. He gave her a deep, hard pump of his hips, burying himself to the hilt. He picked up the tempo while increasing the depth of his thrusts, loving the way her body responded so readily to him.

He could feel her orgasm building along with his own. He felt her mounting pleasure in the heavy drum of her heartbeat and in the echoing throb of their bond. The first shudder overtook her, and she gripped his shoulders as a trembling sigh escaped her parted lips.

She moaned and bit her bottom lip. "Oh, you don't play fair. You're going to make me come too fast."

Normally, he'd be in no rush to finish making love with Jordana. But it was past sundown, and while the Order's patrols were called off for the night, the Boston command center was anticipating the arrival of important visitors any minute now.

"Tomorrow we'll start earlier," he promised. "That way, I can make you scream all day."

She looped her arms around his neck as he pumped into her. "Why? Because it's my birthday tomorrow?"

"No," he said. "Because I love you. Your birthday only comes once a year. We both know that's not nearly enough."

She laughed, but it was swallowed up quickly by the gasp and rising cry that heralded her release. Nathan kept up his relentless rhythm, pushing her toward the brink, then toppling her over the edge with him as his own climax gripped him in a tight, pulsing fist.

They were still flushed with passion twenty minutes later, after they'd shared a quick shower and gotten dressed and ready to join everyone who had gathered in the war room that evening.

All of the North American–based Order and their mates were there.

Sterling Chase and Tavia. Nathan's teammates, Rafe, Elijah, and Jax. Carys and Aric.

Nathan's mother, raven-haired, delicately beautiful Corinne, was there with her big, golden-eyed Gen One mate, Hunter, who headed up the New Orleans command. They had arrived from the D.C. headquarters with the Order's leader, Lucan Thorne, and his mate, Gabrielle, as well as Gideon and Savannah, and the New York chief, Tegan, who was there with his beloved Elise.

Nathan's recently mated friends Kellan and Mira had arrived with her adoptive parents, Nikolai and Renata, the longtime couple only weeks away from welcoming a new son, their first child together.

The rest of the stateside warriors and their mates—Dante and Tess, Rio and Dylan, Kade and Alexandra, and Brock and Jenna—had all assembled with the others for the express purpose of meeting Jordana.

And to see firsthand if her suspicions about her father's secrets were correct.

The object at the center of that question now sat on the war room conference table.

As soon as Nathan and Jordana had returned to Boston, she'd gone back to the museum to switch the pieces and bring Cass's remarkable fake to the Order.

More than one pair of eyes drifted to the innocuous-looking sculpted terra cotta as Nathan made the introductions among his family and extended kin of the Order and the extraordinary female who had become his mate.

His mother was visibly moved, tears glistening in her eyes, which were the same bluish green as Nathan's. She came toward him tentatively, conditioned by her son's damaged past to be careful when it came to affection and motherly warmth.

To see her caution now shamed Nathan. Truth to tell, it broke his heart a little.

So, when Corinne approached him, he moved first, bringing her petite frame into his arms.

"Oh!" she exclaimed, then instantly wrapped him in a sweet, loving hug. "Nathan, I'm so happy for you."

She was laughing through her tears as he released her and made her introduction to Jordana. The two women greeted each other warmly, and seeing them embrace was a balm Nathan hadn't realized he needed.

Nathan reached out to Hunter, clasping the former assassin's hand in a firm shake. "I understand now," Nathan said. "I didn't know it would be possible to feel—"

The massive warrior only nodded. No need for more words.

They'd both come through the fire of a terrible upbringing in Dragos's labs.

Both men now stood in the light of a redeeming bond.

As Nathan and Hunter watched their mates get acquainted, Dante, one of the Order's former Boston members, who was now commander of the Seattle operation, strode over hand in hand with his Breedmate, Tess.

The pair had been talking with their son, Rafe, but now walked toward the sculpture sitting in the center of the conference table. Jordana and Corinne, Nathan and Hunter, all joined them near the piece.

Tess's smile was wistful as she looked at *Sleeping Endymion,* then back to her dark-haired warrior mate. "Twenty years ago, we met in the art museum, in front of this very sculpture. Do you remember?"

Dante grunted, his mouth quirking with private humor. "I remember it was the second time we met. The first time, I greeted you with my fangs in your throat and you, in turn, stuck a syringe full of animal tranquilizer in me. Well deserved, I might add."

Tess laughed. "Not exactly a Hallmark moment, was it?"

Dante shook his head. "Hearts and flowers were never my style. Fortunately, I have other gifts."

"Oh, yes. You definitely do," she said, wrapping her arms around him in obvious devotion.

As they all conversed and reminisced and more of the group gathered close, Gideon and his Breedmate, Savannah, came over to greet Jordana and Nathan.

The Order's resident genius had had the good sense to make gentle but strong Savannah his mate some fifty years ago. The mocha-skinned beauty's kindness and intellect were her abiding traits, but she also had an insatiable curiosity. One that was aided by the Breedmate's extrasensory talent of psychometry.

She studied the sculpture for a moment, then glanced at Jordana, a fervent, impatient eagerness in her soft brown eyes. "Would it be all right . . . may I touch it?"

"Of course." Jordana nodded. "We can do whatever we like with it. The sculpture—and any secrets it might contain—belongs to the Order now. You're all my family now. Whatever I have belongs to all of us."

And Jordana had a lot.

A vast wealth in priceless art, as it turned out. Soon after their return to Boston, Nathan and Jordana had gone to see Martin Gates. Jordana wanted the Breed male to know that she was grateful for the life he gave her as his daughter, and assured him that he would always be her family—the father who raised her.

No more secrets. No more lies.

The only unknown that remained was the terra cotta piece on the table before them.

Savannah reached out cautiously, settling her hand lightly on the sculpture. No one spoke in the long moment that followed.

Then she shook her head and withdrew her touch. "I don't feel anything. It's as if there's something standing in the way of my ability. Blocking it."

Lucan grunted, his dark brows knit in a heavy scowl. "We need to know what this sculpture means. Not only to the Order, but to the Atlanteans and the rest of the world." He turned his sober gray gaze on Jordana. "If this contains what you suspect, we need to understand its power and either harness it or, if necessary, take steps to destroy it."

Carys glanced at her best friend. "Do you really think there's an Atlantean crystal in *Endymion*, Jordana?"

Jordana looked up at Nathan before meeting the expectant eyes of everyone gathered in the war room. "There's one way to find out."

Lucan gave her a resolute nod, but Nathan noticed the Order's leader protectively pulled his Breedmate closer to him. The rest of the warriors did likewise with their women, everyone braced for whatever was about to occur.

Jordana lifted the sculpture in both hands.

With an indrawn breath and a confirming glance at Nathan, she released it.

The terra cotta hit the floor at her feet with a hard crash. It shattered into pieces.

In the center of the rubble lay a polished metal box about the size of her palm.

"Titanium," Nikolai guessed, the blond warrior well versed in the material, having handcrafted custom bullets and blades out of the precious metal for the Order over the years.

Jordana bent down to pick up the box.

With an encouraging look from Nathan and the rest of the Order, she carefully unfastened the latch and opened the container.

A smooth, silvery crystal the size of a hen's egg rested inside.

It was remarkable, otherworldly. A thing of cosmic power and beauty.

Just like the woman holding it.

Jordana rose, looking up at Nathan and smiling. Wonder and amazement danced in her ice-blue eyes.

"The crystal," she whispered, as everyone moved in closer to have a better look at this extraordinary treasure.

Jordana handed it off to Lucan, and Nathan took the opportunity to pull his mate into the shelter of his arms.

He kissed her, relished the feel of her body against him. Savored the feel of her heart beating in time with his.

And as he held her close, he understood with his whole heart—with his entire being—that whatever power the crystal might contain, with Jordana at his side, loving him as she did now, he already possessed the greatest treasure any world would ever know.

About the Author

Lara Adrian is the *New York Times* and #1 internationally best-selling author of the Midnight Breed vampire romance series, with more than 4 million books in print and digital worldwide and translations licensed to more than 20 countries. Her books regularly appear in the top spots of all the major bestseller lists, including the *New York Times*, *USA Today*, *Publishers Weekly*, Indiebound, Amazon.com, and Barnes & Noble.

Her debut novel, *Kiss of Midnight*, was named Borders Books best-selling debut romance of 2007. Twice her novels have been named among Amazon.com's Top Ten Best Romances of the Year and have been twice nominated for Goodreads Choice Awards for Best Romance of the Year. Reviewers have called Lara's books "addictively readable" (*Chicago Tribune*), "extraordinary" (Fresh Fiction), and "one of the best vampire series on the market" (*RT Reviews*).

With an ancestry stretching back to the *Mayflower* pilgrims and the court of King Henry VIII, the author lives with her husband in New England, surrounded by centuries-old graveyards, hip urban comforts, and the endless inspiration of the broody Atlantic Ocean. She is currently at work on the next novel in the Midnight Breed series.

www.laraadrian.com
Facebook.com/LaraAdrianBooks
@lara_adrian
www.pinterest.com/LaraAdrian/

About the Type

This book was set in Berling. Designed in 1951 by Karl-Erik Forsberg (1914–95) for the type foundry Berlingska Stilgjuteri AB in Lund, Sweden, it was released the same year in foundry type by H. Berthold AG. A classic old-face design, its generous proportions and inclined serifs make it highly legible.